Praise for *Most Secret*:

"Carr's storytelling magic is irresistable."
—*The Times*

"An ingeniously invented mystery puzzle."
—*Saturday Review*

Also by John Dickson Carr available from
Carroll & Graf:

The Bride of Newgate
Captain Cut-Throat
The Curse of the Bronze Lamp (by Carter Dickson)
Dark of the Moon
Deadly Hall
The Devil in Velvet
The Emperor's Snuff-Box
Fire, Burn!
In Spite of Thunder
Lost Gallows
Nine Wrong Answers
Panic in Box C
Papa La-Bas
Scandal at High Chimneys

MOST SECRET

John Dickson Carr

Carroll & Graf Publishers, Inc
New York

Copyright © 1964 by John Dickson Carr

All rights reserved

st Carroll & Graf edition 1989

hed by arrangement with Harold Ober Associates, Inc

Graf Publishers, Inc.
venue
Y 10001

42-6

United States of America

CONTENTS

EDITOR'S NOTE

Well, how much truth is in it? Anyone who reads the ensuing narrative may wonder whether Colonel Kinsmere (rest his soul) was not glorifying his grandfather by building the sort of vague legend found among many families into a lyric edifice of lies. This is the verdict of one of his descendants, Mr. Herbert Darlington, who has assisted me in preparing the record, so that in suggesting it I am in no danger of getting myself sued for libelling somebody's ancestor.

Primarily, the story was designed to amuse young people at Blackthorn during the troubled month of June, 1815. The bogy of Napeleon Bonaparte was abroad in Flanders, and three members of the Kinsmere family were shortly to face him in the army of Field-Marshal the Duke of Wellington. Boney's drums could be heard even in that quiet library by the Avon. Whether the story was in part invented by an old gentleman of exuberant fancy (Colonel Kinsmere had celebrated his eighty-third birthday on the previous 11th of April), or whether every incident really occurred as he swore it did, is a question to which no answer can be supplied.

And yet, though certain details may be stretched or elaborated, we need not necessarily doubt everything. To-day's experience suggests that, in matters of diplomatic hocus-pocus behind the scenes, the melodramatic explanation is usually the true one. Besides, when Colonel Kinsmere told his tale in 1815, research into the records of the seventeenth century had attained only a rudimentary stage; even Pepys's diary was not yet decoded.

The real-life people to whom Colonel Kinsmere introduces us behave so much in accordance with the discoveries of present-day scholars as to afford proof that he heard the details at first hand. The same may be said of topographical detail: the London background, the Devil tavern, the arrangement of rooms in Whitehall palace. Though it is impossible to discover whether a performance of *Julius Caesar* was given by the King's Company on the date he assigns to it, those actors and actresses who appear with Dolly Landis in chapter IX were all authentically members of the King's Company at that time, playing the parts that would have been given them.

Again, Colonel Kinsmere's characters talk so entirely in the style of the seventeenth century that Mr. Darlington and I were somewhat tempted to woo readers by modernizing it. But this, as contemporary letters and diaries attest, is how people really did think and speak in the year 1670; it makes very easy reading when long sentences are punctuated into short ones and we have decided neither to alter nor to apologize.

Finally, it might be interesting to quote extracts from the diary of Mrs. Anne Kinsmere Darlington (1799-1868), who took down the narrative verbatim. She declares, in her diary, that she finds it a shocking story, though there is nothing in the least shocking about it. Whatever the lady's views, it is to her interest and industry that we owe its preservation; certain marginal notes indicate she might surreptitiously have wished for herself the broad charms and amatory adventures of Dolly Landis. In any event, here is the tale as Richard Kinsmere told it; the reader may be left to determine how much probably happened, how much might have happened, and how much could never have happened in this world.

PART 1:

THE RAREE-SHOW

"Rares choses à voir! Rares choses à voir!"

Cry of the Puppet Show-Man
Seventeenth Century

I

He was a sizzler, was my grandfather.

I am aware that this modern term "Sizzler" might seem to lack something of the veneration we are taught to accord grandfathers in general. The memories we retain of our own grandsire, as a rule, are few. To a child he occupies the awesome and unaccountable position of being father to our father, and therefore presumably capable of twice as hard a caning.

We regard him, in fact, as something between a saint and a bad dream. His white hair and beard confuse him in our minds with a mysterious personage out of the Bible, who is always stalking about very excitedly in a species of nightshirt, and preaching something to somebody. Though he seems a more sedentary sort of being than this, he has a shrewd taste for asking questions; besides, we are forever offending him. We somehow contrive to land a cricket ball in his cup as he sits down to tea, and all the aunts seem turned to stone when he swears. Then the aunts look sorrowfully at *us*. They convey the impression that it hurts them beyond words to hear a boy cursing so viciously at the tea table.

This, I gather, is the sort of cloudy memory most young people retain. I do not think, however, that you can regard *me* in such fashion. And if you think I am tolerably active for my age, and an unpardonable old rip of a grandfather into the bargain, then, Lord love us, you should have seen your great-great-grandsire as I saw him all those years ago.

Ah, yes. Yes, indeed!

I remember the night I heard him tell how he fought Captain Harker in the dark at the old Devil and St. Dunstan tavern in Fleet Street. He recounted the tale in 'forty-two, seventeen-forty-two; I am sure of it because they were sending me away from the Hall to school in the same week, and they had let me sit up at table with the gentlemen when the port went round after supper. The vicar was there that night, and Squire Redlands from Cyston Court down Gloucestershire way, and Major McCartney of the Life Guards; I remember Major McCartney's red coat and fine gold epaulets.

" 'Twas thus, mark you now!" says Rowdy Kinsmere.

For my grandfather not only told that rousing story of the fight in the dark; he borrowed Squire Redland's sword and illustrated it all over the dining room, with the sword in one hand and a glass of port in the other, whooping out comments as he did so. When old Silver came in to suggest that it was bedtime, he was so excited that he fired the cut-glass decanter at Silver's head, and very nearly hit it at that.

(Indeed, considering the length of our dining room here, I do not think I have ever seen a better shot: except perhaps when Scrope Wiley wagered two thousand pounds he could throw a toasting fork and spear the Lord Mayor of London exactly in the seat of the breeches at a distance of sixty feet; and did it, too, during the Procession of 1756. In Parliament it was called attempted assassination.)

Anyway, on this night I was telling you of, they sent me up to bed after I had drunk all a boy of nine years can conveniently carry. I went to bed, but I was awakened by some noise just as the stable clock was striking four, and I crept out and peeped over the banisters into the main hall.

In the main hall (which was paved with flagstones at that time) there stood my grandfather, and Squire Redlands, and Major McCartney, and the vicar, with their arms round each other's shoulders, singing Macheath's song from the *Beggar's Opera*. Squire Redlands and the vicar, of course, were put to bed in the house, but Major

10

McCartney had to ride to Bristol that night. So my grandfather propped him up on his horse, and saw that he was pointed in the right direction, and then stood out on the drive in the autumn mist and hallo'd him out of sight.

"Poor fellow, being obliged to leave us," says Rowdy Kinsmere. "Ah, poor fellow!"

Upon my solemn oath, he was up drinking his ale at the breakfast table next morning, no whit the worse for it. And he had celebrated his ninety-second birthday on the previous 15th of May. Later he came to help them pack my box, which was to be put on the London coach for school. My mother had forbidden me any pocket money beyond the four shillings a term prescribed by the school; but he roared, "Hell alive, woman!" and crammed my pockets full of gold sovereigns, telling me to be sure not to spend 'em for anything sensible or he would birch me when I came back. He also made out a list, and showed it to me, of things at school for which I should receive a bonus. One, I remember, was for a prize in fencing and riding competitions; one for any completely new cheat or bubble I could devise to devil my housemaster; but the others I cannot call to mind.

Yet I can still see him in the room I occupied then: the little panelled room up under the eaves of the west wing, which Edward's son has now. To the end of his life he would never wear anything except the clothes that were fashionable in his youth. So I see him standing by the window, in his great black periwig of Charles the Second's time, his black camlet coat and the lace at his throat, reading that list through his spectacles, and the ilex tree throwing a shadow on the floor.

Now when I say to you that he was, in the language of 1815, a Sizzler, I do not refer to him in his old age. I would tell you of him as he went up to London in those distant days when the throne of England was graced or disgraced by a king whom some called Old Rowley. For you may be assured that, even in a family whose most conspicuous talent lies in its spontaneous ability to become embroiled in devilment, nobody ever had such a taste for it, or experienced so much of it, as your great-great-grandfather.

There are others, of course. You will perhaps have heard of my uncle Charles, his second son, who used to go

11

to those private theatricals Queen Anne loved, and once hired a conjuror to find three gold watches and the Duchess of Marlborough's garters in Dean Swift's hat. But they didn't know the man was a conjuror, you see, so that my uncle Charles was compelled to depart for the colonies in some haste.

And so I would tell you my grandfather's story, young ladies and gentlemen, partly to beguile the time for you while your elder brothers are away in Belgium with Lord Wellington, and partly so that you may tell *your* grandchildren you have heard the true things out of a century and a half gone by: of what manner of men they really were who diced and jested, and fought and bussed wenches, at the court of Our Sovereign Liege Charles the Second.

It is very real to me. I heard it all, being Rowdy Kinsmere's favourite. At my first duel he insisted on standing by with the surgeon, holding the cloths and the water basin. I had the good luck to run my man through the shoulder during the first minute of play. Afterwards my grandfather escaped from those who were supposed to keep an eye on the old reprobate; he was inviting the whole village to take beer at his expense in the taproom of the local tavern, and singing a duet with the blacksmith, when they found him.

His first name being Roderick, it was shortened to "Rod," or "Roddy," and became, almost inevitably, "Rowdy." By my parents—a somewhat sanctimonious pair, though worthy people—he was regarded as a fierce old villain, past comprehension and damned as well. In actuality, a kinder-hearted or more muddle-headed person never lived. He made much of that little pinprick of a duel, and afterwards (I was fifteen) treated me as a man grown.

"You are blooded," declared he. "It is better so."

But was it?

The quarrel leading to the duel, I recall now, was with poor Bunny Whipstead, Squire Whipstead's son, who never did anybody the least harm. The last time I saw Bunny must have been close on forty years ago, at Alexandre Man's Coffee-House behind Charing Cross. We got drunk with a pair of actresses from Covent Garden, and I cannot call to mind whether or not he married one of 'em;

but, anyway, a few weeks later he went off with Johnny Burgoyne to fight the Americans, and got killed somewhere.

However, speaking of tippling with actresses in taverns reminds me of my grandfather again, and of the time they discovered the dead man in a cupboard: the question as to the identity of the skulker with the bone-handled knife, and the relationship borne by such events to the Secret Treaty of Dover.

In order to understand all this from the beginning—especially a small matter of piracy in the English Channel—I must tell you first of the ring. It is the ring which explains the whole affair.

Fetch the lamp, now, and hold it up to his portrait over the mantelpiece. This is Rowdy Kinsmere as he looked when Kneller painted him in 1678. You see the heavy peruke falling to his shoulders, the dark-grey velvet coat and silver-grey waistcoat, his pleased expression as he seems to open one eye and say, "Damme, sir, did you mention a cup of wine? Why, hang me, sir, I don't mind if I do."

You have seen it a thousand times, but I wonder if you have ever observed that ring he wears on the left hand resting on his sword hilt?

The painter shows it as a vague blue stone. It was actually a very fine sapphire, almost (as you shall hear) a unique sapphire. King Charles the First, of Glorious Memory, gave it to his aide-de-camp, Roderick Kinsmere's father, after Newbury fight in the Great Rebellion. The sapphire was cut into the likeness of the king's head, an astonishing piece of craftsmanship, some dozen years before the king's real head fell under the axe outside the Banqueting House at Whitehall. But that ring is not in the possession of our family now, though "Buck" Kinsmere, whose true name was Alan, handed it down to his son. It is buried in the coffin of the woman . . . no matter. Set down the lamp again.

Buck Kinsmere, my great-grandfather, was in no great danger of persecution by Cromwell's Protectorate. Still, he followed Charles the Second into exile two years after his own son was born and his wife died here at Blackthorn. You might have thought he had done enough already, having fought in every major engagement since Edgehill, lost an arm at Naseby, and flung away his fortune in the king's cause; but he only did what many another gentleman did, quietly, in the mysterious ways of faithfulness. After the Restoration he returned here and presently died. He was weary, and always a trifle puzzled that the oak trees should look the same on the lawns, and the summer rains still whisper, whether a Stuart sat on the throne or no.

Meanwhile my grandfather had been brought up (with casual proddings, now and then, as you would doze before a fire and give it an occasional poke to make sure it doesn't go out) by his uncle Godfrey and a tutor named Dr. Harrison.

This Harrison was a great scholar, and also a notorious toper. He used to get fuddled every night at dinner, and then go down the south meadow to the Avon and recite Virgil by moonlight. One night in the sixteen-sixties he was ripping out something especially noble, Dido's funeral pyre or the like, and thrashing his arms above his head, when he fell into the river and was drowned.

This occurred just at the curve of the valley where we have put the stone bridge now: where the Avon is narrow and very still, and dark green with the reflection of its banks. So they buried Dr. Harrison in Keynsham church-yard, and all his scholarly cronies staggered to the funeral. I remember my grandfather telling me that one of them read a fine Latin oration over the doctor's grave, which brought tears to everybody's eyes. But it concluded my grandfather's classical education just at the point where all he could remember was that *virgo* does not necessarily mean "virgin," and some complicated business about the movements of the sun and the earth—he could never remember exactly what, or anything about it, except that you demonstrated it by means of oranges.

Of religious education he had, I regret to say, little. This was partly due to a curious circumstance which nobody has ever explained. The land, it is true, was under the domination of the Puritan clergy. And these Puritans, although sour enough fellows, were either not so tyran-nical as we suppose nowadays, or else they had a suspi-cion it was not altogether safe to cross a Kinsmere; in any event, they made few attempts to enforce their form of worship on the people at Blackthorn. But they would send missionaries, in steeple hats and grey worsted stockings, to exhort with the godless. Being a hospitable sort of man, my grandfather's uncle Godfrey would at least have admitted and fed them, except for the circumstance I was telling you of.

Uncle Godfrey had a favourite bull terrier named Goblin. Now Goblin, everybody agreed, was a tolerably mild-mannered dog, as dogs go. Yet it so happened that the very sight of a clergyman of any sort seemed to drive him into a frenzy. Nobody could control him. No sooner would he see a steeple hat coming through the lodge gates and up the hill than down he would streak after it in a fury of cannibal glee.

"Eh, Goblin," they would all cry. "Parson, Goblin! Go it, boy!"

And Goblin took that advice to the letter. He chased one nimble Man of God across two meadows, a cornfield, and the river, and finally treed him in the apple orchard; and the stablemen had to go down with pitchforks to get him off. My grandfather told me that this particular divine must have been the fastest sprinter in holy orders, because so fine a performance never occurred again. Anyhow, what with Goblin pursuing clergymen at the first sight or sniff of a square-toed shoe, and a standing bet with the head gardener as to which portion of each one's anatomy would receive the most damage, I regret to say that Roderick Kinsmere was accorded no vast amount of ghostly counsel.

Indeed, you will perceive that even for those times Blackthorn was considered a somewhat careless and demon-infested place. The village hanged a witch or two among our tenantry; but at Blackthorn they believed in witches, and regarded this as fair enough. Otherwise it was a lazy life. Nobody paid great heed to the weeds or nettles, or the fact that pigs would escape through the kitchens into the house; I can remember this occurring in my own time.

When Buck Kinsmere returned after the Restoration, of course, they made some attempt to put a better face on it, because Buck Kinsmere was a great diplomat, and a fine soldier, and polished with the airs of court. Yet, beyond the few duties he would hold to, he seemed to take little interest.

Sometimes he would assemble his household in the

15

great oak library, which later was so much damaged by fire in sixteen-ninety-one, and he would offer up thanks for the safe return of Charles the Second, confusion to his enemies, and prayers for the soul of Charles the Martyr. The morning sun would just be touching the mullioned windows of the room, not lighting it greatly. My grandfather remembered him standing with his back to the hood of the tall stone fireplace, in his long curling hair and lace collar. His eyes would be shut, with one hand extended towards the windows, the gilt-edged prayer-book under his empty left sleeve; and the household all kneeling, silent, around him.

Then sometimes he would take my grandfather into the main hall, to show him his pistols hung up on the wall, and his old breastplate with the rusty bloodstains upon it. He would bid my gradfather never to forget two things: the loyalty he must bear to his king, and the memory of his mother who was dead. Buck Kinsmere said quietly that, when his son came of age, the boy must at length go to court among the noblemen, and that the inheritance from Roderick's mother had made this possible.

She must have been a clear-headed little lady, Mathilda Kinsmere. She had been Mathilda Depping, the shipman's daughter; her father owned a stout fleet of merchant vessels which put out from the port of Bristol to trade in rum and slaves. When Edward Depping died, and she married my great-grandfather, Mathilda Kinsmere had the fleet sold so that there should be no taint of trade in the family; but she would not allow her husband to throw all her fortune as well as his own into the royal cause. Thus it came about that a part of this fortune, approximating ninety thousand pounds, was put into trust for my grandfather with Buck Kinsmere's friend Roger Stainley, the head of the great Stainley banking house, which is known all over the world nowadays.

Their destinies were to cross in singular fashion, because . . . but no matter for that, now. This inheritance was the precaution Mathilda Kinsmere took. You have seen her portrait in the Long Gallery, all stiff with lace after the Dutch style, with her red cheeks and merry eyes. But she died notwithstanding, of rust that got into a cut finger: she and Buck Kinsmere still loving each other so much that his was the worse heartbreak when he knew she had to go.

Still!

I do not wish to tell you of the ghosts and shadows you may find here, but of my grandfather growing up and going to London for his great adventure.

He had a pleasant time of it at Blackthorn. His uncle Godfrey taught him the use of small arms, particularly the four-foot double-edged rapier and the new-style, much lighter cup-hilt—narrow of blade, without cutting edges but needle-sharp for play with the point alone. They used to practice on the bowling green, where it was shady. The serving-girls would run to the windows, and Dr. Harrison sit under a plum tree with his pipe and a jug of cold punch, to watch some pretty rapid fencing matches there.

But what drew everybody round to shout, especially the men from the stables over the way, were the quarterstaff bouts. To see a whirl between two well-matched fellows, each with a seven-foot staff shod in iron, is a rare thing nowadays. When I was down from school once I saw Jem Lovell, the West Country champion (he was a Somerset man, though he settled in Devon), fight a Welsh challenger at the fair on Hanham Green; but today the sport has pretty well given place to boxing.

There was small notion of social dignity at Blackthorn after Buck Kinsmere died; and, my grandfather having acquired great proficiency in the quarterstaff art, a circumstance occurred which brought him wide notoriety in the country.

This fell out in the year 1669, when he was past his twentieth birthday: a genial, easygoing young fellow, with a knack of using long words in addition to his other accomplishments, and a nice eye for a wench.

Of his nimbleness with the quarterstaff Uncle Godfrey was especially proud. So it fell out that one night at a magistrates' meeting Uncle Godfrey drank a bottle too many, as old gentlemen will do. He got up on the table and offered even money on his nephew to crack the skull of any man in Somerset within half a stone of his weight. Whereupon a visiting landowner from the Mendips instantly offered two-to-one odds on a promising carter of his village, and a match was arranged—under terms of the most absolute secrecy—to take place at Blackthorn.

It so happened that this same carter (as the Mendip gentleman well knew when he made the wager) had been accustomed to drive twenty-odd miles every week in order to ogle a certain pretty dairy maid of our village. Which dairy maid was already—most reprehensibly, I grieve to say—a safe conquest of my grandfather, and well satisfied with the arrangement. Being informed of this fact did not please the honest carter. To the contrary, he swore by all his gods he would "smash yon yoong zur's poll for 'ee, and lay 'ee down dead, look." The J.P.'s felt themselves justified in expecting results of a tolerably lively nature. They had arranged for the presence of a small chosen group to watch the encounter on the bowling green: all very secret and orderly, as befitted their magisterial dignity.

You will, no doubt, anticipate what occurred.

On the appointed date, the whole countryside roundabout bore the general aspect of fair day. The good peasantry, still exulting in the free-and-easy reign of King Charles the Second, were full of what we should nowadays describe as "beans." Having already wagered their shirts on this bout, they were out to see fair play. They came flocking in, horse, foot, and wagon, in their best clothes. They rang the church bells, shot off squibs, hanged unpopular characters in effigy, danced in the taverns, and generally fortified themselves for the occasion. They also contrived to catch a bailiff and hold his head under a pump.

My grandfather, it need hardly be said, was immensely well-liked in the district. By nine o'clock in the morning he was down among them, settling the score for their beer, saluting the women, and inviting everybody to Blackthorn for the mêlée.

The opposing faction—consisting of a strong body of Mendip backers—arrived drunk towards one o'clock in the afternoon. They marched up the High Street singing "Here's a Health unto His Majesty," and broke a number of windows by way of diversion. Certain delays ensued, due to the outbreak of sporadic fights, and the discovery of one unlucky fellow (suspected of having been an exciseman for the late Commonwealth's tax on ardent

18

spirits), who was chased as far as Kingswood and thrown into the pond.

The bout took place at three o'clock, and was an epic. It lasted for an hour and twenty minutes, 8 1/2-foot staves bound in iron, without either the carter or my grandfather being able to land a blow that would stretch the other insensible. By this time they were both so furious, what with the futile whirling and cracking of quarterstaves, their own injuries, and the spectators' goading yells, that they could endure it no longer. They flung away weapons and went for each other fists, claws, and teeth.

This was the true battle. It shot and fizzed round the bowling green like a grounded skyrocket, the spectators buckling out to make way for it, and then closing in behind with howls of encouragement. It rolled away off the green, making the manure fly in clouds and scaring the very wasps out of the flower beds. It got up presently, danced a trifle, and reeled past the smithy (which stood where the summer arbour stands now). Here my grandfather stumbled on a wagon wheel, and they pitched forward into the dust again. The carter tore loose long enough to lay hold of a light hammer and throw it, which might have won the day for him; but it sailed through the forge window instead, and did no damage. Eventually the battle wound up in a horse trough over against the stables, both contestants being hauled out exhausted, half-drowned, and almost unrecognizable, when Squire Thunderman decided it was time to cry quits.

After a consultation Squire Thunderman mounted to the stable roof and stood up against the gilt face of the clock in the tower, where he made a speech declaring all bets void. Uncle Godfrey followed him, being whistle-drunk by this time, and the politest man in Somerset always.

"A few words, good people?" appeals Uncle Godfrey. "A few words, under favour and by your leave?"

"If that be your desire, have at it," says Squire Thunderman. "And yet the hour grows late. You will be short, sir?"

"Oh, ay," cries Uncle Godfrey, striking as much of an attitude as his years and weight would permit. "There need be no fear, dear brother-justice. I will be short; depend on't."

19

True to his promise, therefore, the old gentleman held forth for less than an hour in the most graceful terms, thanking the spectators for their presence there and congratulating both sides: he invited everybody to drink his health in the dining room, as well as my grandfather's for good measure; and concluded (in the course of a complicated oratorical gesture) by falling off the roof.

Thus amicability was restored, and all went right merrily until well into the following morning. Indeed, my grandfather liked this carter for his fight, and discovered him to be a most excellent fellow; shaking hands with him warmly, and saying, "By God, man, I am thy brother!" He also made him a present of a fine team of greys, feeling a trifle guilty about that dairy maid; and would have handed him the girl, too, if she had permitted it; and so passed the day.

You now have some notion of the calm pastoral life Roderick Kinsmere led, and of the elements that went into his making. It will not do to dwell on this, since there are mighty things a-brewing in the great world beyond Blackthorn gates. The time has come to speak of him—some eight or nine months after his fight with the carter—when he must pack his saddlebags and ride up to London to claim his inheritance.

From the strongbox in the library he took the letters his father had written for him years ago, notably a letter to His Grace the Duke of Buckingham at York House, one of the most powerful noblemen at court; and also from that strongbox he took the fine sapphire ring. His uncle Godfrey presented him with a letter to Mr. Roger Stainley, a pouch full of money, and a new sword.

All the tenantry had assembled to see him go, lined up deep before the old grey house. Under pretext of addressing parting injunctions to his nephew, Uncle Godfrey did not lose the opportunity of holding forth to them at considerable length.

The old gentleman stood on the steps under the arched doorway out there, carved with heraldic beasts as you see it now, and wiped a vinous tear from his eye as he exhorted. Uncle Godfrey bade him to be of good cheer; to remember the manners of his father, and his father's famed civility; to reflect on and hold dear the ancient Kinsmere name, its honesty and its worth; and manfully to smite in the eye any ill-disposed thus-and-so who doubted it. Uncle Godfrey further counselled him (rather unexpectedly) to remember that flesh is but grass, and man travelleth a weary road throughout his life, and liveth but to die; and after some minutes of this vein he had got both himself and the tenantry into such a depressed frame of mind that he fell back overcome.

During the harangue my grandfather sat quiet on his horse, with his hat off out of politeness. But he refused to be cast down; he could taste the air of springtime and see the green meadows warm under the sun. So he replied that he would strive to remember all this advice; he bade everyone good-bye, and rode down from the house with the tenantry cheering behind him, in a very tolerable good humour with himself and with the world. Mingled in the cheers he could hear the bells of Keynsham Church ringing far away, and the friendly pigs honking by the roadside; and this was in the green month of May, being the Year of Our Lord one thousand six hundred and seventy, and the tenth since the return of Our Sovereign Liege Charles the Second.

II

But now I must tell you of London, of its masks and fashions, of its squalor and glitter, as my grandfather first saw it all those years ago.

They caught the highwayman Claude Duval one night in January, at the Hole-in-the Wall in Chandos Street: as they catch knaves, almost always, whose tongues clack too freely in public. Claude Duval was the graceful cutthroat who played the flageolet on Hounslow Heath; who stopped the coach, and danced a coranto with the lady on the smooth turf in the moonlight before he relieved her husband of much booty.

But they took away his own money pouch and pistols, clapping him into Newgate. Then arose a great uproar and to-do; ladies in vizard masks came tearfully to visit him. Claude was a hero. Claude postured with ease in the dock at the sessions house, speaking up mighty jocosely to the red-robed judge above the bar, who felt his own importance when he fitted on the black cap.

And then one raw morning the great bell boomed at St. Sepulchre's. They put Claude into a cart, with the sheriff going before and the javelin men around; they presented him with a bunch of flowers as the procession moved out along roads that ran two and a half miles through the countryside to Tyburn gallows. A vast crowd saw Claude turned off after an affecting last speech, but his honours had only begun when his legs ceased to twitch.

Wailing their lamentations, his admirers arrayed him in finery, put him into a mourning coach, and set his body to lie all night in state at a tavern near St. Giles's, with eight wax tapers burning about the bier and eight black-cloaked gentlemen in attendance. This, then, was at the turn of the year, at the beginning of the second decade in the reign of King Charles the Second; and Claude with his dancing master's airs might have been put up as a model for the time, like the status of King Charles at the New Exchange.

It was a noisy time, a posturing time, a time of jigs and of bludgeoning wit: a cruel, swaggering, credulous, clever time, for smoky London on its mud-flats. This New Exchange, on the south side of the Strand, made a shopping centre for the western end of town, waxing rich on my lord and my lady's passion for gewgaws. Four galleries, inner and outward walk, upper and lower walk, held a clamour of damsels crying finery at their stalls. Very good gloves and ribands, sir; choice of essences, rings, clouded canes with silken tassels; the true wigs of Chedreux, sir, and our dusky Lower Walk very useful for assignations. In the courtyard pigeons fluttered round a statue of His Majesty's self, looking stately in the dress of a Roman emperor.

But for the finest knick-knack wonders, the trinkets of China which my lady must have or die of shame, they went further. They went into the darkest City, to Leadenhall Street, where the India House held its sales, its auctions, its raffles and tea drinkings. A prosperous time, this, for the fat merchant companies: for the Turkey Company, the Russia Company, the Africa Company, the newly formed Hudson's Bay Company; most of all, for the great East India Company. Would my lady have a fall of Mecca muslin, woven with gold and silver? A dragon in speckled porcelain? A caged nightingale? Some gilded jars of snuff

22

and pulvillio, or the stuffed sawfish everyone so much admired?

It was all there for her. She had my lord's purse, or somebody's purse. On any day she could go rolling in her huge springless coach to the India House, where the rafflewheel spun, and spices were burned in the fire, and opulence served tea out of cups like tinted eggshells.

A season of prosperity, too, for the toymakers round Fleet Street, who could charm the most sober minds with a jack-in-the-pulpit or an ingenious climbing monkey. His Majesty the King much prized an artfully fashioned clock which was made to run by the motion of rolling bullets down an inclined plane; he would roll bullets for hours at a time. His Royal Highness James Duke of York—who not many years before had been putting bullets to a rather less domestic use, in the war against the Dutch—sat on the floor with a bevy of ladies, playing "I Love My Love with an A," or enjoyed the Cromwellian pastime of cushion pelting.

Give us, cried fashion, all manner of toy wonders. Even the Royal Society, under the aegis of their silver mace, gravely played at science with clocks, barometers, vivisection, and chemistry. They exhibited mummies and the livers of vipers. They conceived plans for a steam engine, a housebreaker alarm, and a tinderbox that turned into a pistol; they injected sheep's blood into a man's veins, to see what happened, and puzzled their wits over His Majesty's query about the fish in the water pail. Very remarkable grew the debates of the Royal Society at Gresham College, until they gathered up their flasks and loadstones to run westward before the roar of the Great Fire.

The fire swallowed thirteen-thousand-odd houses in that year '66, when Prince Rupert and the Duke of York were scorching the Dutchmen's tail feathers at sea. *Annus Mirabilis,* Mr. John Dryden called it when he wrote the poem, in his natural enthusiasm and desire for preferment. Mr. Dryden even had the wondering fish raising their heads out of the water to contemplate the spectacle. And from this ruin a new town had begun to take shape. Kennels were no less foul, sewage as bad, and paved streets as few. The tanneries, the lime kilns, the soap vats still brewed a murk of oily smoke, raining soot flakes as big as your thumbnail and making a fog all the year round.

But the new streets were raised and widened; the new houses were built of brick, not pitch-coated matchwood; and the plague of '65 had been burnt out of every hole. Back crept the vintners to Three Cranes, the mercers to Paternoster Row; Cheapside once more raucously rang with the cries of 'prentices, and coaches rumbled again past the rails round the black-gutted stumps of Old St. Paul's.

In fine, none had fared better through evil days than those same merchants I was speaking of. Their tables grew heavy with gold plate, and four Flanders mares drew their coaches to the Royal Exchange. They were the aldermen of that powerful body, the Corporation of the City of London. As symbol of their pomp, my Lord Mayor rode to the feats at Guildhall in scarlet robe and black velvet hood, with the gold chain around his neck. His trainbands numbered twelve regiments of foot and two of horse; the corporation's own poet laureate rhymed (somewhat optimistically) the splendour of his name in future ages. Hence your merchant-lords, watching the throng of bubbleheads who bought their gauds in such profusion, could scheme better bargains at Lloyd's Coffee-House in Leadenhall Street, and drink the soot-black delicacy out of a dish.

Already a multitude of glass lanterns had appeared before the coffee-houses. A glass lantern was its sign, as a red lattice indicated a tavern. Presided over by pretty jillflirts of accommodating character, they were fair quarters for the inhaling of tobacco and snuff. Though the best of them in the money-changing area might be accounted Garraway's, off Cornhill; yet these dusky rooms of high-backed settles were the forerunners of all our clubs; and, to taste the true flavour of an institution uniquely British, any foreigner went westward.

He took an uncertain footing down Ludgate Hill, where the hackney coaches splashed a jolting passage. From here to the Strand, under painted gables, rolled a din of barter and brawling. They cried rotten fruit, jars of usquebaugh, and scrofulous-looking sausages. They hawked mackerel and rosemary, their voices rising as harsh as the clank of passing-bells.

"Have you," bawls a tinker, after his rattle of ghostly knocks at somebody's door, "have you a brass pot, iron pot, skillet, kettle, or frying pan to mend?"

"No, we have not. Be off!"

"Come, mistress, a word with you. I'll adventure it."

"Will you so, God damme? Gardy-loo, jackanapes! 'Ware slops below!"

This may have been witty; it may not. Yet any pedlar, you conceive, must be nimble in more senses than one. Here rattled the crooked lanes of street signs, bright-painted, gilded, carved to huge goblin shapes a-creak in high winds; and an imp-black dwarf of a chimney sweep tripped up an incautious baker, coloured all silver-grey from the dust of the basket on his head.

Now God help, in all pious sincerity, any impertinent foreigner who went to find the good talk of the coffee-houses in Fleet Street. They always took him for a French-man, what they called a Mounzer, and they hated him. They knocked him under waterspouts, pelted him with rams' horns out of the kennel filth, mashed his toes with the barrels that draymen were rolling into cellars. Does he clap handkerchief to his nose against the smells? Won't he let the bootblacks brighten his shoes with a polish of soot and rancid oil? That beggar at the corner of Water Lane, who has burnt sores in his own face and festered them to hideousness with powdered arsenic: that bundle of ulcers wheedling on his knees, with white eyeballs uprolled—is the foreigner heedless of his whining.

"French dog!" screech gamin and slut. "Mounzer! Papist! Lousy spy!"

Mounzer's periwig is fouled with beer foam or twitched off as a trophy. Mounzer, who can find no coach, bolts over Fleet Ditch, past Bridewell Prison and the scaffolding round new St. Bride's Church, which Dr. Wren is fashion-ing for the peace of God; up the long slope toward Temple Bar. The clatter of pursuit, battering through Fleet Street like a 'prentices' football chase, will bring Bully of Alsatia shouldering out of his den to see the sport.

He was all too familiar a figure, Bully of Alsatia: a greasy, swaggering, chin-jutting, many-oathed bravo. They knew his flopping hat, pinned up at one side; his frowsy linen and sandy weather-beaten peruke; above all, the scandalous iron sword rattling at his heels. Alsatia, his stable, made a small plague spot bounded on the east by Water Lane, on the west by the wall of the Temple, on the south by the Thames, and on the north by Fleet Street: a dozen-odd stinking lanes in a corner, the sanctuary for every unhanged rogue in town.

No bailiff's footstep shook the flies off a dead dog's carcass inside Alsatia; no bailiff dared come. Even a magistrate would not venture among such mephitic houses without a company of musketeers behind him. Let any suspicious stranger be detected here, and they set on him a-whooping with swords, spits, bricks, and broomsticks. They battered him senseless, tossed him in a blanket to point the lesson, and flung back the pulp to Fleet Street.

In this rabbit warren, down by the mud-flats where the stench of tannery smoke hung thickest, Bully ruled supreme above his crew of pickpockets, thimbleriggers, pimps, cutpurses, and bankrupts. He had been (he said) a soldier. He knew the ways of fashion. That ruined gentleman, sobbing draggle-haired across a chair, "Our Father, which art in heaven," who needed half a pint of raw Hollands to quieten his shaking guts and steady his hand for dealing at cards again: that ruined gentleman was Bully's closest friend. Bully jostled the timid when he ventured forth. He swore By the Hilts; he went sometimes to the bear garden at Southwark across the river, there to guzzle warm wine while dogs tore out the throat of roaring Bruin, or two fencing masters made each other's blood fly in a cut-and-thrust with double-edged swords. When he had a shilling or two to wager, he visited the cockpit in Shoe Lane. Meanwhile, at the George above Hanging Sword Alley he shook out dice among the quart pots, with his fuddled harlots around.

Bully and his cronies kept up an incessant feud, for one reason or another, with the stately old institution next door. Side by side with Alsatia, separated from it only by a brick wall, lay the premises of the Temple. Here the Templars—young men they were, mostly—lived in a sort of university, with the Benchers as dons and the Treasurer as Chancellor. *In mentibus parentorum,* they studied law. In actuality, they did almost anything else.

Through courts and cloisters swarmed a pack of robust, arrogant students as formidable as Bully himself. Questionless, there must have been somebody of studious habits—Roger North says his brother Francis was. Tucked away up two pairs of stairs, in an airless petit chamber with a tallow dip, you might perhaps have found one earnest young man poring late over Littleton, Manwood on Forest Law, Coke's Pleas of the Crown and Jurisdiction of the Courts, Fitzherbert's *Natura Brevium,* and other delectable uses of *hic, haec, hoc.* A most exemplary fellow, this, who kept vast commonplace-books, practised putting causes in the Common Pleas, had a weak smile and fluttery hands, nor ever got drunk except with a judge.

But the Templars in general, being three-bottle men, were lads of a different kidney. They paid five pounds entrance fine to get five years' sport before they assumed wheedling airs and a scarlet gown at Westminster Hall. If an officious Bencher tried to make them behave, he was held under a pump. Even my Lord Mayor, who essayed an entry in full panoply with the sword of state before him, got his sword of state beaten down and himself booted out, and provoked a riot for whose quelling he must appeal to the king and whistle up the trainbands. Your Templars gave much patronage to fencing-and-dancing schools. They were fond of a hand at basset over a late tobacco pipe and half a dozen of claret; they ate cheese-cakes; they pursued with gusto masked nymphs in the Mulberry Garden or picked up a fashionable disease among the trulls at Whetstone Park.

If a poor Bencher complained to the judges about them, he was frequently snubbed. And why not? Those were great days (say four or five years after the Great Fire, about the time when Sir Matthew Hale became Lord Chief Justice of the King's Bench) for the brethren of the long robe. Anybody, from the nervous barrister with a first brief to the eminent serjeant-at-law in his black coif, could tell you that advancement did not lie in knowledge of the Year Books.

"Keep on the good side of the judge, young man," shrewd counsel would have run. "Know the judge; study the judge; let your client lose his cause without a word, but for God's sake don't cross His Lordship or dispute with him when he shows signs of having a bee under his peruke."

Or, as a litigious widow once put it:

"Come, Mr. Blunder, pray bawl soundly for me at the King's Bench. Bluster, sputter, question, cavil; make sure your argument be intricate enough to confound the court, and then you may do my business."

But, *imprimis,* coddle His Lordship. Even our rigid-minded old Puritan Hale, as a result of dexterous smoothing, has a partiality for drunken Will Scroggs, whose tipple is claret, and for drunken young George Jeffreys, whose tipple is anything. Above all, for the long run, strive by judicious toadying to win the favor of a patron: first among the powerful aldermen of the City and then—if Providence is kind—among the all-powerful lords of His Majesty's court. You may be Chief Justice in half a dozen years, and perhaps Lord Chancellor in ten.

Anyhow, it made a pleasant interval for shrewd lawyers in the haunts south of Temple Bar. Towards evening, when a mist crept up from the gardens along the river, Fleet Street grew warm and bright with the red lattices of taverns. Over against the Middle Temple gate stood the famous Devil and St. Dunstan, which Ben Jonson knew in James the First's time. Not far away was the Cock, where the actress Mrs. Knepp ate lobster with Mr. Pepys of the Admiralty before they took coach for some amorous fondling at Vauxhall; the Globe, at which Mr. Henry Vaughan scribbled verses "in a chamber painted overhead with a cloudy sky"; the Bell, Peele's, and the Greyhound. Hard by Temple Bar stood Dick's, and the Rainbow that was the second oldest coffee-house in London. At the corner of Chancery Lane—its double balcony overlooking the pillory in Fleet Street—you might see the notorious King's Head tavern, at which the Green Ribbon Club would scheme its Whiggeries in later years.

Not the taverns of the courtliest wits, these. For such you must pass Temple Bar, far westward into the world of fashion. Hereabouts you would seldom find Jack Wilmot, "Little Sid," or Gentle George Etherege. These arbiters of the witty word visited Fleet Street only as preparation for a night's scouring through the City: to wrench off door knockers, belabour the watch, or smash the windows of blind old Mr. Milton's house in Holborn.

But the company could be rare enough, after the thunder of wagons had ceased in the street. It was a fine sight for Jack Pauper, shivering outside these snug boxes, when the sharp air steamed the windows at nightfall, and he could see the fire gleaming on pewter pots, rich cheeses, and nets of lemons; when sparks fluttered up among the dark old chimneypots, like the brown-peruked, white-waistcoated, purple-cloaked young sparks gesticulating inside; when, as you passed by in the street, you could smell the roast sizzling in gravy on its spit over the fire, and a fragrance of hot spiced ale.

Presently, in the thick dusk, mummified heads were no longer visible atop Temple Bar. Presently lackeys came trotting from the opposite direction, holding up flaring links to light the way for my lord and my lady borne east in gilt sedan chairs. They swept past shuttered shops, turning left up the court and plying the knocker of the licensed gaming-house in Bell Yard. My lady raised a claret-coloured curtain of her chair to show—briefly, in the blaze of torches—large eyes peering out, paint, and patches. Through the mud-and-kennel smells of everywhere trailed a scent of orange pomade.

The visitors moved on. A last torch shone on the face of somebody hunched in the pillory, forgotten by the constable; he had been insensible since midday, from a blood-caked gash over one eye, and still hung limp with his mouth open. In Bell Yard the iron knocker banged again; the door opened. Presently laughter and calling died away with the barking of dogs.

Once outside Temple Bar (Dr. Wren built it, where formerly there had been only posts and chains across the road) you were en route to Westminster by way of the Strand. On the south side of the street, from here to Charing Cross, stood the great town-houses of the nobility.

Look at them, now, as you might have seen them then.

Under the eaves of the noblemen's houses, stuck like a poultice to every buttress, are the little shops and stalls: the merchant very dignified in his flat-topped cap, rubbing his hands and yodelling. Round the rails of St. Clement's Church you watch them a-bickering, as thick as the sparrows that twitter above its porch. Here too are some mountebanks: fire-eaters, raree-show-men, ballad singers hoarsely warbling.

But of this hubbub it is only in part that I would speak. The world my grandfather came to know lay still farther west, within a quarter mile or so round Whitehall Palace.

Charing Cross at that time was a vast open space, bare brown earth underfoot, with the Royal Mews, where the soldiers were quartered, stretching along the north side. If you stood with your back to the Royal Mews, you could look straight down King Street to Whitehall. On the left, where the Thames curved, a crazy, ancient hodge-podge of a palace—all architectural styles, though in the main of red brick or dressed stone—straggled for half a mile along the waterside. So much without plan had they built the old rookery that one of its principal gates, the Holbein Gate, stood slap in the middle of King Street and blocked the road; but the public had a right of way through it to Westminster.

If you followed the crowd that debouched past Spring Gardens (good glades and arbours for dalliance, and Rhenish cost only eightpence the bottle), you would plunge into the bustle round Whitehall Palace. Across King Street on the right were stationed the Horse Guards, two troopers in breastplates and blue sleeves, sitting their horses motionless on either side of a grey stone gate; and beyond them, acre upon acre, rose up the trees of St. James Park.

Over the main body of the palace, opposite on your left, the sky would be tumbling with smoke from half a mile of chimneypots: high and low, little and big, singly or in clusters, out of every cranny whence smoke could issue. Beside the Banqueting House opened another gateway, called the Palace Gate, which constituted the entrance-in-chief. Sedan chairs waited there to be hired, the chairmen smoking their pipes and lounging in the shade of trees that hung over the wall.

There was always much commotion at the Palace Gate. You found there a throng of pedlars with wares of every sort, from a string of glass beads to a swearing parrot. (My grandfather bought a fine swearing parrot once, and was very proud of it; but his friends used to throw water over it to make it swear, and they did this so often that the parrot caught cold and died.) Pedlars and mountebanks were supposed to be forbidden in this quarter, because they made such a crush that the gentry could scarcely enter. Quite often a pair of sentries would come out raging and prod at them with pikes or halberds, but they always pressed back. After all, the public had another right of way here: this time through the Great Court to the waterside.

Does that shock you, dear grandchildren, in our wellbehaved year 1815? But it was true.

There stood the dirty white gatehouse, with lodgings for the king's almoner. Beyond it lay the Great Court, which smelt most powerfully of cooking; the palace kitchens and buttery had been built along its north side at the rear, and steamed all day above a noise of clanking pots and mysterious knockings at casks. If you had an errand away from Whitehall, you would push your way across the cobblestones and go along an open passage with the kitchens at one side and on the other side the Great Hall, which had been turned into a public playhouse. At the end of this passage the public stairs descended to the water and to the swarm of boats clustering there. At a very modest price you could take wherry for anywhere in the City, with none to hinder or say you nay.

But if you were merely one of the ragtag throng, and had no errand or thought of one, you would only swear at the watermen and stick your head round the corner for a glance along the waterside. A little southward lay the private landing stairs, which the king and his household used. At the top of these private stairs, up a ten-foot ladder, the queen had her volary; and, when anybody began to descend, the birds would set up such a clatter and song that it was as loud as a herald crying the royal presence.

(She was very fond of birds, was the poor Portuguese queen, and of all gentle things. She had a retreat built on the flat roof near the private stairs: her bedroom windows opened on this. It was from this retreat that they watched the river pageants or processions—the king fingering his chin, patting the heads of his spaniels, and sometimes saying, "God's fish, madam!" while Queen Catherine sat with her hands folded in her lap. She was a quiet, dark, illfavoured little lady, with protruding teeth; much given to piety, and fortitude, and unobtrusiveness. My grandfather was once escorted, with much pomp, to see her chamber. He said she had nothing in it but some pious pictures and books of devotion, her holy water in the alcove where she slept, and at her bedside a clock with a lamp burning inside it, so that she could tell the hour at any time in the night. I have heard that sometimes, in the night, she cried.)

Oh, yes. It was a town in itself, this careless, brawling, loosely managed hive of a palace. I told you the Great Hall had been turned into a public playhouse. There was also (unknown to the various chancellors or grooms or such-like dignitaries) a public dram-shop smack in the middle of the palace, under the very stairs leading up to the king's Presence Chamber. They only discovered it by accident, years later. During the reign of James the Second, in looking for a place to put the queen's sedan chair, they came upon a parcel of tipplers earnestly boozing underneath the stairs; and nobody (including the proprietor) could tell how long the place had been there.

This is the atmosphere my grandfather found when he strolled into the Great Court one evening in May of the year one thousand six hundred and seventy. He was moving along pleasantly and good-humouredly, thumbs in his sword belt, whistling a country air, and at peace, or so he thought, with all the earth.

He walked into trouble five minutes later.

III

It was, then, one of those warm days when the blood stirs, the trees seem more green, and even the geese strut their ways saying "boo" to each other. My grandfather, Roderick Kinsmere, had been wandering through town since early morning, having taken up quarters at the Grapes near Charing Cross and stabled his horse there.

To him London seemed a vasty fine place, if far from overclean. In his heart of hearts he was not easy, and perhaps a trifle struck with awe. But this is a state of mind which no Kinsmere has ever relished, and he resolved not to betray it.

In the morning, too, he had gone to attend the Duke of Buckingham's levee at York House, as he had been instructed to do. He had no difficulty in finding York House, which was also near Charing Cross on the south side of the Strand; nor had he imagined that the rest would be difficult either.

"Come!" you could imagine His Grace of Bucks saying. "A good welcome, let all take note, to the son of an old friend! Sit you merry, young man; and, ecod, what's your pleasure in the choice of drink?"

That, he had thought to himself, was how matters would be carried by George Villiers, the second duke; it was how they carried matters in Somerset, and what he himself would have done.

But nothing of the sort occurred.

On the contrary, when he arrived at York House he found himself swallowed up in a great mass of struggling suitors. York House proved to be a splendid place beside the river, having many lawns and coloured awnings; it was divided into two buildings by a court whose terraces descended to the water gate.

With no tipstaff on guard to question him or even observe him, he entered a great foyer or anteroom. From its floor of veined marble, slippery enough to run and skate upon, pillars of polished wood and gilding rose up at some height to support a roof all painted over with sky and clouds and fat naked goddesses reclining there.

Though the whole place was full of people, they showed no disposition joyously to skate on the floor. They displayed no joyousness at all, being too preoccupied or even anguished. All their attention seemed centred on a pair of carved double doors at the west side of the foyer, guarded by large flunkeys with supercilious eyebrows.

There was much loud talk, a continual swish-swish of feet on the marble floor, and a smell of perfume, not very pleasant, with no good tobacco smoke to lighten it. At intervals one or two of the guests would make a rush at those closed double doors, as though attacking a fort. Most often they were fended off by the arrogant footmen, but sometimes they would worm through; the doors opened briefly and closed again.

Still nobody paid the least attention to my then-young grandfather, which is not good for a man's ease of mind. At the far end of the foyer, where there were deep windows towards the terraces above the river, he saw a neat little elderly man in a dark periwig, snuff-coloured clothes, and white stockings. This gentleman took no part in the loud talk. He stood in the embrasure of a window, his hands folded behind his back. His face, though something

33

cynical and pitted with wrinkles about the forehead, was not unkindly.

My grandfather liked his appearance on the instant.

"Give you good day, sir!" says Kinsmere, with much courtesy and heartiness.

The small elderly gentleman made a leg, by which I mean he bowed.

"And to you, sir," he answered with equal courtesy, "a very good day in return. If you are come to attend His Grace of Bucks's levee . . ."

"Indeed, sir, I apprehend I am."

"Have you by chance a petition to offer, may I ask?"

"Petition, sir? I have no petition, nor desire aught at his hands. The noble lord is *there*, we must suppose," cried Kinsmere, stabbing his thumb towards the carved double doors.

"Yes, yes! The noble lord is there, and takes his morning chocolate."

"But, damme, sir, how does one wait upon him? What's the password to admit us?"

Kinsmere's companion drew a deep breath and cast one eye round, like a man who has much patience but needs all of it.

"Why, as to that," he replied. "If you are a near friend of His Grace, or bear tidings he desires to hear, you have but to present yourself at those doors. If you are a suitor in some kind, or he owes you money," and here the small gentleman twitched up bony shoulders, "you are not like to see him at all. 'Tis a thing far easier to gain audience with the king. His Majesty pays no debts, on my life; but at least he is mighty affable and civil in putting you off."

At this moment there was a sharp kind of scuffle at the double doors. Both of them were knocked open at once. The aggressor at the doors, changing his demeanour so quickly that he seemed struck by paralysis, adjusted his wig and faltered inside.

My grandfather had one glimpse of a large, thick-carpeted room with a canopied bed. In that bed, choked round by a lace-collared nightgown, a stout man with a red face and several chins, his shaven head swathed in the silk scarf of dishabille, sat propped up against the pillows with a silver chocolate service in his lap.

Many persons had gathered round him, including a

plump fancifully dressed woman who had very little bodice to her gown. But Grandfather Kinsmere did not look with any attention at those still in the room. He looked at those who were just leaving it.

Out from the great bedroom, all abreast, stalked four men of fashion.

All were young. All wore their hats indoors, as the custom was. But, whereas three of them carried the garb of beaux—fringed pantaloons, much lace, light cup-hilt rapier slung just inside the skirt of the coat—the fourth man, at the extreme left, was a very modish captain of dragoons.

The identity of the three beaux my grandfather never knew or needed to know. This dragoon captain, on the other hand . . .

He was a tall man, was the captain, perhaps an inch or two taller than Rowdy Kinsmere. Under his long red coat, with black frogging across the buttonholes, you saw cavalry boots with wide tops to prevent the leg being crushed in a charge. Instead of the dragoon's heavy backsword, as though to emphasize his modishness he wore over his coat an ordinary cup-hilt on its gold-embroidered baldric from right shoulder to left hip.

Clean-shaven, unlike most cavalrymen, he had a long nose that flared into wide uptilted nostrils above a narrow mouth. He was so remote in his own sense of superiority, a kind of congealed sneer, that quite literally he did not *see* anyone else as the four fashionables marched abreast. He did not see my grandfather.

And then it happened.

Kinsmere had turned partly sideways, bending down to speak to the little elderly man in the window embrasure. The four fashionables wheeled, making for the front of the foyer; the dragoon captain wheeled at the end of their line. As he swung, staring through my grandfather as through a windowpane, his strong right shoulder rose up. With a great thump and jar it struck Kinsmere just under the chin.

Kinsmere's shoe slid wildly on the polished floor; his hand seized at air. But for his excellent balance, and a cat's quickness on his feet, he would have been knocked flat.

"Come!" said the little man, extending a hand to help.

35

"That was ill-done! That was plaguey ill-done of so fine an officer, if I may say so!"

"Why, damme, you say true. And therefore . . ."

The four fashionables were now some distance away, uncaring.

"Stay!" cried the little man. He seized Kinsmere's arm as my grandfather made an instinctive movement. "Stay!" he repeated, in dignity shot through with alarm. "Where are you going? What would you do?"

"I would follow him, that's what. I would follow him, and remonstrate with him. If he won't hear remonstrance, curse me, I would knock his head against the wall and teach him manners."

"Stay, I tell you! You must not, young man; at all costs you must not! To provoke a brawl at York House were the sheerest folly."

"Is it so?"

"It is so, believe me. You would gain short shrift from any of the sycophants here. At best you would be beaten from your five wits; at worst you would see Newgate or Bedlam."

"Must I endure it, then?" shouts Rowdy Kinsmere. "Must I receive all and give nothing?"

"Ay; 'tis to be feared you must."

"Why?"

"That's the way of the world and of courts, young man. You may mislike it; *I* mislike it. But that's the way of things; we can't mend 'em, and must suffer 'em. Besides—Come!" urged the other, his wizened face taking on the heartiness and the earnestness of peacemaking. "You forget your errand here, surely? And that must not be. You had intent, had you not, to wait upon my Lord Duke of Bucks?"

Kinsmere looked across at the carved doors, which were again closed.

"I *had* intent to wait upon him, it's true. But I have altered my mind."

"Altered your mind?"

"All such fuss and turmoil," exclaimed Kinsmere, "to see *him?* Why, hang me," says he in a surprised way, "I have been put at less trouble to see the five-footed calf at Bristol fair. Or even Hamid the Strong Man, whose feats were most prodigious. Besides, having once glimpsed that

36

fat red-faced jackanapes in the bed there—was it my Lady Shrewsbury, his *chère amie* as they say, astir betimes and beside him?—I am not persuaded that the spectacle much allures me. My lord duke? Be damned to him."

Whereat the young man clapped on his hat.

"And now, sir, for an errand of more moment," he continued. "With many thanks for your courtesy, can you direct me to Lombard Street? I must wait upon an eminent banker-goldsmith, who is in some sense a guardian of mine. I am to claim an inheritance he holds in trust, to the amount of some ninety thousand pounds or the like . . ."

"For God's sake, young man," interrupted the other, "pray lower your voice!"

"Hey?"

"Be not so free in your ways or speech, I counsel you! Be not so open as publicly to mention a sum of that size, else in our honest town they'll be at you like leeches to drain you of it. Discretion, ever discretion! Hem, now!"

"Well, but . . ."

"You would know the way to Lombard Street, you say, and you would wait upon a banker of that district? Pray pardon my seeming inquisitiveness, but may I hear the name of this banker?"

"To be sure you may. His name is Mr. Roger Stainley. He—"

"And your own name, sir?"

"Kinsmere. Roderick Edward Kinsmere, of Blackthorn in Somerset."

The small shrewd-faced gentleman nodded, drawing my grandfather into the window embrasure. From the pocket of his snuff-coloured surcoat he took a spectacle case, extracted a pair of square spectacles, and fitted them on with so deft a motion that he disturbed not a curl of his wig.

Kinsmere never forgot how he looked at that moment, in the sunlight of the window embrasure. The glass of the great window was a little crooked and of a faint greenish tint, set in a multitude of small round panes with metal edges. They threw wavy shadows across the oak wall of the recess and across the face of the man in spectacles—who had turned sideways, one knee slightly advanced, left hand behind his back, studying his taller companion. For the first time my grandfather looked well

37

at him. He remarked, despite this well-wisher's sober attire, the handsome gold watch chain and the fine fall of lace at his throat.

"Hem!" said the sober-resplendent man in spectacles, and cleared his throat once more. Whereupon he smiled, making a very stately and courteous bow. "Why, then, permit me to hope that we are well met," adds he. "You were not expected for some days, but 'tis no matter. To speak a truth, Mr. Kinsmere, I myself am the banker you would wait upon. *I* am Roger Stainley. My boy, I rejoice to see you."

"Burn me!" exclaimed my grandfather, as they shook hands. He was delighted; he felt a real burst of affection, and all but yanked the prim Mr. Stainley off his feet. "Well met? Burn me, I should think so!"

"And now . . ."

"Why, we'll go hence and drink hearty. What else?"

"Drink?" said Mr. Stainley, frowning and pinching at his underlip. "Drink, did you say? Hem, now! Tush, tut, and again tush! This is a matter of business, young sir, and must be done in good order.

"Stay, though!" he added in some disquiet. "We are not private enough here, I fear. Tongues wag and clack about us, as your ears will provide evidence. We may be overheard, and that must not be. If you will give yourself the trouble of accompanying me . . . ?"

Stiff, sober, and yet bustling, the banker took his arm and led him from the window embrasure. Mr. Stainley then guided him to an arched doorway at the back of the foyer, along a passage to the rear door and the open air, and thence to a bright flower garden overlooking the water gate, where no eavesdropper could possibly have approached.

Here Kinsmere gave him the letters of identification, one from Uncle Godfrey and one which his late father had written years ago. While the banker read these letters with great care, my grandfather watched little boats moving against the smoky sparkle of the river. Mr. Stainley finished the letters and handed them back.

"Good, that's established!" says he. "You are Alan Kinsmere's son, you show it, and I consent thereunto. The sapphire ring on your left hand were proof enough in itself." Then he cast up his eyes in thought. "To our

38

business, now! As regards your accounts . . ."

"My accounts? What of 'em?"

"They are prepared for your inspection," answered Mr. Stainley. "You made reference (most injudiciously!) to ninety thousand pounds. I may tell you privily that the moneys intrusted to my keeping, by fortunate stewardship of investment, now amount nearer to a hundred thousand than to ninety. It is a handsome fortune, which you must guard well against rogues. How will you employ it?"

"Sir, does that matter?"

"Does it *matter,* you declare?"

"Indeed, I declare it," says Kinsmere. "Oh, damme! I was bred up in the country, and want little. So long as there are a few good coins in my purse," and he slapped the pouch at his right hip, which gave forth a satisfying chink, "who knows or cares for the future?"

The little banker was much shocked, as well he might be.

"Come, this is mighty unbusinesslike! This will never do! You were bred up in the country; granted; so much is evident. Yet you aspire, past doubt, to become a man of fashion?"

"Sir, I do not. If we may make judgment from the four sneering elegants who sailed at us in the foyer (including our bold dragoon captain, damn his uptilted nose), I would have as little truck with such cattle as I conveniently may."

"And yet you must," retorted Mr. Stainley, "because this is an obligation you may not shirk. Come! I'll not deny you may be in the right of it; I'll not deny that in my heart I may agree. And yet—duty! Your father stood high in the esteem of the late King Charles the First, and was favourably known to His Present Majesty. You must be presented to the king; you must take your place at court. It will entail certain preparations. Those clothes of yours, for instance . . ."

"Clothes, sir?"

"They were well enough, past doubt, at Blackthorn amid the folks of Somerset. They will not serve, pray credit me, for the galleries and withdrawing rooms at Whitehall." Again a look of satire and cynicism pinched down Mr. Stainley's eyelids. "Not that I care, God knows, or that the king will care. His Majesty, notoriously, is the most slovenly man at court. But I hold myself to some degree responsible for you. And I must give you the outward seeming of a man of fashion; I must see you fitted out with foretopped peruke, with satin waistcoats, with clouded cane and Venice-point and finger watch, to save my very conscience!"

There was much more in this strain. Mr. Stainley talked at some length, answering the questions he himself asked, while the morning sun strengthened on the river and the bright flower beds. They must first do much buying, Mr. Stainley said. They must visit tailors, and wigmakers, and jewellers, and swordsmiths, and hosiers, and heaven knew whom else, until his listener's head began to reel.

All such suggestions were pleasing rather than otherwise to my grandfather. He was resolved never to become a spark of fashion. But he rather looked forward to bedecking himself (briefly) in this manner, as he would have looked forward to donning some wildly outrageous costume, just once, for a masquerade ball.

And then, the banker declared in some anguish, they must find him proper quarters to live in. It must *not* be known that he was lodged, even for one day, at a common tavern. Mr. Stainley suggested (somewhat uneasily, you might have thought) that Kinsmere should come to lodge with himself and his wife and daughter in Lombard Street, until such time as he should find a place in the fashionable world.

But this offer my grandfather opposed with heat. For you must know he had his eye out to certain amusements for that night, not unconnected with wine bottles and willing dames. Prim and elderly people, however kindly, are almost always opposed to such diversions; he wanted no watchful eye upon him. So he protested with warm civility that he couldn't, burn him in hell if he could, so inconvenience his good friend, and the rest of it, burn him to a cinder.

He had a pretty fair notion that Mr. Stainley suspected his reasons; but the banker only shut up one eye and nodded, with what looked like relief, and they were mighty considerate of each other. Well, then, the banker said, no doubt conscious of having done his duty; well, then, at least his young friend would sup with him at nine o'clock? His young friend would, with pleasure.

"Enfin, as it may be," Mr. Stainley concluded, adjusting his flat-crowned hat as he prepared to depart. "I shall be much preoccupied with business for the rest of today. At best of it, you will allow, we can't go a-buying until the morrow. Meanwhile, young sir, will you take advice from one who is older and pehaps wiser than yourself?"

"I will take advice from *you.*"

"Come, that's better! That's seeming hopeful!" And the banker pondered. "You must see the sights, I suppose. But keep to yourself, I conjure you, as much as may be. Go not a-buying at the New Exchange; mingle little with your equals among the quality until such time as *I*, though of humble birth and small consequence in this world, shall be close at hand to give counsel. Above all things, since you seem not oversupplied with prudence, I would urge upon you the need for self-control. These impulses of yours, when you think yourself jeered or insulted, to knock somebody's head against a wall . . ."

"What of the impulses, Mr. Stainley?"

"They are unworthy; they are unseemly; resist them! A last word in your ear, Roderick Kinsmere. Do you honour your father's memory?"

"I honour it and I cherish it, sir, with all my heart."

"Would ever Alan Kinsmere have behaved as you desired to behave? Would Alan Kinsmere have stooped oafishly to assault a dragoon captain and knock his head against the wall?"

"My father, rot me? *He'd* have measured the jackanapes with a sword blade."

"But not, I think, for an offence which may only have been of accident or heedlessness? Never, never without just cause?"

"No, never without just cause."

"Upon your father's memory, my boy, will you give me a pledge to walk warily?"

"Upon my father's memory," cried Kinsmere, lifting his hand to take the oath, "upon my father's memory, damn me, I swear I will."

And he meant this, too, when he said it.

"Well!" observed Mr. Stainley, and fetched up a deep sigh. "The rest must be left to fortune and to your own native good sense. There are some safeguards which God Himself must provide. I can't provide 'em. Until nine

41

o'clock this evening, then! Mr. Kinsmere, I bid you good day."

My grandfather was not altogether sorry to see him go, the little man walking with great precision and stateliness up that series of terraces, to hire a sedan chair at the entrance of York House. Kinsmere remembered that he had money in his pouch, which was a good thing; and that he was free of observation now, which was a better. Whistling, he set out on foot for Charing Cross, followed the crowd, and came presently to Whitehall Palace.

Round the Palace Gate rose a great dust of commotion. And to his ears floated the music of fifes in a quick-step march. From the Horse Guards down the road a company of foot soldiery, flintlocks on their shoulders, swung out through King Street to the lilting clear fife music and a rattlety-tap of drums at every tread.

Kinsmere thought them very fine indeed. He liked listening to music; he liked watching well-drilled troops; he wondered if it would repay trouble to follow them. But, since the press of people had elbowed him, almost through the Palace Gate, he decided to go in. And so, amiably sauntering, he entered the Great Court.

"Now hang me," he said to himself, "hang me, but this is rather a curious sort of palace, if in fact it *is* the palace?"

For the place steamed with dirt and offal, as I have indicated at another time, and this Abram-seeming crew had scarcely the appearance of courtiers. But it was dinginess and splendour all jumbled together. Under the arches of a brick gallery you could see several great gilded coaches, and a number of private sedan chairs with varicoloured silk curtains. Over the way from the kitchens the noble spire of the Chapel Royal rose up high above a glow of stained-glass windows in the sun.

"Come!" says Rowdy Kinsmere, to nobody in particular, "*is* this the palace?"

A loud, hoarse, wheedling voice spoke somewhere behind him.

"Attend to *me!*" cried the voice. "Oh, good gentlemen, oh, brave gentlemen, oh, all sharp wits and steely hearts of the true breed, do pray for sport's sake attend to *me!*"

My grandfather turned round.

Bright sunlight streamed through a rain of soot flakes from the smoke of so many chimneys. Near the arches of the brick gallery, where the sunshine lay warmest, a greasy man with a pitted face stood leering and ducking his head. Round his neck, on leather straps, he carried a wooden board like a pieman's tray. Several greasy playing cards lay on it. The man with the pockmarked face spoke as though to a multitude, though he addressed Kinsmere alone.

"Behold," he continued in a kind of passion. "Here's the do; here's the game; here's the challenge. I vouchsafe this, for sport's sake, at great risk of loss or beggary to a poor man. Yet I offer it, though it ruin me! And what is't I offer?"

"Well, my bucko? Eh, yes, halloa? What is't you offer?"

"Find the lady!"

"Find the lady?"

"Ay, in all conscience," cried out the other, fixing Kinsmere with a hypnotic eye. "I have here three right royal cards." And he snatched them up. "You mark 'em, brave sir? Knave of clubs, king of diamonds, queen of hearts? Queen of hearts above all: that's the lady. They are put face down: in this fashion. They move, they mingle, they alter their places: *so*. Now I would hazard a sixpence . . . a shilling . . . ay, even the half of a crown piece . . . you can't say which is the lady. Would *you* hazard this wager, most noble gentleman?"

They were attracting some attention. Other ragtag figures had gathered round to stare. Up to the mountebank hurried a stout, blowsy girl with fixed smile and a leer of great would-be lewdness. Dirty, bepainted, in a battered straw hat and draggled finery, she edged between Kinsmere and the three-card man.

"Oh, he would!" cried this newcomer. "He would, Tom, but you must not!"

"I tell you, Chelsea Bess . . ."

"Nay, Tom, you must not! 'Twould be no trick at all for *him* to find the lady. He'll outwit you, Tom; you'll starve!"

And then another voice spoke.

"Country bumpkins, it would seem, are come to town in great numbers."

My grandfather had never heard that voice before. Yet he almost guessed whose it was. He whipped round with

43

greater quickness than he had turned the first time.

Not far behind him, as though fated to be there from the first, stood the tall dragoon captain who had thumped him aside so unseeingly at York House.

The captain still did not look at Kinsmere, or seem to look, though his eye may have strayed to the glitter of the big sapphire ring. On the coils of his periwig he wore a dragoon's beaver hat with a flat plume round the brim. His nose was lifted above the thick upper lip, the narrow mouth, and the congealed sneer; he stared blankly, incuriously, above my grandfather's head.

An argument had burst out between the three-card man and the stout slut in the draggled finery.

"What you say, Chelsea Bess, may be gospel truth . . ."

"It is, Tom; I vow it is!"

"Should he have a good eye, as no doubt he has, I venture much and rashly against a fine noble gentleman with a full purse. Still and all, Bess! 'Tis a short life, and what's money? Then I'll tell you what I'll do," declared this generous-minded mountebank, as though with sudden inspiration. "Shall it be a first wager of one shilling, now, to make a tack at finding the lady? What d'ye say, sir? Will you bet, sir?"

"No," replied Kinsmere, "I will not."

"*You'll* not bet, by the Hilts?"

"On all else, yes. On the lady, never again. At Pie Powder Court in Bristol, once, when half a dozen of us had spent fifty pounds in an endeavour to find that lady, we commenced to suspect something must be wrong. How we served the rogue who mulcted us, after he had been turned upside down and the coins shaken from his clothes, you will be spared the pain of hearing. Yet the lesson was a salutary one. By which I would intimate, good friend," says my grandfather, "that the charitable offer on which you pride yourself can be little else save a bubble and a cheat."

The mountebank uttered a hoarse scream.

"Bubble, is it? Cheat, is it? By the Hilts, Bess, here's impudence! Tom o' Bedlam am I, with my license under the hand and seal of Sir Henry Herbert, Master of the Revels to His Most Sacred Majesty. Tom o' Bedlam am I, most honest of all the honest, who—"

The dragoon captain spoke again, this time addressing

the three-card man and the doxy.

"Hold your clack, carrion," he said in his harsh, bored voice. "Now be off, and no skreeking about it, lest I summon guards to take you in custody."

"Tom o' Bedlam am I, by God's death and Christ's body, the most honest of all the honest . . ."

"D'ye question *my* orders, fellow? Or you either, wench? Must I be at pains to repeat it? Go!"

It completed their demoralization; both turned and fled.

Now the captain faced towards my grandfather, but still would not look at him. In the sun-and-smoky courtyard, as antagonism flared, something sizzled between these two like a match to a powder train. The captain, nose higher still, kept his glazed little eye fixed at a point somewhere past Kinsmere's shoulder. He spoke as though to an invisible third party.

"Rogues and trulls of such kidney are not welcome at Whitehall Palace. But less welcome, it may be, are country bumpkins too grasping or cowardly to risk their poor shillings at a wager. Country bumpkins have no place in a world of fashion; they also had best begone too."

"Had they so? And who will compel this?"

"They had best be off, I said. Country bumpkins must not threaten."

"Do *you* threaten, my bold dragoon?"

"It is not needful"—still the captain addressed his invisible auditor—"to make threats against oafs and clods. Who threatens a poor blackbeetle in a kitchen? It is ignored, no more, until stamped upon and squashed. I have given myself the trouble to say: DEPART."

"And I am still here."

"If there be any poor clod who thinks himself jeered and insulted, who aches and burns to settle a score with his betters . . ."

"Oh, come!" said Roderick Kinsmere, with a little pulse jigging in his arm. "*You* are the man desirous of trouble, my bucko. You will force a quarrel at any cost. Yet why should you wish this, against one you never saw before. Why?"

"If there be any such lout, and he should have anything he would desire to say to me, let him walk quietly at my side and say it. Let him not raise hand like a stableboy; let

45

him try to behave, though he can't, as a gentleman might. Let him walk beside me, I repeat." Then the bored voice grew louder and harsher. "This way. This way. *This way!*"

IV

For the first time the captain looked full at him, bending forward a little to do so. They measured each other. The glazed dark eye, the long nose, the thick upper lip to narrow mouth: all these, framed in the coils of a great periwig, were thrust almost into Kinsmere's face.

Then the captain, muscular and sneer-poised in his long red coat, baldric and rapier gleaming against it, lifted one shoulder and stalked carelessly towards the southeast part of the Great Court.

At the southeast end of the courtyard an open passage—perhaps a dozen feet wide, with muddy cobblestones underfoot—stretched between blank walls towards the public water stairs above the Thames.

On one side of this passage, your left as you entered it, ran the brick wall of the palace kitchens. On the other side rose up the stone wall of the Great Hall itself. It would be only an hour until midday-dinner time. Though no sound issued from the Great Hall, which they used as a playhouse, the whole length of the kitchens clanked and smoked at meal heat.

After looking round sharply, as though to make sure they were unobserved, the captain led Kinsmere into this passage. It was gloomy here; gnats buzzed in their faces.

And then:

"Stop!" cries the captain, half wheeling.

"With right good will," says my grandfather. He halted with his back to the kitchen wall. "But how now, Bold Sir Captain and Cock of the Sneerers? Do you deign at length to mark the bumpkin's existence? Hath it penetrated into your noodle that I am alive?"

The other seemed almost convulsed.

"Alive!" he repeated. "Alive! It breathes; it moves; it speaks almost intelligibly, as though the clod were a human being. Yes, poor bumpkin! You are in some sense alive, let's allow, though for your insolence to me you are not like to remain alive. Now hearken well, good lout, while your betters shall put a question. You wear a sword, like so many who can't use 'em. You wear a sword, but do you know swordplay?"

"Yes. A little."

" 'A little,' says he. A little!" Again the captain seemed almost convulsed. "Come, here's a jest. Come, gods and omens of all this earth, here's a jest most monstrous rich! Of swordplay, the lout saith, he knows a little. Ay, good bumpkin, I may guess how very little. And yet, if the thing can be managed discreetly or without noise, I may take pity. I may award you more honour than you deserve."

"More honour than I deserve? What honour?"

"The honour," retorted his companion, "to be spitted through the guts by my sword."

And he lunged forward, breathing hard in Kinsmere's face. With his gloved left hand he pinned my grandfather's right shoulder against the wall.

"I address you, bumpkin," he said loftily.

"Remove your hand! Desist! Stand back!"

"Have you ears, oaf? I said I address you!"

"The words were heard. Will you remove that hand?"

"I use my pleasure at all times."

"Do you so?"

"Indeed I do," said the captain, leering close.

And that did it.

"I have pledged myself to good deportment. I have sworn an oath to use civility towards all. And yet, by God, this goes something too far. For the last time, will you drop your hand?"

"Ay, good zany. But I drop it, mark me, only the better to do *this*."

The captain's left hand fell. His right hand, also gloved and its fingers open, he swung round savagely to whack Kinsmere across the side of the face.

That blow never landed, being parried by an upflung left arm.

Kinsmere's left hand darted behind the captain's back. His right hand shot out, fingers closing round the underside of his companion's bony jaw. His hand cradled that jaw as a man nowadays might cradle a cricket ball. Bracing himself, settling a little with weight on his right foot, he opened both shoulders in a mighty throw.

47

The captain, for all his muscular surefootedness, flew backwards across the passage as though caught beneath his jaw by the heaviest of all mallets they used at the game of *pêle-mêle*. The heels of his gambado boots made squashing noises on muddy cobblestones. His hat fell off. His back struck the wall of the Great Hall. His sword scabbard rattled as he sat down hard in mud.

And Kinsmere, feeling a lightness in the legs as well as a great hollow inside his chest, swerved sideways with left hand dropped to sword hilt.

"Shall we try," says he, "how devilish little I know of swordplay? Lug out, Cock of the Sneerers, and we'll despatch our business now."

Yet he scored very little of triumph.

The other man rose up instantly, hat on again, all poise and menace, no whit of assurance lost. From the direction of the Thames, into which all the town's refuse was emptied, a foul smell arose and blew through to poison the good steam of cooking.

But it was the captain who held attention in that dim passage. Towering, formidable, his every movement betraying the expert swordsman without pity or bowels, he circled catlike against what light entered from the river end.

"Lug out, you say?" His utter and low-voiced contempt was like a blow in itself. "Lug out, eh? Is that what you'd do?"

"I said it, yes! Why not?"

"With three royal edicts to forbid duelling, with the king as fixed against it as a man may be in this world, you'd provoke a brawl in the very premises of Whitehall Palace? Dog! Spawn of the dung heap! Draw but half an inch of iron from that scabbard there, and I will not even stir myself to spit at you. I will summon guards, as I would have done for the other scum, and have you clapped into a gatehouse gaol where you belong. And yet you need not think to escape me, oaf. You have jeered me, which is not done with impunity; you have dared to lay hand on me, which is not done at all . . ."

"Now, damme," says Kinsmere, "but what mighty grandee have I so offended? Who are you, bold fellow at employing your mouth? How do you call yourself?"

"My name, oaf, concerns you not. My deeds shall concern you much. Are you acquainted with Leicester Fields?"

"I saw Leicester Fields today."

The captain moved forward, facing Kinsmere with one shoulder lifted high and the gnats round his wig.

"Leicester Fields, the north side towards the Dead Wall," he said, "and the clump of trees within the gate? Eh, lout? There will be a moon this night. Shall we meet there, eleven of the clock as men of breeding do, to settle the differences between us?"

"Yes!"

"You'd dare venture this, poor fellow?"

"I would not miss it."

"There need be no seconds to fight beside us." Here the captain all but spat in his face. "Shall I call *my* friends to meet the cattle *you* would bring, and demean myself before all? But 'twill not take long, I warrant. A pass or two, and I run you through the guts. Or, in meantime, should heart and courage fail together . . ."

"A truce to boasting, Corporal Ninnyhammer," snapped my grandfather. "Go on much more in this strain and, royal edict or no, there shall be a whack across your chops to make you lug out HERE."

"And if I shout for the Yeoman Ushers?"

"Then shout, God damn you!"

The captain opened his mouth; had he uttered a sound, Kinsmere would have sprung for his throat. Again hatred flared between these two, another lighted match to a powder train. For all this cavalryman's disinterested manner, he had an almost maniacal light in his eye. Then both controlled themselves.

"Shall we set the seal on our bargain, then?" jeered the captain, lifting his right shoulder still higher. "Tonight? Leicester Fields? Eleven o'clock?"

"Tonight! Leicester Fields! Eleven o'clock!"

"Through the guts you shall be punctured, mark me again. Through the guts you shall be punctured, and die slowly. I can trouble myself with you no longer until then."

The captain turned round. Dismissing all, contemptuous of all despite the mudstains on his coat and breeches, he marched straight and high-shouldered towards the water stairs. You heard the noise of his boots on the steps; then he was gone.

"Young sir," interposed a new voice, "may I beg the favour of a word with you?"

In from the Great Court end of the passage, attempting a complicated kind of bow as he did so, lounged a burly, middle-sized, middle-aged man of remarkable ugliness.

He had a portentous air and a rumbling voice. He was dressed in rich if slovenly fashion: plum-coloured velvet coat above wine-stained waistcoat of canary yellow, silk stockings, silver-buckled shoes, and a finely carved hilt to his rapier. The coils of his brown peruke enclosed a countenance high-coloured with tippling, battle, and hard weather. And the newcomer's presence brought reassurance. Even his ugliness was of the fetching and engaging sort; it compelled your liking even as you grinned.

"Eh, now!" continued this newcomer, surveying Kinsmere with a ruminating eye. "Forgive me; do forgive the impertinence I utter! But—are ye strung on a wire of tautness, may it be? Does that heart knock at your ribs, and your legs know a certain trembling at the knees?"

"In candour, sir, I must own to being a trifle distraught. Should it not be so; do you mean? Is this caitiff behaviour after all?"

"Nay, don't say it!" returned the other. "Don't think it, even, since you are much mistaken. I too am a man of peace, though I seem always to walk incontinent towards trouble. And yet, for all my many years of finding broils or being found by 'em, I feel the same knocking heart and the same light legs on each occasion."

"Well?"

"Forgive me, young sir, but I saw it all. I saw your broil with Pem Harker . . ."

"Pem Harker?" demanded Kinsmere. "That's the tall fellow with the nose and the bad manners?"

"It is."

"What's his station, then? Who is he?"

"Captain Pembroke Harker, First Dragoon Guards, is a man of rare good birth. He is much at Whitehall, more particularly in the Matted Gallery. He hath some esteem, and is indulged by nearly all . . ."

"Because he is so well liked, can it be?"

"No, for the very reverse cause," says this burly newcomer, "Pem Harker, d'ye see, is the sort o' type"—he

50

turned it into a French word, pronounced *teep*—"for whom most people will stand aside, and to whom they'll even grant a mort o' favours, because they *don't* like him at all. We have all known the teep, have we not?"

"Truly we have."

"Well, then! I saw and heard. And what you did was bravely done. But Pem Harker? Harker set on you with great deliberateness, to force a quarrel. Why did he do this?"

"I don't know, for the life of me; I can't say!"

"We must discover it; we must sound the depth of this business. Harker swore he would run you through the guts; and I dare vow he'll make a tack at it. But not, it may be, in quite the way you think he will. Eh?"

"Sir," Kinsmere cried out, with bewilderment thickening round his wits, "I have no doubt you are certain of your own meaning. I am not. However, I thank you for the compliments you pay."

And he bowed.

"Yet we must sound the depth of the business, believe me. That's one reason why . . . Come!"

Here the burly stranger, showing considerable agility for all his stockiness, wheeled round and bowed in reply. At something of a flourish he led Kinsmere back into the sun and smoke and commotion of the Great Court.

". . . one reason, good my lad, why I desired a word in your ear. Now permit me," adds he, with a manner of stiff and profound courtliness in contrast to his great voice and many-coloured face, "permit me one further impertinence. You have engaged yourself to fight a duel with Pem Harker?"

"I have."

"Tonight, at eleven of the clock, in Leicester Fields?"

"It was so agreed."

"Ah!"

The other man screwed round his thick neck out of a cabbage-leaf series of laces, peering in a mysterious manner up and down the courtyard. Then he lifted a large forefinger, tapped it twice against his nose, and smiled still more mysteriously.

"Come, then, here are perplexities! Unless word of honour be set at naught, you are to meet Harker this night in Leicester Fields. Well, so am I."

51

"What's that you say? Did the damned fellow challenge you as well?"

"He did. For the same time, at the same place, and also without seconds or witnesses. Wherefore, being old and skilled in the ways of war and statecraft, I must ask myself—mark, alas, the Gallic influence!—I must ask myself the reason on't. Eel muh fo demanday," roared out the burly man, with a somewhat non-Gallic accent, "why Captain Pembroke Harker, First Dragoon Guards, should be at such pains to pick a quarrel with two people in our trade . . ."

"*Our trade,* is it?"

"Ay, ecod, what else? *For* the same place, *at* the same hour, in hole-and-corner fashion to boot! There you have it in a nutshell, perhaps with hints of what's a-brewing. Sir, do I speak plain now?"

"Sir, you do not."

"Ah, discretion!" rumbled the other, again tapping his nose. "You'd be oon omm tray discreet, I know, and it does you credit. Still! In some matters, permit me to say, you use small discretion at the best o' times. Wearing that ring, now! Harker's motives we don't know; but 'twas the sight of the ring set him on you."

"Now, what a fiend's name *of* the ring? Had Harker a mind to steal it, do you think?"

" 'Tis possible; all is possible, no doubt, though this would add but fresh perplexity. Come! Be advised by me. You are young; you are new to the trade of—you are new to the work. Allow me to present myself," says he, taking off his flat-plumed hat and sweeping it across his chest. "I am Bygones Abraham, at your service. Sir, will you drink?"

"Sir," my grandfather replied right heartily, "those are the first comprehensible words I have heard you speak. I will drink."

"But we'll not betake us to a tavern, where we might be overheard. No, never. I have been given lodgings in the palace," announced the man called Bygones Abraham, brushing up his moustache with much complacence. His thick chest swelled. "Which should mean (you apprehend?) a new errand ere long. By your leave, then, shall we visit my lodgings for a bone santy?"

52

"By *your* leave," says Kinsmere, "and with much pleasure, we will."

Beyond a hope that he had not encountered a wandering lunatic he did not reflect overmuch on the matter. Grinning, chuckling, with every exaggerated courtesy Bygones Abraham led him across the Great Court. But on one thing his new friend insisted. He must remove the sapphire ring from his finger and conceal it in an inner pocket.

"For it would be a plaguey ill thing, you concede, if in evil hearts suspicion were roused of you, or of me, or of a certain exalted figger whose name we don't speak unless 'tis needful. Hey?"

Thus Kinsmere was escorted under the arches of the brick gallery, where stood the private coaches and sedan chairs. Beyond this gallery, in a huddle of buildings at the far side of the Great Hall, double doors opened into a foyer full of liveried attendants. In this foyer—dusky, illuminated only by small windows of stained glass, but richly carved and painted—a noble oak staircase rose up from the black-and-white flags of the floor.

A throng of people, gaudy in their plumage, had begun to drift down these stairs. Certain doubts assailed my grandfather. He had promised Mr. Stainley he would not mingle too freely with . . .

"Under favour, Mr. Abraham," says he, "but who's here and what's here? Where, in precision, are we bound?"

"Abovestairs; where else? Past the Guard Chamber, and through . . . Great body o' Pilate, lad!" The other man broke off. "You're familiar with the palace, to be sure?"

"To speak a truth, and between ourselves: not over-familiar, I fear."

"Well! Well!" Bygones Abraham relished this jest. "But you are new; you are unfledged; this is none so surprising. This morning's levees are all but finished, you'll observe. If you would learn, hearken well. I am the man to guide you; I will be your sisserony. Hey?"

Bustling, almost at a strut, lowering his voice to a confidential growl, he continued to speak volubly as they mounted the staircase; and he pointed out every detail.

It is all dust, now. Near to three decades after my

grandfather first saw it, a huge fire destroyed all of Whitehall Palace save only the Banqueting House, In these halls, in the maze of galleries surrounding them, there had been an end of revelry long before the fire. The fiddle strings were all snapped, the candles blown out, on a grey February morning when Charles the Second died.

But it would be fifteen years until that evil winter. Here at the top of the stairs rose spacious windows, and arches of wood so polished that they threw out gleams of red. Here were the doors to the Guard Chamber, a lofty room with a gilt ceiling. Beyond this, an inner room, lay the Presence Chamber of the king, where those allowed entry must preserve the strictest behaviour.

The doors to the Guard Chamber were closed as Bygones Abraham and my grandfather went by, the king's levee being over. But they had actually to pass the queen's Presence Chamber, and the old soldier bade Kinsmere glance in.

Half a dozen maids of honour, in taffeta gowns, were playing at cards round little tables. Over the back of one chair lounged a handsome stripling who Bygones Abraham said was the young Duke of Monmouth, the king's natural son by an old affair with a brown-faced Englishwoman in Holland. But Queen Catherine herself sat facing the windows, near a hanging cage of canaries, and they could not see her face.

However, as they passed the door, a dark-haired woman with a train of handmaidens came sweeping and rustling out of the room. Bygones Abraham, looking stunned, made a deep obeisance which she ignored. She was not (as you will see her in the portrait by Sir Peter Lely) pensive and languishing, head against one shoulder, looking up with deep, heavy-lidded brown eyes. She carried her head high, the face as haughty and dusky as a Spaniard's. Round her mouth there were lines of anger as faint as though drawn with a needle. Dark and plump, all a flash and fire of eyes half shut up, she whirled past in her gown of yellow satin. Her hair was set in the short wired ringlets called heartbreakers, and trembled against her cheeks.

"Eh! Now it's a very odd day," said Bygones Abraham, at a kind of musing rumble, "it's a very odd day when my Lady Castlemaine pays her devwar to the queen. Ecod, lad, there walks a fine woman!"

"My Lady Castlemaine?" says Kinsmere. Even in Somerset they had heard much of this charmer, who for a full decade—in part, at least—had captivated the king's fancy. "The Countess of Castlemaine, was it? Why, damme, though, sir: she's *fat*."

He said that because he refused to admit how much he had been struck. For she had an allure, all fleshly and lewd-suggesting, which spread round her as she walked.

"I would not asperse her," says he, "and such words are plaguey ill to breathe. But the woman's FAT, damme, and there's an end on't."

"Pish!" roared Bygones Abraham. "Pish, tush, and what d' *you* know o' fine women? A fig, say I, for all your thin jillflirts with no more shape than a washboard. Give *me* a woman I can lay hold of."

"Oh, granted. At the same time . . ."

"Stay, though!" interrupted Bygones, checking himself and shaking his head. "I must not forget Dulcinea. My passion for Dulcinea," cries he, with a watery and sentimental light blurring his eye, "is *spirituelle*. Ah, Dulcinea! Sound of lutes and—er—lutes. It's a deep secret, yet I confide in you."

"Dulcinea who? Not Dulcinea del Toboso, I suppose?" says Kinsmere, who knew and loved *Don Quixote*. "Which Dulcinea, then? What's her name?"

"I don't know."

"You don't know?"

"Nay, how should I? Having seen her but at a distance, and finding none acquainted with her to present me? But many times I have drunk her health in ink. And once in a mixture of barley water and soot."

"Come, friend, these are strange tipplings for an old soldier! Ink? Barley water and soot? Wherefore such japes as that?"

"Because 'tis ah la mode," returned Bygones. "I am a man of the mode; I have ever resolved to be one, though God He knoweth why."

"Well, then?"

"Well!" said Bygones, huffing a little. "With a love spiritual or ennobling, hark'ee, it's the new fashion to drink your Dulcinea's health in some compound . . . not nauseous or *too* disgustful, it may be, but one no man o' parts would think to quaff for his pleasure. And you must write her verses telling her how cruel she is, and how much she won't love you.

"But my Lady Castlemaine," he pursued, "needs no verses to fetch her down. Report saith they're to give her a duchess's coronet ere long. Yet she's a damned fine woman; it's a pity."

"Well, but," protested my grandfather, "where's the pity in it?" He still would not have admitted he was thinking of that yellow gown going past, of the eyes sweeping left and right, of a black patch near the small, heavy, duskily red mouth. "Where's the pity," says he, "in the awarding of a coronet for devoir well and truly done?"

"Oh, as to that! Her enemies say this is no more than a pension, since she hath outlived her usefulness. 'Tis not as in old days, they say, when the king cared much and was tied to her shift strings. If she shows open fondness for Mr. Wycherley or for Charles Hart, the actor, they say it's all one to our Charles of Whitehall Palace. We live in a maze o' galleries, each one a whispering gallery. *They* say . . . always they say . . ."

"Do they say true?"

"Well!" retorted Bygones, and began a complicated oratorical gesture. "The king is but forty years old; he still knows hot humours; what would they have? Certes there are others. Here's Nelly (the play-actress, d'ye see?) being this month brought to bed of a child. And Moll Davies as well.

"But what's that to my Lady Castlemaine, who can ever whistle him back when she's a mind to? There's none to compare with her, ecod, there's not! She is still mistress-in-chief, strike me blind and don't you forget it; of all amorous zhongloors she is still the woman."

Here he broke off, with some pride, to draw attention to his lodgings.

Having negotiated many more passages, they had emerged into another gallery: a long, dusky gallery which ran east and west just above the private landing stairs to the river. The Shield Gallery, it was called, because of certain remaining shields and banners—from the ancient times of tournaments in King Harry the Eighth's day—which were still hung up along the walls.

Sunlight touched stained-glass windows at the eastern

end, where a balcony had been built out over the water stairs; the maids of honour, on state occasions, stood cn this balcony to throw flowers at the royal barges coming to mooring below. Here the singing of birds in the queen's volary rose at its loudest.

"You'll observe, hey?" Bygones swept out his arm. "The queen's apartments are on *that* side, the north. The king's apartments are *here,* the south—where I also (mark'ee, lad) have the honour to be. Here's the door, and this fellow with the staff, we'll send about other business. Come! Rare fine lodgings, or so I think?"

There were two rooms, guarded outside by a porter with a tip-staff. Though the bedchamber might be small and stuffy, the withdrawing room was a spacious place of panelled walls adorned with tapestries. Its two windows looked down on a little garden full of statues, the Volary Garden, round which stretched the private apartments of the king.

There were chairs in some dark polished wood, much carved, with seats and backs of woven straw having body cushions for comfort. Silver candlesticks stood on a round table scored over with the marks of glasses. Between the windows was a sideboard bearing tankards, goblets, a brass-bound tobacco box, three or four long clay tobacco pipes, even a few books. It was rather warm here; dust motes danced above the sideboard.

"Come, here it is," cries Bygones, indicating a chair beside the centre table. "Sit you merry, friend; take ease! Rare fine quarters or so I think?"

"Yes, most noble of aspect."

"And, now I call it to mind, there's another set o' chambers vacant to the west o' these. No doubt, matters standing as they do, they'll invite you to occupy 'em?"

"Invite *me?* Why a pox should they lodge *me* at the palace?"

"Is this another mystery? Bend your wits to the question; you'll divine it. Now, then!"

Fetching up a deep sigh and shaking himself, he loosened his coat, his waistcoat, and the fall of lace at his throat. He removed hat and peruke, revealing stubbly grey hair that made another contrast with the red or purplish hues of his face. The peruke he draped across a wig block on the sideboard.

They must drink sack, he said, meaning the wine we now call sherry. From the top of the sideboard he took two pewter tankards each holding a pint; from the lower part he fetched out an armful of bottles. With these he marched back to the table.

"Ayagh!" said Bygones Abraham, clearing his throat and opening bottles. "I had thought, d'ye see, we should first descend to business. But we will not. We will drink a health to the king, as loyal men should, and pledge him long life. Hey?"

"We will."

Bygones filled the two tankards and pushed one across the table. The gurgle of the wine as he poured seemed to fire him with eloquence. Said he, striking a great attitude:

"I have drunk his health, lad, in prosperity and in exile: as an excuse to start and as a reason to continue. I have drunk it out of tankards, mugs, goblets, glasses, pint pots, quart pots, great jacks, small jacks, gingleboys, and other receptacles whose names for the moment escape me. Down this throat have flowed libations in which England's star ascends, so to speak, with reverse motion. Long life; down she goes; God for King Charles!"

Up tilted the tankard; back went his head. His Adam's apple had scarcely wriggled twice before his face, redder than ever, flipped back into view. He puffed out his moustache. Beaming, he turned the tankard upside down and ticked its edge against his left thumb. One drop slid from the empty vessel and exactly covered the thumbnail.

"Ha!" And he snorted with pleasure. "There's the proper way, d'ye mark it? One drop on the nail. No more, no less. Now, lad what do *you* say?"

Not to be outdone, my grandfather rose to his feet and stood straight.

"You have said it, Friend Bygones; I have but to make echo. May he live long years, and . . . God for King Charles!"

He lifted his own tankard. In four swallows he drained off the full, mellow, not-too-sweet wine, which sent a pleasant warmth through him as though waiting until it reached his stomach before it cried "Huzza!" He drew a deep breath for air, ticking over the tankard and leaving one drop on his left thumbnail. Then he threw out his chest under Bygones's approving glance.

"Sir," said Kinsmere, with much earnestness, "I come of a cavalier family which, whatever its other failings, has paid distinguished service in the matter of health-drinking and all loyal toping. There was a Kinsmere," says he, stretching his imagination, "there was a Kinsmere dead-drunk under the table at the signing of Magna Charta. A Kinsmere saw the Spanish Armada all over Plymouth Hoe ere they persuaded him 'twas a vision born of a bottle.—Thank you. Since you seem so insistent, I *will* take another."

Bygones stayed his hand in the act of pouring again, and stared.

"Hey?" he demanded. "Your name, now! Your name, you said, was . . . ?"

"It is Kinsmere. Roderick Kinsmere."

"Kins—" And Bygones smote his forehead. "And your father's name, his Christian name! Was it the same as yours?"

"No. My father, whom they called Buck, was named Alan."

"Of the West Country, or so I think?"

"Of Blackthorn, in Somerset, near Bristol."

"And commanded his own troop of horse at Naseby fight? Ay! Left arm shattered, and they cut it away . . ."

Bygones Abraham sat down. He put his elbows on the table and his fists against his temples. For that brief time sombreness had come on him; his battered face wore a look of pathos near the comical.

"Buck Kinsmere's son!" he said. "And with no better luck at Whitehall than to meet a posturing old hunks like . . . Into what drunkard's boasts do I betray myself, at *my* age? *Your* father, Roderick Kinsmere, was the noblest of the noble. How is he, lad? He fares well, I trust?"

"He fares well, I am sure, though he has been dead almost ten years."

"God rest him, Roderick Kinsmere!"

"Amen to that, Bygones Abraham!"

"He never knew—?"

"Ah, but he did! He lived to see the Stuarts restored to their own, and took much comfort thereby. You knew my father, then? You were acquainted with him?"

The wigless man threw himself back in the chair.

"I am out of old times, lad. I am passy. Even these,"

59

and he touched moustache and chin tuft, "are passy and not ah la mode. Nay; I had no acquaintance with your father, save by sight. I was no fashionable beau then, whatever I may affect to be now. I carried a pike in Langdale's Yorkshire Foot, the ones who lost us that last battle. Your father was of Prince Rupert's Horse; and they helped much in the losing of it, as the hell-riders they were so proud to be. When they'd broke Ireton's line, as they designed to do, not a man would stop or draw rein until he got to the baggage wagons. By the time they were back again at full gallop, Black Tom and Oliver had piled horse and foot against our centre, and some fool gave command to march to the right . . ."

Bygones Abraham rose to his feet.

"I can't say," he added, rather wearily. "I've heard 'em describe it, including a parcel of men who weren't there. It was a blazing hot day, with much dust, and my head ached worse than the back-sword cut I took from one of Noll's Ironsides. But what befell, or how it befell, I can say no more than though it happened in a dream.

" 'Tis the common feeling of any ranker, the lowest of the low. You're choked and near blind. You stand holding a sixteen-foot pike elbow to elbow with the next man. Then the charge comes down out of smoke. It may be they'll trample you, it may be they won't. There's naught to be apprehended save confusing and firing. Then you have some dull notion 'tis all over. You walk a-stagger along a road somewhere amid much blood and screaming from those who are left. The trees seem strange; the road is strange too; and your only thought is to wonder how the devil you are come there at all. That, d'ye see, that's war."

V

"Mistrust me not," pursued Bygones, who had grown more cheerful. "I'll not say there's no glory, though it's small part o' that a foot soldier ever sees. 'Close ranks! Stand fast! Here they come!' Yet 'twould gladden my heart to *remember* a little, or as other than a clout across the noddle inside a smithy. Besides, ayagh!" And he snorted. "Where are all the airy cannon balls a-bouncing harmless, the cupids and gods and goddesses and such-like, in the heroic pictures? Figgeray voo and je muh demand! What's the answer?"

"Why, as to that," replied Kinsmere. "A man of shrewdness would suspect your cupids and gods and goddesses are to be found only in portraits, like the uncommon kind of horse that can stand on its hind legs long enough to be painted so. Or maybe," says he, "it's only the generals can see 'em. Let us drink the sack you have so generously poured, and reflect on this matter in all its aspects."

But Bygones had turned adamant.

"We'll quaff a bumper, and more than one, when it's meet and fitting we should do so. It is not meet and fitting so soon. The time passes; the clock presses; eel fo proceed to business."

"Business?"

"Ay, to be sure! There are mighty strange circumstances here, now I think on 'em."

"As—what circumstances?"

"You are Buck Kinsmere's son? Well! If you're Buck Kinsmere's son, you should have lands. You should have estates. You should have coin and cuffs at the least of it. Yet there's no air o' grandeur about you, and small air o' prosperity either. How came you into *this* trade for your living?"

"What trade?"

"Oh, body o' Pilate," roared Bygones. "But where's the use of this pretence with *me*? Look at this; look well!"

Fumbling inside waistcoat and shirt, he produced a little leather pouch suspended round his neck on a leather thong. From this he took out a gold ring with a blue stone. My grandfather, sitting forward for a closer look, saw that it seemed identical with his own sapphire ring. Then Bygones snatched back the bauble and replaced it inside his shirt.

"You observe, young man? You mark it? 'Tis *my* ring, the second ring, the *other* ring. Accredited sign of a King's Messenger, one of the only two messengers employed by old Rowl—employed by His Majesty's self for devious work beyond the Channel in France. Why, then what o' *your* ring?"

"Now, burn my body and soul, but this is confusion worse confounded."

"Is it so? What o' *your* ring, I say?"

Whereupon Kinsmere told him. He told the truth. But, as he spoke, his companion's expression changed still more. Bygones stood there with shoulders humped, head forward, an ugly look in his eyes and his hands hanging hooked at his sides.

The bad moment grew worse. My grandfather had just concluded, "It has no meaning, believe me; or, at all events—" when suddenly Bygones was across the table, as quick as a snap of your fingers, and had a dagger at his throat.

"Did I betray myself, rogue? Or did you? Are you in truth Buck Kinsmere's son? Or are you an impudent, lying coxcomb, come foully to set traps for a true man? God strike me dead!"

"Sir," said Kinsmere, "it is a most grievous thing to find you behaving in this fashion, since you are a hospitable gentleman to whose company I have taken a fancy—"

"Filch secrets from a King's Messenger, ecod? It was a jape, a piece of stage-acting, that pretended broil between you and Pem Harker? Strike me dead," snarled Bygones, almost choking, "but you'll regret this, rogue, and so will the villain who set you on me. Who was it, knave? What high courtier employed you?"

". . . None the less," Kinsmere continued, "I am not enamoured of having a knife point against my Great Vein. And if you are not short to remove it, when again I shall ask you civilly—"

He brought up his left arm as the other man lunged across the table; he caught Bygones Abraham's wrist, and whirled sideways as he rose to his feet. They stood at grips, locked together, looking each other in the eye.

"You're right surprisingly strong, sir," pursued my grandfather. "It would be chancy, I think, to bet on a wrestling fall against any such—"

"Have a care, jackanapes!"

"No! *You* have a care!"

They reeled against the table. Several wine bottles clattered over, one of them rolling wide to fall and smash on the floor. Still these two contestants stood locked at grips amid disturbed dust motes. They veered away from the table; my grandfather went on wrenching, with shufflings and crackings and grunts, until the sharp point was turned outward from his throat.

"Forbear, now! Put up your dagger!" And Kinsmere released him. "Ay, keep it at hand, if its presence shall comfort you. I desire only to disabuse your mind of certain fancies, and also to offer proof. Will you hear me?"

Bygones Abraham cursed him with some comprehensiveness, gasping for breath as he did so. But his wrath seemed to be cooling into a puzzled stare. He hesitated, returned the dagger to a sheath inside his coat, and fell back a step.

"Well, young man?"

"Rogue I may be; that's a matter of opinion; though with no plot against you or against anyone else. A Kinsmere of Blackthorn assuredly I am. Come! Here's my own ring, which you bade me hide away. Will you be good enough to examine this, and to look inside?"

The old soldier stared with protruding eyes.

"Look . . . *inside?*"

"Faith, yes! The stone in its setting turns upward on a hinge. The king—the late king, that's to say, whom they are now pleased to call Charles the Martyr—gave it to my father after Newbury fight in the Great Rebellion. On the gold inside the setting, with another dagger point, he scratched the letters C.A. Will it please you to test this?"

"Mr. Kinsmere," Bygones said abruptly, "almost I am persuaded to believe you."

" 'Almost'? Faith, at least we make progress!"

" 'Tis to be hoped so." Bygones held up his hand. "And now, if I may?"

Kinsmere threw him the ring, which he caught with a flat smack against his palm. Bygones carried it to the left-hand window, through a whole legion of settling dust motes.

" 'Tis known—sub rosy, as they sat in Latin—two of these rings are in existence. Lingard, that was once the cunningest jeweller in Cheapside, made 'em more than forty years gone. The late king, ere his barbarous murder by the Roundheads, passed 'em both to *our* Charles. Hark'ee, though! I've heard report of a third ring, said to 'a' been lost. True, false; ecod, what can't we hear? Still! If what you say is true, this is like to be the third ring, the sup-

63

posed-lost one. *If* what you say is true . . ."

"Yes?"

"King Charles the First, of glorious memory, had a most distinctive way o' fashioning the letters C.R. Let's adventure it!"

Holding up my grandfather's ring against the light from the window, he opened the sapphire on its hinge, stared long at the inscription inside, and shut it up again.

"The ring *I* carry," he said through his teeth, "I have long worn next my skin without suspicion the jewel is like a lid. If this should open too . . . ?"

Muttering under his breath, Bygones braced himself. He took his own ring from the leather pouch. He held it up beside my grandfather's. With gentle fingers he prised at the setting. The stone opened at once.

"Oh, body o' God!"

"Sir," said Kinsmere, "will you drink your wine with me now?"

"Drink it?" echoed Bygones, turning round. "I'll do better than that, ecod! I'll bid you to dinner at the Devil
. . ."

"Come, damn me no damns. Can't we make an end of cursing each other?"

"I meant no damns, pray credit me. I am all honest apology, as full of excuses as a man may be. My reference was to the Devil tavern, a haunt of good people. We'll dine there; we'll take aboard good cargo of strong waters; we'll be off in ten minutes. And yet . . ."

Bygones returned to the table through a pungency of sack fumes, past a great star of spilt wine on the carpet and glass fragments from the smashed bottle. Some of these glass fragments he kicked aside; the rest he ignored. He set upright the tumbled bottles on the table. With great respect he handed back Kinsmere's ring.

But he did not touch either of the tankards, being far too deeply troubled.

"Oh, this is a parlous thing! Oh, this is a most damned thing!"

"What is?"

"I have been indiscreet," roared Bygones, striking a fine attitude in spite of himself. "I have not stood on my guard; I have fallen a-ranting; I have discoursed of things best kept dark. It would go very ill with me, lad, were you to repeat what you've heard in this room. Nor is that all, though it's the worst part.

"This night I am pledged to a duel with Pem Harker; ay, come to think on it, so are you! Harker marked down your ring; past doubt he thinks, as I thought, you're a King's messenger too. Is this even worse than its seeming? D'ye see the unrolling of a design? Come what may I am committed to fight Pem Harker, and you're committed as well."

"Why, so I am!" Kinsmere admitted.

"Now, sir," he went on, when both of them had pondered hard for a moment, "I have no more curiosity than most folk. But you have stated it with exactness. I am committed to fight a man I don't know, for a reason I can't fathom, in what seems a mere dance of lunacy. Perhaps there's no harm in what we do. It may be your own notion of wholesome sport. And yet my curiosity has come near a mania. I would give a pouchful of guineas for some intimation as to what, by the sixty-eight bonfires of hell, may be the meaning of all this."

"Statecraft!" said Bygones, looking still more portentous and shutting up one eye. "These may well be matters o' statecraft. Even could I guess at 'em, lad, would you understand?"

"Faith, then why not try me?"

"Try you?"

"Yes; why not speak plain? Must those versed in statecraft always be so squint-eyed mysterious, like parents instructing their children in things appertaining to the lusts of the flesh?"

"Matters of statecraft, for the most part, are not complex at all."

"I rejoice to hear it."

"Some people would persuade other people to spend money, and call 'em clods or traitors if they say it's too much. That's for the most part, certes, and in general of the great hocus-pocus. But this—oh body o' Pilate!—this is different."

"Different how?"

"This is secret. This is gunpowder. This relates to foreign affairs. The king . . . I'll not call him old Rowley, as others do; that's too much of disrespect . . . the king, God bless him, walks devious ways with designs kept dark

65

from his ministers of the Cabal. To this end he employs two messengers. Shall any minister of state, even the most important like my Lord Arlington or His Grace of Bucks, be acquained with who these messengers are, or where old Rowley sends 'em? Well, then!" pursued Bygones, lowering his voice, "ontry noo and all in confidence, where *are* they sent?"

"Yes? Under favour, where?"

"To France; where else? And to whom are they sent? To His Majesty's sister, called Madame, who dwells at the court of Versailles and hath the ear of the French king. And what do they carry? Dispatches, writ in cipher and torn in two halves, each half carried by a King's Messenger so that none shall be the wiser should either half miscarry. Come, lad! I would not be indiscreet, you apprehend . . ."

"No, no, for God's sake don't be indiscreet. All the same!" says Kinsmere, who was growing more excited as he grew more uneasy. "Since you have been a *little* open in this matter, let's study it. There are two King's Messengers for foreign service, of whom you are one. So be it; but who's the other?"

"I can't say; I never learned; I mislike to guess. Still! There are grim things a-brewing. As you say in your innocence, and as I myself made pronouncement some while ago, we'll study the business and sift it for truth. To that end . . ."

Bygones Abraham hitched up his sword belt. He lumbered to the sideboard between the windows. Taking his peruke from the wig block, he fitted it back on again and skewered his hat to the wig with a long pin.

"Lad, lad! You are newly come to London, as I construe it. Are you familiar with players and play-acting?"

"I have seen strolling players at an inn in Bath. But no such spectacle as is said to exist here. Two companies of players, are there not?"

"Ay," the other said grandly, "of most excellent good skill. The King's Company and the Duke's Company. Wherefore, since 'tis time for our departure . . . ?"

"Friend Bygones, what have you a mind to do?"

"Why! After dining at the Devil, well padded with drink and comfort, we'll take ourselves to the play at the King's House. Not for the play, mark'ee, though it's a sight you must see. We go beyond it and behind it, to the tiring room where the actresses dress 'emselves. And we'll hope for speech with Dolly Landis."

"We'll hope for speech with . . . ?"

"Dolly Landis, ecod!" Bygones spread out both hands. "Mistress Dorothy Landis, an actress of the King's Company. Born in Coal Yard, 'tis true; but under teaching by Hart and Mohun she can ape a lady with the best of 'em. A pretty girl, and pleasant and fetching too; though not, as she could scarce be, so fine a woman as my Lady Castlemaine."

"But how does Mistress Landis concern our purpose?"

"Because she's Pem Harker's wench, or so they say. She is Pem Harker's woman, and he holds her fast."

It was as though, into that spacious room with the tapestries and the French carpet, there thrust through at him an image, lip upcurled under nose, of Pembroke Harker's face. My esteemed grandfather swore loudly.

"Captain Harker, eh?" he said. "Our bold, clever, all-conquering dragoon officer . . ."

"Ay! Don't mistake it, lad: he *is* a clever fellow, and a man of parts too."

"Even so! Allowing all vagaries of fancy to the sex, is it possible any woman save a mother could be fond of an object like Harker?"

"Fond of him, ecod?" Bygones echoed. "D'ye truly think Dolly Landis is *fond* of him?"

"Then how does he hold her fast?"

"How does he gain most of his ends?" returned the other. "Think on that, lad! I'll not pursue further a matter where I only suspect and don't know. But think on it; think well. This afternoon, good fortune attending us, we'll try to prove whether old Bygones is quite so much a fool as he must oft-times appear. And there is another question too."

"What question now?"

"The question," said Bygones Abraham, "to which we must find an answer before we visit the playhouse at all."

And he would say no more.

At Whitehall Stairs they took a wherry downriver. They sat in the stern sheets, the boatman at the oars facing them with his back to the prow. Though the river itself was odorous, few smuts and smudges from chimneys blew so

67

far out. Amid a multitude of small craft, some with little white or reddish sails, they were carried down half a mile to the Temple Stairs.

It was not much past noon. Bygones, strutting ahead at a good pace, led Kinsmere up through the Temple gardens, underneath the arch of Middle Temple Gate, and across a crowded road to the Devil—properly speaking, the Devil and St. Dunstan—tavern just opposite on the north side of Fleet Street.

Two floors and an attic of black beams and smoke-darkened plaster, with many-paned windows opening out like little doors, upreared to the west of St. Dunstan's Church, not far from the turning of Chancery Lane. The inn sign that swung above, once bright-painted in red and black and gilt, showed St. Dunstan seizing the Foul Fiend by the nose with a pair of red-hot pincers.

"Heigh-ho!" says Bygones Abraham.

Noise and heat smote out at them from this famous haunt, three generations before so loved by rare Ben Jonson that Ben, to be near it, took lodgings above a comb-maker's hard by. John Wadloe, the present proprietor, kept an ordinary or eating-house as well as a tavern; the atmosphere was pretty thick from meat roasting on spits in the underground kitchens. Since you might smoke tobacco in any room you pleased, not merely in some poky hole above a dish of coffee, the atmosphere had grown thicker still. And there were many of these rooms, each named for some pagan god or goddess.

"Well . . . now!" says Rowdy Kinsmere.

Bygones plunged first into the Apollo Room, to the right of the passage leading from the front door. Tables, stools, oak settles were well filled. The tapsters or skinkers—waiters, we should say nowadays—slid past with armloads of flagons and drinking jacks. Through the blatter of talk ran a *click-click* of snuffbox lids and an incessant tinkling from little bells hung over the leathern beer jacks called gingleboys. In a niche over the chimneypiece stood the bust of Apollo which Ben Jonson had caused to be put there, with Ben's verses painted large on the wall above:

Welcome, all who lead or follow,
To the Oracle of Apollo . . .

All his Answers are Divine,
Truth itself doth flow in Wine.
"Hang up all the poor Hop Drinkers!"
Cries Old Sim,* the King of Skinkers.
He the half of Life abuses
That sits watering with the Muses.
Those dull Girls no good can mean us,
Wine, it is the Milk of Venus . . .

Though at Bygones's insistence they put down a good
deal of drink, mainly sack out of pint pots, no mention
was yet made of food. My grandfather, whose head
buzzed a little, had begun to despair of getting any.

And one aspect really troubled him. In Somerset he had
been accustomed to playing host everywhere, and much
enjoyed this; but Bygones would not permit it here. It was
always, "Nay, I'll pay our shot!" or, "*This* reckoning's
mine, hark'ee!" as they made a tour of the downstairs
rooms.

"Oh, ecod, it won't do! I, who know everybody, see not
one man I'm acquainted with. And yet the question must
be answered . . . there's no escaping it . . ."

"Damne, man, what *is* this question so insistent to be
answered?"

"The King's Company play today, whatever the piece
they've chosen. But does Dolly Landis appear with 'em?
There's a sight o' pretty young actresses at the King's
House, all eager for their chance. There's Peg Hughes,
there's Mary Knepp, there's Ann and Beck Marshall. If
Dolly don't act, if the play's not right for her, we lose our
labour and what's to be done? Besides! He ought to be
here; he should be here; he's always here; where is he?"

"Who ought to be here?"

"Tom Killigrew, the master and manager of the company! A saucy fellow, a deep fellow, suffered much indulgence by His Majesty's self. Therefore I ask myself . . .
Stay, though!"

They had returned to the Apollo Room, each carrying a
sixth tankard. Bygones Abraham stopped short.

"Oh, body o' Pilate! He *is* here; he hath been here the

---

* Simon Wadloe, proprietor of the Devil in the very early seventeenth century.

whole time; veritably my eyes abuse me. D'ye mark it, lad?"

"Where?"

"Alone? By the chimneypiece, under Apollo's bust?—A good day to ye, Mr. Killigrew! A most happy and prosperous good day!"

At a table before the empty fireplace, trying hard to look inscrutable, sat a wiry little man with a pointed chin and monkey-bright eyes. He was older than his youthful clothes and bearing would have indicated, being in his late fifties. He rose to his feet and ducked a brief bow, not very cordial.

"Mr.—Mr. Bygones Abraham, I think?"

"The same. And this is most auspiciously met! Sir, will you dine?"

"With much thanks, I have already dined. A bumper of brandy," and Mr. Killigrew lifted his heavy goblet of dark-green glass, "a bumper of brandy, judiciously swallowed, does some little to offset the ill humours of cooks."

"Your health, then!"

"As you please." He drank and sat down, adjusting his laced pantaloons. "Now, sir, how can I serve you?"

"If I may crave the indulgence of a great favour . . . ?"

"If you must, I suppose you must. But be short, pray; I am much vexed and harassed. What's the favour?"

"I would present a young friend of mine. Mr. Kinsmere, may I make you known to Mr. Thomas Killigrew, Most Worshipful Master of the King's Comapny of Players, true wit and true judge of skills? My young friend, sir, would desire—"

"Would he indeed?" The little man's monkey-bright eyes lifted to survey my grandfather. "Well, Mr. Kinesear," he said, "and what will you read for me?"

"Read?"

"You are a brisk and hearty-seeming young man, not ill to look upon. It will be no fopling's role you would essay, I'll warrant, nor yet a comic one. Shall it be Celadon in *The Maiden Queen?* Almanzor in *The Conquest of Granada?* Or some harsher and cruder part, Hamlet or the Moor of Venice, from the old plays that begin to disgust our refined age?"

Against a rattle of voices in the background, the

tinkling of little bells on several gingleboys rose loudly and then died away.

"*Tapster,*" bellowed a distant voice.

"*Sir?*"

"*Tapster! Did you not hear those bells stop? The jacks are empty, God damme, Tapster!*"

"*Anon, sir! By and by, sir!*"

"Mr. Killigrew, Mr. Killigrew," Bygones Abraham exclaimed with horror, "already we are neck-deep in misunderstanding. My young friend is of the Cavalier landed gentry. He gives his patronage to the stage. But he is not an actor."

"Zounds, zounds, much thanks for *that.*" Tom Killigrew sighed. Drawing a gold comb from the pocket of a green velvet coat, he fell to combing the curls of his dark-brown peruke. "Could you guess how much my time is wasted by dolts and jack-puddings, you would pity me from the bottom of your heart. Well, well! Mr. Kinsear is no dolt or jack-pudding. But did he desire only the favour of being presented to me?"

Bygones, standing against the table, lowered his head above his tankard as though he prayed.

"If we might have," he rumbled, "perhaps a trifle of information?"

"Say on, then! But be short; I am much vexed and harassed."

"My friend did this day request me to accompany him to the King's House. Will the performance repay our trouble?"

Mr. Killigrew stopped combing and suppressed a yawn.

"The play is but *Julius Caesar,* one of the old stock pieces we share with the Duke's Company. And yet! To guide and govern these wilful stage folk, I do assure you, is no light or simple task. Behold! Look upon this!"

From another pocket he took a crumpled note, and spread it out on the table.

"Look upon this, I say! Saw you ever the like?"

Thos. Killigrew, Esq.,

Sir:

Beg leave to inform you the whole Roman Senate are getting drunk at the "Rose," and swear, Damn their eyes if they'll play today.

Yrs. respectfully,
J. Meaney

"Now what a thing," cried Mr. Killigrew, "is the temper of the artist! Even my stage hands are afflicted with it. Unless you be strict with 'em, as like as not they'll dash on and interrupt somebody's dying words by fetching away the bed. And, if aught more than another galls the artist's mind or exacerbates his spirit, it's to have his dying words cut off before he has thoroughly expired. However! You will do well to give 'em your countenance this day. The king and the court are to attend."

"You are sure o' that, sir?"

"I had it from His Majesty's self this morning, while he was being shaved. I acquainted him with our difficulties. (Zounds, zounds, was ever a man so vexed or harassed?) 'We must make shift as best we can, sire,' I said, 'since it's your pleasure to find new words and postures for so many of our actresses.' Yes! King and court will be there: you may depend on't. My Lady Castlemaine, I fancy, would demonstrate she has lost nothing of . . . Come, no matter! And I think, gentlemen, I can promise you the piece will be well acted. With Mr. Hart as Brutus and Mr. Mohun as Cassius . . ."

"But the women's parts, good sir! What o' the women's parts?"

"In *Julius Caesar*—faugh!—the women's parts are nothing. Yet there may be some small heat in Fop's corner," said Mr. Killigrew, and went on combing his wig, "when Mary Knepp appears as Calpurnia and Doll Landis disports herself as Portia. That's to say, if Mistress Landis is indeed with us when 'tis time to go on."

"Ay, but . . . body o' Pilate, Mr. Killigrew," roared Bygones, "what's all this? If arrangement has been made for Mistress Landis to enact Portia, why shouldn't the lass play?"

"Perhaps no reason. Yet you have heard, beyond doubt, of her attachment to a certain well-born if truculent

72

young captain of dragoons. And also, as I speak to you, she is here."

"HERE?"

"At this moment," replied Mr. Killigrew, putting away his comb, "she is abovestairs, in a private room, at dinner with Captain Harker. I don't meddle in that quarter, thank'ee. I have no wish to lose more of my company, but I don't meddle. The man who crosses Pembroke Harker is guilty of a great act of folly. Take warning, gentlemen! The man who dares even ruffle the feelings of Pembroke Harker—"

Bygones Abraham set down his tankard with a thump.

VI

"Eat?" said the woman's voice. "But I can't eat, Pem! I vow I have no hunger at all."

It was only two minutes since Kinsmere and Bygones Abraham, after receiving directions from a tapster, had crept quietly up the rear stairs at the Devil. Here they found themselves in a darkish cross passage, with a line of closed doors, which ran left and right along the back of the house.

Following the direction of Bygones's stabbing finger, they turned left into this passage. They moved on tiptoe over creaky boards, holding up their sword belts against clinking, with more doors now on their right. There was no other noise except a muffled clatter of activity from below.

"Sh-h!" hissed Bygones, making a hideous face in near-darkness.

"Very well; I'll sh-h. Where are we?"

"The back windows of these rooms," and Bygones gestured, "look out on an alley that runs in east from Chancery Lane. Beyond that alley is the back garden o' Serjeants' Inn. Sh-h!"

"As you like; I'm whispering. What do we do now?"

"You heard what the tapster said?"

"Yes, but . . ."

"Harker and his Dulcinea, so called, are in the Cupid Room. That's the last room down the passage. Next door

73

is Hebe, which has been vacant all morning, and that's our vantage point. What do we do, hey?"

"Yes?"

"We spy on 'em, that's what! Private rooms were created by God to be spied upon, else they'd not *be* private rooms, which is the first rule of diplomacy. Ontry noo, there's devilish few of 'em without a knothole in the wall. Oh, ecod! Is anything amiss with you?"

"Friend Bygones, ought we to do this? If those two are only disporting themselves . . ."

"Disporting 'emselves?" jeered the other, all but strangling with the violence of his own whisper. "At midday, d'ye think? At midday, or not an hour past it, and in a tavern given over to men at meat and drink and carouse?"

"No, no, no! There's other times and places if they'd a mind to dalliance. It's in *my* mind, right or wrong, they're here for discourse sake; and to hear that discourse may be very much to our purpose. Stop! Sh-h! Here's the Hebe Room. Be silent; walk warily; pray for luck!"

Gently he lifted the latch and pushed open the door.

The room into which they tiptoed was not quite as dark as the passage, though it swam in dimness. On its two windows in the tavern's rear wall, facing the door by which they entered, the shutters were still closed from the night before. Thin little spears of light, through tiny round holes in the shutters, slanted down dustily to a solid floor which did not creak.

And the room had been used for a carouse the night before, nor had anyone troubled to clean it. From a square wooden table in the middle, on which stood a big glass punch bowl filmed over inside with what had been drunk, four chairs were pushed back and one overturned. Round the bowl, amid squat glass goblets, lay scattered playing cards and the fragments of broken pipes. The whole place had a dreary, sticky look; it reeked of stale punch fumes and tobacco smoke. On the right-hand wall was pasted a copy of the king's proclamation against the drinking of healths.

From the left-hand wall, which was also the wall of the Cupid Room next door, had been built out a cobblestone fireplace with a brick flue. Bygones, finger to lip, gestured in that direction.

Also from this wall, a little distance to the left of the

chimney-piece, was built out a wooden cupboard whose door stood open. With hooks inside for the convenience of hanging up cloaks or coats, the cupboard was large enough to hold at full length any insensible toper who might see daylight through a knothole below the line of hooks, and they heard a murmur of voices.

Two seconds later they were both inside the cupboard. Bygones, after bending down and peering through that large knothole straightened up and motioned Kinsmere to look in his turn.

"Eat?" said a girl's voice. It was a beautiful voice, which might ordinarily have been warm and caressing, though it held little of either quality now. "But I can't eat, Pem! I vow I have no hunger at all."

And then he saw her.

Dolly Landis—little Dolly, if not so extremely little at that—sat at one side of the table, her back to the two windows. She had pushed aside a heaped platter, together with knife and two-pronged fork. Nearby stood an untasted glass of the wine called champagne, which had been imported from France only since the Restoration a decade ago.

Dolly put both elbows on the table. She had thrown back the cowl to a grey cloak; the ringlets of dark-brown hair were a little disarranged. Underneath the cloak she wore a blue-and-orange taffeta gown, much frilled with lace and cut low at the bodice. Kinsmere thought he had never seen a prettier face, or a better figure than the one compressed into the blue-and-orange gown.

Ah, Dolly!

She had a pink mouth, with very little lip salve. Her brown eyes—long-lashed, intense, luminous about the whites—were fixed steadily on her companion.

"No hunger?" said Pembroke Harker. "Or thirst either, it would seem."

"No, nor thirst either!"

"Well, madam—!"

Captain Harker, opposite her, sat back at ease in his long red coat. Hat and sword baldric were laid across a chair. His gloves protruded from his pocket. He had done himself well with a dish of roast mutton and potatoes, and finished several goblets of wine.

"Well, madam!" he said. He sat up straight; then rose

to his feet and looked down at her. "Well, madam! If you won't eat or drink, let it be so. Therein you must please yourself. It is no concern of mine."

"Have you *any* concern for me, pray?"

Harker lifted one shoulder.

"You will do as you are bid, Dolly, in whatever way may prove useful. You will obey my commands instantly, unhesitatingly, with as little cavil or ill humour as may be. That is my concern; it is all you need to know."

"Then my welfare or happiness . . . ?"

"Your welfare?" echoed Harker, and addressed the ceiling. "Oh God save us, *your* welfare or happiness! As though *you* mattered two straws in this world, to me or to anyone else."

"I am of no consequence, I know. Yet I might wish I did matter to somebody."

"Madam, madam, what a poor wretch you are!"

"Yes, I—I daresay." Dolly regarded him strangely. "Do you complain of me, Pem?"

The indomitable Harker stared back, forcing her to drop her eyes.

"Complain?" he said, as though wishing to be fair. "Do I indeed complain of you? Come! Let me think on this, and consider it well!"

He left the table and strolled towards the windows, whose shutters were folded back open. There, a few yards behind Dolly's chair, he turned round. Poised, utterly indifferent, he stood with his black periwig outlined against a window and a tangle of rooftops beyond. Then he took a few steps back and stopped. To see his face, as evidently she wished to do, Dolly was compelled to twist sideways in the chair and look up at him over her right shoulder.

"Hear my verdict, dear madam. On the whole, it must be confessed, I have no great cause for complaint. I might wish, perhaps, you showed greater relish for my company . . ."

"Do you show relish for *my* company?"

"I show relish for nobody's," Harker informed her. "Herein I could read you a lesson, little one, save that in your weak good-nature you'd not heed it. If you would learn how to triumph on this earth, let all men see the utter contempt in which you hold them. Spit on them, elbow them, jostle them, kick them aside as you would kick a

76

mongrel cur into the kennel, and they'll fawn on you as mongrel curs ever do."

It was plain that tears had risen to Dolly's eyes. But she did not speak.

"I could also wish," Harker pursued, "that in our more intimate moments you showed greater transport of joy. I could wish you did not lie so like to a dead woman, betraying no sign of pleasure or even of life."

"Oh, fie! Am I a strumpet too, that I should countefeit what I don't feel?"

"Yes, madam, you are a strumpet. What other word describes you?"

Dolly, near sobbing, seized both arms of the chair.

It had grown warm and stifling in the dark cupboard on the other side of the wall. Bygones Abraham glared at Kinsmere, who had lifted both fists, and Bygones enjoined silence by gripping his right arm.

"Let us have none of this huffing, little one!" said Harker. "Your feelings count for nothing, as you must be aware. You serve your purpose, whether you lie quiescent or writhe in transports like Barbara Castlemaine herself; you'll serve me in still another way ere this day be finished. Yes! You serve your purpose, and I would not be unkind. I don't in the least dislike you, Dolly. Indeed, in my own fashion, I may tell you I feel a certain indulgence towards these vapours . . ."

"How *kind* of you!" Dolly burst out. "Oh, God and damnation, how wonderfully *kind!*"

"No huffing, I said. And none of your Coal Yard insolence, lest I be obliged to chasten it."

(*"Let's strangle him. Let's . . ."*)

(*"Sh-h-h!"*)

"And therefore," continued Harker, "I will use you with all indulgence. Come, then!"

He returned to the other side of the table. He sat down. Picking up a knife, he tapped its edge lightly against his empty goblet.

"Come, then! Be open with me, Dolly, and you'll find me understanding enough for any purpose within your comprehension. What's amiss?"

"Amiss?"

Dolly's fine shoulders were bent forward, elbows again on the table. The pink mouth trembled. Her face, hitherto a little flushed either from the heat or from some other cause, had grown rather pale.

"Amiss?" she repeated, squirming in the chair.

"What quells your peasant's appetite, madam, and dries your usual thirst for strong drink? Why did you mutter to yourself, and all but refuse to accompany me here? In fine, where's the trouble?"

" 'Tis because I am affrighted, Pem. Oh, Christ ha' mercy, I am all but frightened from my wits!"

"And wherefore frightened?"

"I am a play-actress, Pem. Folk speak us fair and freely: 'What does't matter? She's but an actress-harlot of the King's House or the Duke's House.' We hear much of report and rumour, though sometimes 'tis hard to remember whence it came. Oh, Pem—bold, sweet Pem—what is this report of a design you've set your hand to?"

"Design?"

"A design," Dolly bent farther forward, "against the king, against the 'body politic,' whatever that may mean. There's report of vast subtility (so 'tis named) of a plot here, of great and secret workings in the dark, of much I can't fathom or let pierce my head at all. And that you have set your hand to this for gain, for coin or money or the rhino, since what else moves your heart or hath ever moved it in any fashion?"

"Do *you* scorn money, Madam Landis? *You,* of all on this earth?"

"Nay, I have never scorned it! But—"

" 'Design.' 'Plot.' 'Against the king.' 'Against the body politic.' These things be formless and shapeless, madam: as formless and shapeless as the reason in your own muddled skull. Can't you speak plainer than such hazy maunderings? Can't you put it into a word?"

"If it were put in a word," answered Dolly, "then I think the word would be 'treason.' "

"Treason!" said Harker, and struck the knife sharply against a glass.

But he was not stirred or taken aback. He merely surveyed her.

"In plays on the stage," said Dolly, "we talk much of this. We spout of it; we rant of it; we make fine speeches and lift our arms thus. But I never thought of it as real or

78

true. In our own country, among our own people, that any man should so think and so behave—foh, it's not possible!"

"Possible or not, Dolly, where heard you this rumour? From whom?"

"I can't remember!"

"You had better remember." With his left hand he reached across the table to touch her shoulder, and she flinched back. "While you endeavour to do so, I will assist you with a hint. Does the word 'Puritan' convey meaning to your mind?"

"Puritan?"

"In the tiring room, where you dress or undress yourself for the play . . . ?"

"Stay, Pem! A canting sanctimonious fellow, crying out all manner of pious utterance, but most lewd with his hands when he can put a woman into a corner."

"Was he called Gaines? Was he called Salvation Gaines?"

"Truly I think so! Yet—"

"Mr. Salvation Gaines, who is by way of being a gentleman, hath employment as a scrivener at court. It is not surprising, madam, you should have heard of this design from Gaines. I told him to let fall a hint."

"You *told* him?"

"And wherefore not? I have need of your service this day. *You'll* not betray me; have no fear of that; and outside our circle there is no other person who knows or suspects."

"Our circle? Oh, in the name of all pity and decency, what is this gabble of 'our circle'? What . . . ?"

Dolly Landis sprang to her feet. She flung her cloak back over the chair. She would have run from the Cupid Room, the watchers felt, if Harker, putting down the knife, had not also risen and taken her by the shoulders.

"Madam, sit down."

Harker did not debate or argue. With icy indifference he threw her away from him. She stumbled, groped, and then huddled back into the chair.

"For traitors, sweet strumpet, they provide a public gallows and a disembowelling knife and a quartering block. Here, I must take it, is the cause of this sore affright. Not for me or my safety, as would befit the loving friend you are not, but lest their lawyers and judges think you yourself concerned."

" 'Tis a horrid thing, surely?"

"I could wish you a pleasanter end. And yet you need not fear it."

"Oh, God ha' mercy!"

"No, Dolly, let *me* have mercy." Once more Harker picked up the knife. "*I* am the one you need fear, and the only one. Now, my unskillful drab! Now, my dead-woman bedfellow! Let's look a little at the design. As for Salvation Gaines and *his* part in this affair—"

"Salvation Gaines!" Dolly, in tears and breast heaving, almost spat out the words. "By all that's hyprocritical and clammy, Salvation Gaines! Is he so near a friend of yours?"

"He is an underling of mine. D'you mark me well, woman?"

"If I must!"

"So be it, then!" said Harker, and continued to tap knife against glass. "Certain men at court—notably the head of the group, who commands us by virtue of his position are not content either with Charles Stuart or with Charles Stuart's managing of public business."

"And you, dear Pem, are one of those not content with an ill king?"

"Now, what a pox is this?" Harker demanded. "Shall I concern my feelings, one way or t'other, so long as I be well rewarded for what I do? Let me tell you something of myself, little one. Not much; you are faint of heart and deserve little knowledge; but enough so that you may assist me without undue risk. Already you are acquainted with me as a man well-liked and well-received at court, having the ear of all and the indulgence of most. Do you know what else I am?"

On the other side of the wall there was a kind of silent commotion.

("Now there," Kinsmere said to himself, "now there, by crowns and continents, is a question should be answered in a loud, clear voice. Do we know what else you are, Captain Pembroke Harker?")

But Bygones Abraham had seized his arm in a wrestling grip. Bygones bent down himself to peer through the knothole and then, at Harker's next words, urged Kinsmere back to it.

"I am a King's Messenger for foreign service," Harker said. "Enough of vapours, madam; I'll bear no more. Dry your tears and observe this ring."

From his waistcoat pocket he had drawn what was unquestionably a duplicate of the other two sapphire rings. After holding it out for Dolly's inspection—she was too blinded to see—he returned it to his pocket.

Tap went the knife against a glass goblet. *Tap, tap* . . .

"Up to this morning I had believed there were but two of us. And I still hold the same opinion. A small complication of accident arose in the Great Court at Whitehall. But have no fear; I'll resolve it! It will be all one to our plans, madam, and all one to you and me."

"Our plans? You and me?" Dolly burst out. "Lord, Lord, must I be drawn into your schemes as well as your bed? Is there no end to this business of 'you and me'?"

"No end whatever, until it shall please me to grow weary. However! I spoke of a second King's Messenger with a ring like mine. The man in question is not acquainted with *my* identity, although I know his."

"One of your malcontented group, belike?"

"He is not, being a grotesquely loyal king's man who can't be corrupted. But he is a fool, and will pay dearly for his folly."

"Stop, Pem; for God's sake, stop!"

"Nay, attend to me! This other messenger is called Bygones Abraham: a gross fellow of low origins, once a common soldier, who has contrived in some measure to better his position. By only two things may you mark him out. He talks great nonsense in the most florid of ill-chosen words. And, though none might suspect it from his clumsy bearing, he is a noted swordsman."

Harker looked down at her steadily.

"We ply our separate routes between Whitehall and Versailles, each carrying half of a dispatch writ on thick paper and heavily sealed over. The king pretends no knowledge of our existence. He meets us only in secret, in his private cabinet abovestairs from the Great Bedchamber. Who knows of this clandestine correspondence between Charles Stuart and King Louis the Fourteenth—in particular with a proposed French treaty which by every sign to be read is now afoot between them? Who knows, or suspects this, let it be asked? Apart from myself and perhaps the other messenger, not one living soul."

"Pem, Pem! You bleat of one who talks nonsense. And yet *this* is great nonsense, at all events!"

"Do you indeed find it so, madam?"

"Even *I* am aware," Dolly screamed, "the king hath advisers and a council. If these are documents of state—ay, a treaty . . ."

"They are not documents of state," Harker answered; "and *this* treaty is of different sort. The king's closest advisers (need I speak it?) are five men the first letters of whose names form the letters of the word 'cabal.'

"The 'C' of the Cabal is Sir Thomas Clifford. The first 'A' is my Lord Arlington. The 'B' is my Lord Duke of Bucks. The second 'A' is my Lord Ashley: our most cunning 'little man with three names'—born Anthony Ashley Cooper, but a decade ago created Baron Ashley of Wimborne St. Giles . . ."

Tap, tap went the knife. *Tap, tap, tap . . .*

"Whereas the last name, Dolly, give us the 'L' for my Lord Duke of Lauderdale: a brutal fellow and a ruthless, but beyond doubt with wits in his head, who—"

"Lord, lord, I understand not one word of all this!"

"Patience," said Harker, "you need understand very little. Now, it is remotely possible that Sir Thomas Clifford, being a Roman Catholic as well as a lover of France and monarchial principle, may have learned some details of the proposed treaty. The others—never. These others are united in their passionate hatred of Popery, or at least in their hatred and distrust of France. The king rides high; he may ride for a fall. If the others were to learn of what goes forward, and if all England came to know it as well . . ."

There was a sharp crack as the knife edge smote the goblet. Glass pieces flew wide above a broken stem; Dolly Landis cowered back.

"*Habet!*" Harker said.

"The latest dispatch," he continued, "will be sent this night. I had my information three days ago. I had it from none other than Rab Butterworth, Second Page of the

Back-Stairs and assistant to the more notorious Will Chiffinch, First Page of the Back-Stairs and procurer for His Majesty. The man Abraham will be told late today.

"On each occasion when dispatches are sent, Chiffinch and Butterworth thinking it only some trumpery affair of amorous notes or *billets-doux,* the custom is ever the same. At ten o'clock I present myself at the last door on the south side of the Shield Gallery. I scratch at the door. When it is opened, I pass in my ring to identify me. I am conducted abovestairs to the private cabinet. My ring is returned to me—this is most necessary!—together with half of a much-sealed cipher document in the king's own hand.

"Forthwith I am off to Dover, with horses provided at posting stations along the road, and I take ship for Calais. The ring (that insignificant ring!) is my badge, my sign, my touchstone to open doors. It carries me to Calais, to Paris, to Versailles, and to Charles Stuart's young sister, Madame la Duchesse d'Orleans, who is the go-between for the French king.

"But what of our second messenger, the man Bygones Abraham, carrying the other half of the dispatch?

"He is instructed in much the same way, though he shapes a different course for France. He waits upon the king at half past ten, so that neither messenger may see the other. Once he has received his half of the document, the rest of his journey is by water."

"By water?" Dolly exclaimed.

"In the main, yes. A wherry at the private landing stairs bears him downstream to a sloop, the war sloop *Saucy Ann,* lying below London Bridge. The sloop weighs anchor for the Narrow Seas. And yet much time must elapse ere he need even leave Whitehall Palace on his mission. Do you know why?"

"What this to me? Shall I know or care?"

"You had better know. The sloop must wait for the tide, which is at a quarter hour past midnight. Even the wherry does not call at Whitehall Stairs until the quarter hour *to* twelve. Do I speak plain?"

In the gloom of a cupboard grown ever more stifling, his back and legs cramped from bending to that knothole, Kinsmere glanced sideways at his companion. A tiny shaft

83

of light through the knothole touched Bygones's mottled face, and Bygones nodded confirmation of what had been said.

Back went my grandsire's gaze to the scene in the Cupid Room.

"The man Abraham," pursued Harker, "has therefore a full hour and a quarter between the time of receiving his half-document and the time of his departure at Whitehall Stairs. Therein, sweet strumpet, lies our most fortunate circumstances. Therein he finds his death, and we have him."

Sheer horror had seized on Dolly.

"Finds his death? *We* have him?"

"Come, madam! What choice is there? Be not troubled; your part in the business occurs elsewhere. But mine is with the man Abraham. If I am to gain his half of the dispatch, so as to present the complete and damning document to a plotter-in-chief who so much desires it, have I any alternative save to remove it from a dead body? Zounds, madam, this is only good sense! Will you try to be reasonable?"

"Reasonable? Oh, God kill me!"

"Nay, dear drab, seek not so hard for surcease. It will arrive soon enough, I do assure you."

"I—I begin to hope it will."

"The man Abraham is a fool, as I told you." Harker's lip curled up. "The nature of his folly is a passion to be thought a gentleman. No gentleman, in this lout's solemn belief, refuses even a challenge to fight."

"Yes?"

"And so I challenged him: that he meet me (alone) in Leicester Fields at eleven o'clock tonight. He will be there, make no mistake, and with the half-letter upon him. From Whitehall Palace to Leicester Fields is but ten minutes' journey on foot, the half of that by horseback. The man Abraham, in his conceit, will think he has ample time to kill or wound me and yet return to Whitehall for the wherry that awaits him at a quarter hour to midnight. He is a famous swordsman, as I freely grant . . ."

"And yet you'd fight him?"

"Now, why should I give myself the trouble of fighting him?"

Dolly stared and stammered, colouring up in confusion. "But—but . . . !"

"Tut!" interrupted Harker, with a gesture of such supreme assurance that it would have daunted anyone. "I *could* come fairly at him and kill him; am I not a master too? Yet where is the virtue to run needless hazard? If I am anything at all, I am a man of good sense.

"No, madam! He shall have his deserts; 'tis so arranged. There are bullyrocks and bravos in plenty; two of these are already hired. They follow him from Whitehall towards Leicester Fields. In open ground beyond the Royal Mews they take him; they knock him on the head; they bury him deep. They may have his watch or the coins in his purse; *I* take the half of a cipher dispatch to give over to our plotter-in-chief for a somewhat richer reward.

"Afterwards, Dolly? Mark well what I say!

"I go abroad, in exactness as planned. I disappear, or seem to disappear, awaiting the issue of what happens. By the king it will be assumed that both loyal messengers have been robbed and slain. If the plotter-in-chief shall triumph over Charles Stuart, I still hold over him a threat of exposure such as he holds over Charles Stuart. If the king triumph, as may well be the case, I return in honour with some befitting tale for his ears. In either case my fortune is made; *I* triumph, as always; in no event can I lose."

"Oh, P-Pem, but this is a pretty business! And is that all?"

"No, madam. We are come to your part in this affair, since there is another lout to be dealt with besides the man Abraham. Your trull's talents, such as they are, shall find proper employment at last. I don't persuade or cajole; I give you my command; and it will go very ill with that pretty neck unless you are strict in carrying them out."

Bygones Abraham, chest heaving, bent towards the knothole. Kinsmere drew away. From the Cupid's Room issued the scrape of a chair being pushed back. Harker's harsh, bored voice died away. But Dolly Landis uttered a cry. Then there was silence.

Silence, aching and interminable, except for a faint gasp. In that darkness Kinsmere could see only the little line of light that fell across Bygones's one staring eye.

VII

Such kegs of gunpowder were packed into that cupboard, with Harker blowing on a lighted fuse each time he spoke, that you might have wondered why they failed to explode.

Kinsmere wondered too, in his cramped position with wobbling legs. He knew they must keep cool heads; they must do nothing precipitate. But it was very hard to remain quiet. Every word, every look of Dolly Landis went to his heart and stabbed there. He wanted in some fashion to lash out. He wanted to burst from the cupboard and face Harker. He wanted . . .

And yet the gunpowder did not explode—for a few moments.

"Come, that's better!" Harker said unexpectedly.

With a great heave my grandfather pushed Bygones to one side.

Harker began to stride up and down the Cupid Room, his spurless gambado boots a-clack on boards. Dolly had risen to her feet, and stood watching him.

"This morning—" Harker began. Then he checked himself.

"Art disturbed, Pem? Art so very, *very* disturbed?"

"Nay, who saith I am disturbed at all?"

"Perhaps *I* say it. And yet who am I to speak aught save at your bidding? Stay: no matter! 'This morning . . .'?"

Harker stopped pacing and returned to the table. He still carried the knife, which he threw down beside his plate.

"This morning, in the Great Court outside the palace, I had chance encounter with the second lout: an oaf, an ill-looking fellow, a very country bumpkin come to town from his rustic bog. He was young, younger than myself. And yet he wore the ring of a King's Messenger.

"A third messenger, was it, some cursed royal servant unknown even to me? I could not believe this, Dolly; I still don't believe this; and I know I am in the right of it. I misliked the man at sight; we quarreled; he provoked it and laid hand on me, for which he shall suffer in good time."

"He laid hand on you, did he? Is it indeed so? This reckless bumpkin *dared* so great an outrage?"

"No insolence, madam; he will pay dearly."

"With money, like the plotter-in-chief?"

"No insolence, I said! Yet this encounter gave me insight to explain. For all his boorishness he spoke well; I allow it; those who brought him up have been people of some culture if no manners. And the ring, therefore, the meaning of the ring . . ."

"Ay, the ring?"

"The meaning of the ring, madam," retorted Harker, his self-control slipping a little, "is that it hath *no* meaning of import to you or me. The ring is imitation gold and sapphire, perhaps: a trumpery heirloom handed down from some rustic Old Hunks to his still more rustic son. We have met accident, coincidence; no more!

"Notwithstanding, I much wondered. I had left my bumpkin and begun to descend the water stairs at Whitehall when a fortunate instinct caused me to turn back. There stood my bumpkin in the passage, deep in talk with none other than the man Bygones Abraham. Though too far away to overhear, I followed them on their departure. They walked together into Whitehall Palace. Again I wondered."

"Wondered what?"

"This Abraham, as I have named him, is a fool in his mania to pass for a man of fashion. But by otherwise he is not over-stupid. Were these two in league together? Was this by some chance a trap? Did the man Abraham suspect *my* motives? Was he grown suspicious . . ."

"Was he grown suspicious, in fine, you would so blithely betray the king who trusts you?"

"Charles Stuart trusts nobody!"

"Then that . . . that . . . oh, God Damn me, have it as you will!"

"There is no suspicion," Harker told her. "There is no trap. Of this I am certain. But we'll establish it, woman; we'll make the business sure. You said, I think, you are to play today?"

"I am Portia in *Julius Ceasar.*"

"Well, well, let be: we'll allow you that indulgence! Do you enact the virtuous Roman at the theatre; you shall become your true self soon enough."

"My true self? How?"

"I must make shift to discover who this young bumpkin is, and where he lodges. It should not prove unduly difficult. You will call on him early this evening. You will make yourself known to him. You will be at him horse, foot, and artillery, with every female weapon you own. You will use all such methods as are needful (*all*) to learn what secrets he knows or possesses, which will be none whatever. You apprehend me, woman? You will do this?"

"No, Pem, I greatly fear I won't."

"Come," said Harker, knocking his knuckles against the table, "I am not sure I have heard aright. If this is more huffing at virtue . . ."

"Nay, when have I ever pretended to be virtuous? Indeed, I think I was born otherwise."

"Then what—?"

Even Harker broke off. Dolly was laughing.

She stood there, head back, ringlets-a-dance, and chortled with honest mirth. Her shoulders, rising in polished pink-white shapeliness from the bodice of the blue-and-orange gown, shook and trembled. The brown eyes were half shut up as though again with tears. Her roguish look—half ingenuous, half hoyden-knowing—reanimated a face rapt, flushed, and lovely enough to turn a man's brain.

"I was sore afeared," she said, "but I am afeared no longer. I'll not do this, Pem, because I'll not be put upon. I can't say why, but you have abused my confidence. You have mocked me; you have jeered me; you have told me a very nosegay of lies!"

"Lies, madam?" exploded Harker. "Lies concerning the man Bygones Abraham or the oafish youth whose name we don't even know?"

"Nay; concerning the King of England and the manner of man you think he is. Are you truly acquainted with the king, Pem? Have you ever exchanged ten words with him?"

"Have I ever . . . ?"

Harker, so taken aback he could not continue, merely lifted a hand to adjust his wig.

Dolly was not even listening. Always at her best in comedy, she played comedy by making her eyes appear long and sleepy-looking. She rubbed her nose as though that also were long, and walked her fingers across her upper lip in the manner of one feeling at a thin line of moustache. Finally, she drew in her chin to mimic a very deep voice.

"God's fish, sir!" This from far down in her throat. *"Let me have fiddle music, with bawdy songs. And a wench. God's fish, Mr. Chiffinch, fetch me a new wench!"*

Then all mimicry dropped away.

"Mistake me not!" Dolly cried in her natural voice. "I use no disrespect towards the king, or at least not much. He hath a good heart, and is no zany. 'He could see things if he would,' as the exiled Lord Clarendon is reputed to have said. He is but a lazy idle saunterer, with little to occupy him save sport or whoring. Yet he owns good enough natural wits, all declare, could he be persuaded to turn 'em towards seriousness."

"How penetrating is this," said Harker, "that you in your wisdom should find him not *altogether* a fool!"

"A fool? Nay, I expressly denied it! Shall you change his nature, though? Was it not my Lord Rochester, that most insolent young wit in the fair periwig, who wrote a mock epitaph and affixed it to the bed curtains in the Great Chamber? I think it was; I remember the epitaph, and sure never was character better summed up.

"Here lies Our Sovereign Liege the King,
    Whose word, no man relies on—
Who never said a foolish thing,
    Nor ever did a wise one."

"There you have it, true-writ by an intimate friend. Pem, Pem, why do you jeer me?"

"Jeer you?"

" 'Unthinking Charles!' 'Old Rowley!' The idle good-for-nothing who chased a moth with my Lady Castlemaine while Dutch guns came up the Medway! Yet this is the man you would limn for me as ceaselessly employing his wits, as deep in hidden craft, as one who may outwit a plotter-in-chief at Whitehall and might even outwit the King of France himself."

"In truth he might," said Harker. "It has not occurred to you, I see, that Charles Stuart is the shrewdest man in Europe?"

"Oh, bah! Out upon it! If you would persuade me . . ."

"As I am not here to persuade or cajole, madam, neither am I here to argue. You have received your orders."

" 'Plotter-in-chief!' 'Group of malcontents!' God's death, a truce to such moonshine! If there should truly be in any sort a plotter-in-chief, who is it?"

"Perhaps I may tell you, since you find it so fantastical. Meanwhile, you will obey my commands. You will throw yourself at this young oaf from the country. You will conquer him, lie with him, drain him of what he knows. And, then this shall prove to be nothing . . ."

"Ay, what then? That *he* may be followed by bullyrocks and knocked on the head from behind?"

"No, madam. He shall have more honour. Him I will meet in Leicester Fields by moonlight, since I challenged him too. Only at the second or third pass, being merciful, will I run him through the guts and leave him to die as he deserves."

"Because he dared raise his hand to this sacred presence? God, Pem, what a low foul bitch's spawn you are!"

"Now if I am so, madam, what of you? Whore you may be or no, since you make fine distinctions in such things, but this is mighty high posing for an unhanged thief."

"Pem, I . . ."

"Dorothy Landis," said Harker, pointing a long finger into her face, "how old are you?"

"I am twenty, near to twenty-one."

"When you were thirteen or fourteen, like your near friend Madam Gwyn—'Madam' Gwyn, save the mark!—a drunkard mother 'prenticed you as table servant in a brothel, to serve strong waters to the gentlemen. Is this so?"

"Indeed, it is! What then?"

"At sixteen, as I also think, you became an orange wench at the King's Playhouse. While still an orange wench, even as old Michael Mohun began to instruct you in the craft of acting, you one night picked the pocket of young Sir Aubrey Fairchild."

"*I was hungry.*"

"No matter for that; you picked his pocket. Sir Aubrey knew this, and wrote a complaint against you . . ."

"Because you compelled him to! Because poor, well-meaning Aub Fairchild feared you so much, and grovelled before you as all others seem to do. Am I a strumpet and a poor thing? Well! Did I but meet a man of good heart who cared a little for me, and was not one whit afraid of you or your great sword, I think I would love him until I died. And *he* should learn whether in truth I am like unto a dead woman. As for the written complaint against me, 'tis burnt and destroyed."

"It is not destroyed, as you know well or you'd not have been so complaisant. I have it here." Harker tapped the left side of his chest. "In sheath pocket inside the coat, where others bear a dagger, *I* carry evidence for the magistrate and the hangman. An end of cavilling, you foolish woman! This means Tyburn Tree, and your slut's corpse handed over to the knives of surgeons, unless straightway you are content to obey my commands. What do you say?"

"I say again that I'll not do it! I am utterly weary and sick of you!"

"Then a magistrate had best be summoned. Since *I* say again, and for the last time, that I am not here to argue."

Harker moved to one side of the table. With his open hand, scarcely looking at her, he struck her hard across the mouth. Dolly's arms flew out; she herself flew back into the chair; and chair and girl went over backwards with a crash on the oak floor.

And, at the same moment, Kinsmere lifted his fist and rapped sharply with his knuckles on the communicating wall.

Harker whirled round. He was no longer quite so impassive. For a moment or two he stood motionless, a frozen, sly, almost half-witted look framed in the curls of his peruke.

"Who's there?"

"I am the country bumpkin," Kinsmere said to the knothole, "who is to have steel through his guts. And the time for it is now come. Need I go in there to your dinner table, Captain Brag-and-Blow, or have you still sufficient huff to dare meet me here?"

Harker cast up his eyes in delight, nose lifting above the thick upper lip. He did not condescend to speak. He took his sword baldric from the extra chair, draping it over his coat from right shoulder to right hip; he wheeled round, and walked at an unhurried pace towards the door.

"Ecod!" breathed Bygones Abraham. "Oh, ecod!"

Kinsmere stalked out of cupboard into the Hebe Room, with Bygones following. Though the air of *this* semi-darkness was a little less close, the reek of stale tobacco fumes and arrack punch closed round like a hand at the throat. My grandfather stopped by the mantel-shelf above the cobblestone fireplace, on which shelf stood a tinder box and a tallow dip in a pewter candlestick. He kicked at one of the andirons in the fireplace, disturbing dead ashes.

"Lad, lad!" rumbled an overwrought Bygones. "Body o' Pilate! If there needs must be fighting, here and now and damn the consequences, 'tis no part of yours to be foremost. *I'll* meet him."

"You will not. I have taken a great fancy to the wench in there, and this bold captain is mine for a measuring."

"But . . . but not here in this room, surely? Or at least open the shutters! 'Tis all but dark! You'll barely be able to see him."

"Or he to see me. If he is in fact as formidable a fellow as he boasts of being . . . ?"

"Ay, he's an uncommon good swordsman. Braggarts are not always liars and cowards, as so soothingly we find 'em in legend."

"Then it may be just as well. No, don't touch the shutters!"

"Lad, lad! I have put no questions heretofore. Since you are Buck Kinsmere's son, I had thought ye trained to swordplay as soon as you could walk. Tell me truth and speak home: *have* you skill?"

"I am no master of the blade, as was my uncle Godfrey ere he put on so much weight. But my fencing is more than respectable."

"How many times have you been out? Measured points on a green? Met your enemy in true duello?"

"Faith, sir, there must be a first time for all of us."

"*Never* before? NEVER, ecod? Rot me, I'll not allow . . ."

"By God, you will!—Go and see to Dolly Landis! If he hurt my Dolly, hurt her even in the least degree . . ."

"Lad, lad, where's the need for fighting at all? He has spoke enough treason to damn him ten times over. If we fetch a Foot Guard officer from Whitehall Palace, or even a magistrate of the civil law . . ."

"And have Dolly taken in custody as well? Go and see to her, won't you?"

Muttering and cursing hard under his breath, Bygones lumbered towards the door. There were footsteps in the passage outside. The door was flung wide open; it struck the wall and rebounded. In the aperture stood Pembroke Harker: towering, little more than a blur to be seen, right hand across on his rapier hilt.

"Two of you, then?" he shouted. "*Two* of you to set on me in ambush?"

"Only one, Captain Loud-Mouth," Kinsmere yelled back. "Or at all events one at a time. Your own concern for fair dealing has already been noted. Mr. Bygones Abraham, whom you would have had assassinated, will be close at hand but to attend you should you put an end to me."

"Which will be almost immediately, dog."

Harker, without seeming to notice Bygones, took two steps inside. Bygones stalked by him into the passage and clapped shut the door. Kinsmere, tightening his sword belt, moved out from the fireplace, between the table with its punch bowl in the middle of the room and the thin, dusty little spears of light through closed shutters at the back. But he turned sideways, so as not to be too much silhouetted.

They were alone now. Harker must come round the table and face him sideways. Neither would have advantage from what blurred light existed. Kinsmere could hear the breath whistling in Harker's nostrils. He could sense like a presence or an odour the delight with which Harker closed in for the kill. Again there was a great hollow in his chest and a lightness about the legs, with a pulse beating somewhere . . .

(Dolly! Little Dolly!)

Harker stopped beside the table, still facing forward.

"This is the end of you, bumpkin. If you would pray, do it now. If you would cry quits, you can't. This is the very last—"

"Save your breath to help your swordplay! Lug out!"

Both of them did so. The light ran along the blades.

"Do you know what will happen to you, oaf? Can you guess or conceive this? You will be . . ."

Still as he faced forward, the fingers of Harker's left

93

hand slid down underneath the glass punch bowl with its sticky dregs. And he sent that heavy bowl flying to the left. There was a bursting crash of glass as it struck the chimneypiece just above the fireplace opening; fragments rained and rattled on the hearth.

"Smashed," he roared. "Smashed and smashed and *forever* smashed."

"A damned error, Captain Loud-Mouth. You should have thrown it at me. Or are you like the ancient Chinese—Chinese, Japanese, which?—who thought to conquer their enemies by making noise?"

"Is it only noise, oaf? Think well: is it *only* noise?"

Then he was round the edge of the table. The instant they faced each other, bodies sideways at guard position, Harker flung out his great reach at full-length lunge for the middle of the belly.

The blades clacked together. Kinsmere, jerking his wrist to the left, parried beyond the centre line and drove back in riposte for the left side of his opponent's chest. He heard the stamp of his own foot, then the recurrent stamp and steel slither of full engagement—thrust, parry, riposte, thrust, parry, riposte—as a great dust rose round snaky light flashes on the swords.

Rapier play in my grandfather's time was much brasher and cruder than the polished business we learned towards the end of the eighteenth century. What it lacked of skill or finesse it made up in murderous fury. And yet these two could not go on at such a pace: all out, near-blind, breathing poisoned air, with every thrust aimed at a vital spot.

Kinsmere, no doubt overreckless, had begun to press his man back towards the wall which held the royal proclamation against health-drinking. And Harker nicked him.

For Kinsmere had tried a feint, his eye clouding. Harker, anticipating this by instinct, broke it and shot forward in vicious full-length lunge for the heart. But his foot slipped, or *his* eye clouded too. Though the point pierced, it struck high and wide of the mark.

Instantly Harker disengaged and drew back. His boots did not clack or thump; he took little shuffling steps; the tall figure seemed almost to melt and disappear. Then it did disappear. Death and damnation, where was he?

Kinsmere felt no consciousness of hurt. Sweat stung his forehead, his eyes, his ribs. From somewhere at the top of the left shoulder spread a warm, thickish wetness which could not be sweat at all.

But where was Harker?

He's back against that wall. It's my accursed eyesight that I can't see him. But he's coming out; I heard him shuffle. He's coming out; he's moving slowly; he . . .

Take care!

What Kinsmere saw shocked him awake and alert.

Harker loomed up, an avatar of terror. His right hand held the blade poised and slanted at guard. On his left hand was—a glove, to be sure! One of the black-leather cavalry gloves which previously had been in his pocket.

He was about to try an old trick, a famous trick of which Kinsmere's Uncle Godfrey had given warning, and which would win or lose you your life.

You thrust at your adversary, no matter where. After parrying his return thrust, in the brief moment when the points were disengaged, you deliberately threw yourself inside his guard. You seized his blade in your left hand; with your right hand, shortening your sword, you stabbed him through the chest at close quarters. If you missed and failed to seize the blade, he had you at his mercy.

This was the manoeuvre Harker had prepared to execute, and would execute at any moment . . . that is, unless Kinsmere beat him to it by using the same trick first. He had no glove, but he needed none. The swords, though needle-sharp of point, had no cutting edge. You could cut yourself if you were careless, admittedly. Also, if he groped wildly and missed the blade . . .

He found himself looking into Harker's eyes.

"Art prepared to die, oaf?"

"Have at you, Captain Loud-Mouth!"

Harker's back was still towards the wall with the royal proclamation. Kinsmere kicked at an overturned chair that all but tripped him. He lunged out at his adversary, blindly and rather low; he darted back at guard, to await the return thrust he must parry before he could spring forward and seize the sword. That return thrust never came.

Then he stared incredulously.

Harker, head bent far forward, had sunk down on one knee. For a moment he remained there, gasping.

Kinsmere's heart jumped up in his throat. He had hit Harker vitally, but he had no notion how; he had not felt the point go in or come out.

Still doubled forward, the dragoon captain lurched to his feet. He stumbled against the overturned chair. His rapier wavered, turning slowly round his hand, its cup-hilt and quillons reflecting dusty light. Then it clattered to the floor.

Harker had started towards the fireplace. A stricken, ghostly figure in red coat and black periwig, he went stumbling across through gloom. He stretched out his hand for the mantel-shelf, but failed to reach it. Abruptly he staggered again. He pitched head foremost into the fireplace, across dead ashes and shattered glass. His head struck one andiron as he fell. A little puff of ash blew up and settled round his head.

My grandfather himself was trembling all over and could scarcely hold the sword. His left shoulder felt numb; the thick wetness ran from arm and shoulder down to ribs. He pulled himself together, or tried to, when a heavy footstep stirred from the direction of the door.

"Friend Bygones, is that you?"

"By the laws of all youthful foolery, and o' mad Bedlamite champions in a first duello," rumbled back the oratorical flourish, "it can be affirmed that 'tis none other. Lad, lad, how d'ye fare?"

"Pretty well, I thank you. But could we have a window set open, do you think? It is devilish hot here, and I am not so fine a fellow as I imagined. How is it with the divine Dolly?"

"She's a-weeping and a-cursing, as might be expected, in the customary female proportions. But we have her safe, and all's well."

"Was she hurt?"

"Be easy; not one bit! The lass did desire to witness issue of the fight, looking in reverse direction through that same knothole past the open cupboard door. She could not face what she could scarce have seen, but fell to skreeking out with a noise like 'Eee!' and forthwith hid her face. And yet, when she learned 'twas Harker suffered scathe and not you, she was so wild-relieved she fell to skreeking again.—Lad, lad, it was bravely done; but where did you hit him?"

"The only honest answer," retorted Kinsmere, "is that I don't know and can't remember. Below the belt, I think, though even with Harker I would never deliberately have aimed there."

"Below the belt? Ay, that would account—!" Bygones stopped.

He blundered across to the rear wall, folding back the shutters on both windows and pushing open their sashes like little doors. Daylight entered; cleaner air blew through. Below the windows an alley stretched in some distance from Chancery Lane away on the left. Beyond the alley, northward, ran the old brick wall round the gardens behind Serjeants' Inn, their plum-trees heavy with ripening fruit.

But Kinsmere had no time to observe this. Bygones—his face fierier, pulling hard at moustache and tuft of chin whisker—was muttering as he peered round the room. His gaze travelled to my grandfather, past him to the overturned chair, across towards Harker, and back to Kinsmere again.

"There must be deep drinking belowstairs, and a rare afternoon's carouse. Not a man heard the noise o' this, though it was like to shake the house. Below the belt, you think? Ay, ay! and yet . . ." Suddenly his eyes bulged out, "Great body o' Pilate!" he roared. "What weird fantastical circumstance is this?"

"Eh?"

"There's no blood on your sword," said Bygones Abraham.

Kinsmere peered down, moving his rapier blade as though he had never seen it before. There was not one drop of blood. Bygones, muttering again, hurried to the chimneypiece. With a wrench he rolled Harker face upwards.

"Insensible and deaf to all sounds," Bygones grunted, "from the cause that he cracked his head against the andiron in falling. Here's the bruise of it below the foretop of the wig. But—but . . ."

Once more Bygones peered round the room. He looked at the overturned chair, he looked back at Harker and the glove on Harker's left hand; then with a great surge of triumph he smote his thigh.

"This man," he said, "is not even wounded."

"What's that?"

"He was not even touched! And here, let it be asseverated and proclaimed of all trumpets, is the luckiest and most fortunate circumstance e'er befell two wights like you and me. Lad, lad! D'ye see what happened?"

"No, I am hanged if I do! Harker doubled up quite suddenly; he went down on one knee . . ."

Bygones pointed to the chair, with its legs turned obliquely upwards.

"The glove gives sign, eel sote ohz yuh, he seized for your blade to stab you at close quarters with his other hand. And the chair was there. Is this so?"

"It was what he had intent to do, yes, and what I would have done myself! But there was no time for either of us. We—"

"Had *intent* to do, d'ye tell me?" roared the other. "It was what in fact he did do. Harker was caught below the belt, God knows. But not by you. He parried your thrust in seckowned; he leaped to seize your blade—"

"And beat me to it?"

"Ay, ecod, if you'd put it so. He leaped, I say, but missed his grab. He slipped; he fell, and went down with his full weight on the sharp leg of that chair. 'Twas the andiron struck him senseless. He'll be up in an hour, belike, to meet charges of treason from a sterner judge than you."

Whereupon Kinsmere began, like St. Peter, to curse and swear.

"Now what, pray," he continued, "is so lucky or fortunate in all this? Here's my first duello, as you were so quick to observe. I am resolved to carry myself well, to fend off or even defeat this mighty braggart, to gain credit in the eyes of my divine Dolly. Do any of these things occur? They do not. I succeed, I gain my triumph, only because the great swordsman trips over his own feet and goes down with a chair leg striking hard into his . . . into his . . . Bah," shouts Kinsmere, "bah, yah, with another bah to crown it all. And be damned to you, Bygones Abraham, for the grinning clown Harker said *I* was!"

"Oh, lad! Pish, tush, and again pish! You'll not win out against me—no, nor against the lass either!—should it come to a swearing match. And it *is* most unholy fortunate, say what you will. We can still move in secret against King Charles's enemies. Scant harm has been done; Harker is much alive; and you, a loyal king's man, are embroiled in no fatal brawl to earn the displeasure of the king. Besides," added Bygones in a voice of awe, "consider the nature of the punishment already meted out to Harker! Mah fwha! We have gained much—we have gained—"

"Yes, now I think on it," Kinsmere interrupted, "we may have gained something greatly to be desired. Stay a moment!"

He returned his sword to the very light shagreen-covered scabbard swung on two tiny chains from his belt. He went over to the chimneypiece, where Harker lay sprawled face up amid dead ashes and the broken fragments of a punch bowl. Kneeling down, he felt for the sheath pocket within the left-hand side of the coat. From this he drew out a much-creased paper, several years old and growing frayed, which showed many lines of writing when he unfolded it.

"Come!" Bygones rumbled above his shoulder. "Is it Sir Aubrey Fairchild's statement against the lass? Was it more of Harker's huffing, or did he speak truth?"

"He spoke truth. *'I, Aubrey Fairchild, of Monkshood Hall in the County of Hampshire, do depose and testify that, on the afternoon of 8th September, 1667, being at the King's House for the witnessing of a new play called* She Would If She Could, *I detected the orange wench known as Dolly Lands or Landis when she did insinuate her hand into the pocket of my camlet cloak and abstract therefrom—'*Bygones!"

"Ay?"

"On the mantel in front of you you'll see a tinder box and a tallow dip in a pewter holder. Will you be civil enough to strike a light?"

"Ay, with pleasure. Would you do what I think you'll do?"

"Indeed, I would, when you've lighted the candle too. We burn this on the instant. Then let Harker—or another, or a whole parcel of 'em—make shift to prove what they can!"

"Ay, with still more pleasure! Good luck in all you do. We'll make a King's Messenger of you yet, lad, once you've soaked up the sun of my presence. Here."

The lighted candle was handed down. Kinsmere

touched flame to the paper; he watched it curl up and blacken; he ground the ashes to powder in his hand, scattering them on Harker's coat, and handed the candle back up.

"And now . . ." he continued, rising to his feet and feeling a slight dizziness as he did so.

"Why, there should be a coil of rope for use in case o' fire! We'll tie Harker most securely. We'll roll him into the cupboard. We'll tell the tapster, should any inquire, he is sleeping off the fumes of too much drink. Then we'll sit down and study what's to be done. We'll—" Bygones, staring at him, broke off with a look of alarm. "Body o' Pilate, lad, are you hurt? Did he hit you?"

"Yes, he hit me," admitted Kinsmere, who had been brooding on this. "Though 'tis of small import and I had much worse in a quarterstaff fight with a carter. But he hit me, curse him," explodes my grandfather, "and all *he* got was . . ."

"Come, my Bedlamite champion! Come, my moonstruck roisterer! Never make light o' what *he* got. We'll —No, stop! *I'll* do the tying and disposing. Do you make haste to the next room and speak to the lass. But—"

"But what?"

"Nay, ecod, I am NOT troubled. Yet she's a woman, and deestray. Use her gently, as your father would ha' done. Be not amazed at any wild talk."

"What wild talk?"

"No matter; will you linger here? Make haste, I say!"

Kinsmere, far from easy in his mind, went out into the passage and along it to the closed door of the Cupid Room, where he tapped lightly at its panel.

"Madam—" he said.

"No!" cried Dolly's voice from behind the door, with a touch of anguish he could not resist. "No! Be off! Go 'way!"

He opened the door, walked in, and closed it behind him.

She was sitting in a righted chair at the far side of the table. She had been sitting with her face down on her arms on the table, but she twitched up her head as he entered.

Dolly was one of those girls who can cry streams without it in the least puffing their eyelids or destroying their beauty. If he had been attracted before, he was bowled over now. She looked so intense, so alluringly pretty, with her long-lashed eyes and her fair complexion and her pink mouth, that my respected grandsire's heart sailed like a paper dart out a window.

"Sir, begone! Do pray be civil and begone! I won't see you. Oh, sweet Jesus, I am so utterly discomposed that I *can't* see you!"

Down went her head into her arms, the brown ringlets tumbling forward; then, almost instantly, she raised it.

"But he said you were ill-looking!"

"Madam?"

"Pem said you were ill-looking!"

"He said true. My beauty, madam, has not hitherto been generally remarked. To the contrary, a conspicuous lack of it has led various people in my family, when sufficiently provoked from one cause or another, to draw such comparison as ape, crocodile, or similar creatures of no vast personal charm. However! As touches this matter of looks—"

"Stop, stop! I'll not hear you!"

"Perhaps not. And yet, madam, although circumstances have not allowed me the honour of being formally presented to you, still I hope you will forgive me, Mistress Landis, when I say you are beyond question the loveliest wench I ever saw."

"Do you think so? Oh, truly, do you think so?"

"With all my heart. And therefore, madam, I apologize—"

"Now wherefore should you apologize? Because you beat him? Or was it because," her mood changed, wrath and tears joining together, "was it because, in my pitifully overwrought feelings, I said what I did say concerning the man who *should* face him unafraid? Are you so like to the others, then? Would you seek to gain advantage from that?"

"I seek no advantage, God knows. I apologize because the son of a wh—because Captain Harker addressed you with so many words you must have wished had not been overheard. He even proposed, worst of all, you should set yourself at a blundering object like me. By consequence, if you were well and truly insulted . . ."

"Insulted?" repeated Dolly, sitting up straight with the tears running down her face. "You are not displeasing to me; I own this; wherefore, if I am honest, should I have cause to feel myself insulted? And yet I think I could kill you. Why, why, must you make a noise and interfere?"

"He struck you!"

"Ever since I can remember," Dolly said in her beautiful voice, "somebody or other has been a-striking me and a-walloping me. And a-calling me fool and strumpet and much else I must seem and perhaps am. But why, why must you cry your challenge to Pem, when I had all but wormed from him enough information to give the king?"

"When you had wormed from him," yelled a thunderstruck Kinsmere, "enough information to give *whom?*"

"The king, strike me dead of a pox, who else? 'Twas His Majesty set me on Pem, to trap him if I could. Sure you guessed I was leading him on? I had no notion 'twas so big a plot as it's like to prove; I *am* afeared, though not for the reason I said. I know Pem suffered no hurt, save for a certain mishap we won't discuss; could I not hear you and Mr. Bygones talking through the wall? I know you burned that paper writ by Aub Fairchild; and truly, truly I am grateful. But was it of such very needful help?"

"Madam, for God's sake—!"

"No matter what I had done, the king said, he would pardon me could I but even in part confirm his suspiciousness of Pem Harker. Come!" said Dolly, with a little smile flashing through tears. "You are *not* displeasing to me. Sit down, dear boy; we'll hold soft discourse of other things. And yet, notwithstanding that at one moment I could have killed you for your interference, perhaps I am not truly sorry after all."

Kinsmere said nothing. He bowed to her, almost reverently, and sat down.

PART II:

THE GRAND DESIGN

"Le Roi de la Grande Bretagne a une manière si cachée et si difficile à pénétrer que les plus habiles y sont trompés."

Ambassador Barillon to King Louis XIV

VIII

There had been a deal of talk, and even some little action, before the bells of the City clocks struck two. While Kinsmere was still pondering the relation of Dolly Landis, Mistress Dolly discovered the wound in his left shoulder, and "Eee'd!!" in a most hair-raising way.

The wound was actually of small consequence. Harker's point had nipped through some loose flesh at the top of the shoulder blade; beyond a slight stiffness for a day or two, there could be no ill effects. But there was a fair amount of blood, which enables us to persuade the ladies that death may be imminent. And so my grandfather fetched up a dismal groan or two, rolled his eyes glassily, and felt not displeased at all.

She was in a passion of concern, was Dolly. From the table she took a large pewter soup tureen and emptied its cold contents out the window, to the audible dissatisfaction of some gentleman passing in the alley below. Then Dolly took the gallon jug of boiling water she had bespoke from a tapster; she flung half the boiling water out the window, by way of reply; and this time the unseen gentleman stood and passionately addressed the window for some minutes.

Under the blue-and-orange gown Dolly wore an astonishing number of petticoats. From the topmost one she tore strip after strip, turning round and round like a cat chasing its tail. Having thus obtained clean bandages, and a quantity of lukewarm water by mixing boiling with cold in the soup tureen, she proceeded to bathe and dress Kinsmere's wound. Dolly's nearness as she bent over him had an irresistible effect. Once the bandage had been adjusted, and his shirt and coat put on again, he could contain himself no longer. He rose to his feet, took the girl in his arms, and kissed her at some length.

Again, young ladies and gentlemen, I perceive your shocked expressions. For this is the Year of Grace eighteen hundred and fifteen. Pious old King George the Third, however mad and blind he may be, is still alive. But our true ruler is His Royal Highness the Prince Regent, whom I once saw at a prizefight when he was still a youth and I the mature colonel of my regiment. And I am sure that the Regent would be in no sense shocked. He is recorded as having remarked that King Charles the Second was the only one of his predecessors whose company he could have tolerated as a gentleman.

But I was telling you how Rowdy Kinsmere, on that May afternoon of the year sixteen-seventy, for the first time kissed Dolly Landis. Nor did Dolly herself display the least coyness or reluctance, clasping him tightly round the neck and furthering the process with her tongue after a fashion of which you, young ladies, will doubtless hear when you are a little older.

They were in this position when Bygones Abraham walked into the Cupid Room.

"Well, strike me blind!" roared Bygones, stopping short.

"Sir and madam," says the exalted Kinsmere, "it seems necessary that we drink."

"Can ye spare the time?" says Bygones. "It would grieve me to interrupt a teet-ah-teet merely with mention o' something relevant. Howsobeit! I have tied Harker securely, with my sash round his head by way of a gag, and shut him in the cupboard with the door latched. He'll be tractable, we can warrant, for lack of the power to be anything else."

Whereupon Kinsmere bethought himself of what Dolly had told him. He went on to inform Bygones, who at first refused to believe it.

"Have a care, lass, if this is more deceit! Deceive Pem
104

Harker all you like; but if you'd deceive us too . . ."

" 'Tis no deceit, I do solemnly swear! You are an ugly old cat o'mountain. Yet I like you; I would not deceive you. And could I dream of deceiving this boy here?"

('Boy, damme? Now who are you calling a boy?')

"Indeed," confessed Dolly, shivering all over, "I was sore perplexed and afeared as to how I *should* proceed. Knowing, as I did, there was some person listening at that knothole . . ."

"You knew that too?"

"For sure I did! But who was the watcher? And was it a spy on *me?* And who sent him to spy there? Was he put there by . . . by . . . ?"

"By the king, would you say? Oh, body o' Pilate! D'ye fancy the king (God bless him) would set a spy to observe the postures of his own spy?"

"I don't know and can't say. I am not so familiar as some people with the ways of conspirators. And yet, having been acquainted with His Majesty some matter of a month or six weeks, I vow I think he might do *anything.* Nor was it an easy task I had. When Pem ceased speaking so much treason, I must prod him on again by making mock of the king as an idle good-for-nothing."

"Which we know he is not."

"Oh, sir, I greatly fear he is not!"

"You fear it?"

"Ay, truly I fear it!" Dolly answered. "He is much given to idling and laziness, as which of us is not? He loves the sins of the flesh, as which of us does not with the right person for company? But he is endowed with so great a crowning of brains that 'tis frightening and not sootheful."

"You yourself, lass, are not altogether lacking in *that* respect. How much have you learned of this conspiracy at the palace? Of the band o' malcontents and their plotter-in-chief?"

"Only what Pem boasted of. And some few hints from His Majesty's self, which did but mislead me. What else *should* I know?"

"Come, Madam Landis! Are you a loyal king's man?"

"Oh, I am! Pray believe I am!"

"Why, then," said Bygones, uprearing in eloquence,

"I'll tell you what it is and must be. We will form, here and now, a defensive band o' counterconspirators. We will exchange bits and pieces of guess or knowledge, like three more deities on this Olympus at the Devil. We will command dinner at long last, and take a deep cup or two to drink our own prosperity. Hey?"

"Oh, this is lovely; this is most pleasant!" Dolly beamed at him. "I am ripe for a drinking set, or carouse if it must be. But be sure we don't o'erdo it. Pack me off to the theatre by four o'clock, I implore you, and sober enough to play."

Afterwards they had fine memories of that little hour or more in the Cupid Room: partly because they got on so well together and partly because Bygones poured wine with a liberal hand. (He and Kinsmere drank claret; Dolly drank champagne.) In a niche over the chimneypiece stood a small figure of Cupid, painted pink as the bust of Apollo downstairs was painted blue. Beyond open windows, beyond the alley, lay the romantic garden of Serjeants' Inn. It is true that every fresh breeze sent in neighbouring chimney smoke like somebody making a skilful stroke at billiards, that flies buzzed round the food and that a hitherto sunny day began to grow overcast.

But, so far as my grandfather was concerned, it could be called idyllic. Up had been ordered a comfortable meal, which commenced with a roast calf's head and a couple of geese, and ended with a large Cheshire cheese. Though in Dolly's presence Kinsmere had believed himself no longer hungry, yet he was constrained to partake of most courses and to finish at least one grilled fowl down to the bones.

It was pleasanter still to sit at table beside Dolly, observing how the brown eyes would constantly return to him as she ate or drank. She was telling them something of her history; nor did she speak solemnly in the telling, since Dolly was always inclined to laugh at herself rather than to laugh at anyone else.

She told them of her late home in Coal Yard, Drury Lane; of her late mother, who had been a kind-hearted soul and a good enough mother in all conscience, except when she belted Dolly because there was no money to buy drink, or else had the horrors from too much drink and chased everybody in sight with a manure fork. A drunken cobbler taught Dolly to read and write. The identity of her father she never learned. There had been several brothers and sisters, so far as she could remember; but all these had died naturally or been killed somehow: according to the fate, Dolly said, which usually overtakes such.

Of her apprenticeship as table servant at the brothel—Mother Fenniman's handsome establishment in Red Lion Fields—she made good comedy. As for her second apprenticeship, an orange wench at the theatre, she did not slur over the fact that she had picked the pocket of Sir Aubrey Fairchild. Orange wenches for the play, either under Killigrew at the King's House or the late Sir William Davenant at the Duke's, received pay too wretched to live without other means. There were always men to get money from; and yet Dolly, though she made no pretence at being better than others, would not go with a man unless she was fond of him. It seemed the more ironic that somebody like Harker, of all people, should fasten on her with his grisly threat of the gallows, and should hold that threat for nearly three mortal years.

"Until *you* met him and beat him! And, oh, I am so very happy!"

"The plain fact, madam, is that I did NOT beat him. 'Twas the merest accident, sweet heart, as you are well aware. Also, to speak a truth, I was somewhat frightened of the fellow."

"Oh, be bothered!" cried Dolly, or words something like it. "Did you fight him, dear boy, or did you not?"

Clang smote the great bell at the Church of St. Dunstan-in-the-West, clearly heard from Fleet Street on the opposite side; it went on to strike two.

Bygones Abraham, who had been stuffing himself until his face assumed richer purplish-red hues than ever, here settled back with a look of drowsy comfort. A moment later he leaned forward, poured out and disposed of two tankards in rapid succession, hiccuped, patted his stomach, and settled back again with an expiring sigh. As he watched Kinsmere and Dolly lean towards each other, their fingers touching as though reluctantly, a watery and sentimental light began to grow in his eye.

"It was 'way far and gone' in forty-three—!" Bygones

107

said, so abruptly that the others jumped.

"What was?"

"Ay!" muttered Bygones, in a sepulchral voice like a prophet. "There were men in those days, lad! Men, I tell ye!" He contemplated the wine bottles in a gloomy and mysterious way. "Tempoura mewtanter, ate nose something-or-other in illus! Faith was stronger, causes were spiritualler, a more noble scale struck a chord in the forefront of human existence. A good backsword at your hip in a cavalry charge, taking care the grip don't turn in your hand when you rise in stirrup to hit 'em; and skill in all the arts and diplomatic tongues of this earth.—What is Love?" inquired Bygones, changing the subject.

"Come, here's d-drollery!" chortled Dolly, and lifted her glass once more. "The talkative gentleman, I do protest, is grown most remarkably drunk."

Both to Dolly and to Kinsmere this notion seemed so extraordinarily funny that they leaned towards each other and roared. But the old soldier would have none of it.

" 'Tis rank slander!" he declared. "Bygones Abraham, pride of the cavalry, become foxed on a few pints of claret? Zhommy duh lah vee! It's a habit o' mine, when much discourse must be spoke on weighty matters, to oil the muscles of my eloquence with some choice words beforehand. Have you never seen runners before a race? Springing up and down in such fashion, freely unlimbering 'emselves?"

"And an excellent habit I pronounce it!" said Kinsmere. "The question before us, good friends," he continued, with some recollection of his uncle Godfrey, "hath been propounded as 'What is Love?' " He looked sideways at Dolly, his head spinning. "Love, good friends, may be described as—"

"I am already unlimbered," Bygones cut him off. "Nay! Zoot ellers! Assay duh saw! And as for *you,* lass!" Indulgent yet judicial, Bygones also contemplated her. "What you say is of much interest, may be, but it's not to our purpose. Let us hear instead of plots and counterplots: how you met the king, what he said to you, and what was determined thereon."

"You'd hear it *all?*"

"I would," said Bygones, with sudden grimness striking

through, "and every word of it. Well?"

"Well!" replied Dolly. "It was about the beginning of April, I think, and at the theatre. I was Olivia in *The Mulberry Garden,* which they'd played two years before but were playing again."

"Ay, lass?"

"There was a great throng in the pit, the middle and top galleries filled too, and all the court in the side boxes come to see us. The king was applauding hard, though 'tis no very comical play; and he was applauding *me*, though he'd not aforetime cast a glance in my direction.

"All of us were in a flurry and dither: especially Mary Knepp, who took the part of Victoria and had a song to sing. I played badly, I know; I forgot some of my speeches to Ned Kynaston (he was Jack Wildish) and needs must improvise with jeering speeches out of other plays. And, whatever this portended or might not portend, I vow I felt much more alarmed than I felt pleased."

At the end of three acts out of five, Dolly explained, she was changing her dress in the tiring room when Mrs. Knepp brought her an unsigned note and said: "Lackaday, Doll, there's good fortune in store for *some* people." The note, which was from the royal box, she could not have disregarded even if she had wished; and it requested her to be at home that night could she find it convenient to do so.

In her more prosperous days now she had lodgings off Bow Street, with a cage of canaries in the window. And so she swept, dusted, and polished in a mighty to-do. Then she put on her best gown, doused herself with perfume, painted and patched her face; and sat down in apprehension to await her visitor.

He arrived secretly, after the clocks had gone eleven. She heard him walk up the three flights of stairs whistling a country air, which hardly seemed dignified, nor did he have any escort except a few bad-tempered spaniels. He had to stoop to enter the doorway; he wore a plain dark coat much behind the fashion; and yet by his manners, she said, you could tell he was the King of England.

She had heard (Dolly continued) that the best way to please King Charles was to behave naturally in his presence—as though anybody could!—and even jeer him a lit-

tle. She contrived the mockery pretty well, drinking a good
deal of wine to keep up her courage. Yet he seemed so
comfortably at home as he sat there, his great voice urbane
and his long legs stretched out, that she did behave
naturally, forgot fears, and found herself more frank than
she had expected to be with anyone.

Dolly fetched out her most cherished possession, a
music box which played "Cuckolds All Arow" when you
wound it up. He was so pleased with this that he wouldn't
let it go, but played it over and over until he almost broke
the works, shaking it beside his periwig when it ran down,
and tapping his foot in time to the music.

For his part, he said, he liked tunes a man might keep
time to; and he asked her if she could sing. Dolly, all fear
gone and able to troll out a rollicking measure with the
best of them, promptly produced a beribboned cittern. She
sang him a number of well-known airs, full of hey-ding-a-
ding-dongs and fa-la-li-la-las. She sang "Here's a Health
unto His Majesty" and "The Man That Is Drunk Is as
Great as a King," whereat her visitor wagged his head and
joined in the chorus. Then she sang one with which he
said he was unacquainted, Grainevert's song out of
Suckling's play.

> Come, let the State stay!—
> Drink merry away,
>   There is no business above it;
> It warms the cold brain,
> Makes us speak in high strain—
>   He's a fool that does not approve it.
>
> The Macedon Youth
> Left behind him this truth:
>   That nothing is done with much thinking;
> He drank and he fought
> Till he had what he sought:
>   The world was his own by good drinking!

At this he fell silent for a time, with the spaniels curled
up at his feet. "Ay?" says he. "It may be true, though the
matter is debatable," so that she wondered if she had offended him. But he only bade her sing him another strain,

110

which she knew but had never liked, it being a queer and solemn song by John Shirley. It surprised her, Dolly thought, that *he* would like it. She plucked at the strings lightly, feeling for the tune.

> The glories of our blood and state
> Are shadows, not substantial things . . . .

That was how it went, as the bells were tolling midnight:

> The glories of our blood and state
> Are shadows, not substantial things;
> There is no armour against fate—
> Death sets his icy hand on Kings . . .

In the quiet of the little room King Charles sat motionless, with his wig black against the candlelight and his swarthy chin in his hand.

"But that, madam," says he, "is a melancholy business to contemplate." And he reached over and took the cittern away from her.

Whereat Mistress Dolly, being a rational young woman and thinking she knew what move would be next, smiled at him, albeit she was a trifle disappointed. For this was the king, who had a great reputation among the ladies. And yet she felt, astonishingly, no more drawn towards him than towards several others who (for one reason or another) she had obliged.

"Madam," says the king in a thoughtful way, "we are now, at the least of it, made acquainted. What's your opinion of me?"

"Sire," says Dolly, "I think I may say I like you."

She cursed herself in bitterness for not more nimbly exercising her charms. Here was such stupendous opportunity, such opportunity as would be offered to few wenches in a dozen lifetimes, that any sane woman would have hurled herself at him without more ado. She could have wept with vexation for being such a fool. Yet it stuck in her throat that a man who approached her fair and friendly, without arrogance on the one hand or foppish struttings on the other, should not get a straight and

111

friendly answer. And so she spoke out of her very hatred of too much coyness. "Sire," says Dolly truthfully, "I think I may say I like you."

Bygones Abraham and Rowdy Kinsmere, listening to her recital, gathered that at this point the king must have observed her furious face. But Dolly only reported that he smiled, plucked at a string on the beribboned cittern, and explained that his errand here was not what she had supposed.

"Madam," says he with great civility, "pray don't exert yourself. I am an old fortress, unconscionably easy to capture. I do not think there has been a watchman awake these twenty years. But that," says he, rubbing his nose, "is precisely the difficulty. Already there are so many conquerors feasting inside that I am not at all easy in my mind. Too many more assaults might bring down the walls or wreck the powder magazine—which would be, you must own, some little of a catastrophe."

And he looked at her with sardonic raised brows.

"Madam," pursues he, "let us change the metaphor. I am addicted to a weakness called sauntering: which leads me, more often than not, to no happy valley. But tonight I would speak of graver matters. If you were granted one wish of all things in this world, what would you wish for?"

She would wish, Dolly felt at the time, for the return of that damning deposition which Pembroke Harker had forced timorous Aub Fairchild to write, and which he still held over her as a threat. But she could not say this—not yet. She asked him, with respectful humility, why he wished to know. Nor would the king himself pursue it further.

"Well, let be!" he said. "Yet I have heard report of you, madam, as one who can hold her tongue if need be. It is possible (God's fish!), it is possible we may speak of this another time."

He did speak of it another time: ten days later, when he invited her to sup at the Rose in Covent Garden. They were not altogether alone that night. In the next room two of his younger and madder cronies—my Lord Rochester, author of the mock epitaph, and Sir Charles Sedley, who had written *The Mulberry Garden* with a brace of *their* wenches—were getting howling drunk and smashing furniture, while assuming the king pursued his latest conquest with Dolly Landis. What King Charles actually said was:

"You are acquainted, I think, with a certain Captain Pembroke Harker?"

"Pem Harker? *Him?*"

"You do not appear overfond of this man!"

"*Overfond?*"

"Nor am I happy, between ourselves, with report of disaffection in the army, or of schemes on foot to take the militia away from my control. My father lost his head because of such measures. I will not let the army pass from under my command, not even for half an hour. If Captain Harker be concerned in this, plotting treason against me . . ."

And then, presently, Dolly blurted out her whole story.

"God's fish, madam, here is no trumpery business of a stolen purse! Do you watch him, madam, and mark him well. Bring me the least indication my suspiciousness is correct, and, whatever you have done, I will pardon you should you be betrayed. It is probable you will be pardoned in any case. Bring me full proof of this man's activities, with the requisite witnesses, and with the pardon shall go the fulfilment of whatever wish of yours it is within my power to grant."

At this point of her recital, in the Cupid Room of the Devil, Dolly Landis set down her glass with a shaky hand.

"Yet it was not disaffection in the army?" she cried.

"Nay, less," rumbled Bygones Abraham, "though matters may come to that pass in future. 'Twas a greater thing by far."

"He misled me, then? He misled me deliberately?"

"That would appear probable."

"Now wherefore," cried Dolly, "should the King of England trouble his head to deceive the likes of *me?* Because he is become earth's greatest jester?"

"Not so," retorted Bygones, and slowly rose up. "Because he is become earth's greatest cynic."

Chimney smoke blew through the open windows into Bygone's face, but he paid no attention. He lumbered to the fireplace, wheezing, and turned round with his back to it.

"Come!" he said. "You are both too young to have

113

clear recollection of the Restoration a decade gone. What happened, hey? I'll tell ye.

"Charles Stuart, elder son of the man they executed outside the Banqueting House at Whitehall, returned from exile in so-called triumph. For fifteen years he and his brother, the Duke of York, had been eating poor relations' bread and salt at half the courts in Europe. He had been an awkward fellow in those days; they let him see it. Not only France, but tuppenny courts as well, laughed hard at him and made sport of his suit for the hand of a tuppenny princess.

"Here in England, under the Roundheads, they could sing psalms and huff high as long as Oliver was Lord Protector. But Oliver died; they were bankrupt; the psalm singing had a sound most unholy sour. Within two years they made discovery that 'twas all a hideous mistake: that they craved the son of the old king, had craved him all the time: and that, unless he made haste to return, they'd die o' broken hearts.

"What did he think, d'ye fancy, when they fetched him back from Breda amid the lit bonfires and the bells going mad? Oh, ecod, what did *he* think? In this same country he had been chased through ditches after Worcester fight. All the lean times, the years of sitting in draughts . . ."

"It's to be supposed," said Kinsmere, while Dolly merely cursed, "this had not sweetened his view of human nature?"

"Nay, lad, it had not. 'Since you love me as much as this, I wonder I have been so long away.' But he walked amiably enough. He kissed the Bible they gave him, and said he loved it above all things in the world.

"Past doubt he knew, as he could not help knowing, that many a rusty old Cavalier had lost land and goods and all else, and done so with the greatest cheerfulness, to see the dawn of this blessed day. Such men, the true-loyal, would gain small preferment when rogues flocked in for plunder; as, d'ye see, the rogues always do. And what of the king, who himself needed money? Parliament voted him huge subsidies, which were never collected or could never be collected save in part. And Parliament would turn on him in an instant, as it had turned on his father, did he show signs he'd a mind of his own. On what course,

114

therefore, was he hence-forward resolved?"

"Why—"

"Why, I'll tell ye!" roared Bygones, striking right fist into left palm. "It was to meet roguery with roguery, and deceit with the greater deceit. 'God's fish, they have put a set of men about me; but these shall know nothing!' It was to rule in his own fashion, letting no man be aware he ruled, with all ill acts attributed to his ministers. To raise money independently of Parliament, and be free of 'em: bribes, titles, pardons, sale of Crown lands or appointments, everything in his power. He sold Dunkirk to the King of France. And now, if I read the signs aright—Harker read 'em aright—he fishes in more dangerous waters still."

"Will you try, in all this," Kinsmere roared back, "to speak one plain word of fact? What's the king's design, then? If negotiations with France should be on foot, what does he hope to gain by them?"

"A subsidy paid in secret by that same French king," answered Bygones. "In my time, lad, I have seen all kinds of fighting and uproar and bloodletting. If there is any manner o' dispute that here in England would cause more than another of fighting and blood-letting, 'tis a dispute concerning religious faith: in particular, of the Roman Catholic faith. Stay, now! Don't ask how this concerns us! Let's assume, for the moment, that here's theory and no more. But do I speak truth?"

"You do."

"I can't claim to know the rights and wrongs of it, not being myself a praying man. I have no dislike for Roman Catholics; nor has the king. These Papists have ever stood his friends, in good fortune and in bad; when he was a fugitive in his own country after Worcester fight, a Papist priest saved his life. For my own part, I hold enmity only towards Puritans and all their works; nor have I yet met a Papist who could abide Puritans either. What's your feeling in the matter, lad?"

"Much like your own, I think. And yet—"

"And yet," interposed Bygones, hitching up his sword belt, "and yet, as you'd doubtless say, the feeling is not common in this nation. 'Tis a very hobgoblin with 'em, is Popery! They think of racks, and ropes, and thumbscrews. They'll limn for you, in all fantastic luridness, fires burn-

115

ing again at Smithfield. And they'd slit the throat of the man who would make it our state religion. Is *this* true?"

"It is."

"*Your* view, lass?"

"God bless the Church Established!" cried Dolly. "Though I say that so glibly, and don't in the least know what it means, still . . ."

"Still," said Kinsmere, slipping his arm round her as they both rose up, "still, theory apart, how is this to our purpose? There has been much talk of a 'treaty.' "

"One treaty, fairly new and thought to be binding, already exists."

"With France?"

"Body o' Pilate, no! It was signed by England, Holland, and Sweden; it is called the Triple Alliance; it exists to promote 'peace, trade, and prosperity' among three Protestant nations. However!"

Bygones, oratorical finger lifted, turned round to address the figure of Cupid in the niche over the fireplace; then, becoming sensible of the incongruity, he swung back again.

"King Looey Catters of France, 'tis widely reported, would like well to see that treaty broken. He would have England again at sea war against the Dutch, allied to France in secret treaty if need be."

"*Could* such a secret treaty be brought about?"

"It could, lad; it probably will. Ayagh!" snorted Bygones. "The Dutch have cut our throats on every trade route; you can't beat a Dutchman at bargaining; there's powerful companies in the City would have this altered. It may not be long ere we again hear ships' guns off Lowestoft, as when the Duke of York blew up Opdam in his own two-decker. Moreover . . ."

"Well?"

"Should such an arrangement be one item in the secret treaty, then all five members of King Charles's Cabal would sign it. *But—*"

"Hang me, what are all these 'buts'? What are you gabbling of now?"

"Gabbling, am I?" roared Bygones. "Attend to me! Another item, the most secret and the most dangerous, could be told to two members of the Cabal alone. To Sir

116

Thomas Clifford, he being a Papist; to my Lord Arlington—ay, Harker was wrong there—my Lord Arlington having Popish sympathies under his mask. The other three, Buckingham and Ashley and Lauderdale, must never learn it in this world. The terms of this most secret item shall be known only to the King of England, the King of France, and the King of England's sister as negotiator."

"Bygones, for God's sake! Can't you EVER speak plain?"

"I will do so," said Bygones. "In return for the payment of an enormous subsidy, King Charles will promise France that he will introduce the Roman Catholic religion into this country: by persuasion if possible, by the use of a French army if necessary."

"Stay a moment!" said Kinsmere. "Whatever else the king may be, is he stark mad?"

"Not so; far from it! He knows he can't *do* this; he knows he dare not; nor would he ever see foreign troops on this soil. But he will promise it; he will play against time and the clock; he will forever put it off. Are these plain words now?"

"Then hark to some other plain words," says Kinsmere. "If he would so much as promise this, even without will or intent to carry it out, then the King of England must be fully as great a rogue as any who . . ."

"Since when is statecraft honest? Or ever has been? Also, if we be loyal King's men, which of us is to judge him?"

"I preach no sermons. And yet—"

"Well, nor do I debate or defend: I only tell you these things are true. Here are the terms of a treaty which Harker and I were this night to have carried to France in two halves of a divided document and which somebody else and I must still carry!

"D'ye see, lad? Great body o' Pilate, here's more gunpowder than Guy Fawkes ever dreamed of! And we three are sitting on it, because we know too much. Or put it that we're between two sides: the king on one side, and on the other a band of malcontents led by a plotter-in-chief whose identity we can't guess at. As for Harker in there—"

Abruptly Bygones Abraham paused. His eyes swung round towards the knothole in the wall, as though he had heard a noise from the next room. Then his eyes bulged.

"Harker! Oh, ecod! If . . . Wait here, both of you!"

He was across the room before either of them could speak. The door to the passage opened and closed behind him; they heard his footsteps move towards the Hebe Room.

"What is happening?" cried Dolly, and then lowered her voice. "Oh, so-and-so it all, what *can* be happening?"

"I don't know."

"But it's no concern of ours, is it? (Hold me closer!) Sir—dear boy—it can't in any case concern *us?*"

"I can't say that either. And yet, madam—sweet heart, that's to say!—we are slap in the middle of whatever trouble there is."

Bygones's voice, speaking through the knothole, struck at them with muffled thunder.

"Lad!" he said. "Come in here at once. You, lass, remain where you are!"

Releasing himself from Dolly, who was frightened and had no wish to be released, Kinsmere hurried to the door. Then he ran. In the next room, not far from the partly open cupboard door, Bygones awaited him with a face of wrath and near-collapse.

"Harker!" he said. "*You* did him no hurt. *I* did him no hurt. And yet—" He pointed to the cupboard. "Who did this, lad? Who *is* the plotter-in-chief? God damn my soul."

Kinsmere, conscious of flies buzzing near, threw the cupboard door wide open.

Pembroke Harker, trussed round with ropes which were no longer necessary, lay face down at full length. Also unnecessary was the plum-coloured satin sash wound twice round his mouth and tied at the back of the head. At the collar line below the sash's knot, through the curls of the periwig and through a great flowing of blood, jutted up the yellow bone handle of a heavy knife.

As he lay trussed and helpless, someone had stabbed him to death through the back of the neck. Already a dozen flies were gathering and buzzing round the blood.

IX

The King's House, Little Russell Street, Drury Lane. Friday, May 20th, 1670. Four o'clock in the afternoon, and the performance about to begin.

Stand at the back of the pit, now, and look at it. It will be a gala afternoon, since today most of the court attend the play. Nowhere will you get a better view of so many of these people gathered together, with an edge of wax-light on their faces; and you will see representatives from half London too. Grandee and Grandee's Lady in the side boxes; in the pit, Fop and Trollop and even respectable young Man of Affairs, with wife (Mr. Pepys of the Navy Office is a good example); Sedate Citizen in the middle gallery; Unnameable Public in the top gallery.

Never expect, as you enter, to see anything like our modern theatre of 1815. There'll be no drop curtain, as you observe; no floats or footlights to shine on it; such things have not yet been invented. Merely a raised platform of a stage, with double doors at the back and a smaller door flanking them on either side; above the stage, on ropes so that they may be raised or lowered, two chandeliers with crowns of candles.

Nor is there any scenery, except such articles as are necessary for the action. You must use imagination, letting the scene be painted with words. And some costumes on the stage might startle the uninitiated. An actor—Mr. Hart, for instance—will play Macbeth in the periwig and red coat of a seventeenth-century Guardsman. However, since today the play is *Julius Caesar* and Roman dress well known from the number of London's statues in toga or tunic, some attempt will be made to present this as it might have looked in Julius Caesar's day.

Standing also at the back of the pit, so as to keep a wary eye out for riots at the door, is Tom Killigrew, the manager. He can look with pride on this theatre. It is a commodious place, capable of seating nearly two hundred people, and even has a glass cupola to protect the pit from rain. That cupola will be necessary soon. Despite a sunny morning, it has grown so dark and thunder-fraught that the wax candles have been lighted above the stage, throwing shaky illumination towards spectators too.

Killigrew's French musicians—ten of them—are already in place below the stage, tuning their fiddles. There is a sharp tap for attention. Then the fiddles, aided by a horn or two, strike up a country dance as though to silence the buzz of the crowd.

It is a large crowd and a well-behaved one—barring, to be sure, those congenital brawlers who always make an uproar at the door, and say they'll pay their money when they get inside. A shuffling from the pit is drowned by the tumult of the top gallery, where the crowd whoops and whistles and stamps like a cloudful of angels on a spree. There sit 'prentice from Eastcheap, jack-pudding from Ludgate Hill, bullyrock from the stews of Alsatia: critical, not-to-be-cozened public, with their wenches along.

Grave-faced and quiet is the middle gallery, showing no female company. Any respectable woman may go to the play, provided she wear a vizard mask. But the Sedate Citizens of the middle gallery hold different views. Here are government men of all but the highest rank, country gentlemen, bankers, trade princes from the City. They don't bring their wives; they won't bring their doxies. They wear five-guinea perukes above sober finery; or they wear skull caps, gold chains, and grave fur gowns. They may be raised to the peerage one day. Meanwhile they whisper to one another, bending forward in dim light. Yet they are none the less eagerly glancing towards the side boxes, left and right, upper tier and lower, not yet filled by the court.

The fiddles dance into a merrier tune; the clamour in the pit grows louder. Come, there's your fashion! Camlet cloaks are jostling together; a bottle passes from hand to hand. On the stage itself, in Fops' Corner—chairs or stools there, as in the side boxes; no benches as in the rest of the house—several furbelow'd gentlemen have raised gold quizzing glasses, and are ogling ladies in vizard masks who sit well to the front of the pit.

Above singing fiddles you can hear the cries of the orange girls. *"Oranges! Will you have any oranges?"* They are pretty, bare-armed wenches with roving eyes. *"Oranges! Who'll buy my oranges?"* Standing with their backs to the stage, they swing baskets covered with vine leaves. *"Oranges!"*

It has grown much darker now. A rumble of thunder shakes the glass cupola, setting candle flames atremble. The atmosphere is close, rather foul; dust rises; a lack of washing becomes evident. From the gloom of the pit you can hear scuffling noises, laughter, and the sound of a slap. *"Let be, you! Oranges!"*

There is a burst of laughter at the door. Killigrew turns round; the top gallery cheers; Sedate Citizen cranes his neck. For the court parties are arriving. At the head of them, looking round complacently as he enters his side box, is a portly man with a light tread . . .

George Villiers, second Duke of Buckingham: Master of the Horse, minister without portfolio, but a very powerful minister indeed. Complacent, vain, witty, persuasive, monstrously energetic: a large-nosed and light-footed conqueror, whose brain boils with a hundred interests at once. He thinks himself a great soldier, though of scant military experience, and a great statesman, though he is nicknamed Alderman George. One day he will be working with chemistry, swearing he has discovered a means of fixing mercury; the next he will sit down and write a play to ridicule Mr. Dryden, or a set of derisive verses against the king, whom he holds in some contempt.

In his youth this Bucks was a slender daredevil, adroit at disguise and at tweaking Puritan noses. Though brought up in the household of Charles the First, he had small liking for poverty and exile with the old king's son. In '57, still with a price on his head, he returned to England under Oliver's Protectorate. To regain his confiscated estates, at least in part, he won and married the daughter of Black Tom Fairfax, that eminent Commonwealth general. Despite his father-in-law's favour, after more escapades they clapped him into the Tower and would have executed him (he said) if Oliver had not died. But Parliament released him; and he had afterwards, or so he also declared, no small share in promoting the Restoration.

You see him now at forty-two, surveying the King's House as he might have surveyed the king's domain, and turning to joke with Sir Robert Howard. You see him padded with good living: the heavy reddish face, the double chin, the magnetic eye half shut under a great brown periwig. He wears claret-coloured silk with much lace, and he gesticulates. Who overthrew Clarendon? In whose hands is Parliament as wax? Who, as unofficial chief minister, in effect rules England and directs its policies? All the cheering from the top gallery—he is popular with the mob, and knows it—all this waving of handkerchiefs by masked ladies, might to his mind give answer in one mighty shout: "You!"

And why not? If there were any such fantastical vessel as a ship of state, then George Villiers might be pictured as captain with spyglass and master gunner too. It is the sort of double role he would enjoy. Though he hates Popery, and would allow liberty of conscience only to Protestant dissenters, he has vast admiration for the French king. He will be off to France soon. In his honour Versailles will bloom with fêtes, and masques, and lighted fountains; he will be made the gift of a jewelled sword valued at twenty thousand crowns; even his mistress, Lady Shrewsbury, whom he won by killing her husband in the famous and scandalous duel at Barn Elms, will be awarded a pension of ten thousand *livres* a year by His Most Christian Majesty Louis the Fourteenth.

Thus Buckingham, whom the gods love. He glances once more round the house, and with a gusty laugh sits down to await the play. My Lord Rochester has called him the sort of man who, when he goes out of a room, always leaves the door open so that he can come back in again.

Young Rochester? *He* will be there, close behind in a noisy group, though at this hour he is customarily so drunk that he will be quite unable to remember it afterwards.

"I am at no pains or trouble, gentlemen," says John Wilmot, Earl of Rochester, "to arrive at a given place. But 'tis awkward to recall whence I have just come." And at first you may not see him amid the other wits and sparks thronging round.

There's Etherege, for one: affable Mr. (not yet Sir George) Etherege, the playwright, who wrote *Love in a Tub* and will be an ambassador one day. In far future he is to have the glory of dying for gallantry. One night in Paris, aged fifty-six, he will be lighting a lady out of his bedchamber; walking backwards and holding up the taper, he will fall downstairs and break his neck. Which is a tolerably severe punishment for devotion to good form. But he also wrote *The Man of Mode,* and should have been satisfied.

There's Charles Sackville, Lord Buckhurst, who was Nelly Gwyn's first protector. There's the smallish and dark-faced Sir Charles Sedley, "Little Sid." And who's the woman, the masked woman in the hooded cape, beside Little Sid? Is it "Chloris," to whom he wrote the graceful song in the third act of *The Mulberry Garden?* Or is it "Celia," whatever her real name may be, to whose amatory skill he has paid still higher tribute?

> Then why should I seek further store
> And still make love anew?
> When change itself can give no more,
> 'Tis easy to be true.

Would that we could all so ingeniously salute our own Celia or Chloe!

The Earl of Rochester is visible now, a lanky youth in a fair periwig, staggering into his box behind Lord George Orrory, and refreshing himself with a pull at a stone bottle. He stops; he stares out . . .

One of the gallants in the pit has bought half a dozen oranges from Flip Jenny. This gallant tosses them to everybody within reach, and then draws the orange girl down into his lap. At such a strategic move, the cheering in the top gallery becomes a frenzy. There are yells of advice (not very practicable under the circumstances), intimations of doubt, and critical suggestions cut through by one staunch cry:

" *'Follow your quarry, and upon this charge—!'* "

"Sh-h! God damme! Sh-h!"

Tom Killigrew grits his teeth. The hiss of "Sh-h!" increases in volume. Along the rear benches ripples a rapid whisper, in which the word "king" is vaguely audible. The head of the Chief Fiddler appears above the stage, like an apparition out of a witch's cauldron, and peers anxiously round. After an irreverent greeting from the spectators, it disappears again.

The music stops abruptly. Another call for quiet is followed by a hush as the roar dies away. This pause is

123

broken by a rustling, breathing, scraping noise of people pushing back chairs or benches and rising to their feet.

Silence.

Then three sharp taps for attention. Horns and fiddles, as ecstatic as though they sang the words, burst out together.

> Here's a health unto His Majesty,
>   With a tow-row-row and a tow-row-row—
> Confusion to his enemies,
>   With a tow-row-row and a tow-row-row ...

In the side boxes they draw back and bow. At first you will observe only a dim company moving chairs. Then a figure walks within the edge of candlelight and stands motionless, hand on box rail over against the stage.

He has not quite reached his fortieth birthday, but the cropped hair under the periwig is already grey. He is six feet tall, of athletic frame, and grows more lean as others grow paunchy; for at his "wonted large pace" he walks where others ride, and gets up at five in the morning to play at tennis or *pêle-mêle*. Leaning now on the box rail, he moves his shoulders under an old black cloak lined with red, and wears a flat-plumed black hat also lined with red.

His face is long and swarthy, with sharp furrows drawn from nostrils to the corners of the mouth, and a thin black line of moustache. Blinking out into the candlelight, he surveys these people of his with what seems uncritical indolence. He looks up at the top gallery, across at Buckingham, down at the spaniels stumbling round his heels. The newcomer's eyes are his one good feature: an odd shade of red-brown, deep and perhaps satirical. What goes on in this man's brain, he alone could say. Who is he and what he is, anybody in the house will tell you. Dabbler with yachts, chemistry, music, clocks, dogs, and mistresses. Called King of Great Britain and Ireland, Defender of the Faith, dubiously by the grace of God. Called old Rowley, his own designation, after a favourite stallion. Called "a merry monarch, scandalous and poor," the second Charles of England.

And he that will not drink his health,
I wish him neither life nor wealth,
Nor yet a rope to hang himself—
With a tow-row-row, and a tow-row!

The soaring note breaks and falls against a profound hush. The fiddles sweep on into a plaintive melody, "To All You Ladies Now on Land," written at the time of the First Dutch War. The king steps back urbanely to set out a chair for Queen Catherine. And other members of the royal party become visible.

You see, beyond the king's shoulder, the tall and strong-jawed man in the brown wig, his face slightly pitted by smallpox scars, with the ugly woman beside him? He is James, Duke of York; the woman is his wife, Clarendon's daughter, Ann Hyde. A tight-lipped fellow, the Duke of York, with flaring nostrils and an uncertain eye. Not the genial companion of his younger days. Not even the captain in half-armour of five years ago who came back, hearty and burned red by the sun, from the battle off Lowestoft in the North Sea.

It is not certain that he has yet been converted to the Church of Rome, but assuredly he is about to be; and most men know it. Buckingham hates him, my Lord Ashley hates him; if you listen well, you can hear much whispered to his discredit by Sedate Citizen in the middle gallery. And some might consider this unfortunate. He has sincere affection for his brother; he will fight Charles's battles when he has scarce strength to fight his own. He is invaluable to the navy, knowing more of ships than any man in the nation. He can be an unswerving friend, if a relentless enemy. James Stuart is merely overdetermined and not very intelligent, with a genius for adopting ill-chosen courses.

In the royal box, standing behind his wife, he taps his fingers on the back of her chair; *she* taps her fan against a stout brocaded bosom; occasionally both of them try to talk to the dark-faced little queen, who is a Catholic and an ally. But the queen speaks no great number of words. Often she glances at the king, and smiles apologetically while he sits playing with the spaniels. Once or twice she tries to get a look into the box overhead, which is impossible; so she only settles back again with a ghostly grimace round protruding teeth, murmuring into her throat whatever may be the Portuguese for "Deliver us from our sins." My Lady Castlemaine has been at court for ten years, longer than has the queen, but Catherine of Braganza is not quite reconciled even yet.

And Barbara Villiers, Lady Castlemaine—that goddess in the box above—herself frowns and mutters. She will look like fire if the king notices another woman in public. You see her up there, splendid in an orchid-coloured gown, her face ornamented by patches cut to the shape of hearts and diamonds. She is marking and noting everything, though not seeming to do so. She knows how much she is admired by Fop, Sedate Citizen, and Jack-Pudding alike, by a discreet buzz rippling from pit to gallery. And yet—

"Oh, I am so monstrous vexed!"

Barbara, once the wife of plain Roger Palmer but soon to be created Barbara, Duchess of Cleveland, straightens her shoulders. She calls for her pomander ball, to keep the odour of the crowd from her nostrils. By some freak of memory recalling Roger Palmer, she remembers a duty to another man of the same Christian name. She turns that imperious stare, and at length nods coolly to Roger Stainley, the banker, in the middle gallery; it will make Old Sobersides happy for the day. She has overdrawn the large sums placed to her account by King Charles; she is head over ears in debt.

Bankers, being troublesome people, are not subdued so easily as kings: by raging tempers, or a threat to knock out the brains of one's child against the wall. Still, since she owns a fortune in jewels, it is other fears which sometimes haunt her. Of the flesh growing flabby, of wrinkles round eyes and neck: the sharp little fear which is not always repressed by day, and which always returns in a sleepless night. It is unfair and untrue! It is not to be borne. It is someone's malicious talk . . .

Now the rain, threatening for some time, begins to fall. It drums on the glass roof of the cupola; its noise thickens to a roar, fades a little, and steadies to a steady downpour which goes all but unheard. Whistlings and stampings from the top gallery call for a beginning of the play. Cross draughts have blown out a number of candles; the stage is no brighter than it should be.

My Lady Castlemaine looks across and down at the lower stage box opposite the king's, where His Grace of Bucks sits at ease. But her glance does not linger, Buckingham being her cousin and her enemy. In the box above *him*, included in that sweeping look, are two gentlemen without attendants.

Both these gentlemen are leading spirits of the Cabal. The Cabal, however, is only a name; they are also, like Bucks himself, members of the official Privy Council. Political grandees, no doubt meditating!—although, since they have so many opposed views, it is a little surprising to see them together.

The one on the right, that stoutish elderly man with the too-sombre manner and the lozenge of black plaster across his nose to hide an old scar, is Henry Bennet, Lord Arlington. He has a Dutch wife but Popish sympathies; he is rich, and would be still richer. Though they mock much at his bearing, like that of an astrologer prophesying doom, those who mock at Lord Arlington find themselves usually on the short end of a bargain.

"My lord, it seems to me—"

"And I, my lord, can only suggest—"

The grandee at the left, of merry face and pointed chin under a flaxen periwig, is Oliver's "little man with three names," Anthony Ashley Cooper, Lord Ashley. He has suffered much from an abscess in his side. But his tongue is as well hung as ever, his mind and behaviour as slippery. He has turned his coat many times; he will turn it again, remaining consistent only in his hatred for France and Popery.

What are they saying? You can't hear, even if you would. Ashley rises, as though to take his leave; with much ceremony he backs away.

Another candle puffs out: Ashley disappears. The fiddles strike up a last flourish before leaving off. And the play at last commences.

Julius Caesar. Act 1, Scene 1. Rome—A Street.

Most of the audience, already familiar with the text, are able to picture the street as well as though they saw columns or colonnades. Enter Flavius, Marullus, and

—rather precipitately, as though pushed—a number of Commoners. All Commoners wear the full imperial toga, with the exception of one sturdy old Roman who has got on the costume generally used for King Henry the Eighth. This does not trouble the dictators of pit or top gallery. But they sit coldly silent while Flavius and Marullus exchange words with the punning cobbler. Pit and top gallery would get on to business.

It is not until the second scene that things grow more lively. Enter, in procession with music, *Caesar; Antony,* for the course; *Portia, Decius, Cicero, Brutus, Cassius,* and *Casca:* which should be enough celebrities for anybody.

It is certainly so for this house. At mere mention of Caesar's name, such a roar of applause goes up that Caesar (Mr. John Lacy) comes downstage and bows until hauled back into place by a somewhat glowering Mark Antony (Mr. Edward Kynaston). Afterwards the audience is heart and soul with the play. This may be accounted as fortunate; the Large Crowd of the stage directions carries itself awkwardly. Cicero, in fact, seems a good deal the worse for drink. Luckily he is not required to address the Roman Senate, though a critical observer would suspect the members of that august body as being in a condition little more sober than himself.

Once the clutter of supernumeraries has been cleared off, the weight of the play is carried by Charles Hart as Brutus and Michael Mohun as Cassius. Mary Knepp as Calpurnia is well received. And there is a fine display of thunder and lightning: the first produced by metal well shaken, the second by a lavish use of firework powder which (this time, at least) does not set the whole place ablaze.

A great cloud of smoke has been accumulating, through which the players stalk and declaim. The loudest applause, as a rule, will be drawn by any speech of patriotic fervour. When Cassius lifts one arm towards heaven, and soars into earnest rhetoric concerning his love of country, the top gallery responds with cheers. This reaches its height as Brutus, looking mournfully at the plant-in-a-tub which serves as his Orchard, strikes his breast and says:

"Every drop of blood that every Roman bears, and

nobly bears, is guilty of a several bastardy if he do break the smallest particle of any promise that hath passed from him!"

They all love that. Though the side boxes give only token applause, too much enthusiasm being below the court's dignity, King Charles the Second may be seen listening with as close and respectful attention as any.

But pit and top gallery are waiting for their favourite. They will not be satisfied until Dolly Landis has come on. A while ago there has been a whisper in Fops' Corner on the stage—nobody knows how it started—that something is wrong with Dolly, despite her brief appearance in the crowd during the second scene: that she is not well, that she plays some other drama of her own: a dozen conjectures which rustle among the chairs, and down along the benches in the pit.

When she does come on, in the second act, this feeling at first is intensified. The scene is still Brutus's Orchard by night. In appearance Dolly is much the same as ever, playing the Roman matron in a blue-and-orange gown.

But a curiously sensitive place is the theatre. At her first words of, "Brutus, my lord—!" there is an instant hint of something beneath the surface. It is not the slight trembling in her voice, as though it sought to find the right level. This is not illness, perhaps, or even drunkenness. And yet—something. Certain people in the pit, groping underneath benches for nosegays or bouquets they have kept to throw at her when she shall make her exit, find themselves much puzzled.

Dolly plays most of her parts with a certain hoydenish innocence. Usually there is a touch of burlesque, a suggestion of mouth twisting or a wink, at the end of some florid speech. But she is speaking every word as though she meant it: a surprising, rapid, heart-felt performance, which strikes the house quiet within thirty seconds.

With this fervour she begs Brutus to tell what is wrong with him: why he is gloomy, and what dangers there are. She crosses towards the royal box, within a few feet of where the king is sitting; then she turns, and hurries back. "I entreat," she says to Brutus, that he tell her

> . . . what men to-night
> Have had resort to you; for there have been
> Some six or seven, who did hide their faces
> Even from darkness.

It is quickly finished, no very long scene she has to play. She has started across the stage before the knocking of the conspirator. Pit and top gallery wake up with a roar of applause. Dolly hesitates, almost as though expecting this, and comes down to the front of the stage.

Three or four bouquets are hurled up at her from the pit. All but one fall short, tumbling among the fiddlers. The bouquet which lands at her feet she picks up. Her next move, unless you have cause to observe it, you will never see at all. A small, folded paper is thrust deep among the flowers of the bouquet.

As though glad to be rid of the Roman matron, a graceful figure in blue-and-orange goes dancing across the stage. She stops where she has stood once before, facing sideways towards the royal box.

"Hail, Brutus! Hail, noblest Roman!"

Dolly holds up the bouquet for all to see. She postures in a kind of triumph. She flings that bouquet over the edge of the stage, over the box rail, and into the lap of the king.

And now they think they understand.

The audacity of it is such that the whole audience stares with the breath stuck in its throat. Even Nell Gwyn, as impudent a baggage as ever appeared here, has never dared go as far as this. Nelly has imitated my Lady Castlemaine to her face, copying gown and speech and gesture. But to throw a bouquet to the king in public, with Madam Barbara sitting in the box above, is a piece of effrontery which risks every lightning bolt from backstage.

Grandee keeps an expressionless face. Sedate Citizen gapes. Fop cranes his neck uneasily to look towards the royal box, and then up in the gloom at Lady Thunder sitting motionless, her pomander ball at her nose. But, with a sudden and shattering roar, not-to-be-cozened Public in the top gallery comes to life. It cheers. It whistles and stamps and makes sounds indicative of osculation. Down pours that noise in a cataract, flooding the wits of Sedate Citizen.

And King Charles, let it be confessed, King Charles responds well to the challenge.

Nobody sees him take something from the bouquet and slip it into his pocket. The rest may be seen by anyone. He rises. He sweeps a bow to the queen sitting beside him and hands her the flowers.

Afterwards there will be people to tell you that never, in all the years she has lived and is to live in England, did Queen Catherine wear such a look as she did (for an instant) then. Perhaps they exaggerate. Perhaps they were not here. But this dark-faced little lady would seem, momentarily, to have had fine eyes. Otherwise she gives little outward sign, save for a pinched and ghostly smile. The bouquet—which is only the common field flowers anyway, and much bruised as well—she takes carefully into her hands. When she dies in Lisbon, nearly forty years from now, they are to find the withered stalks among her possessions, along with the pious Latin books and the crucifix.

But at this moment the actors, who have been shifting about in a restless manner during the uproar, betray a certain impatience. Mr. Hart bawls out, for attention, a repetition of his last speech to Portia: *"Leave me with haste!"*

He motions to Lucius (Mr. Robert Shatterell), who bends close to his ear and shouts, "Here is a sick man who would speak with you!" They bring on the sick man, a truly ghastly-looking fellow who nevertheless can yell as loudly as anyone else; and all three contrive by lung power to quell the tumult. The King, his chair tilted back, regards everything with great amiability.

The play goes its relentless way. Caesar is stabbed, relapsing suddenly into a couple of Latin words at his dying moment; Mark Antony praises Caesar and buries the conspirators, who are already bound for the plains of Philippi. Still rain beats on the cupola roof. The remaining candles burn low, flaring out in sheets of grease. It is as though you could hear, off-stage, an ominous clang of arms. The king still has not moved. He allows several acts to be played before he takes a note from his pocket, unfolds it, and scans it casually.

Inside the tent of Brutus, represented only by two chairs and a table with a lighted taper, the quarrel between

131

Brutus and Cassius breaks out. There is more talk concerning the honour of Rome. Hart, tall and shadowy, with his helmet gleaming, turns from the table. He strikes the short-sword rattling at his hip.

> For I can raise no money by vile means.
> By heaven, I had rather coin my heart,
> And drop my blood for drachmas, than to wring
> From the hard hands of peasants their vile trash
> By an indirection. I did send
> To you for gold . . .

King Charles looks up with a curious expression. He rubs his long nose. For a second or two he regards the stage inscrutably. Then he tilts back his chair again, and falls to fondling the necks of his dogs.

X

At Whitehall, in one corner of the Palace Yard, the great bell called Old Tom struck eight. Its voice was muffled by the falling rain, but they heard it distinctly in Bygones Abraham's lodgings off the Shield Gallery. Bygones and my grandfather sat in the withdrawing room, with two candles burning in silver holders on the table between them; and once more they waited.

Much could be told of what befell in the few hours after they discovered Pembroke Harker stabbed through the back of the neck in the cupboard. If I need not recount this fully, it being a grisly story, there are reasons why parts of it must at least be indicated.

Kinsmere never afterwards forgot standing in the Hebe Room at just before three o'clock. He remembered the sky darkening towards storm outside the windows, the cupboard's open door, the trussed and gagged dead man lying face down in so much blood, and the buzz of the circling flies.

"Ay!" said Bygones, from deep in his throat. "It's a pretty sight, as you were thinking: a most wondrous pretty sight! 'Now sacrilegious murder hath broke ope—' "

There was a light footstep outside the door of the Hebe

Room; the latch was lifted; Dolly Landis stood in the opening.

Kinsmere leaped at the door of the cupboard. He shut and latched it, but not before Dolly had seen. The colour drained from her face: it was plain that her knees must be trembling like her mouth. She took a faltering step inside, and jerked out her elbow to close the door behind her.

"Pem! Is he—?"

"Yes!"

"Dear God, b-but what happened? Who did it?"

"While we were a-sitting idle in there . . ." Bygones began.

You could still hear the flies buzzing inside the cupboard. Kinsmere went forward to grip Dolly's arm.

"We don't know what happened or who did it. But no oracle is needed to foretell the future. If anybody but you had walked in, it would be said I did it."

"Not so!" retorted Bygones. "You're concerned enough, in all conscience; let's own it freely and damnably; yet not as actor-in-chief. Never think it: they'd call *me* the culprit!"

"YOU?"

"Lad, lad, think further on this!" Bygones lumbered in the direction of the windows, his feet crunching in broken glass; then he swung round again. "Here's all the signs of a duello: behold 'em. There's you with a wound in your shoulder, there's Harker with blood on his sword, *but also*," and he pointed, "there's Harker stone dead of a stab never made in any duello.

"D'ye see how they'll read it? You engaged him, which is true enough. He wounded you: likewise true. Then, when he'd ha' spitted you on the point, I stepped in from behind and finished him with a knife. No matter that this is false: no matter the lass can say it's false! Who'd believe her? And no source of help to you either. This is a great business, a wicked business, a hanging business; they'd nub us both together on Tyburn Tree. That's where you're in the right of it. If any person was to come in here and find him—"

One of the flies, loose from the cupboard, rose up and brushed Kinsmere's cheek; he flinched as though he had been stung. And, at the same moment, somebody outside

133

in the passage tapped softly but insistently at the Hebe Room's door.

If he flinched at the touch of the fly, which was wet and glutted, still he did not hesitate. With a gentle hand he put Dolly to one side, and instantly yanked open the door.

Outside stood the tapster who had served them with their meal in the other room. He was a small, bald-headed, servile man, with his sleeves rolled up and a splashed apron round his waist. He had a quick, eager, squeaky voice.

"Please, sir," says he, "I am come for the thing in the cupboard."

Bygones Abraham lumbered forward, but his help was not needed.

"Are you so?" spars Kinsmere, feeling the fly hover back again. "Now what hell's nonsense is this? What d'ye mean, fellow?"

"If you please, sir," wailed the tapster, "don't look so! I studied no offence . . . it was only the gentleman . . ."

"What gentleman?"

"He passed me on the stairs, sir, and did pluck at my sleeve. The lady and the two gentlemen in the Cupid Room, he said, had left in the cupboard here a certain thing they would doubtless desire to have carried downstairs. A box or portmanteau, was it? Some parcel of bottles, or the like? Sir, sir, can I tell fortunes or read minds?"

"Attend only to your proper business. Did the gentleman say anything else?"

"Nay, sir; but he laughed."

"Laughed, did he? And what was he like, this fine comical fellow? Can you describe him?"

"Sir, sir! 'Tis dark on the stairs, as you must be aware! Had a gentleman's voice; 'tis all I know. Besides!" The tapster's little eye rolled up. "Under favour, and most humbly craving your pardon, *need* I describe him? For sure the gentleman was of your party?"

"He attached himself to us, God knows," returned Kinsmere. "But not for long, I am glad to say. And sure *you* can recognize a jest when you hear one?"

"A jest, sir?"

"Did we not tell you, when you served us," interposed

Bygones, in so menacing a tone that the tapster shied back, "did we not tell you a friend of ours—aforetime in the Cupid Room with this lady—had drunk himself insensible, and was put by? Did we not tell you this?"

"Ay, sir, truly you did!"

"He is in that cupboard," said Bygones, "and hears nothing. But he is a proud man; he would not care to be seen as he is now. As for the merry joker who spoke to you, his jest was none so comical as he made out. Still, if it diverted the rogue . . . !"

"Well, sir, your friend's score is paid. He paid it to Big Mike. I know, when he was served with roast mutton. You'll not leave him in the cupboard, though? If I fetched other tapsters, we could—"

"No, let be!" interrupted Kinsmere, as the other set foot inside the door. "We'll stand guard between this room and the next, and decide what's to be done. Meanwhile, be off! Here's something for your trouble; but be off, I say; see to it we are not intruded upon again!"

And he slammed the door in the tapster's face.

Afterwards it was not easy. A sluggish line of blood had crawled out from under the closed cupboard door. Though it was all but invisible under the darkened sky, with puffs of warm air blowing through, more flies had gathered for a feast.

"And there we are, ecod!" Bygones indicated it. "Lad lad, that was well done! You can face a mort o' troubles and stand like a rock, though you turn queasy when it's all over. Meanwhile—"

"*Was* it well done?" says Kinsmere, feeling the nerves jerk again in the calves of his legs. "And *is* it all over? I am not convinced of this. Damn those flies!"

"Will he come back, do you think?" said Dolly, who still breathed hard but had regained some part of composure. "You gave him money; will the tapster come back?"

"For my part, lass," Bygones told her, "I am more concerned with a mighty humorous fellow who laughs on the stairs when he has just done a murder. Ayagh! Should he carry his tale to a magistrate, and make report of our misdeeds in full . . ."

"He'd not dare, surely?" Dolly cried. "When he needs

135

must give his name and say how he knows? He'd not dare?"

"This joker, in the solemn estimation o' Bygones Abraham, would dare almost anything. Oh, body o' Pilate! He might not make report, 'tis true; he's done what he came to do, and all is fair and rosy; but lay no wager thereon. Meanwhile, what's to be done? We can't leave Harker there forever, yet we can't smuggle him belowstairs with the place still filled and roaring. Meanwhile, I repeat, what *is* to be done?"

"Let *me* suggest it," answered Dolly. "And don't, pray don't call me fool and rattle when I say there's but one course to pursue! We must have counsel in this; we must have assistance in this; and there's only one person . . ."

"If you mean the king—"

"I do indeed mean the king. And—"

"Lass, lass!" Bygones was horror-stricken, making volcanic noises in his throat. "This must never be! This presumes too much!"

"You are on his service. In some sense—foh, we are all on his service! And whose interest but the king's is so deeply bound up with what has passed this day?"

"There's sense in what you say, it may be. But . . . oh, ecod! Dare I approach His Majesty with my tuppenny woes? Or, even if I dared, *could* I do this?"

"Nay, not easily! As King's Messenger, save on frequent occasion when you must risk your life, you are not even presumed to exist. As for this dear boy here, this mighty swordsman who met Pem and beat him when no other durst do it, he is utterly unknown at court and would never get near the king. Besides, there is the question of time. Have you marked St. Dunstan's clock for the past quarter hour or more? Have you heard it?"

"For the past quarter hour," Kinsmere admitted, as Dolly lifted her eyes to him, "I would not have heard the Last Trump had it sounded then."

" 'Tis gone three and well beyond! His Majesty will set out soon for the play; and I must be off too. Well!" said Dolly, rapt and carried away. "You should not approach him, either of you. But I can do it!"

"You?"

"Even I! Attend to me!" Dolly ran her hands up to his

136

shoulders, looking him in the eyes. "I can send him a note, unseen and unsuspected by anyone. Never mind how! There's an elderly man in the pit throws me flowers each time after my first exit, no matter if 'tis an ill day and I play badly. I can convey a note to the king, asking for private audience. Oh, please, may I do this? You have done so much for me! May I not do this small and trifling thing for you?"

That look, so pleading and ingenuous and yet proud, would have moved anyone. Yet all it did was turn Kinsmere's brain.

"No, you may not!"

"Sweet, sweet! And wherefore not, prithee?"

"Because already you have been too much in fear and hazard. Because this is no small or trifling thing. Be not moved, Dolly, by any sudden and foolish feeling of gratitude, simply for the reason that . . . that . . ."

"As God sees me," said Dolly, "you have no notion how I feel towards you, or what I would not do for you if I could! This is not gratitude, foolish one. And I run no hazard; truly I don't. Let me feel—oh, let me feel!—that in some idiot's way I can serve and assist you! Is there nothing, nothing at all, I can do for you?"

"Yes. You can give me a kiss."

"Oh, body o' God!" roared Bygones Abraham.

He stumped over to the windows, cursing viciously, and then returned.

"I am a long-suffering man, mark'ee. My patience is of the angels. I would see all young people happy and at fornication. But here's a man murdered with a knife in his neck, here's a hangman awaiting both of us unless the king interferes; and what *she* can do, ecod and strike me blind, is to 'give you a kiss.' Lad, lad, your destination would be Bedlam if it wasn't Tyburn. And there's good sense in what the girl tells us."

"No, I say!"

"But I say yes," pleaded Dolly, clinging to Kinsmere and speaking at Bygones past his shoulder. "Indeed, there is the most wondrous good sense, and you at least will agree I'm in the right."

"Ay, lass, it may be so. Still! Should the king think it not prudent to concern himself—"

"Do you read him so? *I* don't. And this I tell you too. You have spoke much of a wicked jester would run any hazard or do any act. But what of the king's self? He is a careless man, belike. Yet he sails so close to the wind, even by ordinary, his councillors must shake in their shoes and clap hands to their periwigs lest the whole craft overset. Save that he would have no violence and order no man's death, there is not an imprudent deed on earth he would not risk either. Be of good heart, both of you. I will do what I propose; I will be of some use and service; I will do it!"

And so, of course, it was eventually decided.

Dolly left them at half past three, not even permitting Kinsmere to accompany her belowstairs. He and Bygones must stand guard in the Hebe Room, as both were agreed. Dolly, rapt and exalted and starry-eyed, flew into the next room and returned with several still-unopened bottles of claret. Then she was away in her grey cloak. She would send them word by note, she said; and, should it be necessary to refer to the king in writing, she would show herself conspirator-subtle by designating him as "R" for old Rowley.

Afterwards they waited.

They gathered up the scattered playing cards of the carouse last night. They set right the overturned chair. They lighted the tallow candle in its pewter holder, and put it on the table. And so, while the dead man lay in his cupboard and the flies still quested for his blood, they sat down with the cards to play at piquet.

"Well, lad, here it is. We may fillip up, cross or pile, as to what shall happen now. If that comical fellow did in fact seek out a magistrate, and send him with a couple of constables to seek us out . . ."

"Well, if he did," says Kinsmere, "we shall know soon enough—and see gaol soon enough too. Meanwhile, there's no damned measure we can use save to keep our heads."

"Ay, lad, fair enough! Spoken like a true King's Messenger!"

"What's this again of King's Messengers? Cut for deal, can't you?"

At just past four o'clock the rain tore down. Doors

banged belowstairs; footsteps stamped and voices rose; once they heard a drunken man being put into the street. On another occasion foot-falls approached their door, but went past to the Cupid Room and returned without stopping.

The minutes crawled by, and then the hours. No magistrate arrived, but no word from Dolly either. St. Dunstan's clock went on striking interminably. It had just banged out the quarter hour past six when there were more footsteps, and a light rap at the door. My grandfather leaped up as though burnt; then controlled himself and strolled across to it. The servile tapster, his forehead all but touching the floor, handed in a sealed note addressed in painful lettering to "Young Gentlman in Hebby Room."

"Ay, lad? What's the word?"

Kinsmere broke open the note and spread it out on the table.

" 'Deare boy,' " said Dolly's crooked handwriting, which sprawled all over the paper, " 'Deare boy I dount knowe yr name. Dount feare, all is well. Goe back with A. to his lodgings. Leve H. where he ys, he will be taken care of by R.'s order. Staye with A. till you have word from R., you have don well he saith. Much love, D.' "

Bygones Abraham expelled a deep breath.

" 'He will be taken care of,' " Bygones quoted in a heavy voice, " 'by R.'s order.' Y'know, lad, the man *could* have left us stranded."

"He could. I much feared he would."

"Well! He *could* ha' done that, I say. And yet, arrive what may for the future, he hath behaved with much exactness as the lass said he would. That's a fine brisk honest lass too!"

"Am I not sensible of it?"

"Come then!" said Bygones, wheezing still more as he poured out two bumpers of claret. "Considering certain remarks of yours a while ago . . . Will ye drink, can ye drink, the toast I proposed this morning? Here it is, then: God for King Charles! Can ye drink that?"

"I can, with all my heart. Dolly above all, but—God for King Charles!"

Again they both looked at Dolly's note. While Kinsmere, at last permitted to pay for something, went to

139

the door and bawled for the tapster so that he could settle their score, Bygones Abraham pushed aside the cards, fetched out his dagger, and fell to carving a large VIVAT REX in the top of the table.

And so, as the great bell called Old Tom struck eight in one corner of Whitehall Palace Yard, that same note from Dolly lay on another table, but a round table and not a square one. It was the table in the withdrawing room of Bygones's lodgings off the Shield Gallery, where they had drunk their first toast that morning.

Spacious and pleasant the room was, with its tapestries, its French carpet, and the sideboard between two dark windows looking down on the Volary Garden below. Under the stone hood of the chimneypiece against the east wall, a fire of Scotch coal had been lighted against the damp. Someone had cleaned and tidied the place since morning; on the table near the note, where two wax candles burned in silver holders, stood a new and freshly opened bottle of sack, together with the two tankards and Bygones's brass-bound tobacco box.

Bygones himself—mottled face fresh-shaven, his periwig combed and a clean fall of lace at his throat—sat at the far side of the table, smoking a long clay pipe.

"Six, seven, eight." He counted the strokes of the clock, heard through softly falling rain. "Time a-getting on; and no word yet, ecod, as to what I'm to do this night! Come, then!"

Kinsmere himself felt pretty comfortable. He also had got a shave; and washed all over with water out of a tub in his companion's bedchamber adjoining. His bloodstained shirt had been exchanged for one of Bygones's most resplendent shirts. His shoulder pained very little; nothing to speak of. Having just finished a pipe of tobacco, he put it down on the table.

"Well?" says he.

"Where's the lass now, I should like to know? What did she say to the king?"

With the stem of his pipe Bygones pushed round the note so that Kinsmere could read it from the other side.

" 'Go back with A. to his lodgings. . . . Stay there till you have word from R.' And, 'You have done well.' That means, as safe as anything you can bet, we shall both be

140

summoned to see the king. But what did she *say* to him? Stop, stop; what are you at now?"

For Kinsmere had picked up the note, folded it, and stowed it away in an inside pocket beside his sapphire ring.

"It's the only thing I have that belongs to Dolly. I am keeping it safely, by your leave."

"Oh, ecod! You'll see the lass herself soon enough: can't you guess that?"

"It's devoutly to be hoped so. Meanwhile—"

"These outpourings o' sentiment may be proper enough and excusable enough," snorted Bygones, "but when they become moonstruck sickliness they vex all nature and give me a pain in the behind. Come, let's be practical men!"

Bygones drew smoke into his lungs and hoisted himself to his feet. Then, pipe cradled across his left arm, he began to pace back and forth, tugging at his moustache and tuft of chin whisker.

"We may be sure the king (God bless him!) knows there's a conspiracy against him. Ayagh! But what do we know, or think we know from Harker's speaking too much, of that same conspiracy?"

"Well . . ."

"Imprimmus, there's a band of malcontents. Who they are, or how many of 'em, we can't say. The only name Harker mentioned—"

"The only name," interrupted Kinsmere, "was of a canting Puritan named Salvation Gaines. Salvation Gaines, Harker said, had employment as a scrivener at court."

"Has he so, lad? *I* am acquainted with no such man, and I know everybody at court."

"Yet somebody employs him! He exists; Dolly is acquainted with him. Did you mark what Dolly said? 'Most lewd with his hands,' she said, 'when he can put a woman into a corner.' Now burn my soul in the bonfire," yelled Kinsmere, who was simmering with rage, "when *I* think of a clammy-fisted Roundhead . . ."

"Lad, lad, enough o' this maundering! Take your mind for two seconds from the wench, and pay some heed to business!"

Bygones stopped briefly to look at the red-leather fire

141

bucket hanging beside the mantelpiece; according to palace regulations, you were subject to a ten-shilling fine if you let a chimney catch fire. But immediately he resumed his pacing, drawing deep lungfuls of smoke from the pipe.

"At the head of this band," he continued, "there's a plotter-in-chief. Body o' Pilate, it might be anybody! We've no means of knowing who he is . . ."

"No; but we know something of what he did."

"Ay, lad? What did he do?"

"The plotter-in-chief was suspicious of Harker. Others, including yourself, have been suspicious of him. A hired bullyrock was sent to follow Harker and observe him. When Harker's tongue wagged too freely, because he thought Dolly would not dare betray him, the bullyrock—"

"Stopped his tongue with a bone-handled knife?" supplied Bygones. "No, lad! Never in this world!"

"Wherefore not, o Sounder of Mysteries?"

"Imprimmus, hired bullyrocks kill on hire, *and* on instructions. They don't take it into their own heads to make decisions o' that nature; and Harker had given satisfaction, you may depend on't, up to the time his tongue wagged before us. Eyetem, hired bullyrocks are not described as 'gentlemen' by tapsters who meet 'em in the dark. They make no merry jests touching things in cupboards that must be carried downstairs. They—"

"Oh, burn everything! Do you tell me," demanded Kinsmere, "that the comical fellow on the staircase must have been the plotter-in-chief himself?"

"No, not that either! It might ha' been, and yet I doubt it. Shall I say why?"

"If you can."

"Ayagh!" snorted Bygones, puffing more smoke. "I pose not as Sir Oracle; and, when I speak, let no dog bark. Still! There's coruscating conclusions to be drawn here. Eminent men do in fact visit common taverns; this is not France; 'tis a free-and-easy society. But they don't let their hands be seen so fully and freely; they don't mock and jeer with tapsters in public, as this comedian did when he'd used his knife.

"No, I would lay my life on it! The man who stabbed

142

Harker is someone else in the band of malcontents: not so highly placed as the plotter-in-chief, but concerned enough and knowing enough to make his own decision when he found Harker could blab."

"You may *have* to lay your life on it," says Kinsmere. "These people kill as quickly as a dog gnaws bones or as you and I drink. And both of us—yes, and Dolly too!—have acquired more information than is good for health's sake. At risk of being cast again into outer darkness, shall I name the one thing we assuredly know about the plotter-in-chief?"

"Ay, lad?"

"He wants a document in cipher, setting forth certain terms in a secret treaty, of which Harker was to have carried one half and you the other half. Yet you say you have received no instructions about a mission to France?"

"Nay, friend, you know I have not! That is: not yet."

"Harker said he took *his* instructions from someone called Butterworth, Rab Butterworth."

"Mr. Robert Butterworth," Bygones reared up and rolled out the name, "is Second Page of the Back-Stairs to His Majesty. Will Chiffinch, the First Page, meddles not in affairs of the body politic."

"Do you get your instructions from Mr. Robert Butterworth?"

"No, though I have seen him once or twice in the king's private cabinet."

"Then how do you get 'em?"

Bygones halted abruptly and made a fierce gesture for silence, finger to lip.

And it was of silence that Kinsmere became most aware. The rain had ceased; it pattered no more against windows or into the dark Volary Garden. At the back of it you were conscious of a vague stir and mutter from this great hive called Whitehall Palace. Otherwise silence had descended like an extinguisher cap on the room, on the Shield Gallery, on the palace itself.

Silence, that is, except for a padding of soft little footsteps that approached in the Shield Gallery outside the closed door. There was a rustle of paper; something white was pushed under the door sill.

Bygones lumbered over, picked it up, and returned to

the table. He displayed a letter—another letter!—but this one of a sort somewhat different from Dolly's. Large, clean, and oblong, having no superscription, it was folded over once and closed with black wax bearing a plain seal.

"Come!" said Bygones. He put down his pipe, which had gone out. He broke open the paper and held it near one candle flame to be read. "Come, this is something like business!"

The note, unsigned and in small neat writing, was very short. It requested that at nine o'clock that night, if convenient, Bygones Abraham, Esq., and the young gentleman accompanying him (name unknown) would present themselves at the westernmost door on the south side of the Shield Gallery. To no one would they mention this communication, which they would be good enough to destroy as soon as read.

"Well!" continued Bygones.

As Kinsmere had dealt with Sir Aubrey Fairchild's deposition against Dolly, so Bygones dealt with this letter. He touched it's edge to the candle flame. It flared up into a sheet of fire, throwing wild yellow light across the walls, and crumpled to black flimsiness. Bygones crushed it in his fist, letting the ashes sift down on the table.

"Aha!" he added, with a triumphant look and a conspiratorial wink. "I would offer ye two guesses as to who sent this, save that ye may save one of 'em for future use. Eh?"

"True enough. We need no Sir Oracle to tell us who sent it. But what's its meaning?"

"Why, it may mean only that His Majesty would desire to learn details of what befell this afternoon. Or, which is a thing far more likely, it means his plan for France will go forward this night. I carry one half the cipher dispatch: well and good! Then, by the claws of the Eternal, who should carry the other half but you?"

"*Me?*"

"Ay, lad, and who better?"

"But he has no knowledge whatever of me! Since he intrusts so few people, would he intrust a total stranger?"

"Come! From what the lass must ha' told His Majesty, he's not the man I think if he has many doubts. For one thing, you've shown you are a loyal king's man—"

"Am I?" says Kinsmere, in some perplexity. "I suppose I am. All my family have been, God knows."

"Well, are you not?" demanded the other. "If not, ecod, you take mighty strange ways o' showing it! Why have you behaved as you have done this day, then? 'Twas not all the wench, surely. Why have you behaved as you have done?"

"In all candour, I don't know. It must be laid at the cause, in all likelihood, of an utter inability to keep out of trouble. And yet, looking back on the events of the day, I fail to see I could have behaved in any other way. The king (God bless him! as you would say) . . ."

"Lad, lad, whose side *are* you on? A plain question, now! Should His Majesty graciously request you to carry one half of this document, would you do it?"

"I would. Mark this, Bygones! If you are right touching the terms of this secret treaty to be proposed . . ."

"I am right; depend on't!"

"Then the king (God bless him) would appear to be almost as great a rogue as the enemies leagued against him. But that," Kinsmere added sharply, "is beside the point and signifies nothing."

"Beside the point, ecod? Signifies nothing?"

"Or at least very little, damn me. Let him make a treaty with King Louis or with Prester John or with the worms that shall feed on us after death! For I am on the side of my friends. And, if you and Dolly Landis are loyal king's men—why, then, by the sixty-eight bonfires of hell, so am I."

"Now here falls on our ears," observed Bygones, "the sound of a most handsome sentiment. To this old hulk it calls for libations, which shall distil the lucubrations of a manly heart, and make blooming the sandy wastes of the throat. Lad, tilt the bottle."

Kinsmere poured sack. There was not enough to fill both tankards. But they clinked pewter together, drank off the wine, and had set down the tankards when Bygones made another fierce gesture.

"Hush!" he whispered.

"Burn me, but is this more mysteriousness? Is everything mysteriousness?"

"I don't know what it is. Hush, for God's sake!"

145

More footsteps could be heard in the Shield Gallery. They did not sound the same as those of whatever person had brought the letter a little while ago. They were brisk, questing steps, as of square-toed shoes a-clack. They approached from an easterly direction, not a westerly, and passed. There was the noise of somebody knocking at a door not too far away. Then a long silence.

Bygones, lifting his shoulders to dismiss this, had started for the sideboard in search of another bottle when the footsteps returned and stopped just outside. There was a sharp, self-important fusilade of knocks at the withdrawing room door.

"Ay?" called Bygones, turning. "Who knocks there? And 'tis not locked; set it open, if that please you."

The door swung wide. Only a few wall candles were burning down the length of the Shield Gallery, making a dusk in which the figure on the threshold showed only as a silhouette.

"No tipstaff is on guard here," said a snappish voice. "Or anywhere else, it seems." Then the snappish tone changed. "Good souls, good souls, will you suffer a poor sinner to enter? My name is Salvation Gaines."

XI

In swept a lean, middle-sized man with an iron-grey periwig.

"Now *His* ways be praised!" intoned the newcomer, uprolling his eyes. "He shall be pleased to take the crafty in their own net, yet set the feet of the righteous upon paths of godliness and peace."

Mr. Salvation Gaines hurried to the middle of the room. There he stopped, peering at each of the others in turn.

"Think not that He is mocked!" the newcomer said. "As hell and Rome contrive snares for the unwary, so the Lord in His own time shall circumvent the one and chastise the other for their souls' good. Do I address Mr. Bygones Abraham?"

"You do."

"The man Bygones Abraham, hanger-on at Whitehall? Of no known occupation, yet in receipt of a certain in-

146

come from the Privy Purse itself? Are these things true?"

"They're true and I can't deny 'em, though they might be put with more civility."

"Now what have I to do with civility?" snapped Salvation Gaines.

There were several contradictions here. Though his phrasing was the usual cant of the old-line Roundhead, Independent or perhaps Fifth-Monarchy man, he had none of that through-the-nose twang by which "Lord" became "Laard" and "God" became "Goad." His speech and pronunciation were those of culture. If bearing, clothes, and periwig indicated an elderly man, his actual age could have been no older than the very early forties. He would give a little run forward, as though to peer closely at something, and then dart away. After a snuffle of humility, he would throw back his shoulders and send a glance anything but humble from sharp little red-rimmed eyes.

Then he rounded on my grandfather.

"And you, young man! You are Roderick Edward Kinsmere, of Blackthorn Hall in Somerset?"

"Just Blackthorn will suffice."

"Now tell me, young man! Hath your soul been plucked from Satan as a brand is plucked from the burning? Are you saved and among the elect?"

"I can't say. But I should think it most unlikely."

"So young! So young! And yet already a man of blood. Oh, the pity of this!" Gaines snuffled, moaned, and then flung away his hands from his own eyes. "You must be chastised, I fear; yes, you must be chastised! Further tell me: how have you employed your day in this sink of abomination called London? Not in pursuit of lewd women, I hope?"

"If 'tis any of your business . . ."

"It is the Lord's business, boy, and therefore mine. Speak home; don't think to evade! How have you employed your time in this very stench of abomination?"

"I passed most of today at the Devil tavern."

"Indeed you did, as I know. Oh, the pity of *that!* 'And the smoke of their torment ascendeth up for ever' " —Gaines stopped. "I have sought you everywhere in this wicked town. I have this moment come from seeking you in your lodgings here at the palace, and you were not even there!"

"My lodgings here at the palace?" exploded Rowdy Kinsmere. "You are very free with damnation, Mr. By-God Gaines, but what hell's nonsense is *this?*"

Gaines whipped round.

"Man Abraham," he said, "can you deny that adjoining these rooms there is another set of chambers until today unoccupied?"

"If I could deny it, you canting ninnyhammer," roared Bygones, "be sure I would!—"

"A worse man of blood! Shall not the godly expect this?"

"But I can't deny it," said Bygones, pointing to a closed door in the west wall, "because I told the lad about 'em this morning."

Gaines whipped back.

"And *you*, I dare suppose, will deny you occupy those chambers now?"

"Though it's no concern of yours, I never so much as set eyes on 'em!"

"Indeed?" said Salvation Gaines.

For some reason he bustled to the chimneypiece, where he examined the red-leather fire bucket hanging on a nail beside it. Then he went to the table. After looking hard at the black ash fragments where Bygones had burnt the king's letter, he caught up one of the silver candlesticks. Snuffling and blowing, holding the light high, Gaines scurried across to the door in the west wall.

It was closed, but not locked or bolted. Gaines threw it open and crossed threshold, with Bygones and my grandfather following.

The rays of the taper disclosed another withdrawing room almost exactly like Bygones's, hung and carpeted and furnished in the same way. A round table bearing candlesticks stood in the middle; there were chairs with body cushions. Another sideboard stood between two windows looking down on the Volary Garden. The sky above the rooftops had cleared; before long, as night deepened, a full moon would rise above Whitehall Palace.

"Here are few signs of occupancy," cried Salvation Gaines, "and no fire or lights. But let us look a little beyond!"

148

He gestured with his taper towards another door opposite the one by which they had entered. It must lead, Kinsmere thought, to a bedchamber corresponding with that in the other set of rooms, save that Bygones's bedchamber opened towards the east and this second towards the west.

Gaines scurried towards it.

"If they have told lies because they are misguided, there may perhaps be mercy after chastisement! But if they have told lies sinfully, and of their wicked malice . . . ! Oh, and in tears I say it, what is here?"

Kinsmere, hastening after him, looked into the bedroom. And, not for the first time that day, he found his wits whirling.

The room, though small and stuffy, was very comfortable. It had a neat carpet. One tiny window showed a glimpse of the sky. Otherwise it was almost filled by a large bed with a tester, a dressing table bearing bowl and ewer for hot water, and a big chair beside the bed. Across the chair hung Kinsmere's own well-filled saddlebags, having the initials R.K. burned into one corner of the leather with a red-hot poker.

It was towards Bygones that he turned.

"How came the saddlebags here? I took up quarters at the Grapes, near Charing Cross, because Uncle Godfrey recommended it and said my father was used to visit there. I have not seen my possessings since early morning. Had I known they were here, I had scarce need to borrow your shirt."

"Well! It was none o' *my* doing or knowing," roared Bygones. "Can *I* command lodgings at the palace, being here only on sufferance myself? As for the shirt, be pleased to keep it. 'Tis a tastefuller shirt than any you'd choose for yourself. Still, all the same—!"

Salvation Gaines went back to the table in what unexpectedly appeared to be Kinsmere's own withdrawing room. He set down the lighted candle beside the two unlighted ones. The palms of his hands were damp; he rubbed them together, and wiped them down the sides of his neat dark-grey coat. But his little eye did not waver.

"Not know they were here?" said Gaines, with a sneer whistling through his nose. "A likely story, is it not, with which to affront the ears of pious men? Beyond there, or

149

so I understand," he waved his arm towards the west and south, "beyond there, all but surrounding us, lie the state apartments of the king himself. And tonight, in the Gallery—" when any person said *the* Gallery, and not Stone Gallery or Matted Gallery, he meant the great Banqueting House—"tonight, in the Gallery, they play at their accursed games, ombre or basset or the like, for gaming stakes which stink in the nostrils of the Lord Most High. Oh, what a godless court is all this!"

"Is it so?"

"And *you,* young Master Roderick Kinsmere! What do you do here and wherefore imperil your immortal soul with the filth of lies? You must expound this; expound it at once, I command you, else there shall be no hope for you now or hereafter!"

"Expound it, must I? By whose authority must I expound it? And who are you?"

"The same question," said Bygones, "had occurred once or twice to a cooler head than either of yours. Who in exactness are you, Salvation Gaines, that you impose your presence as though you had a very right to be here? State your business, if any, and then begone."

"Did I address *you,* man of blood? Nay, not so! I spoke only to this wretched addlepated boy, so misguided that—"

"Speak to him, then," interrupted Kinsmere, temper again beginning to simmer. "Who are you? What do you want?"

"In *this* life, which is as grass and lasteth but a day, I am chief clerk to the household of His Grace the Duke of Buckingham. His Grace, you will say, is a man of loose and immoral life. So he is; you are in the right; and so I have told him to his face. Yet there is hope for him," gabbled Gaines, "there is hope for him notwithstanding! He hath the kindest feelings towards men of the true faith, Independents all, who are God's Chosen and shall win eternal life. Above aught else, he will have no truck or traffic with the bloody designs of Popery. We have laws against these Papists—"

"I call to mind," said Bygones Abraham, "that we have also laws against Independents and other fanatics."

"Tchaa! Now what are such laws to me?"

"You are above 'em, that's to say?"

150

"It is only to say," and Gaines drew himself up, "that I have no words for *you*. I address this young man. Attend to me, poor boy; mark well what I tell you!"

The flame of the candle wavered a little in a draught, sending great weights of shadow sliding across the tapestries and across the white plaster ceiling with its black crossbeams. Gaines raised an admonitory forefinger.

"It has been called to His Grace's notice that you waited upon him at York House this morning, but departed incontinent without paying your respects. Do I say true, sir?"

"You do, sir."

"That was churlish of you; let it not happen again. However! His Grace of Bucks, being acquainted with your uncle and your late father, deigns to pardon this. He bids you sup with him at nine this night. Nay, don't thank me; 'tis so arranged A wherry will call for you at Whitehall Stairs in—let me think—a quarter hour's time from now."

"Convey my compliments and thanks to His Grace, but say that this cannot be. I have another engagement for nine o'clock."

"Indeed you have." Gaines almost pounced at him. "Shall I tell you what it is?"

"Well . . ."

"Let him speak, lad!" Bygones interposed, with a strong air of tension. "Let the Saved One speak!"

"This morning, in a window embrasure at York House, you were observed deep in discourse with a certain banker, one Roger Stainley, whose religious views are strongly suspect . . ."

"Mr. Stainley is a communicant of the Church Established!"

"And what is this Church Established but another name for the Whore of Babylon?"

"Nevertheless, since it *is* the Church Established—"

"Be pleased, young man," snapped Gaines, "to hold your tongue when I address you. This man Stainley, though not of the elect, is otherwise of good repute. Since he stands in some sense your guardian, since he would transfer to you a considerable inheritance, since you have not forgotten you were to sup with *him* at nine o'clock . . ."

But Kinsmere had forgotten it. That appointment with

Mr. Stainley (the same hour as he was now bidden to see the king) had been clean driven out of his head. When you consider he had utterly forgotten a meeting arranged for the making over to him of more than ninety thousand pounds, you can conceive the sort of shrewd, farsighted, long-headed man of business my grandfather was. When you add that he had every intention of putting off this meeting until such time as it did not interfere with his adventures, you are still further enlightened.

"Now don't deny," said Gaines, "you are indeed pledged to be in Lombard Street. No more lies on your soul. Don't deny this, I say: you were heard and observed!"

"I don't deny it. But by whom was I observed?"

"By *me*. I am much more than scrivener and chief clerk to a household. There are laws, there are household regulations, to be observed at all times. I watch, I study, that such things may be strictly enforced. My eye, like that of the Almighty, must be upon all men at all times."

"You must find it a heavy labour."

"It is indeed a heavy labour, but shall I therefore complain? Well! Since you are resolved to wait upon the man Stainley, and since this shows at least some degree of filial respect, I will excuse and even encourage it. The wherry shall call for you. Stout men, pious men, shall accompany you to the stairs above London Bridge. They shall escort you through an ill neighbourhood of thieves and footpads, so that you suffer no harm. There! Since that is settled . . ."

"It is not settled, I fear. The pious men will lose their own labour if they come for me in a boat. Wherever I am going at nine o'clock I will look to myself and protect myself."

"Oh, what is this my ears are hearing?"

"They heard correctly. Did the head apprehend?"

"What an ill-regulated place," breathed Salvation Gaines, clasping his hands together, "is this palace of Whitehall, and how ill-regulated is the deportment of those who dwell therein! No porters with tipstaves at the doors! Your fault, the man Abraham's fault! And——what have we here? What have we here?"

Snatching up the light, he scurried to the chimneypiece

in the east wall communicating with Bygones's room. No fire burned here, but another red-leather fire bucket hung beside it. Salvation Gaines peered at this. He stalked back to the table and put down the candlestick.

"There are ways to teach you manners, most impious and impudent young man! Verily, verily there are ways to teach you manners! Not one drop of water in a bucket which by command must be kept filled. What should you do if fire, the symbol of men's fate in the hereafter, were at this moment to burst and consume? And what should you say if I tell you I mean to make report of your oversight?"

"Only that you fail to curdle my blood. Tell me much more and, by the bonfires of hell you are so fond of, I will fill that bucket and stick your head in it."

"Then what would you say," returned Gaines, "to a report of abduction or even murder?"

"*Eh?*" roared Bygones Abraham.

"At the Devil tavern, where I went in search of you." Gaines did not take his eyes from my grandfather, "a person answering your description was seen to leave at half past six o'clock. Captain Pembroke Harker of the Dragoons, who had dined there much earlier, was *not* seen to leave.

"He had paid his score, I made discovery; he might have departed unobserved of his own accord. Yet it is a most strange thing that towards seven o'clock an ensign of the Foot Guards, together with a sergeant and two men—by whose order?—called at that tavern and betook themselves abovestairs. A cart was seen to drive away in the rain from an alley behind the tavern. Was something perhaps lowered from the window? Had Captain Harker, being at best a bullying creature, paid his score in different fashion?"

Here Salvation Gaines began to laugh.

It was brief laughter, not very loud; but it clashed and rang eerily in that dim room before he choked it off to become fanatic-eyed again.

"And this wretched boy!" Gaines added. "Did he tell me, a while gone, that he did *not* this day consort with lewd women? Oh, did he not? When in fact he disported himself and made a tack at the foulest and most aban-

153

doned trull in the whole kingdom of—"

"Salvation Gaines," interrupted Kinsmere, "you could have said anything but that. Bygones, set open the door to the Shield Gallery."

"Gently, lad, gently! We can—"

"Bygones, set open the door to the Shield Gallery."

Bygones did so.

"Stand back!" yelped out Gaines, as Kinsmere advanced towards him. "Take but one more step, and I will . . ."

"Ay? You will what?"

Gaines uttered a screech like a strangled parrot. His right hand darted to the sheath pocket inside his coat. But whatever he may have been concealing there, he had no opportunity to draw it. Kinsmere, taking him by the back of the collar and the slack of the breeches, ran him across the room so fast and hard that Gaines's toes seemed barely to touch the carpet. On the threshold of the open doorway Kinsmere halted—and pitched him.

Salvation Gaines staggered across the width of the gallery, just saved by upflung hands from going face first into the opposite wall. He reeled, fell, and bounced to his feet like an India-rubber cat. He whipped round, the curls of his wig flying out. Once more his hand flew to the inside of his coat, but he checked the gesture.

"The Lord of Hosts," says he, "shall exact vengeance for *this!*"

"Is there anything else of which you would make report?" says Kinsmere. "Well, do you report it as you see fit."

And he slammed the door with a crash.

"Lad, lad," exclaimed Bygones Abraham, "surely that was a thought overhasty? Did you mark his laugh? And at what he laughed? And his voice? 'Had a gentleman's voice,' said the tapster; ' 'tis all I know.' And how twice his hand went to the pocket where most of us carry a dagger? By the great body o' Pilate, I would lay a hundred guineas to a Birmingham groat there's the merry fellow on the stairs at the Devil!"

"Yes; it occurred to me. Still—!"

"If we had questioned him unsparingly . . . Still," argued Bygones, who had commenced pacing, "still, as you say, should ha' learned much or gone far if we had?

154

He can be taken whenever we please, and questioned at Newgate or the Tower by men who know their business. Meanwhile, has he another bone-handled knife awaiting its uses? Of one more thing, though, we can have fair certainty. Come, lad! Into my room, now; 'tis more comfortable for discourse, and we have wine and tobacco. This way!"

He lumbered into his own withdrawing room. Kinsmere followed, taking the candle and restoring it to the table beside its companion. With the rain ceased and the warmth of May restored, a coal fire made the place uncomfortably hot. Bygones did not seem to mind this, though my grandfather did.

"Well?" said Kinsmere. "What's the one other thing of which we can feel certain?"

"Salvation Gaines, that murdering and sanctimonious hypocrite, was never sent here by the Duke of Bucks—either for an honest purpose or a dishonest one. Nay, I'll not credit it! My lord duke may one day become the king's enemy; but he is not an enemy now, unless he plays at a deeper game than any would think him capable of. Gaines comes to see us, either of his own accord or sent by the plotter-in-chief . . ."

"Why did he come? What was he at?"

"He was fishing for information, and mighty crudely too! Has the king intent to see us this night? Will His Majesty help us out o' the scrape Gaines put us in when he stabbed Harker? What's afoot in any case? Remember, save that they set most of the problems and we must solve 'em, they're as much in the dark as we are."

"Which may be called a good deal of darkness. Bygones, who *is* the plotter-in-chief?"

"Lad, am I Sir Oracle? I am not. It sticks in my gullet," retorted the other, "that there may be a dozen clues or indications all about, which we can't see even when we trip over 'em. As to who it *might* be . . ."

He discussed the matter at some length, pacing, with almost unintelligible comments in French and Latin. He took out an ornate watch and held it in his hand. He reviewed names, on which Kinsmere could pass no opinion since my grandfather knew none of the persons mentioned.

"And yet," Bygones said vehemently, "there is one

155

question I would have answered above all. This band of malcontents and their plotter-in-chief: what's the motive for the schemes they spin? If they laid hands on the terms of a none-too-pretty secret treaty, how would they use it?"

"Pull down the king? Destroy the throne?"

"And substitute whom? Plotting, d'ye see, is no mere labour o' love to a parcel of schoolboys, like tipping a beadle into a horse trough or greasing the stairs for your schoolmaster to go untimely down. If there's something or somebody you would overthrow, there must be something or somebody you would put in its place.

"Did they succeed in destroying the king, who'd take his place? The Duke of York? Not so, and not ever! The Duke of York is too much hated because he's suspected—only suspected—of being a Papist. Restore the Puritan Commonwealth? That's still more impractical and as wild as wind, because— Oh, ecod!"

Bygones stopped abruptly, staring hard beyond the windows towards the radiance of a rising moon.

"Come! There *is* a motive they might have and a game they might be at. It never occurred to me, though Pem Harker as good as told us. If you employ your wits, lad, you may see what it is!"

"I have been doing little else, but to no purpose. Something Gaines said was all wrong and misleading into the bargain, and yet for the life of me I can't call to mind what it was. There are other questions too. Where's Dolly now? Who put my saddlebags in that bedchamber, and why? Also—"

It was Kinsmere's turn to stop. Through the night stillness, through the faint rustle which marked Whitehall Palace, clove the voice of the bell named Old Tom striking nine.

"There's the signal," rumbled Bygones, shutting up his watch; "and we are summoned to the king. Put on your ring, lad! In this time of trouble, belike, they'll forgo the ceremony of having me pass in *my* ring for identification's sake. Still! Put on your ring; we'll see what comes of it. And one last word. You'll let fall no hint to anyone—to His Majesty least of all—that you guess at the terms of his secret treaty?"

"No word, no hint. Fool I may be, but not a drivelling damned fool."

"Nay, pox woebeescome! You are no fool at all, accept assurance, when you check haste and bend your mind to business. I hope the lass has been discreet too. This way to our fate, lad. Follow me."

PART III:

THE PUPPET MASTER

Here lies our Sovereign Liege the King,
   Whose word no man relies on—
Who never said a foolish thing,
   Nor ever did a wise one.

John Wilmot, Earl of Rochester

XII

The Shield Gallery, long and wide, was so deserted as to seem ghostly. A few wall candles threw murky gleams as they walked along it. The last door at the far end, in the south wall on their left, proved to be double doors firmly closed. Here the gallery branched to the right at right angles into another gallery: even longer and wider, well lighted, with a stone-flagged floor. Great paintings (Rubens, Correggio, Van Dyck, as Kinsmere afterwards learned) adorned the walls between its doors, and it was of a good height too.

"The Stone Gallery," whispered Bygones, though they saw nobody here either. "By day 'tis so thronged you must mark your step well, lest you butt head into another. Our own destination, these double doors on the left . . ."

"To the Great Bedchamber?"

"To the Great Bedchamber, by way of a withdrawing room. Stay, I'll adventure it!"

Bygones scratched with his fingernails at the panel, waited while you might have counted ten, and scratched again. There was another pause of perhaps twenty seconds. Then the doors were opened inwards by a tall, fragile-seeming, pale-faced man in a fair periwig, wearing much-beribboned clothes of green and white. His left hand carried a cane; his right held up a three-branched candelabrum of lighted tapers.

He exchanged no greetings and asked no questions. Nodding briefly to Bygones and bowing to both, he used the candelabrum to beckon. Once they were inside the withdrawing room, he closed the doors with the hand that held the cane.

"By your leave, gentlemen! His Majesty sups with my Lady Castlemaine, but has bade me fetch him as soon as you are come. Have you yourselves supped?"

"Nay, now!" protested Bygones, repressing hard his inclination towards oratory. "We dined very late, and are not hungry."

"So be it, then. If you will give yourselves the trouble of following me?"

The tall man in the fair periwig led them across the withdrawing room; and, through a doorway covered only by a black velvet curtain, into the Great Bedchamber beyond.

For all its spaciousness it was a stuffy place. Curtains had been closely drawn across the windows; another fire of Scotch coal burned under the chimneypiece's hood. On the hearth drowsed several spaniels, whose wet coats were odorous; they stiffened with a growl as the newcomers entered, but a word from the guide quietened them.

Looking round him, Kinsmere saw an enormous bedstead whose curtains bore the royal arms. On the carpet lay a rolled-up mattress: this mattress, Bygones whispered, was used at night by a Gentleman of the Bedchamber or a Groom of the Bedchamber, each appointed man doing duty a month at a time. But most of all, in the Great Bedchamber, you marked a noise of clocks. There were eight of them, all sizes and constructions, ticking and whirring away together, matching their beats against each other's. One asthmatic clock, far behind the others, was just striking nine.

The man in the fair periwig led them to another door, and up an enclosed flight of stairs to another room whose air was better, though it had a chemical sort of breath.

One window faced southeast above the Volary Garden; the other window, in the west wall, looked across a huddle of roof tops towards the Banqueting House. So still had the night become that, though both windows were set wide open, the flames scarcely stirred on the tapers in two candelabra of six branches each.

"By your leave, gentlemen," said their guide, "you will await His Majesty here. He will be short. And I need hardly counsel you: touch nothing!"

Then he was gone down the stairs.

"Oh, ah!" said Kinsmere, who had been staring round. "That was . . . ?"

"Rab Butterworth, Second Page of the Back-Stairs."

"He was as pale as those candles. Is the fellow ill?"

"Who can say? He is known as a great student of government. Much unlike Will Chiffinch, who troubles his head only with drink and the wenches."

"This is the king's private cabinet?"

"It is."

"His chymical laboratory too?"

"No, no! The chymical laboratory, under Dr. Williams, is in another part of the palace. Yet no doubt he tries experiment here, with whatever comes to hand."

No doubt he did. An open cupboard in one wall showed shelves of pills and physic powders. Underneath this, on a very narrow table, were retorts and beakers and packets of chemical salts, side by side with sheets of paper so very thin as to seem transparent: perhaps serving for some other experiment in chemistry. A ship model of a yawl decorated the top of a carved cabinet. Against the wall near this hung a large clock of curious design, having a spiral of brass tubing above it. *Pêle-mêle* mallets had been stacked into a corner. There were several comfortable chairs, as well as one straight chair which stood before an inlaid writing desk. On this desk rested one of the candelabra, above inkwell, sand caster, sealing wax, seals, and a tray of fine-quill pens.

Kinsmere wandered round examining each object in turn. Then he went to the open window above the Volary Garden, breathing deeply of warm, moist air.

"Bygones! Who would lurk in the Volary Garden, at nine of an evening and moonrise?"

"Come!" the other derided him. "None would 'lurk' there: where would be need or reason? Yet anyone might *be* in the garden; there are four doors. Why d'ye ask?"

"I could have sworn I saw the flicker of a face, and one in a hooded cloak who drew back."

"Oh, ecod! You are not seeing ghosts, it's to be hoped?"

"*I* hope not. This is a rare old rookery, the very place for 'em. Forgive me, though; I was wool-gathering."

He had little time for more wool-gathering. They heard voices from below in the Great Bedchamber: the light tones of Robert Butterworth mingled with the bass growl of a well-known great voice. Up the stairs came Butterworth, walking backwards and holding the candelabrum. Following him, in old black-velvet coat and breeches, black-and-white stockings, dull-red waistcoat, and black periwig, strode the man of whom Kinsmere had heard so much.

"If it please Your Majesty . . ."

"Stay, Mr. Butterworth. Have we not another visitor?"

"Waiting in the Volary Garden, Your Majesty. I—I scarce thought it fitting or proper to . . . to . . ."

"Pray allow *me* to be the judge of propriety, notorious though I am for lacking it. Escort the visitor up."

"As Your Majesty shall direct."

Butterworth opened an all-but-invisible door in the wall towards the Volary Garden, disclosing a very long staircase, or perhaps two staircases, descending between the shell of the walls. He went into the aperture, closing the door behind him. And the other man turned round.

King Charles wore no orders or decorations, no jewels, and only one plain ring. But there was a good deal of lace at his throat and wrists. The expression of his countenance, in repose, seemed severe or even forbidding. Yet when he smiled, as he did now, with the long red-brown eyes lighting up, all the charm of the Stuarts flowed out and was made manifest.

"Your servant, gentlemen," said the King of England.

"Sire!"

Bygones Abraham went down on one knee, pressing the other's hand to his forehead. This was the form of a first salutation, and no hand-kissing, as my grandfather had been taught years before. The king lifted up Bygones by raising his hand.

"And you, young sir—"

Kinsmere dropped on one knee for the same greeting.

"Nay, enough of these genuflections!" said the king. "I will be used with respect, and according to the Rules of Civility. But am I my cousin Louis of France, that men must pretend the sun shines in my presence or retires to cloud when I am no longer seen? Rise up, now! Grasp my hand in friendship, man,"—Kinsmere did so; it was a powerful grip,—"and know that a thoughtless fellow may be grateful."

"Sire," began Bygones, sweeping a great bow, "the agglomerations of honour high-stacked on this auspicious occasion . . ."

"Indeed, yes. Indeed, yes! At the one side, God's fish, we have my old friend Bygones Abraham, who rode with the cavalry in Worcester fight twenty years ago. At the other side . . . you, I think, must be Mr. Kinsmere the younger. Is your name Alan too?"

"Nay, sire, it is Roderick or even Rowdy. But—but, under favour, sire," cries my grandfather, beginning to stammer and then made easy by the other's ease, "I had thought you unacquainted with me. That letter of a while gone—"

"Oh, that! The letter was not writ in my hand, which is a vile one; amid so many listening ears, I deemed it best to use caution. Nor did I in fact know your name until early this night. Howbeit! Immediately after the play, as you must be aware, Mistress Dolly Landis comes to me with a tale I could not disregard."

"Sire, Captain Harker—"

"In the matter of Captain Harker, bear up and be easy! He will be reported as having died while honourably engaged about his duties. Saving a great noise of scandal, what else would you have me do?"

"Ecod, Your Majesty," interposed Bygones, "but this is good hearing for both of us! Still, touching the question of this lad's identity . . ."

"Yes, let's consider it," said the king, looking Kinsmere in the eyes. "You visited the palace this morning, I believe?"

"I did, sire."

"Well! Let any man walk for five minutes through this gossip mart, in particular a stranger, and his postures are observed by all. He need but drink a cup of wine, ogle a servant maid, or do nothing whatever: report of it flies to every nook and corner.

"I was at public dinner in the Gallery," King Charles nodded towards the west window and the Banqueting House, "when they told me of a young man, a stranger, seen in company with Bygones Abraham. I did not heed this or indeed think on it until, much later in the day, comes Mistress Landis with *her* account."

He paused. The door to the hidden staircase opened; Butterworth entered. Butterworth, holding up the candelabrum, stood to one side and admitted a woman in a hooded grey cloak and vizard mask.

It was Dolly herself, as Kinsmere had thought when he caught a glimpse of her unmasked in the garden. His pulses jumped as usual. Under the grey cloak of that afternoon she was now resplendent in a low-cut gown of dark-blue velvet slashed with white, and a string of pearls round her neck. She threw back the hood of her cloak, whipped off the mask, and gave the king a deep curtsy, to which he replied with a bow.

"Give you good evening, Madam Landis. It was kind of you to join us. You are well, I hope?"

"I am well indeed and much honoured to be here, though a thought fearful. Oh, dear! Oh, damme!"

"Nay, madam, it is we who are honoured. Nor need you have any cause for fear.—Mr. Butterworth!"

"Your Majesty?"

"Be good enough to take Madam Landis's mask and cloak. Good; thank you. Put them on the chair there. Then you had better go to the Gallery. In the Gallery tonight," King Charles continued to Dolly, nodding again in the direction where chinks of light glimmered through closed curtains on the long windows of the Banqueting House, "they play at basset and listen to string music. Music with cards makes an excellent good diversion; we can pretend to take no notice when the ladies cheat. Bid them begin without me, Mr. Butterworth! Say I am unavoidably detained, but will be there presently. And—Mr. Butterworth!"

The Second Page of the Back-Stairs, on his way down

to the Great Bedchamber, halted and looked up.

"Your Majesty?"

"Have you by chance seen the key to my writing desk?"

"No, sire; I had thought Your Majesty kept it always by him."

"It is lost or mislaid, then; I have not got it. Come, we'll make no great noise of this! 'Tis a trivial thing, and I an idle fellow who deserve the loss. That is all, Rab. You may go."

Butterworth disappeared, closing the door at the foot of the Great Bedchamber stairs.

For a moment the king's eyes, in a long face almost the colour of a red Indian's, seemed hooded and far away. Then he sauntered towards the writing desk, set the tips of his fingers on top of it, and looked round.

"What was I saying? Ah, yes. God's fish, gentlemen! At the play this afternoon Madam Landis conveyed a note to me by most ingenious means, and would see me in my glass-coach* ere I departed. The tale she poured out, though something lacking in coherence, was a heart-felt one. For the most part in hymned praise of an impoverished young man, a very hero out of Homer, with a taste for fighting noted swordsmen in dark rooms. His name or quality she did not know; but gave me a description of such lyricism, sir, that I spare you the embarrassment of hearing it. God's fish, we have a young lady fairly smitten!"

Dolly, pink in the face, looked across at the ship model on the cabinet with an air of not being there at all.

"Bethinking me," pursued the king, "bethinking me of the young man earlier seen with Bygones Abraham, I put certain questions when I returned home. By some strangeness it was my Lord Arlington—that monument of dignity, that seeming mock-astrologer to look at!—who made answer. '*I* saw the youth,' says my Lord Arlington, 'on my way to the council office at past eleven this morning. He was a stranger, yet bore striking resemblance to the late Alan Kinsmere: who flung away a fortune in your father's cause and your own, if you recall this?' Indeed, I recalled it; Alan Kinsmere was with me on my travels. 'A

---

* A coach with glass windows, a comparatively recent innovation.

son?' 'Most probably.' 'Since how long is he in London? Where does he lodge?' 'I can't say,' replies my Lord Arlington, 'yet Alan Kinsmere was used to favour the Grapes near Charing Cross.' Whereat, after disptaching Ensign Westcott to deal with the business of Pembroke Harker, I caused inquiries to be made at the Grapes. For already I was in a great quandary."

"A quandary, sire?" blurted out Bygones.

"If I have not dealt in entire frankness either with you, Madam Landis, or with you, Mr. Abraham, I ask your pardon. I will now deal with you all as frankly as I dare."

The king walked over and looked down the stairs towards the Great Bedchamber, as though to make sure the door was closed. To Kinsmere it seemed imperfectly latched, but he made no comment.

"Two halves of a certain document must go to France this night. I cannot delay or I am undone. Mr. Abraham will carry one half. Since I had already determined Captain Harker must not have the other, to whom should I give it?

"I put my trust in few people, having small cause to do so. But I would trust a Kinsmere. I would trust the man who carried himself as you did this day at the Devil. Though so many hazards attend it, and the rewards at best must be poor, will you render me this great service?"

"By God, I will!"

("Lad, lad," whispered Bygones, "mind your language!")

"Will you render this service, sir, without asking what it is you carry? Or what I myself am about in my designs?"

"Sire, I will."

"Well! So sure was I of having my humour met that, once your identity was established, I did command your belongings removed from the Grapes to a set of rooms off the Shield Gallery here at Whitehall. It was an unwarranted liberty, I know. Do you pardon it?"

" 'Pardon' it, for God's sake!"

("Lad! Lad!")

"Come!" said the king, with a look of sleepy affability. He sauntered back to the desk, sat down in the straight chair, and stretched out his long legs. "I would not embarrass a needy gentleman with too much talk of reward. And

Parliament contrive, as I have warned you, that my service shall be a poor one. But enter it, I beg of you! Be employed by me; and, difficult or dubious though the employment may be, we can find you a thousand or two a year to lighten the burden, with other preferments in good times. But perhaps this had already occurred to you? I see you took the precaution to remove Captain Harker's ring and wear it on your own finger."

"No, sire, I did not."

"No?"

"The ring you see here is my own property. It was given to my father by King Charles the First, of glorious memory; only by accident is it the symbol of a King's Messenger. And, though I will do right willingly whatever you bid me, I am in no need of money or preferments for reward."

"No need of . . *how?* Sure Alan Kinsmere *was* ruined in the Great Rebellion, as I have good cause to know?"

"He was so, Your Majesty. The fortune I inherit comes from my mother, who was Edward Depping's daughter of Bristol. It is not one of the great fortunes, but it should keep me pretty comfortable for the rest of my life. And also—"

A strange expression had crossed the face of Dolly Landis. If Kinsmere could not miss this, being so intensely conscious of her physical nearness, he was far from sure he knew what it meant. But he had no time to consider her feelings.

A quizzical look lifted one of King Charles's eyebrows. He rose to his feet.

"Stay; I forget hospitality! God's fish, this will never do! Madam Landis, pray be seated. A chair; allow me; so. And you, gentlemen, take chairs as well. First, however, be good enough to give me your rings. Both of them."

In a moment all four were seated. Dolly, in a padded chair with one bare elbow on the chair arm and her cheek propped against her fist, seemed hardly to breathe. King Charles, beside the desk, examined both sapphire rings; and then, evidently satisfied that they were the same, put them down on the desk.

"Oh, this is *wicked!*" Dolly burst out.

"Come, madam—"

"It is wicked and cruel and unfair, and it's just my luck too!"

"Madam, these rings . . ."

"Oh, so-and-so your rings!" Tears rose to the brown eyes; Dolly's mouth trembled. "I would have done so much for him, and now I can't. Dost know," she addressed Bygones Abraham, "dost know what I did, or tried to do, ere the New Exchange should close at nine? I went there and bought him a shirt: a silk shirt with frills on it!"

"*Another* shirt, is it?" breathed Bygones. "Oh, ecod!"

"And a cloak with a pink satin lining. And I would have got him a set of clothes, and shoes as well, save that I could not tell the size . . . !"

"Madam—" the king began.

"It had a pink satin lining!" cried Dolly, completely carried away. "The cloak had a pink satin lining. Was ever such ill-fortune in all this world?"

"God's fish!" said King Charles the Second. "All honest men, madam, will share your misery in the matter of the pink satin lining. Yet you should moderate these transports and your voice. Your presence here tonight is doubtless known. From this fact, coupled with my own failure to be present in the Gallery, divers inferences will be drawn. I do not object to a general belief that I am attempting to captivate you. But I must beg you not to make it appear that I am murdering you in assailing your virtue."

"Dolly—" interposed Kinsmere.

"No, no; go *'way!*"

"Enough of this!" the king said sharply. "You have wits in your head, madam. Have you *no* notion of what else may be occurring around me? Can you make no helpful suggestion at all?"

"I w-would know, then, why there are so many soldiers here tonight?"

"Soldiers? Are there soldiers?"

Dolly, who had pressed a handkerchief to her nose, merely looked at him through tears.

"Well!" said the king, drawing a deep breath and again getting up. "Let me be as honest as I am capable of being. We walk amid rogues and knaves; yes, and amid dangers too. There has been no violence here since the days of old

167

Harry the Eighth; and I anticipate none now, yet—"

There was a sharp *plink* as something struck an upper pane of the window above the Volary Garden. Bygones Abraham was on his feet, rapier halfway out of its scabbard.

"Come, man, this is not needful! Put by your sword until we have some use for it. But it may be that I have set something of a trap. And I think the trap is sprung."

King Charles went to the window, peered out, and made a gesture. Then, moving well to the left of the window, he set open that very inconspicuous door leading to the long stairway hidden between inner and outer wall. He went out on the little landing of this stairway, leaving the door open, and peered down into gloom. Footfalls on stone steps could be heard mounting at a rapid pace, amid echoes rolling inside the walls.

The king bent forward and spoke softly.

"Ensign Westcott?"

"Your Majesty?"

Up into sight, though still shadowed, appeared a hard-eyed young officer of Foot Guards, with black periwig and narrow line of moustache like the king's own. He held a drawn sword in his right hand, and clutched his hat to his head with the other.

The king made a further gesture, whereat Ensign Westcott bent close and whispered in a rapid mumble.

"Where? When?"

Another rapid mumble.

"God's fish, is it so? Did you make search of his person?"

"A little money, Your Majesty, and a key. Nothing else."

"Return the money to his pockets. Give me the key."

Mumbled questions drove at the curls of the king's periwig.

"Do with him, God's fish? For the moment, at least, let him be held below in the garden. I will give instructions presently. And for this aid much thanks."

Booted footsteps went clattering back down. King Charles returned, closing the door behind him.

"Yes, the trap is truly sprung. They have taken Rab Butterworth."

168

"Taken Rab Butterworth!" exclaimed Bygones Abraham. "Ecod, sire—!"

"He would have left us in haste by way of the public water stairs, with the key to my writing desk in his pocket. Save that guards were posted there in case he did. Mr. Butterworth said he was on an errand for me—and lied."

A look less than amiable had pinched down the king's eyelids and deepened the furrows from his nostrils. Holding out a small key in the palm of his hand, he tossed the key into the air and caught it again.

"I have been much vexed," he continued, "by a certain flow of information from the state apartments themselves. Should my love letters to Julia or Araminta be thus indecorously unveiled? But could I damn a man without proof? Nay, that were too much! He must damn himself.

"Enough: I will be less fanciful and come to business. Leagued against us—ask Madam Landis—we have a band of malcontents and their plotter-in-chief. These would most passionately desire to know whether this night I had intent to send a messenger or messengers to France. If honest Butterworth were not so honest, he would listen with all his ears and then make haste to carry away the news. I gave him opportunity to listen, though not hear too much, by sending him on a useless errand to the Gallery. Useless, I do assure you! In the Gallery they have already their instructions. Music and cardplay, as well, are to begin precisely at nine-thirty. And the time now . . ."

He strode back towards the writing desk. From the direction of the Great Bedchamber, past a door imperfectly shut, rose the fluid chimes of a wall clock striking the half hour after nine. Another joined it, and then another. Several clocks were striking at once, including Old Tom in the Palace Yard, when the music of a string trio could be heard too. Distant and yet clear in nightstillness, past windows curtained but open, it rose with the strains of "I Pass All My Hours in a Shady Old Grove."

"Yes, yes," the king said rather snappishly, "*I* wrote the words to that song. Pray don't commend me again; I wish now I had not. Besides, we have affairs at hand."

He unlocked the desk and raised its lid. Taking out two sheets of thick plain foolscap, he lowered the desk lid and put them down.

169

"Before I give you precise commands, gentlemen, I confess this matter of the conspirators troubles me not a little. As regards the identity of the plotter-in-chief I am in some doubt. As for the smaller fry, of whom fortunately there are not many, I could hazard more than a guess. Butterworth? Ay: proved! There is a crawling Puritan called Salvation Gaines . . ."

"Oh, ecod!" roared Bygones Abraham. "Your Majesty has good cause to be troubled. With Gaines here this night . . ."

"The fellow is here? God's fish, why does none tell me these things? He may come and go without hindrance, true; shall I close my hand until I have hanging evidence? Still, notwithstanding—!"

"Sire, he is close at hand! He would have lured this lad away on a fool's pretext. I will take my oath he carries another—"

Bygones never finished. Sudden commotion erupted in the garden below. It was not loud, and was soon checked. But they heard a gasp, followed by choking or thrashing sounds, an oath, smothered speech, and two lowered but desperate voices speaking articulate words:

"Where?"

"Through the arch behind you! Run, but make no noise!"

There was another sharp *ping* as a pebble struck an upper pane of the window and then rattled down on the sill. The king whipped round. Kinsmere, who had been looking at Dolly, jumped to his feet with a cold premonition it needed no soothsaying to induce.

The door to the hidden stairway was now open, and King Charles stood on the landing. Booted footsteps pounded upstairs at a run, yet it seemed minutes before Ensign Westcott appeared out of gloom. This time the king did not trouble to gesture for a whisper.

"Yes?"

"By God and His holy angels," said the pale-faced young officer, "I swear this could not have been prevented. And yet he made escape!"

"Butterworth made escape?"

"Not so, may it please Your Majesty. Butterworth stood between Thompson and Sergeant Drake, they each

holding one of his arms. They did not observe one who
crept on them unawares, from the back. See, here's blood
on my own hand; yet I did but touch him when he fell forward!"

"Who fell forward? What of Butterworth?"

"He is dead or dying, may it please you. He was
stabbed. Through the back of the neck. With a bone-
handled knife."

XIII

The too-sugary music tinkled in the distance. A light
breath of wind sent golden ripplings along the candle
flames.

"Under favour, Your Majesty, look not so black as a
thundercloud! I swear this could not be helped. And yet, if
I am to blame . . ."

"Nobody blames you, Ensign Westcott. But—did you
see this assassin who stabbed Butterworth?"

"Only a glimpse of his back, Your Majesty. He did bolt
under the arch and into a passage west through the palace.
Thompson was after him at once; Thompson is fleet of
foot, and will be like to overtake him."

"What was he like, in the glimpse you had of his back?"

"Middle size; dark clothes; iron-grey periwig, but
moved like a younger man. And must have much blood on
him."

Kinsmere, remembering a man of this description, was
about to intervene. But it was not necessary.

"Ensign, our assassin *must* be found. Is the sergeant
still below?"

"Yes, Your Majesty."

"Bid him convey word to your captain. All guards at
ways out of the palace should be warned. Inside, a search
must be made for such a man with blood on him. Whether
or not he is guilty, there is one person who must be
sought, found, and brought to me for questioning. His
name is Salvation Gaines. He—"

"I know the fellow; I have seen him!"

"Good! Look to it at once. Was the knife left in the vic-
tim's neck? As with Harker? You nodded? Good! Fetch it

171

out and bring it to me. First see that it be well cleansed."

"Your Majesty, I swear——"

"Come, man, you shall incur no blame! Look to your duties; that is all."

The ensign clattered downstairs. Sombre, dark of humour, the lines deepening in his face, King Charles returned to his cabinet and faced the other three.

"God's fish, what a pass we are come to! I would I had more knowledge in the handling of these matters, and may yet have need to call for Sir Orlando Bridgeman. Howbeit, we must do what we can. Madam Landis, I would not too much distress you with talk of blood or knifings . . ."

"Nay, sire, I am not overmuch distressed. And shall I of all people be affrighted at what is against the law?"

"Or the rest of us either, for that matter? Now, gentlemen, as touches your mission to France."

A sardonic smile twisted the king's mouth. He went to his writing desk and sat down.

"I will tell you as much as is needful. Pray believe me that I dare tell no more. Time and arrangements have already been altered. They must be altered a little still more. It may require an hour or so to lay hand on this assassin. Once he is taken and questioned, we should learn much of interest. You had better not go until midnight, either of you. That is near enough to Mr. Abraham's usual time of departure, when he goes downriver to the sloop *Saucy Ann*. You, Mr. Kinsmere, since you are new to this work . . ."

"By your leave, sire: we go to Paris?"

"To Calais only. The situation stands thus. Near the sloop *Saucy Ann* are anchored two warships: *Royal Standard,* fifty-eight guns, and *Rupert,* fifty guns, but these are not to be employed for several days. Some part of the French court is now in the north, at Dunkirk."

"They are at Dunkirk, and therefore we go to Calais?"

"Even so. You will learn in a moment that the matter is not mysterious. You speak French, of course?"

"Only stumbling, sire, and after a fashion."

"Tush, lad!" interjected another rumbling voice. "With *me* to aid ye——"

"Yes, Mr. Abraham, yes! Your linguistic achievements are well known. Yet you travel by different ways, remember."

"I said, Sire, that my own speaking of the French language . . ."

"Well, well!" the king remarked indulgently. "The lady with whom you will deal, Mr. Kinsmere, is English. She is my young sister, the Princess Henrietta Anne; she is married to a fantastical character, the French king's brother, whom I could wish to perdition and beyond. So far as the language is concerned, it will suffice if you can manage, 'An English admirer begs leave to speak with Madame.' "

" 'An English admirer begs leave to speak with Madame.' "

"Yes. On the success of your mission depends the issue of whether Madame d'Orléans shall be permitted to visit this country a few days hence. Should it befall according to plan, on Monday of next week our men-o'-war *Royal Standard* and *Rupert* will sail for Dunkirk to escort her to Dover. Meanwhile, in a French ship called *La Gloire*, Madame d'Orléans pays a brief visit to Calais for the express purpose of a meeting with my messengers. Why, you will ask?"

"But I don't ask!"

"God's fish, why not? Dunkirk and Calais are no great distance apart. My cousin Louis believes a meeting will attract less attention so. He also thinks Calais to be his 'fortunate town,' as I have heard him call it. When Madame d'Orléans shall be at Dover, where I propose to meet her next week, the King of France will be throned in state at Calais should we have need to—to confer with him. Eh, the dignity of my cousin Louis! Now, Mr. Kinsmere . . ."

"Sire?"

"At the quarter hour to midnight, then, you and Bygones Abraham will return here and receive what you are to carry. You already have a horse, which will not be needed. Another horse will be provided; it will be saddled and waiting in the Great Court at midnight precisely. At the top of King Street, near my father's statue, Captain Mather of the Horse Guards Blue will also be waiting. Captain Mather will ride with you east through the City and across London Bridge to Southwark, where he will put you on the road to Dover.

"From London to Dover is something under eighty miles. Here," and the king fished through his pockets, "here, writ on a scrap of paper which the late Rab But-

173

terworth has *not* seen, are the names of three inns between London and Dover. At each of these inns a fresh
horse will be provided when you show your ring. Arrived
at Dover, you will seek Grand Neptune Wharf and an inn
called the Easy Mariners. Here you will find a French
shipmaster, Captain Souter, whose English is fluent as Mr.
Abraham's French. Captain Souter will carry you across
the Straits, and tell you what to do on the other side. Is all
that clear?"

"Very clear."

"Repeat your instructions."

Kinsmere did so.

"That is well; the rest I leave to you. I need not stress
the difficulties or dangers in your path. Ride hard, but
beware of traps; there are those would stop you at any
cost. Nor need I stress——"

All were wrought to such a pitch that all started when
there was a light knock outside the door to the hidden
stairway. King Charles rose and opened it, revealing the
dogged but still uneasy face of Ensign Westcott.

"Well, man? Have you found——?"

"Humbly craving pardon, Your Majesty, but we must
be permitted a little *time!*"

"Have I pressed you so sharply?"

"No, Your Majesty, but——! The search goes forward;
the palace is a large place; there are those in the Gallery
who protest at being questioned or examined. None has
been discovered in any fashion blood-stained, but this is
only a question of time."

"What of Salvation Gaines?"

"He has not been seen, or made attempt to leave the
palace; indeed, with all guards warned, he can't escape;
but this also, if I might urge it upon you, is only a matter
of time!"

"Return to the search, then."

"Right willingly, Your Majesty, and at once. However,
you did ask for *this.*"

Across the palm of his hand he held out a knife with a
bone haft; haft and blade had been washed and then
scoured with sand. King Charles took the knife as the
door closed, and turned it over in his fingers. It was a
lightweight knife with a blade some six inches long, very

sharp and tapering to a sword point.

"Body o' Pilate!" said Bygones Abraham. "If Your Majesty looks to find initials—"

"No; I but wondered at the nature of the weapon. It is not truly a weapon. Such knives are carried by most scriveners. My clerks use them for cutting quills."

"Mr. Scrivener Salvation Gaines. Oh, ecod, do we need more proof than this?"

"No more proof, but the man himself. And we will have him."

With a twitch of repulsion King Charles threw the knife on the desk, where it clattered down beside the thick sheets of writing paper and the two gold-and-sapphire rings.

"And now, Madam Landis and gentlemen, since I myself have much work which must be finished before midnight, I will beg leave to be excused. *You,* madam, trouble me not a little. Though I apprehend no great danger to yourself, yet you have learned more of these plotters' affairs than it is good for any woman to know. I had better send you home in a glass-coach, with running footmen to make sure you suffer no harm."

"If I may speak, sire," interposed Kinsmere, "would it not be possible for Dol—for Madam Landis herself to remain here until midnight?"

"It would be more than possible. It shall be so arranged."

"And if I may speak—?" cried Dolly.

"Yes, Madam?"

For all her air of would-be ease, Dolly had flinched and gone pale when the knife was handed over. She still would not look at it, but she would not look at Kinsmere either. She rose from her chair, taking the cloak off its arm. Candlelight lay softly on her brown hair; it warmed the returning colour of face and throat and shoulders. Yet there was something on her mind.

"You invited me here," she said, "but to provide an excuse for your absence from that place where they play the music. That's all it was!"

"Only in part, I assure you. The pleasure of your company—"

"I am of no use or service to anyone, least of all to *him.*

175

Well, I know that; I don't complain! But I think I had better leave."

"Come!" said the King. "It would be most unseemly, madam, were I forced to show sternness and issue commands. I had flattered myself that *I* was behaving as a noble fellow should; don't destroy the consolation. God's fish, what's this? Here are two young people on a summer evening . . ."

"Bah! Twice bah! three times bah!"

"You have well over two hours before midnight. You have the whole broad palace to roam in; you have a set of rooms at your disposal. If you fail to employ the time profitably, madam, you are not the woman I think you are. And I have but one last word." Hearing a stir in the Great Bedchamber below, he raised his voice. "Mr. Chiffinch!"

Up the steps from the Great Bedchamber marched a hook-nosed Hercules in a brown periwig, somewhat bleary around the eyes.

"This is Will Chiffinch, my First Page of the Back-Stairs, whom you may intrust absolutely. Will, may I make you known to Mistress Dorothy Landis, Mr. Roderick Kinsmere, Mr. Bygones Abraham?—Do you follow me, Mr. Chiffinch?"

"Attentively, sire."

"See to it that one of my glass-coaches shall be ready for Madam Landis in the Great Court at midnight, to convey her to her lodgings off Bow Street. Let it be near the place where Mr. Kinsmere's horse is tethered. For the moment, Mr. Chiffinch, kindly escort this lady, and these gentlemen to the Shield Gallery. I pass all my hours in a shady old grove. Hey, St. George for England!"

The king chuckled to himself. He sat down at the desk. In the last glimpse they had of him, turned dark and cryptic once more, he had stretched out a hand towards the pen tray, and was humming the tune of the distant strings.

Chiffinch led them across the Great Bedchamber and the withdrawing room. When he had bowed them out into the dusky Shield Gallery, shutting the double doors, they stood for a moment in silence. Dolly, cloak across her arm, looked sulkily at a pair of dying wall candles.

"Within two and a quarter hours," announced Bygones Abraham, "a boat o' brisk boys will call for this old hulk and take him down to my old friend and bottle companion, Captain Nick Murch of the *Saucy Ann*. Meanwhile, as befits a man of reflection, I betake myself to the Gallery; I drink a cup or two at leisure; I watch 'em at their cards. What of you two?"

"Now wherefore," demanded a ladylike Dolly, "does this man say 'you two' as though Mr. Kinsmere and I were together?"

"Because we *are* together," said the villain of that name, "and for as long as may be. Dolly, will you walk with me?"

"No, I will not."

"*Dolly!*"

"We-el . . . Walk where?"

"Surely there must be gardens here? Gardens, that's to say, apart from that cursed Volary one of knives-in-the-back, where two of minds attuned may gain a breath of air and a look at the moon in peace and comfort?"

"There are gardens in plenty," returned Bygones. "There's the whole of St. James Park. There are also knives behind trees."

"If you mean Dolly's friend Salvation Gaines . . ."

"*My* friend Salvation Gaines?"

"I affected sarcasm, madam, as you affect things that are foreign to your nature. As for Salvation Gaines, they will have him at any minute!"

"Will they, lad? How if they don't?"

"They will take him, I say! He is a murdering hypocrite; he would kill me if he could; but he is no ghoul or warlock to alter shape and walk past the guards. *Can* he escape, do you think?"

"It may be not," snapped Bygones, firing up. "Still! Venture this night into open spaces, any open spaces; you'll go scarce ten paces ere you are again detained and examined by the military, which is no notion o' pleasure for anybody. If so deeply you crave air and the moon, minds attuned or not, get you both to the balcony overlooking the private landing stairs!"

"Where is that?"

"Oh, ecod! I drew it to your attention this morning. Straight along to the eastern end of the Shield Gallery here, and open the door. 'Tis where the maids of honour stand to throw flowers during water processions; but at this hour 'twill be as deserted as any place you could wish for, strike me dead!"

"Bygones, my compliments and thanks. Madam, this way; accompany me."

Dolly swore she would not, and then promptly went with him. She put on her cloak and adjusted the vizard mask. In silence, Dolly flinching away when their arms touched, they marched to the other end of the gallery and found the door.

They were on a balustraded balcony high above water. For all the fact that smoke drifted at them, that the river could be called little less than a stately sewer, it was a spot to stir anyone. Small craft slid past against the dark Thames, with little lanthorns burning at masthead; the distant Surrey shore lay unveiled in pale light; and above Whitehall Palace hung the old chipped battle lanthorn of the moon.

"Dolly, what's the matter?"

"There is nothing the matter! And what do we do here? Do you so truly desire to look at the moon?"

"I desire to look at *you*."

He removed her mask, which she snatched away and thrust into a pocket of her cloak. In that light her face was pale and her eyes, at close range, seemed enormous.

"As though anyone," Dolly cried, "could wish to look at me! When I am only blundering and silly—when I am of no use or value—"

"You are of the world's value, sweet heart. Because you are the loveliest sight in God His creation; because you are all good nature and dear nature; because head and heart were both lost when I saw you; because . . ."

"Don't do that!"

He disregarded her. "Would you prefer that I refrained from touching you?"

"No, you know I would not! Continue, dear idiot, for ever and ever! But what do we do *here,* I say? You have rooms at the palace, someone remarked?"

"I have, though I never asked for 'em, and they are not far away. Would you go there with me?"

"Would I go there with you? Dear God, would I *not* go there with you? Try me, then; oh, please try me!"

178

And so, it appears, they stumbled their way back along the Shield Gallery. Of the ensuing two hours I have never heard a precise description, nor is one required. But it was an interval of ecstasy, which neither of them ever forgot. Certain persons are so well suited to each other that nothing else seems at all important. They made discovery of this; they discovered it again, and yet again. Time fled past on exchanged wings, or stood still when necessary.

"Is it so ill a thing, Dolly, that I am not a penniless wandering mountebank? That I have no need of frilled shirts or any shirts; and, to say a truth, would not be seen dead in a cloak with a pink satin lining? Is this so ill a thing?"

"No, it is not. I thought it was, but it is not. Nothing matters, dear heart, except—"

"Dolly . . ."

"Yes! Yes, yes, *yes!*"

It was with a shock as of cold water that they heard Old Tom ring the quarter hour to midnight. Presently, after a series of farewells, Dolly got up and scrambled into her clothes by moonlight.

"Are you in such haste to leave, madam?"

"Haste to leave? I would stay for ever! But *you* cannot. Strike a light and dress yourself. You are late already; the time—"

"Where do *you* go?"

"But to inquire if the coach be ready. I will see you away; never fear. And yet, sweet heart . . ."

"No; you have said it; time presses; go!"

Kinsmere, now more in love than he would have believed possible, found that this interfered with speed of dressing. But other clothes were in the saddlebags: a leather jerkin, fustian breeches, and boots to which he affixed the spurs. He wore his usual sword belt, but slung a dagger sheath under his left arm. Finally he buckled a cloak round his shoulders, and discarded his periwig for a broad-leafed hat which fitted his own hair.

It had finished striking midnight when he strode out into the Shield Gallery, on his way to get last instructions from the king. Just outside the door he met Bygones Abraham, dressed in much the same fashion except for spurs, and lumbering in the same direction.

"Well?" Bygones demanded, with a somewhat sinister inflection.

"Mighty well!"

"I am glad ye find it so. I don't, nor do many others. They have not taken Gaines."

"Not taken Gaines?"

"Nay, or any man who might ha' killed Butterworth. *Is* the fellow a ghoul or a warlock, ecod, that he can alter shape and fly out the window? If so, my fine adventurer, look sharp on the Dover road!"

"It will be best to look sharp in any case. Here we are."

They scratched at the double doors of the withdrawing room outside the Great Bedchamber. They did not see the king. But in the withdrawing room they met Will Chiffinch, who told them they were fifteen minutes late but that the king said it did not matter.

Each received the half of a thick sheet of foolscap: folded over, sealed, wrapped in oilskin, and fitted into a pouch with leather thongs which they slung round their necks under the shirt. Each received back his ring. Then they were returning, along the Shield Gallery and belowstairs, by the same way they had come that morning. On the ground floor, near the doorway to the brick arches beside the Great Court, Bygones hesitated.

"Ayagh!" he said. "The king may not be vexed, no; but those tars from the *Saucy Ann* will show a most almighty vexation to be kept waiting. Well, lad, good luck!" Gauntlet slapped gauntlet as they shook hands. "O-revwar and ah-lah-been-too! If all goes well and we cock a snook at the Enemy, we'll be drinking a dram in Calais tomorrow afternoon."

Then he was gone.

Into the Great Court moonlight poured a deathly radiance. String music still skipped and jingled behind the closed curtains of the Banqueting House; there was a stir as of many people. The Great Court, save for coach and horses with the driver sound asleep on the box, seemed deserted. It was not so. Kinsmere had no sooner stepped out under the arches than the glimmer of a lanthorn sprang up; a sentry challenged him. He displayed his ring; the lanthorn light dwindled away and vanished.

Dolly was waiting for him near the coach. Though he

had seen her so short a time ago, he felt his heart beating so powerfully that at first he could not speak. Every one of her humours, her tricks of laughter or intensity, her breathless little ingenuous speeches in the dark, returned to overwhelm him. He took her inside the fold of his cloak, stammering that he must see her into the coach; but she only shook her head, slowly and quietly, with her arms round his neck.

Then he moved over towards a horse that was tethered nearby: a black mare seventeen hands high, restive and skitting its tail in the court. There were saddlebags here too, and saddle holsters for pistols as well. He quietened the mare, inspected the bit, saw to saddle and girths, all without conscious knowledge of what he was doing. In the saddlebags he found a pouch of money, bread and cheese wrapped in oiled paper, with a small flask of rum; last of all, a supply of powder, ball, and wadding for the pistols.

From a holster he drew one of these weapons: the dragoon's heavy wheel-lock, with a barrel over a foot long. The music had ceased; but in night-stillness a great rustling of trees swept from the direction of the park. Bending over to look at the wheel-lock, its silvered mechanism glistening by moonlight, he caught sight of Dolly's face. He returned the wheel-lock to his holster, and swung back to her.

"Oh, I am so afeared!" Dolly whispered.

"Afeared?"

"You are such a *fool:* which is to say you run such enorm hazard and would pull the beard of Old Nick himself if you thought he would try to daunt you. I would not have you different, yet I fear I may never see you again!"

"You will see me again. Great pity though you may regard it, it can't be helped."

"*Great pity,* do I regard it? Dear heart, you will take care?"

"I will take care."

"When do you return?"

"In a day or two, not much more. Since the business is pressing, say forty-eight hours in all. And then, my dear, *and then . . .*"

"Will you look at French women, while you are gone?"

"I will not, even should I see any. But you, Dolly! Will

181

you be waiting, when I do return?"

"You know I will."

Suddenly she put her head down and spoke very low and rapidly, slurring the words together as though she could not get through it fast enough.

"Godbless you and—and guard you, and—and keepyousafe—from harm."

Putting her away from him, he swung into the saddle. The black mare reared, whinnying, and came down with a strike of sparks from cobbles. Then they were off through the gateway. At the top of King Street, near Charles the First's statue, he was to meet Captain Somebody, of the Horse Guards Blue, who would guide him through the City and across London Bridge. What he felt was no triumph, but a great wrench at the heart and almost a sting of tears behind the eyes, as the mare thundered up King Street in pursuit of the Grand Design.

XIV

The moon was setting, sickly and with a faint yellowish colour round its edges, as though it were dying too. A wind far away made faint roaring noises; there was a whisper among sedge and coarse grass. But it did not disturb the mist in hollows of the road.

Kinsmere shifted in the saddle of the fourth horse he had ridden between London and here. The clocks had gone three-thirty; the short night was beginning to pale; he was nearing the Channel.

To have covered above seventy miles in three and a half hours was a pace more rapid than he had ever expected to travel. A salt smell drifted across marshes. Long strips of sea water had got in among the grass, and lay as though stagnant with a flicker of the moon across them. He thought he had never seen so dead or lonely a spot. It was cold, and unutterably still. The latest horse settled to a steady gallop; the sound of its hoofs pounded out against empty spaces where the wind answered with the only noise. Loosening the cord on his hat, he dropped it down his back to let the chill air stream in his face and keep him awake. He was conscious of saddle soreness, of an ache in his joints, and his back and shoulders were tired too. The insistence of sleep crept over him with a kind of rhythm like the hoofbeats. Worse than any of this, he had commenced to feel apprehensive. He must be almost within sight of Dover, and nothing had happened so far.

Nothing at all. Not a blockade or a challenge from the road. Not a shot fired from behind a tree, or a decoy to lure him into dismounting. Only loneliness, and the uncanny road winding out ahead. Yet there was good reason to know the enemy had not abandoned the chase.

For the first part of his journey, after Captain Mather of the Horse Guards Blue had put him on the right road, he spurred in silence. Next, with the memory of Dolly's voice in his ears and the touch of Dolly's lips still on his cheek, he awoke to great exhilaration, and he sang. It was,

> Good store of good claret supplies every thing,
> And the man that is drunk is as great as a king,

Or,

> When in silks my Julia goes . . .

Rollicking and roaring, or adrip with sugared sentiment—such is the kind of song I myself have always preferred—out it trolled into the wide night, substituting "Dolly" for "Julia," and, in the earlier one, expressing his mood with, "I who am drunk am as great as a king."

He was not drunk, save with the memory of Dolly, but it served. He made a frugal supper off the bread and cheese in the saddlebag, and washed it down with a swallow of rum.

In addition to stopping for a fresh horse at the three posting stations whose names were written on the scrap of paper, Captain Mather had told him, he must also stop and show his ring at any turnpike where the turnpike keeper had remembered to bar the road for the night. It might be troublesome, Captain Mather admitted, but it could provide him with directions if he needed them.

And he did need them. Twice he almost lost his way:

once outside Rochester and again beyond a grey town —city, rather—which, by the loom of its great cathedral against the moon, could only have been Canterbury.

For the most part he enjoyed it. He liked to clatter through sleeping villages, stirring up birds and echoes and sometimes the watchman, who stood in the middle of the street and shook an ancient fist. He liked to hear the solitary barking of dogs in farmyards. He liked the oak tree before country inns, with the oak seat running round it. Little grey houses flashed past, or a silvered church spire amid beeches. Only once did he check his gallop without cause. A pretty farm girl, returning from some assignation in barn or grove, had sat down under a hedgerow to put on her shoes before returning home. Since he was seeing Dolly everywhere, she reminded him of Dolly.

"A fine night, my dear. And how are you?"

"Tired," said the girl, making a face at him. "Most bloodily tired! Still, if you'd care to step down—"

"No, my dear. Thank you kindly, but I have other business if worse business. God for King Charles!"

And yet . . .

Few turnpike gates were closed. And yet, somewhere in the flat Kentish lands as a distant church clock tolled two, he rode up hard against a white bar across the road before a plank bridge over a stream. Kinsmere reined in, and hallo'd loudly at the little house beside it. This turnpike keeper, sleepier than most, made much clamour at unbolting and unbarring before he thrust a lanthorn past the open door.

"Hold your damn noise," yelled a surly voice. "And stand out in the glim, there, if you're honest enough to do it. What d'ye want?"

For answer my grandfather held his ring into the light.

"Nearer," snarled the voice, as though working towards a paroxysm. "Nearer, I say!"

"Do you turn your gate, Little Brother of Good Cheer? Or shall I jump it?"

"Oh, b'God! Here's a pretty state o'things for honest men! Another of you, is it?"

"Another?" Kinsmere asked coolly enough, though a qualm shot through him. "What other?"

In a minute or two more he clattered over the bridge and onwards with much to think about. Hours before, the turnpike keeper was bedevilled into saying, a man had ridden past displaying the ring of a King's Messenger. His appearance? He had not noticed this man's appearance, the turnpike keeper snarled, and wouldn't have remembered it if he had.

What with the late hour and the strain of the day, my grandfather's wits were not at their best. But one conclusion clearly emerged. *The man who stabbed Pembroke Harker had also stolen his ring.* This had not been investigated; it had occurred to nobody at the time. And yet the king must have remarked it, since he had asked whether that was not Harker's ring my grandfather wore.

Two sides of Kinsmere's mind were at argument, one side putting questions and the other seeking answers.

'Come!' said one silent voice. 'Salvation Gaines killed Harker because the man's usefulness was over; and he killed Butterworth, who had betrayed himself, for the same reason. After Butterworth's murder, surely, he could have escaped from the palace by displaying the ring of a King's Messenger?'

'No, nonsense!' retorted the other voice. 'Ring or no ring, they looked in particular for Gaines. Gaines has a distinctive appearance; he is known to Ensign Westcott, who would have described him. He could not possibly have escaped from the palace.'

'Oh, but he could!' said the first voice. 'He could have done so with ease, and with his inevitable luck, if he took care to bolt immediately after the murder, in the short time before the alarm for him was raised. And the guard who let him pass would be very reluctant to admit it afterwards.'

Gaines, Gaines, ever and always Gaines? That being the case, what would he do?

And so at three-thirty in the morning, with Dover somewhere ahead and sleep stealing on him like a footpad, Kinsmere tried to hold himself alert against other footpads.

A rope stretched between two trees, at about the height of a rider's neck: that was one possibility. He looked to his pistols and loosened the sword in its scabbard. The

185

cloak flew out behind him, thrumming like a flag in the wind. He rode low when they flashed through belts of woodland, or eased his grip in the stirrups as he imagined he detected movement at the roadside.

His latest horse, a hard-mouthed but not overfresh stallion, was blowing hard and flirting back foam into its rider's face. After what seemed interminable hours, and was in fact less than half an hour, he found the approaches to a grey old cobbled town with hills rising east to the left and west to the right. Turnpike gate ahead, and a flicker of light.

More than one light. When he dismounted, so cramped that he seemed to have no spine, he had an impression that he had walked to the edge of a windy gulf. He thought he could make out reflections on water; a stir and swinging, with black shapes in motion. Outlines were strengthening through the murk; he could see the shape of the castle on the left-hand hill. Dover.

Did the turnpike keeper (already astir, and broiling his morning fish) know the Easy Mariners, Grand Neptune Wharf? He did. He had a son, going out shortly with a fishing sloop, who would be pleased to escort the visitor there. Son, still fuddled from the night before, was tumbled down a ladder; after wheedling the price of a morning nipperkin, he beckoned and ran solemnly beside the stirrup.

At four in the morning, with deep-voiced bells clanging and clashing across rooftops, Kinsmere handed over his horse to an ostler at a tavern on the waterfront. Three chipped and half-beheaded figures, holding up flagons in a horrible kind of gaiety, swung bow-legged on a sign inscribed: "Ye Ea ie Mari e s, by Jos Pennwinke e. 16 1." Its red lattice was alight. He pushed open the door and went in.

They were trying to wake up the derelicts of last night, most of whom rested where they had fallen. One be-whiskered seafarer, sprawled on his back like a dead man, had his face and beard covered with a coat of tallow drippings: apparently the humorous device of more sober friends. Another, whose dirty blue headkerchief had come loose, rose suddenly to a sitting position with his eyes closed, said something about slitting somebody's belly,

186

and then flopped back and snored.

The landlord, who could do nothing with these, kicked at his dog and retired. At a bench-table by the fireplace sat a huge barrel-chested man with rings in his ears, consuming cheese and small beer for breakfast. Occasionally he would glance in pitying fashion at the weaker brethren on the floor. Then he would spit in his beer for luck and go on eating.

Dust-covered, weary, and a little dazed, Kinsmere addressed a pot-boy who was hanging up blackjacks from the rafters.

"I am in search of a French gentleman, a Captain Souter . . ."

The man with rings in his ears faced round, rose up, and kicked his chair aside.

"C'est moi!" he proclaimed in a mighty voice. He smiled ingratiatingly, took a step backwards, and struck his chest with a gesture like Othello stabbing himself.

"C'est moi!" he repeated. "Félix Alexandre Charlemagne Souter, veree mooch at your command!"

Over Kinsmere towered this fat giant, with a cheerfulness of expression which all his villainous looks could not dim or contradict. His broad nose flared up into a couple of furry eyebrows. His black beard spread in cascade; the ends of a black moustache blew out and floated whenever he spoke. An old scar on his left temple had drawn up one eye with an Oriental kind of twist; he shut the other eye in a conspirator's wink. Despite their dirt and disorder, his gold-laced purple coat and fringed red breeches made vivid colour in the taproom. He wore a cutlass slung from a baldric; his gold-laced hat lay on the table. The brass rings danced in his ears as he chuckled and bowed; so did the greasy bits of ribbon with which locks of his long hair were tied.

"Good!" said Félix Alexandre Charlemagne Souter, in very tolerable English. "You are from London, *hein?* You bring wit' you de ring and also de small pack-ette, *hein?* But old Félix must not be deceive. Produce dese!"

"Here," said Kinsmere, "is the ring—"

"No, no, no, no! De ot'er. I tell you why," explained Captain Souter, tapping his nose impressively. "Last night a man comes to me wit' de ring, jus' like yours. But he does not ask for me by name. And old Félix is not one fool, you bet. I am suspicious. I watch. I look. Ha, ha, ha." Crouching and shading his eyes with his hand, Captain Souter leered about the taproom. Then he whirled back. "I say to thees man, 'My friend, you show me de ring. It is good. But 'ow else am I goin' to know you?' Show me also de small pack-ette. I t'ink deep. I am one philosopher. Old Félix wish only to see de seals; den he know.' And thees man refuse!"

"He did, did he? Who was the man?"

"Ah! That I don' know. And I do not ask. Me, I am one philosopher. *You* show me de seals, young man, and I am satisfy."

"Here? In public? When there are people," says Kinsmere, "with such a taste for casual assassination that—"

Félix stared at him.

"Eh? What is it you t'ink, young man? You t'ink anyone will dare to try de dirty work wit' me, Félix on de spot all dees time? Oh, goddam!" he cried, appealing to the ceiling. "Young man, you are not acquaint wit' me. You know what I do to anyone who try dat?"

With a gesture which seemed to fill the room, he yanked the cutlass out of its scabbard. He lunged with the point; he cut viciously at the air, endangering a fish-oil lamp hung from the rafters; and then stood back in a mighty pose as though about to have his portrait painted.

"Voilà!" he said haughtily.

By this time Kinsmere had recovered not only his good spirits but his sense of the ridiculous. After summoning the landlord and calling for something to eat, he took the leather pouch from under his shirt and gave Captain Souter a glimpse of what was inside the oilskin packet.

"Good! All is good!" beamed Félix, sheathing the cutlass. "And that is arrange now. I told you I am not one fool, yes? Now you come wit' me; we go to de private room; you 'ave your breakfas'; we wait for Mr. Garlick. Is de mate of my beautiful ship. At dis moment he is round up de crew. Ha, ha, ha!" Félix said proudly. "I have one damn fine crew, I tell you. One minute dey be all blind drunk, lying out on de quay; rows and rows of dem, all in a line . . ."

Félix looked dreamy. His gesture suggested a vista of

188

recumbent seamen, paralyzed with intoxication, stretching away into the distance like the Great Wall of China.

". . . but one bucket of water on each—one bucket—*plosh!* Dey be up de ratlines like monkeys, ha ha. Nobody slip on de footropes. No 'and will shake at all. Old Félix know! You come wit' me, now, and I tell you why I mus' take good care no 'arm befall you at any time."

Clapping on the gold-laced hat, Captain Souter led him out into a passage and back to a gloomy little room with a sanded floor, a fire, and a pair of depressed-looking candles stuck into bottles. They sat down at the table, where the landlord brought Kinsmere a platter of fried fish and a tankard of small beer.

While my grandfather ate, old Félix assumed a look of great profundity.

"Monsieur," he said, "I tell you. De secret of de 'appy life, la vie heureuse, it lie in two t'ings. You are young, and I tell you. In de beautiful cabine of my ship I have one book. He is a great book. I find him years ago in a prison where dey put me, and almost I am hang. At first I do not understand him, but now I keep him by me always. *De Consolation of Philosophy,* by a Roman called Bocthius. Now tell me, young man: do you know ships?"

"Well! I am a landlubber, I suppose, though years ago *I* was used to make a nuisance of myself on St. Augustine's Wharf at Bristol. If I am not overknowledgeable in the matter of ships, at least I like them."

"You like ships? Ha! When you see my *Thunderer*—ha!" boomed Félix, indicating rapture. "Is solid. Is Dutch-built. Not de best in de world, maybe, but nearly so and who care? Consider! Two-decker. One t'ousand four hundred tonnage. Forty gun she mount—"

"Now burn everything," exclaimed Kinsmere, "but do you tell me we cross the Straits in a man-o'-war?"

"No, no, no! Is privately owned; is armed merchantman. But could be a warship, yes; and will be a warship, I say, when I 'ave finish wit' her! I do all I am commanded, I take care of you, and dat ship is mine. Alors, I am one philosopher; I do it. Through philosophy I achieve my ambition. I own my own ship; I sail on de Account . . ."

"On the account?"

189

"On de Account! What you call—piracy. Hein?" Félix looked triumphant. "I get letters of marque, maybe. Maybe not. Ha, ha, ha. Already there is one damn fine crew. My *Thunderer,* she is ready. I make for de Caribbean, I t'ink. And now I tell you de ot'er t'ing which is needed for de 'appy life. Dat is politeness, always politeness! It will give me a good name when I am on de Account. In de islands dey will say, 'Ah, old Félix! He sink de ship. He take de women. He tie us to de mast for de crew to t'row bottles at, maybe. But old Félix, goddam, he is *al-ways* polite.' Ha!"

A harsh voice said:

"Crew's abaard."

In the doorway, one hand on the doorpost, stood a lean, muscular, sandy-haired man with a sullen eye and a knotted lash swung by its thong from his wrist. Wrinkles struggled across his face from the intensity of summoning up speech. He spat, and snapped the whip.

"A zay, crew's abaard," he repeated, in the speech of Somerset. "Yon's *'im?*" he inquired, jerking the lash towards Kinsmere.

With great ceremony Captain Souter presented Mr. Joseph Garlick, the mate of the *Thunderer.* Mr. Joseph Garlick spat again and led them out of the tavern, while Félix made soothing speeches.

A chill pallor of dawn had come up over the Straits. Salt air lay heavily on Kinsmere's eyelids; the wound in his shoulder, almost forgotten until now, began to pull and smart. What he minded most was the return of his drowsiness. Once he was aboard ship, he hoped, he might snatch an hour or two's sleep. But the enemy had made no sign so far. Where were the enemy, and what would they do?

The wharf swam in mist and half-light. Loud rose a screaming of gulls amid crowded masts; the gulls tumbled as though shot, and then flapped up with a wooden rattle of wings. At a jetty facing south Félix made philosophic remarks as he bowed Kinsmere into a waiting longboat. Oars dipped; the longboat shot out through a poisonous atmosphere, cleaving through sewage of the dim hulls roundabout.

The *Thunderer* lay well out beyond, heaving at anchor.

My grandfather watched her grow out of the mist, and approved. She was strong if not graceful, with square lines from beakhead to sterncastle. Square-rigged and three-masted, she carried mainsail, topsail, and topgallant of sturdy breadth; the clumsy spritsail of her time, and the lateen sail aft. All canvas was white or red. Along her brown-painted hull ran two tiers of guns: the upper on the main deck, the lower at open gun ports well below. Brass bow chasers looked out from the forecastlehead; stern chasers were mounted on the quarter-deck aft. If it came to exchanging sea blows with anything except a heavy line-of-battle ship, the *Thunderer* could both give blows and receive them.

A clear breeze sprang up, sweeping at the mist and then dispersing it; long shafts of sunlight struck through. They touched the gilt of the beakhead, they ran across canvas and shrouds. As the longboat hove to under the lee side, a pipe sounded in the waist; there was a sudden patter of activity, and a Jacob's-ladder came snaking down.

Kinsmere looked round with a good deal of curiosity as he climbed up. Even apart from Félix's determination to sail on the Account, he had fallen into strange company. She was a Dutch-built ship with an English name, and she flew English colours; but her crew appeared to be of all mixed nationalities and grades, alike only in looking knavish or unkempt. One spidery Frenchman sat on a sea chest, binding up his skewered wrist and cursing somebody named Ysobel. Another man (what country?) was being sick in the scuppers to leeward, interrupting this process only to gurgle out prayers in one of the more spectacular Latin tongues. Half a dozen others lay in the waist. Kinsmere had never seen filthier decks, and she smelt no better than the quayside.

But Félix was at his elbow, overpowering in geniality. Félix led him up aft; then down a steep companionway into a dark passage to what he called his *belle cabine*.

It was the master's cabin in the sterncastle, spacious enough for that day. A line of arched and many-paned windows, several lights open, faced aft out of wood much carved and painted, and made a kind of eyrie high above the rudder.

A brass lanthorn hung from the roof. Curtains and

191

upholstery, once a bright scarlet sewn with gilt thread, masked bulkheads alive with black beetles and rats. Into the chart rack were thrust a mariner's cross-staff, a telescope, and another dented hat of gold lace. On a table near the windows, set out in massive silver plate greasy from the remains of last night's meal, lay a copy of Boethius's *The Consolation of Philosophy* in English, with an orange holding open its pages.

"Is magnificent, eh?" demanded Captain Souter, looking round with pride. "You t'ink so, yes? You agree? It is not finer, I bet, in de Duke of York's flagship at Portsmouth. And so, my friend," a great bow, "Félix Alexandre Charlemagne Souter make you welcome aboard de *Thunderer!* You sit down and be comfortable, yes? Now I mus' go on deck. But soon I come down again; we drink de wine and t'row de dice like de good men we are. Until den, until den, until den!"

Out he went, with a last proud glance. Kinsmere, throwing aside his hat, drew up a heavy chair to the table, sat down with his right side towards the windows, and propped his feet against the table's edge. It was warm in the cabin, not altogether unpleasant. The *Thunderer* rolled with a gentle motion, timbers creaking and cracking. Somebody shouted hoarsely on the quarter-deck. A patter of feet went up and down; a confused, dreamy hum which became a premonitory tremble . . .

With deadened brain he tried to think, but his head nodded forward in a doze. It seemed to him that Dolly was here, and King Charles, and Bygones Abraham . . .

Then he remembered no more.

It was the breeze which woke him fully: a clean salt wind, blowing cool through the cabin. That, or the movement of the ship. He could feel the strain and pull of her, the poised drive as though belling canvas would carry her out of the water. She lifted, rolled slightly, and then pitched, with a boiling hiss round her rudder. Above creaking timbers he could hear the deep thrum of the canvas, the blocks a-creak, the shrouds as vibrant as fiddle strings.

Running before a fair breeze, the *Thunderer* was crowding sail. Again she lifted on the shoulder of a swell, held poised, and dipped like a dancing master. Again the wake frothed and boiled; green reflections trembled on the windows, and spray glittered against the sun.

"*Naow*," said a voice from the other side of the table, and shocked him alert.

He was looking across greasy silver plate all a-rattle and motion, across the open pages of *The Consolation of Philosophy,* at a man standing there and watching him.

"Naow, m' son," continued Joseph Garlick, the mate, "A'll 'ave ut letter thee'm got in th' pouch. Quick with 'e!"

Mr. Garlick leaned on the table, and steadily advanced the pistol in his other hand.

XV

Kinsmere's first thought, he always said afterwards, was of how refreshed he felt. Though he could have been asleep only a short time, yet he felt alert, rested, and not even particularly astonished at that pistol aimed towards the middle of his forehead.

His next realization, a bad one, was of his own pistols: lost to him, far away in the saddle holsters of the horse he had left at the Easy Mariners. Then came a thought which might provide balance. Automatically, before dozing off, he had thrust his right hand inside his jerkin close to where the leather pouch lay underneath the shirt. Even now his fingers were touching the haft of the dagger he had slung beneath his left arm.

He shifted his boots slightly in their cramped position on the edge of the table. He pretended to stare and gape like one bewildered. The heavy silver dishes rattled; his chair slid a little.

"Eh?" he grunted. "God alive, my backbone! What did you say?"

Joseph Garlick repeated the order, with a kind of urgent but casual contempt. The red hangings, tattered and begrimed and wine-stained, tilted behind his head with the ship's motion. His sullen eye did not waver, and his freckled left hand was outspread on the table.

"Quick with 'e!" he said. "And don't think to make a fight, m'son; the'm caught. No trick to put a bullet in 'e; and then 'tes done. *They'll* kill 'e if I don't."

Kinsmere blinked.

"Oh, come!" he said stupidly. "I was neatly bubbled, was I? You are all concerned in Captain Souter's first act of piracy, or is it only one of a thousand? And where *is* our good Félix?"

"A zaid, quick with 'e!" snapped the mate, suddenly coming to life and squaring forward. "The'll give me yon letter—"

He was taken a little off balance as the *Thunderer* pitched. Kinsmere, his heels on the edge of the table, kicked it out savagely.

Table and dishes crashed into Garlick's arm a split-second before he fired. The pistol exploded upwards with stunning flash and concussion. Kinsmere, on his feet with the dagger in his hand, was thrown completely off balance by the ship's long pitch. He struck hard for Garlick's right shoulder, to disable the man, and stabbed him to the heart instead.

Then he could hear dishes bumping and rattling on the floor. An orange rolled towards the line of lockers underneath the windows, and bounced back. Kinsmere's ears were still ringing from the shot.

In a harsh mist of powder smoke Garlick stood swaying, his mouth open. The pistol dropped. He scrabbled with both hands at the dagger in his chest; he took one step, and fell forward in a convulsion across the overturned table.

Somebody shouted out beyond the cabin's one door. On unsteady legs Kinsmere lurched over to the door, twisting the great brass key in its lock. A moment more acrid smoke caught at the lungs; then the breeze whirled it away. There was blood on his hand and wrist, he noted; he wiped them on one of Félix's curtains, and went back to Garlick.

The man was dead, by the fortunate misfortune of that blow. Kinsmere hoisted him up and rolled him to one side, where knives, forks, an empty milk jug, and in particular the orange went tumbling in animated fashion round the body. Feet pounded up outside the locked door; volleys of knocks were followed by a shouted question in some language he did not understand.

"Go to the devil, can't you?"

The unsteadiness had left his legs, now battle was joined. What interested him, what roused him to an oath of puzzled admiration, was the conduct of Captain Félix Alexandre Charlemagne Souter. In old Félix you met as jovial and hospitable a cutthroat as ever invited you to his lair. No doubt, out of politeness, he had sent Garlick to demand the letter rather than ask for it himself. What all this portended my grandfather could not determine, but that was not his immediate concern. His immediate concern must be how long he could hold out against the whole crew of an armed merchantman.

He peered out the windows. Any notion of swimming for it could be abandoned; they were too far from land; and, besides, a longboat could pick him out of the water without fuss. The door was a solid one, bound in iron. They *might* come at him by way of the windows, climbing down the carved woodwork from the deck above; in good time they probably would. Meanwhile, he had only his sword and Garlick's empty pistol. If he could find a supply of powder and ball, perhaps another pistol as well . . .

He found a lockerful. He found it just before the furious knocking at the door died away. Heavier footsteps approached it. There was a jabber, a whisper, then a very authoritative knock.

"Allo!" shouted the muffled voice of old Félix. "Allo dere!"

My grandfather did not answer, being engaged in biting off paper wadding for another pistol. He leaned against the locker, with his drawn sword on top of it, and looked over his shoulder.

"Al-*lo*, I say!" roared Félix, kicking at the door. "What is in dere, eh? What has happen?"

Kinsmere finished loading the pistol; he set the hammer at cock, and put it down.

"To say a truth, captain," he called back, "I have been obliged to dispose of the mate. He is as dead as Boethius at this minute. But be polite, Félix! Remember, *al-ways* polite."

The bulkheads creaked and cracked. Dishes, cutlery and a dancing orange slithered round Garlick's body and round a copy of *The Consolation of Philosophy* sprawled face up.

195

"Oh, goddam!" yelled Félix.

"Have an orange," suggested my grandfather. "Most amiable prince of pirates, have an orange. Come in and get it; your reception will be a warm one."

"My dear yoong man——" protested a distressed voice.

"Félix, for shame! Where is your nobility of thought? And what would Boethius say to such japes? 'For as good is ever rewarded in this world,'" Kinsmere read a sentence aloud, "'so is evil infallibly punished.' Is this your fashion of carrying King's Messengers, Captain Souter?"

Beyond the door he heard something like a deep chuckle.

"Young man," proclaimed Félix, "I don' want to 'urt you. I am commanded not to 'urt you, but I don' want to 'urt you either. I tell you, I like your ways. Venez, mon cher! Be good. We only wan' to carry you out at sea where you can't raise no fuss and they don' find you if anything bad 'appen. We wan' something you have got; why should we 'urt you? Alors, be good. You can' escape where you are. And we take you easy if we smash de door, hein?"

"Yes, let us all be in good humour," Kinsmere yelled back. "You want what I have in the oilskin packet, is that it?"

"Ah, my brave one! If you will be so good——"

"Now attend carefully, Félix. As soon as you attack that door to smash it, the packet will be weighted with a salt shaker and thrown overboard out of a window. An even warmer welcome, I had better tell you, awaits the first three or four men who stick their heads inside."

There was a muffled, excited consultation, in which no words could be distinguished. Kinsmere had set out four pistols, all loaded. He kept a wary eye out between the windows and the door which faced them. It seemed to him that subdued activity seethed on the quarter-deck above.

Then, outside the door, another voice spoke in English.

"Now is the wicked one enmeshed to his doom! For the Lord shall set a snare for their feet, and hath done so. He is fast bound in his iniquity, and by us too; and, when he shall learn who *I* am——"

"To say a truth," shouted Kinsmere, "he already knows who you are. Surely that's Salvation Gaines?"

"And if it is?"

"Still filled with conceit, Salvation? Is there anything else of which you would make a report to authority? Fire buckets? Pirates? When you had stabbed Harker and Butterworth, did you call down a fine on some poor-devil clerk for losing his quill-cutting knife? Enter, Anointed One; be pleased to enter!"

"Enough of this child's defiance, wretched youth. Will you allow defeat at last, and capitulate to us?"

"No!"

"What I call down upon you, lewd beyond your years, is the fire everlasting and the worm that dieth not. And yet, ere He shall burn and torment you, there are chastisements to be met on earth. When the crew take you and torment you at their own pleasure, as they will do within a matter of moments—"

"Then why not begin?"

"I say to you—"

Somebody must have plucked at Gaines's sleeve; he broke off; there was a muttered conference, with Félix's chuckle at the end of it. Kinsmere rather liked old Félix; he could not help liking old Félix; at the same time, when he pictured Gaines's reddish eyes and vicious blend of humility with arrogance, it was not easy to contain fury.

"Yes, that is best," snapped Gaines, evidently speaking to Félix. "Let it be done; what do they fear? He is a monument of treason, like his master Charles Stuart. He is a whoreson boy with a kept drab. But he cannot harm them. The Lord vouchsafed me sight of him when you led him aboard; he hath no firearms, and no weapons save a sword or perhaps a dagger too. Give the word, Captain Souter; give the word." Then Gaines screamed: "Your last chance, youth of blood! Will you open this door and yield you, ere they take you and rend you in pieces?"

"Go crawl in the gutter where you belong!"

Footsteps retreated and pounded on a companionway. Kinsmere thrust a pistol into one each of his side pockets, tucked the rapier under his arm, and took the remaining two pistols in his hands. Overhead there was a bump, together with louder voices. All over the top of the sterncastle he heard a stirring and scraping like a cupboard full of rats. They would make their first tack at climbing down.

197

Taking up a position midway between door and windows, his eyes on the windows, he raised one pistol. A song, he thought, might not be out of place. This was pure bravado; he knew it. But he was feeling rather light-headed, either from fear or from some other emotion; to sing in their faces seemed the only way of expressing defiance when they crowded into a corner to kill you.

It was hard enough to stand upright without staggering. The *Thunderer* both rolled and pitched; everything was in motion, including the dead man. A silver drinking goblet skittered past his foot and bumped into the door.

> Here's a health unto His Majesty,
> With a tow-row-row and a tow-row,
> Confusion to his enemies,
> With a tow-row-row and a tow-row . . .

The scuffling over the sterncastle approached closer, with more of caution now.

> And he that will not drink his health
> I wish him neither life nor health . . .

A loose foot kicked against wood. As the *Thunderer* went over in a roll to port, its wake seething and boiling, the fingers of a hand edged over the top of one window whose light stood partway open. It groped farther down. Kinsmere could see the black nails, and took good aim.

> Nor yet a rope to hang himself;
> With a tow-row-row and a—
CRACK!

There was a deafening report. His pistol ball smashed one oblong pane and skewered that hand as neatly as a rapier blade. Through the gust of smoke a few bloody raindrops splashed the window; somebody screamed. As the *Thunderer* plunged and shouldered to starboard, a man shot past the windows, wriggling in the air. Kinsmere saw his mouth and eyes a fraction of a second before his back struck the great rudder. It kicked him into the wake, limply; he did not cry out again, and the white rush bore him away.

A yell went up from above. Past the windows flew the ends of a Jacob's ladder, swinging wide with another man clinging to it and aiming a pistol. With one foot he smashed in a whole window, the glass clattering down, and fired point-blank as he swung. Kinsmere could not tell where the bullet lodged, save that it went wild. Smoke and flying glass briefly blinded him. Then the Jacob's-ladder swept back like a pendulum, its occupant lurching for the window sill with knife in teeth; and my grandfather fired straight at the knife. It disappeared; together with face and figure, just as other hands swarmed round and down.

Two shots gone. He staggered back, last two pistols ready to hand, coughing in the raw smoke. Behind him there were crashings when axes splintered at the door. He could hear Félix yelling, "Don' 'urt him; ne faites pas du mal; don' 'urt him—"

Another figure, cutlass in hand, tumbled in through the shattered window. Kinsmere's third pistol snapped and missed fire. The figure with the cutlass, who seemed all hair and steel, dived down against sun-glittering smoke. Kinsmere fired for the last time; his own bullet went wild as other figures, more hair and steel, pressed in through the window. The first man with the cutlass flung out a savage cut; he parried this with the rapier, but lurched off-balance on his return thrust, and only pierced an arm. Hair and steel jerked back from the sting, doing a fantastic dance as though surrounded by wasps. Other hair swept past and shocked Kinsmere back with its weight. Twice he thrust, at bodies wide open when the arm went back for a cut; twice he got home deeply, and tried to set his back against a bulkhead . . .

"Doucement!" thundered the voice of Félix. "Doucement, j'implore . . ."

In went the door, smashed off its hinges. That was the point at which Kinsmere tripped over the rolling dead man, and arms caught him from behind. In an abstract way he knew he had been struck on the head; he heard a heavy bump or thud, as though it had occurred to someone else; then a great roaring in the ears, an exploding wave of pain, and no more.

Consciousness returned to a blurry sound of voices. His eyes were open; his head had become a mass of pain. He was lying on the floor—deck, rather; let's be nautical—at the foot of a bunk in that same cabin. He tried to move his wrists, and failed because they were tied together. He lifted his head a little, inducing more pain. But at least he had a glimpse of his surroundings.

The motion of the ship was much steadier. The cabin had been put to rights in so far as this could be managed. A humped little bearded man, on hands and knees, scrubbed at the boards and wrung out into his bucket a cloth so black that it scarcely showed bloodstains at all. At the restored table sat Captain Souter, with a silver goblet and silver wine jug before him and *The Consolation of Philosophy* open at his elbow.

Kinsmere closed his eyes against pain. He must have lost consciousness again, though only for a few seconds. He was roused by hands reaching inside his shirt. Hands lifted out the leather pouch on its thongs round his neck, and again he opened his eyes.

Over him bent Salvation Gaines, iron-grey periwig and all. With another knife, not a bone-handled one, Gaines cut the thongs and took the pouch. He stood up straight, glowing with smug triumph.

"You again?" said Kinsmere, who could not quite recover his voice. "If it is you and not a nightmare, be off! You sicken me."

Gaines looked down, studied him, and then kicked him viciously in the ribs.

"Stop dat!" boomed Félix, putting down his goblet after taking a deep pull. "You will do none of dat, my friend. No, no, no! You may be as 'oly as de Pope 'imself—"

"Oh, pity and spare us, but what wicked words are these? As the Pope, did you say?"

" 'Oo else? And if it come to dat, you sicken *me*. You would not go in and take 'im while 'e could still fight. You do not touch him *now*, I tell you." Félix swivelled round in the chair. "Ah, my dear yoong man! Is better, I hope? You go better now, hein?"

Félix rubbed his hands together, chuckling and beaming. And, try as he would, Kinsmere could not feel anything but friendly towards this solicitous old bandit. It was due to Félix, he knew, that he had merely been struck senseless and not killed.

"Well, Félix," he said in Captain Souter's own philosophical tone, "we had something of a brawl, don't you think?"

"I do, I do! Yes, you are in de right. It was one damn fine burly-'urly, you bet. Come!" continued Félix, pouring and draining another bumper. "Soon you get up and be com-for-*table*, yes? We drink de wine and t'row de dice, as I 'ave said long ago. Your are not 'urt; I 'ave look at you. A bump on de 'ead, but it do not bleed. A wound in de shoulder has bleed a leetle; but it is not new wound, I t'ink; you do not get it 'ere. You are well and as good as new."

Here he looked at Gaines, who was swallowing hard as though swallowing bile.

"And *you*, de great 'oliness which rejoice to kill people when dey are not looking? What ail *you*, Salvation Gaines? Already you 'ave agree this yoong man mus' not be 'urt or torture: in part because I will not 'ave it and in part because there is still a use for him. Then what ail you, goddam? Why are you so glum? We 'ave got what we were 'ired to get; it is in your clench now; goddam, are you not content?"

"I do the Lord's work," cried Gaines, with tears rising to his eyes; "therefore am I sustained in all trials. You are a wicked man, Captain Souter, lewd and a Papist too. Yet there is reason in what you say."

He took the oilskin packet from the leather pouch. The pouch he thrust into his pocket. Delicately he removed the oilskin, putting that into his pocket too, and weighed the sealed document in his hand.

"Let there be rejoicing! Here," declared Gaines, "is half of the dispatch that will trap Charles Stuart. Let him henceforward obey the behest of godly men; else he will go for ever on his travels or know the axe and block as his father did. Now are the sinners cast into their pit, and the worthy exalted on high!"

The seaman with cloth and bucket had long ago scuttled out, past a half-broken door which was propped against the bulkhead. With hands none too steady Gaines broke the seals on the document.

"We have but little more to do. We intercept the sloop *Saucy Ann;* we gain the other half of the dispatch. Joy is not complete (no, no!) until both halves are in the possession of the man who employed us. Yet already we may praise the Lord for a consummation. Here—"

Spreading out the document in his fingers, Salvation Gaines stopped dead. His face seemed to grow rigid, the mouth pulled square like a Greek mask. A falsetto screech went piercing up; he flung his arms wide, and executed a couple of convulsive little steps, like the beginning of a *danse macabre,* against the line of partly shattered windows.

"Eh?" roared Félix, starting up. "What is it? What is wrong?"

"What is wrong, you ask?" Then Gaines choked. "Look there, man of sin! Look there!"

He spurned the document from him; it fluttered and fell on the table. The oilskin packet had contained, heavily sealed up, half of a blank sheet of paper.

XVI

Already—blinding headache or no, bound wrists or no—Kinsmere had struggled up to a sitting position with his back against the bunk.

What started him off laughing he could never afterwards be sure. It may have been Salvation Gaines's anguished contortions, like a Puritan clergyman thinking of sin. It may have been the thought of how furiously he had carried himself with sword and pistol to defend a half-sheet of blank foolscap. Anyway, he could not stop. Unlike Gaines's giggling laughter, which was largely a sneer, his full-throated mirth rang in the wrecked cabin. He kicked out his heels. He leaned back and roared until he was near tears.

Gaines looked at him out of sly little eyes. Then Gaines stood above him, taking the sharp knife from an inside pocket.

"You knew this, I think? You knew the paper was blank?"

"I did *not* know it," my grandfather retorted truthfully. "Have I lost my senses, that I would challenge Félix and his whole crew to preserve . . . to preserve . . . " He felt his jaws working, and exploded into the other's face. "Let us show a deep pity, shall we, for anyone who would outwit the King of England? And *you*, Salvation Gaines, and your band of malcontents and their precious plotter-in-chief . . . keeo-whoosh! Haw, Haw, HAW!"

"It will be found less diverting," Gaines felt the edge of the knife, "when necessary chastisement has been administered. Meanwhile, enough of this! You will tell me—"

"*I* tell you," Félix roared suddenly. He rose to his feet, shaking a thick arm in the air. "Always you say what a clever faller you are; but you are one imbécile. No, no, no, I tell you! Dis one 'as not got half de dispatch *because de ot'er messenger 'as got it all.*"

Gaines stood stock-still, fingers at his lower lip.

"Regard!" said Félix, somewhat superfluously. "Consider! T'ink what you yourself 'ave tell me. Dees one is yoong man. He 'ave never carry de dispatch before, eh? And your king is not one trusting faller. But dees yoong man will be one damn fine decoy, yes, and t'row us off while de o'ter messenger go to Calais?"

To my grandfather, now, the scheme showed as both simple and inevitable.

"Is this true, Roderick Kinsmere?" snarled Gaines.

"I don't know; I can't say. Yet I would lay any wager it *is* true. Whereat, gentlemen, you have had your labour for nothing. You are most royally bubbled and undone."

"Does it truly appear so, lewd youth? Tremble; you have cause to tremble! For the Lord is not mocked, nor am I. We are come but to the second part of a plan hardly disturbed. You are an obstinate and stupid young man. In your ridiculous efforts to serve Charles Stuart, which Providence sets at naught, you have killed several men and badly injured others. Yet you are *not* dead, as such behaviour merits. You are *not* hung up by the thumbs. You have not even had your ears cropped or your nose slit to the bone: that is, not yet. I have been most merciful; can you guess why?"

"There is a use for me, somebody said."

"There is indeed a use," Gaines fingered the knife, "even for such as you. We had thought to take half a dispatch in your possession, and the other half from an oafish fellow now aboard the *Saucy Ann*. Our plan is altered but a little: the entire document we will take from the man Bygones Abraham.

"How ingenious is the Lord! The sloop *Saucy Ann* has a longer journey round than we. And we are, by happy circumstance, the faster vessel. With full knowledge of the course she customarily sets and no bad weather to delay her, Captain Souter has reckoned we should meet her in the Straits—when?"

"It be any time now, I tell you," roared Félix. "We sight her; we over'aul her; we take her. Eh, yoong man?"

"Félix, for God's sake! It is you, and this praying murderer—and his Lord too, if you think *Him* concerned— who must completely have lost your senses. An act of piracy in the Narrow Seas . . . "

"Tchaa!" said Gaines, lifting one shoulder. "The law of man, it may be, would apply some such name to it, if indeed we attacked the vessel. But we are about pious work. Shall we use such extreme measures: unless, to be sure, they become needful?"

"By de Virgin and St. Joseph," swore Félix, heaving his chest and chuckling, "by de Virgin and St. Joseph, but I 'ope dey are needful. Hoist de bones! Blood in de scuppers! Rum-tiddlety-um-tum, ha, ha!"

Giving a fillip to his beard, shaking his head so that hair and earrings danced, he peered round benevolently. A knifelike kind of malice edged Salvation Gaines's mouth.

"Enough of this, Captain Souter! Tales of violence from the West Indies must not carry your impetuousness too far. There is a difference, let's allow, between an act of piracy off Barbadoes and an act of piracy in the Straits of Dover. Can you not see the nature of that difference?"

"Difference—bah! It's all water," argued Félix. "Besides, we be very polite."

"Enough, I say!" This time Gaines addressed Kinsmere. "The sloop *Saucy Ann* mounts fewer than twenty guns. She can neither fight nor run away. In a good cause we must employ craft to take the man Abraham unawares, lest he destroy the paper as you so foolishly threatened to do. The better plan, therefore—"

"One man I 'ave got," Félix said suddenly, "wit' de educated voice in six languages. Is called Longstaffe; will be de mate now Garlick is gone. Hah, dass it! Him I will put on de quarter-deck beside me to shout: 'Captain Félix Alexandre Charlemagne Souter present 'is compliments; and you will 'eave to damn quick, please, or he give you a broadside.' What you t'ink of dat, yoong man?"

"I am not inclined to favour it, Félix."

"You are not, goddam? W'y not?"

"It is overhasty, I think; it comes to business with a thought too much of the abrupt. Let me suggest a better one. 'Captain Félix Alexandre Charlemagne Souter presents his compliments, and begs leave to pay a short visit aboard your vessel.' How's that?"

Gaines, pale with fury, made a short, threatening gesture.

"Have you some notion, Roderick Kinsmere, that I speak in jest?"

"Oh, go to the devil! If you have no intent to take and sink the sloop, how else can you hope to trap Bygones?"

"With *your* help."

"Oh?"

"With your help, willingly given," Gaines assured him. "I say willingly, and I do not jest; I mean this. You will even thank me, when I have done. For the Lord of Hosts shall open your eyes, and set your feet towards righteousness at last. Do you mark me now, Roderick Kinsmere?"

"Well?"

"I do not know whether the man Bygones Abraham is aware you are aboard the *Thunderer*. If he is not, all doubts shall be set at rest. When we sight the sloop, by Captain Souter's orders, we will draw close and hail. You will be on the quarter-deck in plain sight. You will call for the man Abraham; you will say that difficulties have arisen, and that he must come aboard the *Thunderer* for discourse with you. Once here, he will be detained; we put back to Dover. Should the captain of the sloop become suspicious, what in pity's name can he do? Thus does justice triumph; thus is a design accomplished without disorder or any illegal act. You see?"

205

"Yes, I see. And now the threats begin, I suppose?"

"Threats?"

" 'Do this, or you will feel the knife.' 'Do that, else your death will be lingering and unpleasant.' I am familiar with your tactics, Mr. Salvation Gaines. They will earn you a hemp collar, but they will do much mischief ere that. With what kind of unpleasantness have you a mind to commence?"

"Now, how I am misjudged!" cried Gaines, uprolling his eyes. "How are the godly reviled and traduced when they but seek to do their duty! Threats, wretched boy? I utter none; I carry none out. I will use only sweet persuasion. For there is hope for you; yea, verily, there is hope for you even yet.—Captain Souter!"

Félix, who had sat down and poured himself another bumper, rolled his head round.

"He can do us no further harm, Captain Souter. Since we must be thrice merciful, since we must forgive our enemies, this poor fellow might be made more comfortable, as you suggested. Pray fetch him up; set him in a chair. If you think it prudent, loose his bonds and give him a mouthful of wine. I would plead with him. I would place certain facts before him, and then.—Captain Souter!"

But Félix had been brooding on a different problem.

" '—present his compliments,' " he was muttering, " 'and beg leave to pay a short visit aboard your vessel.' Hah! H'm! Mabbe you are right," he continued, scowling round at Kinsmere and tapping his nose thoughtfully. "You are educate in de politeness. You should tell de right way, eh? But I don't know. It sound *too* damn polite to me. 'Ow are dey goin' to know I am a pirate?"

"They'll see your bones and death's head, won't they, all merry and bright over the mainmast? Are you prepared with a pirate flag, Félix?"

"Not yet; where I get one? Oh, goddam! De principle is de right one, so who care? Hoist de bones! Blood in de scuppers! Tra-la-li-la-la, all's well! What else you say?"

"Help me up, will you?"

Félix surged to his feet, smote his chest a couple of times, and approached at his bow-legged roll. Though my grandfather weighed twelve stone, Félix lifted him as easily and solicitously as a jug of old rum. He put him into a chair beside the table, using his cutlass to sever the rope at Kinsmere's wrists. Into another silver goblet he poured wine. It was Madeira and sickly sweet, no stuff for a man with a headache, yet it had a grateful warmth once it was gulped down. Kinsmere eased his bruises back into the chair.

"All I regret, me," Félix proclaimed sadly, "is what dey 'ave done to my belle cabine. Dey 'ave smash de window. Dey 'ave shoot bullets in de bulkhead. Somebody step on Boethius, even. If I find de scoundrel dat step on Boethius, I will give him de cat, you bet. Still, is beautiful, hein?" he demanded, and refreshed himself with a look round. "Regard my Spanish chest, wit' de ivory. Nine 'undred crowns I pay for him . . ."

"Near to all the damage was done by *our guest*," said Gaines, playfully thrusting the knife towards Kinsmere. "But we forgive him, don't we? Yes, we forgive him! Captain Souter, sit down and be silent. I have much to say to our young friend."

Gaines's friendliness was as overpowering as his humility or arrogance. In an instant he had become all ingratiating airs and playful ways. He would run into corners and run at you, this time in good will. Then he stood with his back to the window, framed against a tilting white-capped Channel.

"Roderick Kinsmere, you have been unjust! A group of worthy gentlemen, gathered together for the public weal under a patron of most noble motives, you have seen fit to designate as a 'band of malcontents and their plotter-in-chief'!"

" 'Worthy gentlemen,' is it?"

"Oh, indeed, the most worthy and the most laudable. When you apprehend, when you know the truth, you will join our number."

"Join your number, will I? Salvation Gaines, do you care to lay a wager on *that?*"

"I do not lay wagers; 'tis an impious practice. Still, if I did, I would put my very soul into the business. Yes: you will join us in happiness and rejoicing, and indeed you can do no other.

"Come!" added Gaines, uprolling his eyes and spreading out his hands in appeal. "Could I have spoken with you in private yesterday, I could have opened the matter and unburdened my heart. But this could not be; you were for ever in the company of the man Abraham. Besides, if I may say so, these poor hands were somewhat occupied."

"They were occupied, for one thing, with the slaughtering of Harker and Butterworth. Is that what you call worthy work?"

"Poor boy, this had to be!"

"Now, damn my soul—!"

"No blasphemies, I beg!" Gently Gaines touched Kinsmere's forehead with the point of the knife. "Come! When you and the man Abraham skulked in a cupboard at that tavern, was I not close behind you; and unseen as I am always unseen? Did I not hear Harker, out of overweening vanity, boast of his deeds and his knowledge to a shameless harlot, and so betray our group of patriots to what might have been their undoing?

"Butterworth (need I say it?) was a case near as bad. He was a stupid man, a weak man. He had allowed himself to be trapped by Charles Stuart. Only a few questions, only a touch of rough handling at the Tower, and he would have confessed all. Could this be permitted? You know it could not. Is there not scriptural authority if I cry that the end justifies the means? And so, for the preservation of a band of patriots . . . "

Kinsmere repeated the word, in no sympathetic tone.

"Yes, patriots!" retorted Gaines, not so amiably now. "If you like, however, I will rejoice in vile insults as martyrs have ever rejoiced in the arena or the cross. I will accept your term 'band of malcontents' and 'plotter-in-chief.' Who were or are these people? Myself. Harker. Butterworth. There are only two more of us, one of whom I need not mention because he is of no consequence. But the other one, the important one—"

"The plotter-in-chief, then?"

"*I* prefer to say our patron, but have it so. Only I am fully in his confidence: only I know what he means to do."

"Well?"

"Well!" said Gaines, and showed his teeth. "What did the plotter-in-chief design, and doth still design as we approach the hour of triumph? Touching this there has been much misconception, even in our band itself. Harker, even poor Butterworth, died in the belief that it was a scheme against the body politic, a plan to cast Charles Stuart from his throne."

"And it's not that?"

"No, it is not that: unless the King of England shall prove too troublesome when he sees himself ensnared." Gaines stood up straight. "Did we destroy him, whom should we substitute? One day in future, no doubt, a return of the ever-glorious Commonwealth, with some worthy and pious man like Oliver (myself, for instance) raised from modest gentleman's beginnings to the very Seats of the Mighty! Meanwhile, no. Charles Stuart —whoremonger though he may be, Papist at heart though he is—will serve the day well enough. He owns certain graces; he is popular with the vulgar. He will serve, that is, provided he obey the behest of Parliament; provided he walk in sober ways, put aside evil women and cease to squander money upon them; provided, to be short, he does precisely as he is told in all things.

"And he will do this, be assured. Upon one thing His Majesty is resolved: he will go no more on his travels, nor risk axe and block as his father did. Over him, shortly, my patron will hold a document so damning that he will be tied hand and foot. As my patron has a grip fast on the king, so I shall have a grip fast on my patron. Even the godliest man must protect his own interests, else where is he? And you, Roderick Kinsmere," Gaines suddenly cried, "will do as *you* are bid in all things. Do you follow me?"

About the man there was such raptness, such blazing certainty, that Kinsmere felt shaken as though by great hands.

"Follow you? How?"

"You will stand on the quarter-deck of this ship. You will whistle the other messenger to his doom. Afterwards, as a good patriot and one of us, you will do what else I shall bid at any time."

"You think so, do you? Why will I?"

"Because, rash youth who would not be warned," answered Gaines, "*the plotter-in-chief of this band of malcontents is your guardian, Mr. Roger Stainley.*"

Then the pious one's voice seemed to come from a great distance.

"I greatly fear," he said, "I have astonished and even shocked you. You will cry fie and out upon it; you will profess not to believe me. And yet, had you paused but a moment to reflect—as you never have—you would have seen this fact as inevitable."

Wind and sea went by; a quiet wind and a calm sea, with only the wake like a millrace. Captain Félix Souter ("I don't want to 'urt you; I am commanded not to 'urt you") rose up massively and poured Kinsmere a goblet of wine. Again he drank off the sweet Madeira, choking a little, and set down the goblet. He was shocked at Gaines's words, yes; nevertheless, in a tumult of conflicting feelings, was he so very astonished after all?

For he was pursuing other memories, and conjuring up other words.

In his mind rose the image of Roger Stainley: the shrewd, correct, mildly cynical face; the spectacles, the sober elegance, the pitted wrinkles from a troubled mind; of Roger Stainley, at their only interview, waiting in the foyer of York House without hope of being received by the Duke of Buckingham.

If you are a suitor of some kind, or he owes you money, the banker's words came back, *you are not like to see him at all. 'Tis a thing far easier to gain audience with the king. His Majesty pays no debts, on my life; but at least he is mighty affable and civil in putting you off.*

And so he remembered Roger Stainley, clearly taken aback when Kinsmere arrived to claim an inheritance several days too early; Roger Stainley, who had urged him to keep as much as possible out of sight, and to speak with few unless the banker himself could be there.

Aboard the *Thunderer*, now, he listened to the rush of the wake.

"Stop!" he said suddenly. "We thought—"

"*You* thought?" interrupted Gaines, thrusting forward with a barely concealed sneer. "Who thought?"

"Bygones Abraham and I. Or I thought, at all events . . ."

"Is it so? And what did you think?"

"In seeking the plotter-in-chief, I surmised it must be a

210

man of importance. A great lord, that's to say, of power or influence at court. But what *is* importance, and how is it measured? In plottings of this kind, for the motives that prompt it, the most important man is the man who holds the moneybags, and can open or shut 'em at will."

"It dawns upon you at last, does it? This is indeed the person of consequence: Roger Stainley. Remember that, foolish youth, and consider how you will ruin yourself unless you join our group of patriots. What is the fortune Roger Stainley holds in trust for you? Ninety thousand pounds, or is it a hundred thousand? Not to be thrown away, I think. Not even to be endangered by a stubborn whim. However!" said Salvation Gaines. "Since no man guessed what we were about, or in any way pierced the design . . . "

"I will give you odds, damn me, that Bygones Abraham guessed. And I *ought* to have guessed, from the lies you told last night."

"Lies, young man?"

"What else? At Whitehall Palace, in the set of chambers I did not know was reserved for me, you gave details of a private discourse I had with Mr. Stainley. If the king had learned so much concerning me and my affairs, where did *you* learn?

"You said," continued Kinsmere, "you *said* you had overheard the talk between Mr. Stainley and me in a window embrasure at York House. That was as false as you are false."

"Have a care, Roderick Kinsmere; have a care!"

"When we spoke of the things you referred to, we were not in the window embrasure at all. We had withdrawn to a garden behind the house. We were alone in a place of little low flower beds so lacking in concealment that not so much as a dog or a cat could have approached us unseen. When you spun the tale at Whitehall last night, I felt that much in it must be false; yet I could not recall exactly wherein lay the falsity or put finger on it as I now do. Since you could not have overheard what we said . . . "

"Have your say; be not afraid. Since I could not have overheard what you said . . . "

"Nobody could have overheard. You quoted certain things; those things were true. You could have learned such intimate matters only if Mr. Stainley himself had told you. And therefore—"

He stopped.

Salvation Gaines, still holding the knife in one hand, raised both arms above his head and made a kind of triumphant bow.

"Come!" urged Gaines. "Bear up and take courage! These facts, believe me, will do you good. They are sour-tasting; but like all truth they will do you good. Once you have recovered a little from your astonishment and your shock—"

"I am not so astonished as you conceive I ought to be. Shocked I was and still am. Even now, if you think I swallow such statements readily,"—here the ship gave a slight uneasy lurch,—"I must be a worse dolt and zany than you take me for. Roger Stainley, by all the powers? Roger Stainley, the plotter-in-chief of the malcontents? He was my father's friend; my father trusted him . . . !"

"Why, and your father was in the right of it. Who *is* more trustworthy than Roger Stainley, or hath ever been? Are you so dense as not to see that all he desires is the return of moneys rightfully owed him? All he desires is justice, else Stainley's Bank will be ruined in a fortnight. And if, to obtain justice, he must adopt stern measures . . ."

"Salvation Gaines, what is your definition of stern measures? Group of patriots, you say? Patriots how? You are no little Cabal playing at government; you are a parcel of the prettiest rogues and traitors unhanged. And some things I can't believe: rot me, I *won't* believe. That Roger Stainley, of all people, should share this passion for stabbing men in the back!"

"Alas, I fear he is not wise enough."

"Not wise enough?"

"I must confess," Gaines leered across the table, "Mr. Stainley forbade violence. Being unsound in religious doctrine (Church of England, forsooth!), he is always timorous and often unwise. But I, acquainted with the hazards involved and the tall dangers amid which we walk, made better decisions in the common interest. For the rest, shall we argue it? Do you call your trustee a rogue because he would have paid back the vast sums borrowed by a thriftless king: failure to repay which (need I

212

say it?) will encompass the wreck of an honoured banking house and the ruin of so many innocents, including your own self? If this be roguery, what is fair dealing?

"Do you also call him traitor? Here are strange words! Listening in the Hebe Room at the Devil tavern while you and the man Abraham and your notorious strumpet were in Cupid next door (pah, these heathen names!), I heard the man Abraham make shrewd hints as to the plot now going forward between the King of England and the King of France. Knowing what you do know, answer me one question. In two plots opposed to each other, which is the real traitor. Roger Stainley—or Charles Stuart?"

Much as he hated Gaines and all to do with Gaines, this was a home thrust straight through Kinsmere's guard. He did not reply. Again Gaines did a little capering dance, and ran at my grandfather with the knife in his hand.

"It is true," Gaines snapped, "I went last night to Whitehall Palace and spoke much I could not have learned save from Roger Stainley. At York House that morning, speaking to me after he had said good-bye to you in the garden, he bade me follow you lest you be led incontinent towards mischief. Could he guess (nay, could he even dream?) the extent of the mischief into which you would walk?"

"No, I suppose not."

"The details of that day you know or can deduce. By evening I had attained a certain desperation, as who would not? It seemed probable that His Majesty would send you and the man Abraham as his messengers to France. I must fish; I must learn; I must anticipate and set at naught. And so—"

"You showed yourself at Whitehall Palace," said Kinsmere, "with a mythical invitation to me from the Duke of Buckingham. A wherry would call at nine, you announced. If not to York House, then to Mr. Stainley. Why? To lure me away and knock me on the head?"

"Oh, what a stupid youth is this! There was no cause to harm you. Have you not been shown (by Mr. Stainley's command) the most extreme consideration throughout? A wherry *was* ready; it would have taken you to the City. Hired bravos would have guarded you on the way to Lombard Street. I could have gone with you; I could have explained you must meddle no more in the king's schemes lest your fortune be lost you. And I should have succeeded; what man acts against his own interest? But—"

"I refused to go to Lombard Street?"

"You refused; you were not persuaded. And this meant France, almost for a certainty. To Mr. Stainley I wrote a brief line, giving a street porter sixpence to run with it to Lombard Street. Mr. Stainley waited there with the other and last member of our group of patriots. They need not send their wherry, I wrote; let them do with it as they liked. You and the man Abraham would most probably leave on the king's business according to the customary arrangement; I had other plans. What plans, you ask?"

"Yes; I do ask!"

"And yet need you, considering what befell?"

"Possibly not." Kinsmere had forgotten his headache. "You watched and waited, as you had been doing all day. Butterworth overheard the king say we *were* bound for France. Butterworth told you this, after which he walked into the king's trap. You were as alert as usual; you struck like a snake and killed him . . ."

"It was necessary. But was it not beautiful too?"

"Beautiful?"

"Come!" said Gaines—and laughed. "I had near to three hours' start; I am no indifferent horseman; I had Harker's ring. And so I rode to Dover, paying for my own post horses and displaying the ring only when any man would have stayed me. The scheme (genius, I think?) rose full-armed in my brain even as I prepared to ride. At Dover lay this ship; the *Thunderer.*"

Félix Alexandre Charlemagne Souter, who had been listening with varying expressions, here surged up in vastness.

"Yes, de ship!" he roared out. "De ship, you say. What *of* de ship?"

"She is the property of Mr. Roger Stainley . . . "

"No, no, no! She *was* de property of Mr. Stainley. Is mine now, yes?"

"Captain Souter, sit down and be silent! Also, if you will, observe the irony. To Roger Stainley, that gullible man, the King of England has said that his trusting banker will be repaid the sooner if this ship may be put to Charles

214

Stuart's private uses. But how well it fitted into a design matured ere I left London.

"You, Roderick Kinsmere, should be decoyed aboard the *Thunderer*. A slower sloop should be overhauled in mid-Channel to ensnare the man Abraham. Captain Souter, the master of the *Thunderer,* had not hitherto enjoyed the confidence of our band of patriots. Charles Stuart, who himself is *sometimes* stupid, believed him devoted. Yet I felt he could be persuaded, if he were given the ship as recompense. Leaving Whitehall Palace in haste and with no blood on me (I must show you the way of stabbing without attendant bloodstains), I could not wait or delay longer to communicate with Mr. Stainley. Haste was still of the most vital necessity. And so I rode to Dover."

"And so you ride to Dover, eh?" demanded Félix. "No, stop! *You* 'old 'ard and listen. By de Virgin, I 'ave jus' t'ink of somet'ing."

He wheeled round, almost banging his head on the brass lanthorn, and stared at Gaines.

"You!" he said. "You did not comm-u-ni-*cat* wit' Mr. Stainley, you say? You t'ink of all dis and he don' know it? Goddam, last night you 'ave show me one letter from 'im. It say de ship is mine if I do what you tell me, and don' 'urt de yoong man 'oo will arrive. And I *know*. I 'ave got ot'er letters from thees gentleman. You t'ink I do all dis unless I get de ship? No, no, I see de letter. 'Ow else I know?"

"Tchaa!" said Gaines, wheeling to face him. "Calm yourself, Captain Souter; calm yourself, I say, and all will yet be well. I am a scrivener, yet my talent for imitating others' handwriting is not sufficiently well known. Having no leisure to consult with Roger Stainley, I took the liberty of inditing the note myself and of imitating even his more foolish sentiments too."

Kinsmere sat up straight. He looked at Félix, and back at Gaines.

"Félix," he said admiringly, "this fellow is the concentrated distillation of something or other. Confess, you old sinner! He's bubbled you to a nicety."

Félix did not speak; he was incapable of it. There was a long rasp as he drew his cutlass. But Gaines faced him without a qualm.

215

"No, captain, you will not be hasty. You dare not be, and you know it. Perhaps I should have refrained from telling you that. Yet I could not resist making you dance; I could not resist making you both dance. You would be most ill-advised to resent my behaviour, since your only hope is in me."

At the look on Gaines's face, which was of poised malice near to laughter, Kinsmere reached out towards the heavy silver drinking goblet. At least it was a weapon of sorts. But there was something *he* could not resist.

"If I were you, Félix," he suggested, "I should begin by slicing off his ears. That will keep him alive longer. If you commence with his throat, or merely run him through . . ."

"Did you hear what I said, Captain Souter?" demanded Gaines. "You are in our service now. You have attacked a King's Messenger and helped to rob him. Should the law overtake us, you will be the first to hang. But the law will *not* overtake us. And why, indeed, should you not have the *Thunderer* for your own? Mr. Stainley, heaven knows, does not want her. If you obey me strictly, as I think you will, I can guarantee she will be yours. Come, enough of this! Do you want the ship, or don't you?"

A kind of power blazed from him. Félix remained motionless for a moment, his chest heaving. Then with a savage snap he returned the cutlass to its sheath, shook himself all over, and folded his arms.

"Me," he said, "I am one philosopher. Vive Boethius! Hoist de bones! Let it be so."

"And another small courtesy, Captain Souter, ere we pass to graver matters. Fetch ropes and tie this young man securely; tie his legs as well as his hands. I mistrust him; he moves strangely, and has an ill air. Do you hear me, captain?"

"Oh, goddam! After what you say—after all de tricks and wheedles—you ask me—"

"I don't ask; I command. Come, no dawdling! Will you have further violence here, perhaps more damage to your beautiful cabin? (And *what* a cabin!) No matter, though! I will hold him quiescent with the knife; do you keep your cutlass at hand for support. But fetch ropes; make haste; else the wretched youth may be troublesome still!"

Félix addressed the Virgin and Boethius. He swore mightily. But he did draw his cutlass again, holding it with subdued menace. While Gaines swept the drinking goblet out of Kinsmere's reach and stood behind him with the knife point at his neck, ready to drive it through after Gaines's usual fashion, Félix fetched more lengths of thin rope from a locker. Within three quarters of a minute my grandfather's arms were tied behind him, and his legs secured by tying each to a front leg of the chair.

"Now, Roderick Kinsmere of Blackthorn," continued Salvation Gaines, "I have said 'enough' to Captain Souter; and I say 'enough' to you. I have used you with the most exemplary patience and forbearance. Your own father could have been no more indulgent. But we have come to an end to that, wretched fellow! I expound no more; I entreat no more; I tell you.

"When the *Saucy Ann* appears, you will be released to stand on deck and do my bidding. You too are in our service; you will do my bidding at all times henceforth. Even apart from the measures I will employ should you be impudent, you have no choice. Shall you know poverty or even hunger when Stainley's Bank fails, as fail it must unless the king can be persuaded to pay his debts? Shall you see your strumpet leave you in disdain when you have no bright coins to give her? Shall you——?"

Félix suddenly raised his hand for silence.

Feet pattered across the quarter-deck above. The breeze seemed to have freshened; the *Thunderer* pitched a little. Kinsmere could feel the strain and creak of her; he could hear the canvas a-drum, and the crying of gulls about her yards. From somewhere up in the crosstrees came an indistinguishable call, so faint that it was like a gull's cry. A voice answered from the quarter-deck:

"*Where away?*"

"One moment!" cried Félix, whirling round. "Don' go nowhere, eit'er of you! If dat be what I t'ink it is, I will come back in ten second. Yes?"

A fat giant, the rings agitated in his ears, he went at his rolling walk through the gaping door. They heard the bump of his feet on the companionway; then he was gone.

And he made good his word. Salvation Gaines, standing behind Kinsmere and lightly digging the knife into his

217

neck, did not speak because there was not time to speak. There was a heavy thud as Félix, after sticking his head briefly abovedecks, returned by jumping down. Cutlass in hand, blowing like a bearded whale, he loomed up in the doorway.

"Messieurs," he said, "here is time for decisions and time in goddam we make up our minds what to do. Dey 'ave sight de *Saucy Ann.*"

XVII

"Still!" added Félix, saluting ponderously with the cutlass. "It be a little while, you know, before she come up and we can hail her. I go on deck again, now, but I be back again, too, before we be ready to hail her. Mr. Goddam Gaines, who persuade everybody, I leave you thees yoong man to persuade. Don' 'urt him, dough, unless you *mus'* 'urt him to get what we want. I tell you, I like his ways! One t'ousand pardon: excuse me!"

And he was gone.

Salvation Gaines, knife in hand, darted round in front of Kinsmere and loomed over him.

"As I was saying—"

"Need you say it?"

"Yes. As Captain Souter tells us, the time for decision is come. And you have seen sense at last, I pray and believe. Shall I cut your bonds? Will you walk on deck and call to the man Abraham as I have ordered?"

"No, I will not."

"Now, I scarce believe," cried Gaines, with an odd kind of spasm crossing his bony features, "that my ears have heard aright! You'll not obey me in this?"

"No, nor in aught else!"

"Why? Because of your devotion to a wastrel king?"

"No! Because you are you and I am me. Because there are colonies of spiders and blackbeetles that make better company than yours. Because I will see you in hell and beyond ere I obey *any* command you shall choose to give."

"This is Bedlamite talk! This is sheer lunar madness! Have you reflected?"

"Yes."

"Ninety thousand pounds! A hundred thousand even! Gone, vanished, slipped through your fingers and lost to you for ever. What will life hold without money?"

"What will life hold at the behest of such as you?"

"Now the Lord open the eyes of the blind! When you are of our party, and among the elect, your transgressions shall be forgiven. You can escape the damnation that awaits you. Even your sins of the flesh, your gambollings with an accursed harlot, shall be washed away in the waters of pardon. Freely I offer it; freely I promise it; joyously I call you to eternal life. Hath any man an answer to that?"

"Yes. Go to the damnation that awaits *you!*"

With a whistling intake of breath, cradling the knife against his chest, Salvation Gaines hurried across the cabin and hurried back again. He muttered to himself; he seemed to be praying. The rushing murmur of the sea went past; the creak and crack of timbers made no word distinguishable. For what seemed a very long time he paced, as though ordering his thoughts. Then he returned.

" 'The Lord is my shepherd; I shall not want.' Are you truly so staunch in your determination, impious fool? I think not; I think I can move you. How well do you endure pain?"

Kinsmere did not reply. Gaines made a dart at the windows, and darted back.

"Behold, we shall see; for the testing time is come! A while ago, stupid fellow, you spoke lightly and jestingly of cropping *my* ears. Well, you have chosen it! Your own shall be dropped; slowly and at lesisure, but sliced off close to your skull; and your nose slit down to make you less favourable in the eyes of your strumpet. You are struck with panic, I think? You flinched, did you not?"

"Perhaps I did."

"Now the Lord of Hosts lend strength to my arm and skill to my fingers! You have mocked and defied me, impudent youth; let us see how you like the consequences. I will begin . . . "

He was testing the knife blade on his thumb when heavy footsteps clumped down the companionway. Captain Félix Souter, with an odd and strained and wrathful set to his big face, loomed up gigantic through the doorway, cutlass still in hand.

"Come, captain!" said Gaines. "You are in time to witness well-merited chastisement. This stupid fellow refuses! He has refused to aid us!"

"Hah!" said Félix, at the beginning of a roar. "He refuse, do he?"

"And must suffer the penalty. Captain, come and hold him! He is tied, I know, still, hold his shoulders and I can work the better. Captain Souter . . . !"

Félix shouldered in. He made straight for Kinsmere, who had gone hot-and-cold. With his cutlass he severed the rope that held my grandfather's wrists. Bending down still further, he cut the ropes round each leg. Gaines stood teetering to the movement of the ship, stupefaction followed by wrath.

"Captain Souter, what is the meaning of this?"

"You!" roared Félix. "*You!*" He sheathed the cutlass. He reached out and took Gaines by the throat. "You are one damn' fine t'inker, ain't it? You get us into all dis. Listen, Goddam Gaines. Don' you '*ear* not'ing?"

"Hear?"

In a sudden gust of fury Félix lifted Gaines by the neck. The knife spun into the air, flew against a curtain, and dropped. Screeching like a strangled parrot—a sound he had made once before—Gaines was borne across the cabin with his toes just bumping the deck. His face was thrust out of one shattered window, and his neck twisted round to starboard.

"If you don' 'ear not'ing," shouted Félix, "maybe you 'ave got eyes and can see. Look!"

But they all heard another noise now. Distantly a deep crash echoed out across water; a kind of wail grew into a scream overhead, and not far away there was a heavy splash.

"Dat be de second shot across our bows," said Félix, "as a sign we mus' 'eave to. De *Saucy Ann* 'ave come up. And two warships wit' her."

He yanked Gaines back and hurled him away. Gaines, evidently only half comprehending, staggered back against the table. He clutched at its surface, scrabbled at *The Consolation of Philosophy,* and finally regained his balance as the book was knocked to the deck.

220

"Warships?" repeated Kinsmere; he shouted in his turn. "Warships?"

It was all over. He would live; he would see Dolly again. And he was free of ropes. At the same time, when he essayed to stand upright his legs proved momentarily so unsteady that he sat down again.

"Two warships, I tell you," yelled Félix, "which I 'ave seen before. *Royal Standard,* fifty-eight gun. *Rupert,* fifty gun. Each one mount more metal dan we dɔ; toget'er dey blow us up like a powder keg wit' one broadside. Is wonderful, eh?"

This time Kinsmere did stand up. His legs remained shaky, but he contrived it. And then, to his own surprise, he found himself speaking genially.

"Well, Félix," he said, "how does it feel to be a pirate? Hoist de bones! Blood in de scuppers! Have you no mind to make a stand for it? Where is the fighting blood of the buccaneer?"

Félix lifted one fist in a mighty gesture that suggested the beginning of a dying speech. But he checked himself, scowled, dropped his arm, deflated his chest, and ended by scratching his nose.

"No," he said, "no! I tell you before: I am one philosopher. Now I suppose dey are goin' to 'ang me. Well! It 'appen to everbody, and it 'appen to old Félix. But all I care about—*im,*" Félix roared, and pointed a massive finger at Gaines. "De wet-nosed salaud dat carry himself like de Emperor of China, and cause all de trouble for everybody. Should I jump on his face and kill him now, do you t'ink, or should I wait for dem to 'ang 'im wit' me? Regard! Dey *will* 'ang 'im, won't dey?" he asked anxiously. "I don't want to make no mistake about dat. Dey *will* 'ang 'im?"

"Yes, you may feel sure of that: now or later they'll hang him. Most probably sooner than later, though. A drumhead court-martial, and up he goes to the yardarm."

"Ah, dass good. I t'ink, yoong man, we 'ad better go up on deck and talk to your friends when dey send de longboat. I could try to argue wit' dem and swear you are not 'ere, but I t'ink dey know already. Besides," a chuckle rumbled up in Félix's throat, and he nodded, "besides, I tell you, I like your ways!"

"If I were you, Félix," said Kinsmere, "I should not be

inclined to worry or brood too much about your position. You are a thorough-going damned scoundrel, let's allow; but I find *your* ways tolerable enough. Permit me to explain your behaviour, perhaps not with the strictest truth; there is no reason to suppose they'll hang you. With any luck, you will yet live to hoist the bones and sail on the Account."

"Eh? *What you say?*"

Kinsmere repeated it. Félix blew like an exhausted horse.

"Dere *is* justice," he roared at last. "Dere *is* justice, and Boethius have protect me. Come! We go on deck! You too, de damn one dat cause all the trouble! You!"

Salvation Gaines, drawn up and rigid, looked at them loftily from under reddish eyelids.

"If I am to hang, Captain Souter, be sure you will hang too. *I* will contrive that, if I contrive nothing else. But this may not be! It cannot be! The Lord shall lead His anointed out of the sorest of their tribulations. I prophesy——"

"Come!" said Félix. "Come! Or do I take you by de seat of de breeches? Come!"

Gaines paused only long enough to snatch up his knife. Then, with Félix holding one of his arms in an iron grip, they went up on deck.

The *Thunderer* was lying to, her helm hard down and her upper canvas furled. And she was very quiet. The crew, though with a restive and sullen air, had lined up in orderly fashion. No arms could be seen anywhere; no gun match had been lighted.

Kinsmere drank in cool air as he emerged on the quarter-deck and descended to the main deck. The sun was declining towards midafternoon (how much time had elapsed!); lengthening shadows wavered across the boards.

Off the starboard quarter, on a quiet sea flecked with whitecaps, there were other shadows. A shabby sloop, her fore-and-aft rig seeming very lean in contrast to the square-riggers that accompanied her, was also hove to and lowering a longboat. Well out beyond, spaced as though at either side, towered the spars of the two men-o'-war. Even viewing them across the bows, Kinsmere could see the gun muzzles that twinkled along the line of great curved hulls; and from each mainmasthead flew the Cross of St. George.

Kinsmere's heart rose up when he saw it. How these ships had come here he had no idea. He was only grateful for their presence; for the clean air again, and the day. All things had turned pleasant—the luminous sky, the grey sparkling water that turned blue in the distance—all things save one. He glanced at Salvation Gaines, and averted his eyes. It would be no pleasant business to see even Gaines hanged, on a day like this.

The *Saucy Ann*'s longboat, full of armed men, came dipping across the swell. He could see Bygones Abraham's burly figure in the bow, scanning the side; and he walked to the rail to answer the hail from the longboat. Félix bellowed an order; two men moved out to throw down a Jacob's-ladder.

The crew were muttering now; an uneasy movement ran through them. Across the waist to the forecastle straggled a crooked trail of blood where their wounded had been carried from the battle in the cabin. One of their dead must only just have died. They had not thrown him overboard; he lay on straw, his head lolling.

The longboat scraped the *Thunderer*'s side. Somebody screamed out an insult from the forecastlehead; the mutter rose and swelled, and there was a rattle as though of an unseen cutlass unsheathed. Faintly across water rang a sharp command from the *Royal Standard*. She began to come round with deadly slowness, her musketeers in the crosstrees and her gunners at battle station with lighted matches in their hands. The mutter instantly died.

Up over the rail clambered Bygones Abraham. His mottled face wore lines of grimness, and his hat was pulled down to hide a bandage round the head. After him climbed a wiry, middle-aged man in a frowsy jerkin, red breeches, and sea boots.

Bygones lumbered forward to shake hands; then he stood back and surveyed Kinsmere.

"They made a tack at it, then, did they? Body o' Pilate, lad, what befell?"

My grandfather presented Captain Félix Alexandre Charlemagne Souter.

223

"For the honesty of this gentleman, Bygones, I can answer on my honour. He would cut nobody's throat—nobody's!—unless few other courses were open to him . . ."

"Hah!" proclaimed Félix, throwing out his chest and beaming with pleasure. "Yoong sir, dat is most 'andsome. I t'ank you."

"Yet there has been something of a confusion—"

"Already," said Bygones, "I would ha' laid sixpence on it. Ecod, lad, have you had a look at yourself? There's blood splashed all over you, though most of it don't seem to be yours . . ."

"No!" roared Félix, lifting a heavy arm. "Thees is not'ing, I tell you, not'ing to speak of whatever! De yoong man has been playing a little, dass all."

Bygones paid no attention to this.

"Well?" he demanded, looking narrowly at my grandfather. "You have still got it, I hope? There has been no confusion about *that*, has there? You've still got it?"

"Got it? Got what?"

"Your half of . . . Oh, ecod!"

"My half of it?" Once more Kinsmere's wits were whirling. "Why, man, you are carrying it all!"

Bygones stared at him, jaw slackening, and then recovered himself.

"Come! No losing our heads now; or being put off by a misadventure! Surely, lad, there's a place where we can go for discourse in private?"

While Félix with much ceremony offered the use of his beautiful cabin, Bygones presented the wiry middle-aged man as Captain Nicholas Murch, master of the *Saucy Ann*. Then Bygones saw Gaines; such a look crossed the newcomer's face that for the first time Gaines shied back. But the pious one did not get far. Bygones followed Kinsmere below-decks, leaving Captain Murch in command on deck; Félix laid hold of Gaines's collar and brought him along.

If strict privacy was not to be, Bygones hardly seemed to mind now. He inspected the cabin, eyes protuberant against a mottled face, and sat down in Félix's chair.

"Now, lad! Whatever may ha' took place here, and there are all the signs of a past fight royal, 'tis also a fact that *you're* safe. Safe, hale, and hearty enough, if a little knocked about and a little white. Then where's your half of the dispatch? Half of it will be no good to the enemy; and my half—"

"Hell alive, man, are you telling me somebody took what you were carrying?"

"Ay, somebody did. I was hoaxed most neatly and elegantly, rot me! If I had not put two and two together, out of all the bits that were shooting round the firmament, and followed you as soon as might be . . . "

"I tell you, Bygones, you had the whole dispatch! The king (God bless him!) included me only as a decoy. You were the trusted messenger aboard the safe ship. He gave me a blank piece of paper. There it is on the table, with the broken seals. You see?"

Bygones picked up the paper, inspected it on both sides, and dropped it.

"Done," he said. "Done crisp! Scuttled and sunk without a trace!"

"But what befell *you?* You were safe, surely? You said you couldn't have been safer. You said—"

"Gently, now! Ayagh, lad! D'ye recall last night? The wherry from the *Saucy Ann,* d'ye recall, was thought to be waiting for me at Whitehall Stairs from a quarter hour to midnight onwards?"

"Was 'thought' to be waiting? Yet surely . . . ?"

"Gently, I say! It *had* called there, true enough. But we were very late. 'Twas past midnight, well past, when we left the palace. I remarked, if an old hulk's memory will serve, that the lads might be a trifle impatient. Oh, body o' Pilate! But it never occurred to me . . .

"There was a wherry at the foot of the stairs. There were four or five men, muffled up; I could make no recognition of any. They said nothing; I said nothing. I stepped into the wherry; they pushed off. We were a quarter mile down the river, and well out in midstream, when—"

Salvation Gaines, disengaging Félix's hand from his collar, uttered a shrill burst of laughter before he drew himself up like a man inspired.

"Did I not prophesy this?" he inquired. "Stand back, Captain Souter!

"And let there be an end," Gaines added, "to presumptuous talk of detaining me or executing vengeance against me. For the Lord hath saved his own from the fiery furnace and from all tribulation!

"Do you not guess what occurred? I have told these people, man Abraham, that my patron—the head of our band of noble patriots—was in waiting and had a wherry at his disposal. I sent him word you would proceed to Calais according to plan; he must act as he saw fit. Oh, how wondrous and inscrutable are the ways of Providence! For it is evident in what fashion he acted. My patron . . . "

"Patron?" snarled Bygones, right hand flying to sword hilt.

"Ecod, what a name to give him! Lad, lad! Has any told you that the plotter-in-chief of all this business is none other than—"

"Yes, I know," interrupted Kinsmere. "The Lord's Anointed has chosen to reveal all. But did *you* guess it was Roger Stainley?"

"Nay, how could I? I thought 'twas *some* moneybags desiring a hold over the king; and then His Majesty must dance to their piping. The name, no; not until—"

"If you stepped into a false wherry, what became of the real wherry? At all events, what happened in the false wherry?"

Bygones, still gripping the sword hilt, for a moment let his murderous gaze stray from Gaines. A reminiscent, almost sentimental light appeared in his eyes.

"What happened," he replied, "was a fight. 'Fight,' lad, is a mild and modest word for it. A-floating down the Thames by moonlight, when one muffled-up rogue says, 'Stand and deliver,' we re-enacted the part of o' *Paradise Lost* where the heavenly hosts fire cannon balls at each other and knock chips off the starry firmament. 'Twas close quarters for such eruptions; I shot one of 'em with a pistol and ran another through the body; but they were too many for me. One cut the thongs of my pouch and says, 'Jump overboard'; he says to another, 'jump overboard and take this to old Stainley.' 'Nay,' says the other, 'we are not paid for that; throw *him* overboard.'

"And just at the second—

226

"Nick Murch, d'ye see, had given command of the real wherry to a young first officer who was too almighty impatient and fond o' himself. When I failed to appear at the quarter to midnight or at midnight either, the young 'un said my mission must ha' been cancelled. Back they went to the *Saucy Ann,* giving opening to a false wherry full of hired knaves on a different kind o' mission.

"Well! The real wherry reaches the *Saucy Ann.* Nick Murch curses 'em all to a blister; he orders 'em to return to Whitehall Stairs if they must wait all night; in fact, he goes with 'em to be sure there's no other mistake.

"Back they went upriver faster than ever a wherry travelled. Then they saw the end of *my* elegant war, just as I was knocked on the head to be thrown overboard; they joined battle. But the messengers o' darkness had got what they wanted; *they* dived overboard and scooned off. You'd already told me your history, lad. There was I, somewhat bloodied but not quite senseless, yelling, 'Stainley, Stainley,' like a gibbering madman.

" 'Stainley?' says Nick Murch. 'Why, shiver my timbers,'—or whatever Nick did say—'Stainley's the great banker. He owns Captain Souter's ship *Thunderer,* plying the Narrow Seas on royal business like us.'

"And then, lad, I was mighty afeared they'd ha' laid a trap for you too. They'd take my half of the dispatch; but what use would it be (thinks I) unless they had it all? Near the *Saucy Ann* lay the two line-of-battle ships the king had told us of. 'Come!' says I. 'In a day or two those ships weigh anchor for Dunkirk in any case. Can't they anticipate by a little time and escort us to Calais?' 'Not without orders,' says the captain of the *Royal Standard.* Well, we got orders. But did I dare send word to the king I'd been robbed within sight of Whitehall Palace? I did not. My only hope, to keep us from the worst trouble we are like to see in our lives, was that you might be safe. And now . . . "

Breathless, wheezing, he let his voice trail away.

"Now," agreed my grandfather, who could hardly be called happy, "Mr. Roger Stainley has the entire dispatch. The king (God bless him) must needs keep the whole affair hushed and dark, save for dealing with us as we deserve. As for what I deserve, listen!"

Whereupon, while Gaines smirked triumphantly and Félix glowered, he explained everything that had happened.

"Ay!" agreed Bygones. Finding two goblets and a silver wine jug at his elbow, he poured a bumper of Madeira and drained it. Judicially he turned back. "You are right, lad; so is Salvation Gaines. He has thrown the main and won it; we can't touch him. He would have to stand trial; and even at a drumhead one, he would employ his mouth too much."

"If you apprehend that, man Abraham, you are gifted with more understanding than I had given you credit for. Now His ways be praised!"

"Here's a man," said Bygones, ignoring him and addressing the roof lanthorn, "who for combined hypocrisy and viciousness can scarce be matched even among his Lord's Elect. And yet we can't touch him; he's safe."

Bygones laid his cheek against his palm, reflecting with half-closed eyes. Then he chuckled, looking up at Félix.

"Well, moan capeeten, eel fo bid you good day, nest paws? Nome doon peep! Eel fo que we go on to Calais and report to Madame Dorleaon and take our punishment," proclaimed the old soldier, coming down to earth and letting French go after a short grapple. "You're a pretty tolerable good fellow, as the lad seems to think. Ayagh, though! It's cruel hard fate in store for you."

"One moment!" Félix said grandly.

Hurrying across the cabin, pausing only to restore a fallen *Consolation of Philosophy* to the table, he opened another locker under the windows.

"Your sword and sword belt, yoong man," he said to Kinsmere, producing these. "I put dem away, safe and sound for you, in case you are going to play rough again. You permit I restore dem now?"

"Indeed, I permit it. Thanks very much."

"But, monsieur," and in stately fashion Félix addressed Bygones, "I do not understand what is so cruel 'ard. Dey do not 'ang me; dey do not even 'ang dat t'ing dere which would swear 'e 'ad de Pope's blessing if he kill his own wife. No, no, no! If I could 'ave de deep honour to escort you and my yoong friend to Calais, I should be mos' 'appy. Command me! All dat old Félix 'ave—"

"No, captain," said Bygones. "Also with many thanks, it is only fitting that the lad and I should continue aboard the *Saucy Ann*. You are free; ay, to be sure. And yet, from what Captain Murch tells me, it *is* cruel hard notwithstanding. Roger Stainley, d'ye see, sold this ship to the East India Company less than a week ago. Gaines should never have promised her to you."

"Eh?" said Félix.

Bygones rose up.

"If *you* have made an end here, lad, we will take our leave. Captain Souter, I am onchantay to have had the joy of your connaissance, rip me in small moreso if I'm not! We will leave Scrivener Salvation Gaines in your tender care. Doubtless, when we are gone, you will wish to have speech with him."

There was a long silence.

Félix slowly closed one eye. His great chest had swelled, and he smiled upon Gaines.

"Monsieur," he replied, obviously impressed with Bygones's conversational style, "from de bottom of my 'eart, wit' the pearly tear of gratitude which glisten at de corner of de heye, Félix Alexandre Charlemagne Souter desire to t'ank you. Ha, ha, ha."

The knife fell from Gaine's hand and stuck point downward in the deck. Gaines whipped round.

"This must not be!" he cried. "This cannot be! You are a villain, man Abraham; you are no better than a murderer! There are laws to be enforced, and English warships to enforce them!"

He flew towards the windows, shouting, "Englishmen! Englishmen!" It was there that Félix caught him, and tucked him under one arm so that his cries were stifled. Then Félix bowed to the others.

"My friends," said he, "it desolate me dat I may not go on deck and say farewell. But I mus' keep dis one quiet until de warships leave, and den I talk to him. Ah, one moment. Will you be kind enough, Mr. Abraham Bygones, to fetch me de knife 'e 'ave use himself? It is dere by your foot. One t'ousand t'anks, my friends both, and so good day."

Again he bowed as they went out, and they saw the look in Gaines's eyes.

The warships *were* preparing to leave for Dunkirk, as they discovered on deck. But Kinsmere could not think of this; he was feeling a trifle sick.

"Bygones," he said, "where did you learn about Mr. Stainley selling this ship? From Captain Murch, was it?"

"Why," Bygones answered with a meditative air, "so far as I know, he has not thought to recoup his losses by selling her at all. But I called to mind the tortured and elegant principles of diplomatic speaking; it seemed to me the effect was salutary. Let us go aboard the *Saucy Ann,*" says he, "and solace our woes with a bottle of rum."

XVIII

Southward loomed the purple coast of France, and the lights of old Calais were twinkling on the hill as dusk drew in. Idling at a bare two knots, her mainsail dark against a pink sunset, the sloop *Saucy Ann* crept in an almost windless sea. A creak of protest shook through her from bowsprit to rudder, but the quiet water slipped whispering past her bows.

Leaning against the forward rail on the port side, Bygones Abraham and my grandfather watched the light die out of the wrinkled sea; shadows deepened; France grew vaster against the sky. They felt the slight roll, and heard a drowsy flip-flap of canvas. From well aft drifted the noise of an argument about a wench. Somebody was performing prodigies of music with the assistance of a comb and a piece of paper. A hoarse salt-pork voice began humming the tune, and then soared into song.

> To all you ladies now on land
> We men at sea indite . . .

Other voices took it up:

> And yet would have you understand
> How hard it is to write;
> The Muses nine, and Neptune too
> We must implore to write to you,
>   With a fal lal lal, and a fal lal lal . . .

So close were they drawing to Calais that they could hear the bells from the Church of Our Lady. The bells of Our Lady were clanging and jangling, faintly, in slow discord. A peaceful discord over water: as though they were trying to speak both French and English at once; and neither could predominate, but only raised a din.

It would be fitting comment. For possession of this town England and France battled throughout centuries. Arrows sang from its walls before the fourth Edward was king; its name (they say) is written upon Mary Tudor's heart. So the bell clamour from the Church of Our Lady fell *ding-clatter-clang* across roofs and cobbled quais; lights sprang up in narrow stone houses; and even the sea began to turn purple in the mild French dusk.

You would not suspect this sleepy, muddy old town of being at all associated with that most puissant and cold-faced sovereign, King Louis the Fourteenth. King Louis the Fourteenth has not yet attained his thirty-second birthday. But he has long set an example to other kings of slacker thoughts and dignity, or even less fashionable coats. He is a symbol. Awesome in a great mattress of a periwig, propped up on red heels to make him look tall, he is soon to be known, modestly, as the Sun-King.

Across Europe range his lace-hatted generals, Turenne and the great Condé, carrying war to the Spanish Netherlands. At his back rises marble Versailles, changed from a shooting box to the most splendid palace of all the earth. On his lawn Fashion stands tiptoe like a statue; world-shaking commands are issued as to the set of a periwig or the twirling of a clouded cane. Art and music sit at his feet; the *haut-lisse* Gobelins are woven, one square yard a year, to glorify his name. On his private stage the playwrights may be seen beckoning—that so-witty M. Molière, who makes him smile at the antics of a poor *bourgeois* trying to be a gentleman, or M. Racine, with the stately tragedies wherein all the violence occurs off stage and does not disturb his ears with any unmannerly noise.

Between the French and English courts, as represented by their theatricals, there is a curious parallel. If you feel drawn towards the rowdy robust English theatre, with its rowdy robust court besides, you may not be too enamoured of the stiff and brittle clockwork actors on the private stage at Versailles. At Whitehall Palace there is an open playhouse, with a gallery for Jack Public. King Louis would no more think of letting Jacques Bonhomme into Versailles than of letting him into an upper chamber of the Kingdom of Heaven. Jacques's business is to work long and pay taxes, so that for Louis the Kingdom of Heaven may be (as decorously as possible) anticipated. Years afterwards Jacques Bonhomme will commence to think of this, and he will curse the Sun-King's coffin as it goes past in the rain.

But it is young Louis now, at his marble-topped table in a hall of cake-icing finery. Small fair-haired La Vallière worships him; his cunning runs on unchallenged; and three hundred men are required to assist him in the heavy labour of putting on his breeches. At this court there is no place for the mocking laughter of Charles Stuart. A little light music. A little light vice, and certain unpleasant vices as well. A proud little scene to be painted on the ceiling, with gods and clouds and cannon, and all underlings a-tremble. Bow down, ye stiff-necked Englishmen! *L'état, c'est lui.*

Bygones Abraham, hearing the bells of Calais across the water, was in an oratorical mood.

"Nay, lad," said he, in a hollow and doleful voice like an oracle from its cavern, "never speak lightly or jestingly o' the plight we're in. 'Tis no jesting matter, mah fwaa it's not! There's His Majesty's sister (God bless her) waiting in a ship called *La Gloire* for the terms of a secret treaty, and we've not got 'em. She'll not come to England; there'll be no treaty signed at Dover; the king will be several hundred thousand pounds a year out of pocket; and, worst of all, the plotter-in-chief is in a position to make His Majesty dance for ever. Oh, ecod! I hate the thought of facing that lady when we arrive. She looks little and mild; but she's a clever woman, and she has a jaw. Still, it's not much compared to the situation awaiting us at home. What our punishment will be I can't guess, but . . . "

He fetched up a deep sigh, and again had recourse to the stone bottle with which he had been fortifying himself for some time. Calais's lights strengthened through dusk.

The salt-pork voices aft, which had rumbled through several verses, sang on with undiminished zeal.

> Should foggy Opdam chance to know
>   Our sad and dismal story,
> The Dutch would scorn so weak a foe
>   And quit their fort at Goree;
> For what resistance can they find
> From men who've left their hearts behind?
>   With a fal lal lal and a fal lal lal . . .

Bygones handed the bottle of rum to my grandfather, who took a deep pull and returned it.

"Well," Kinsmere said thoughtfully, "I hope we are not expected to go out and hang ourselves or some such nonsense. Because burn me if I'll do it! Now that the dispatch is gone, in spite of our doing our devilish damned best to keep it, don't you find yourself tolerably well pleased?"

"Pleased?"

"In candour, yes. These proceedings were none of the most honest, now, were they? Asking for bribes, selling his country—"

"Shush!" muttered Bygones, peering round as though in fear of an eavesdropper. "Lad, lad!"

"Well, don't you think so?"

"Oh, ecod! This is treason talk, no less!"

"Why, as to that," Kinsmere's gaze searched the crowded masts in the harbour, "let us disregard words and think only of deeds. A considerable inheritance went down the wind when they desired me to go in with 'em . . . "

"Ay, and you wouldn't! Why, lad?"

"I don't know," Kinsmere replied. And, as they both pondered this, it is a sober fact that he didn't know.

"At all events, and in strictest confidence," he continued, "you can answer my question. Aren't you tolerably well pleased?"

Then, presently, Bygones began to chuckle.

"Why," says he, "it may be—it may just be—you are in the right of it. 'Tis the proper happy ending, with the villains all circumvented and the like; although," added Bygones, taking another reflective swig at the stone bottle, "the heroes and the villains seem to have become most un-

233

consciously scrambled. For the life of me, ecod, I can't tell which is which. But it's a profound moral lesson, this is, and shows the perspicacity o' Providence. Whichever were the villains, we see clearly that right and justice have triumphed. This not-entirely-reputable treaty has been put aside or at least much delayed . . . "

Then Kinsmere saw that he was winding himself up with rum for a profound discourse, and about to hold forth at some length.

"Right and justice!" Bygones pursued affably. "Those twin glowing beacons which are as frankincense and myrrh crying aloud in the wilderness to the ears of a multitude grovelling in chains! And what's the odds how the dice fall to rekindle 'em. I may be a-growing old, lad, but I'm not too old to pick up my bed and walk again, as I've been doing since I carried a pike for Langdale in 'forty-five. Wherever there's fighting to be done, or a drop o' good liquor for the belly, old Bygones will be walking not on crutches until they shovel him six feet under.

"And what's the result? Out of this business you get a rare fine lass in Dolly. And I make a friend of as good a fighting man (if you'll allow me to say so) as I could ha' wished for when the cavalry charges.

"Truth and justice, we see, have been a-working from the first. In my lodgings yesterday, when you first told me the story of your ring, I thought you were a liar and a spy. And if," said Bygones, exhibiting on his finger the blue stone of a ring that glittered in the last light, "if Providence hadn't caused both our rings to be hollow so that you could show yourself an honest man—why, we'd ha' cut each other's throats. But here's old Rowley outwitted, and justice triumphant. And all I had to do was pull sharp at the stone in the ring, like this, and it came open, like this, and—

"*Great body o' Pilate!*" roared Bygones, as though stung by a snake.

Kinsmere, still looking ahead at the masts in the harbour, started and whirled round. Bygones stared with bulging eyes at the cavity he had disclosed when he pulled open the stone by way of illustration. Peering down at it, Kinsmere saw wedged inside a small object which looked like very thin paper folded many times over.

"Every time we carried a message," Bygones was saying vacantly, "we were obliged to pass in our rings to His Majesty—Do *you* remember? Last night? He called for both our rings; we put 'em on the desk; we saw 'em not again until we took our leave? Also, whenever a King's Messenger calls on Madame, 'tis the same process.

"Do you further recall, lad? On the table in the king's private cabinet? Sheets of writing paper, fine and strong but so thin you could almost see through 'em? You observed those, did you not?"

"I observed 'em, yes; I thought they were for some kind of chymical experiment, though it's hard to say why I should have thought so."

"And the fine-quill pens on his desk; you marked those too?"

"I did."

"Now open your own ring! Make haste and open it! Quick!"

Kinsmere did so. A duplicate of the much-folded paper lay inside.

"Oh, ecod," gabbled Bygones, "don't you see that with those heavily sealed half-sheets in the oilskin packets we were *both* carrying blank pieces of paper? Pem Harker said a true word: 'Charles Stuart trusts nobody.' But, whoever carried a dummy dispatch with the true dispatch concealed inside, he would guard his ring above all things because he believed it was useful only as a passport. And furthermore—"

Bygones stopped for want of breath. Kinsmere took a long, refreshed look round the deck of the *Saucy Ann*.

"Let me understand this," he begged. "You would inform me, then, that the imposing document which Roger Stainley holds above the head of the king is as virginally white as the one they took from me?"

"That's it! Oh, body o' Pilate, what an ingeniousness of tricks! And—"

"And," supplied Kinsmere, "the terms of the God-damned treaty have been safely carried to Madame after all?"

"They have."

"I see," my grandfather said musingly. "Well, well, well."

235

After a time, while Bygones was still chortling and chuckling and dancing with high glee, Kinsmere continued in the same musing way.

"'Profound moral lesson,'" says he. "'Perspicacity of Providence.' 'Triumph of truth and jus—'"

"We didn't know it, true; but were just as successful as if we *had* known. Eh?"

"'Old Rowley outwitted.' 'Twin glowing beacons.' H'm."

They fell silent for a moment. The voices aft had become silent too. Presently the grin of the Kinsmeres crept across my grandfather's face, and he swung round.

"Ahoy there," he shouted along the deck to the sailor-men aft. "Ahoy there, hearts of oak and such-like! Accept my compliments on your noise. And, should you know it, will you sing the catch I shall name for you?"

An enthusiastic affirmative was bellowed back by the flattered sailors.

"It is only proper and fitting, hearts of oak," said Kinsmere, "that on approaching a foreign port we should make some demonstration of true British feeling and honesty. Let us have 'Here's a Health unto His Majesty,' all the verses. And see that it is good and loud, hearts of oak. It will have cost somebody near to a hundred thousand pounds!"

L'ENVOI

At this point, fortunately or unfortunately, breaks off the narrative which was taken down in shorthand by Anne Kinsmere (Darlington) between the 1st and 18th June, 1815. The circumstance of its breaking off is explained in that excellent lady's journal, and forms an escapade worthy of Roderick Kinsmere himself.

Mrs. Darlington having been addicted to moralizing, her statement is of considerable length; I must beg leave to set down only essential facts. It will be observed that the foregoing story has eighteen parts, each one of which was told by Colonel Richard Kinsmere in the library at Blackthorn (called the New Library) on successive nights. It was a trying time for the whole family, as already explained. Of three young relatives in Flanders with Wellington's army, one would appear to have been Colonel Kinsmere's favourite grandson—Captain Barry Kinsmere-West, 40th Regiment of Foot (Somerset).

From the beginning of June it had become evident that the Allies would shortly face the terrible Bonaparte. Colonel Kinsmere was doing his best to keep the minds of his listeners (and also, no doubt, his own) off the coming encounter.

For eighteen nights, then, he detailed these adventures of his grandfather. He must have been recounting the last chapter when in a distant country darkness fell across grainfields beyond the village of Waterloo, with the Grand Army shattered and in wild retreat.

Colonel Kinsmere did not break off because he was interrupted by news of the victory. News of the victory did not reach England until three days later. He broke off because in the telling of the final part on Sunday, June 18th, he drank so much port that he went upstairs inebriated and singing, and being in his eighty-fourth year, kept to his bed the next day.

He had thoroughly recovered when he heard of Waterloo, together with a citation in the *Gazette* for Captain Barry Kinsmere-West. Then occurred the conduct which so much offended the later Mrs. Darlington. Colonel Kinsmere would appear to have danced a hornpipe before the eyes of his scandalized grandchildren. He then clapped on his hat and sallied down to the village. Hiring a coach at the Hound and Glove, he filled the rear boot with bottles of spirits, invited a number of villagers to ride with him, and himself drove the coach from Bristol to Taunton, crying news of the victory.

We are possessed of thirdhand accounts by old men whose own grandfathers saw him, of that apparition thundering through the countryside. In his youth Colonel Kinsmere was a fine whip, but even as an octogenarian he seems to have outdone himself in the handling of a heavy coach over indifferent roads. He is remembered as sitting up there in a blue coat with brass buttons, his tall hat on the side of his head, singing a song called "I Pass All My Hours in a Shady Old Grove," and drinking brandy out of the neck of a bottle.

237

The narrative was never resumed. Or, if it was, I can find no record of it anywhere. Since it is a complete story in itself, however, we have ventured to let it stand in the present form. Those curious may be interested in the following extract, beyond a bare record of births and deaths in the parish register.

For this I am indebted to the scholarly work of the Rev. William R. Eccles, *Reminiscences of a Country Parish*, privately published in 1882. His account of Roderick Kinsmere, as one of the famous figures out of the past, is fairly brief and highly discreet. After detailing "Rowdy" Kinsmere's ancestry and birth (May 15th, 1649), Mr. Eccles goes on:

"After he had gone to court in the year 1670, his pecuniary resources were embarrassed by the failure of Stainley's Bank. Although this was only temporary, and Stainley's Bank is today one of the great financial institutions of the domain, he never recovered the more substantial portion of his inheritance. Fortunately, however, he was awarded a pension by Charles II, doubtless from one of those happy caprices which make us feel a certain kindliness for that king despite his manifold weaknesses, vacillations of character, and the temptations to which even the strongest wills are prone to succumb in a licentious and profligate age," etc., etc., etc.

"In 1670, moreover, he married Miss Dorothy Jane Landis, a lady of most esteemed birth and happy accomplishments. Though malicious tongues might hint that this lady had been associated professionally with theatrical enterprises in the metropolis, such reports were contradicted by her sweetness of temper, the calm dignity and nobility of her character, which shone about her during her visits to Blackthorn.

"Their union was blessed with four children, viz.: Bygones (1672), Dorothy (1674), Charles (1675), Alan (1680). Due to unhappy eventualities which overtook the two older sons, it fell to the lot of Alan to take into his capable hands the management of the estate. In 1687 Dorothy Kinsmere passed gently from this life, mourned by all who knew her, but leaving behind those tender memories which must cling for ever round the couches of the blest.

"The revolution of 1688 occurring not long afterwards,

her husband retired to Blackthorn, passing the rest of his life in the beauty and serenity of pastoral surroundings. He was much given to study and good works, and set an example to his descendants worthy of being followed in these, alas, much different days. He died November 28th, 1748, and lies amid the eternal calmness which in life his lofty spirit loved so well."

At this discreet summing-up let no irreverent reader commit what the Rev. Mr. Eccles would *not* have called "the vulgar error of a horse-laugh." For us who grub in diaries and try to puzzle out the characters of Sizzlers long dust it is, rather, a solemn thought. Awesome as it seems, this is what they call the Verdict of History—that jack-o'-lantern which has teased so many students. And, in leaving it for the reader's consideration, the editor has one consolation. It is probably fully as accurate as most of the estimates made by the gravest Victorian scholars of the life and character of King Charles the Second.

FINE MYSTERY AND SUSPENSE
TITLES FROM CARROLL & GRAF